Praise for ~~Susan Matthews's~~

previous novel
AN EXCHANGE OF HOSTAGES

"Powerful, insidious and insightful—a singular
accomplishment."
Melanie Rawn, author of the *Exiles* series

"An intelligently written book full of unexpected
moments of beauty."
Sherwood Smith, author of *Crown Duel*

"An absorbing work . . . [that] can stand comparison to
Dostoyevsky's *The Possessed*."
Stephen R. Donaldson, author of
The Chronicles of Thomas Covenant

"An impressive achievement."
Locus

"Absorbing and frightening . . . A very intense novel."
Martha Wells, author of *City of Bones*

"Bold and disturbing . . . Susan Matthews is a writer
to watch—and to keep away from
explosives and sharp objects."
Debra Doyle, co-author of the *Mageworld* series

Other Avon Books by
Susan R. Matthews

AN EXCHANGE OF HOSTAGES

PRISONER Of CONSCIENCE

susan r. matthews

AVON · EOS

AVON BOOKS
A division of
The Hearst Corporation
1350 Avenue of the Americas
New York, New York 10019

Copyright © 1998 by Susan R. Matthews
Published by arrangement with the author
Visit our website at **http://www.AvonBooks.com/Eos**
Visit Susan Matthews's website at
http://www.sff.net/people/Susan.scribens/
Library of Congress Catalog Card Number: 97-94463
ISBN: 0–380–78914–0

First Avon Eos Printing: February 1998

AVON EOS TRADEMARK REG. U.S. PAT. OFF. AND IN OTHER COUNTRIES, MARCA REGISTRADA, HECHO EN U.S.A.

Printed in the U.S.A.

WCD   10 9 8 7 6 5 4 3 2 1

◆ Acknowledgments

My protagonist was raised according to a strict standard of filial piety that includes reverence for his ancestors. I'm not Dolgorukij, but it rubs off. Therefore, taking up a bundle of lighted incense sticks, I clasp my hands before me and face north to bow to my ancestors, who will always have guest-place in my house.

Devra Langsam was my great-grandmother. Joanna Cantor and Lori Chapek-Carleton were my great-aunts. Ellen Blair and Bev Clark were my earliest confidants. I had too many godmothers to count: I can only bow.

To Maggie Nowakowska: for all the extra loads of laundry, sinks full of dishes, plumbers and electricians intercepted, bills written, cars washed, and errands run while I was holed up in a dark room writing, I dedicate this book; with my gratitude for her support in years past, and my hope for her continued companionship in many years yet to come.

◆ One

Fanner Rigs hugged the visioner at his station, fascinated and horrified at once at the sight of the enemy fleet that faced them. The enormity of the task was overwhelming: How could they hope to challenge the Doxtap Fleet, in all the pride of the Jurisdiction's might?

The Bench had left no choice for them.

They had to try.

Eild was their homeworld, and the orbiting artillery platforms that defended it had to be protected from destruction by those mighty warships if Eild was to have any hope of remaining free.

"Our target." It was his brother's voice on intership, Marder's voice. On this little courier they almost didn't need the intership to hear each other—the ship was tiny, built for speed and maneuverability, both of which were crucial to its intended task. They had to get past their target's own defenses, its Wolnadis, after all.

And the Wolnadi fighters were visible even now, clearing the maintenance atmosphere and coming toward them at frightening speed.

"Jurisdiction Fleet Ship *Scylla*," Sonnu's clear calm voice confirmed. It was useful to remember that Sonnu was there. Fanner had often fantasized about marrying with Sonnu, if he could catch her eye for long enough to make his case with her. This was his chance to show her his true mettle.

And still it was a desperate enterprise.

They all knew that.

His party had the most desperate part of it, for while the others in the attack on *Scylla* were to draw the Wolnadis off toward the carapace hull—the topmost shell of the warship—his party was to feint for the carapace, and slip at the last minute through the atmosphere barrier into *Scylla*'s maintenance atmosphere, beneath the ship.

They had the schematic firmly fixed in mind.

If they could only be quick and nimble enough about it, agile and canny enough about it, slip through the startled defenses of the maintenance atmosphere—*Scylla* could not fire upon itself, for fear of damage to the ship—

To fail meant death.

To succeed meant death as well, because if they won through to the main battle guns they could destroy *Scylla*, and everybody on it. Including them.

He would never marry with Sonnu now, but if he could be part of the freedom of port Eild it would not even matter.

"Initiate tactical plan," Marder said; and Fanner engaged the overthrust boosters on the courier, and sent it leaping forward.

Toward *Scylla*, and their death.

If they could only take *Scylla* with them it was worth it.

Snatching a breath as best he could in the close quarters of *Scylla*'s maintenance corridors, Joslire Curran steeled himself for the next desperate sprint. He couldn't stop for long enough to catch his breath. He couldn't afford to. There were Nurail sappers in the corridors, they'd breached the maintenance hull and gotten in through the maintenance atmosphere and if Joslire and his team couldn't stop them in time—

Kaydence Psimas came up on Joslire's left and nudged Joslire's shoulder with his elbow, wordlessly. Joslire nodded toward the access to the recirculation systems, and Kaydence grinned and went, dropping to a roll halfway across the corridor as he was fired on. Joslire checked the cross-fire zone with a swift movement of his head: no blood on the deck. So maybe Kaydence was unharmed.

The Nurail would know where to watch for them now, though, and there was nothing they could do but get across as quickly as they could. The Nurail sappers had only left one man to try to slow them down. The rest of the party would be three corridors away by now.

The only thing that stood between *Scylla* and destruction was the fact that men who knew the ship's architecture from living there could navigate more quickly than anyone else.

Kaydence fired back down the corridor at the Nurail who had pinned them there, as much to remind his fellows that he was waiting as to encourage the Nurail to go away. Erish Muat went across, stumbling on the decking and sliding to safety, Kaydence covering him with a shot. They couldn't afford to use full charge on board ship for fear of starting a fire. The enemy didn't care.

Toska Bederico brought up the rear, but there was no fire at all from the Nurail, so maybe Kaydence had shot him down. It didn't really matter. All that mattered was getting through to the main battle guns before the Nurail sappers could get there.

The main battle guns—lateral cannons forward, in this case—could not be turned back toward *Scylla*'s interior. But they could be spiked. And the resulting explosion would destroy everything within a standard orbital.

Down the cross-corridors now to foodstores three. The sappers were taking the main access corridor, but the back wall of foodstores forward abutted a wastechute that could be vented into armory two levels above. The sappers wouldn't be able to use the lifts. The lifts had been shut down by Engineering as soon as they'd realized that the crew of the small Nurail scout ship that had cleared the maintenance atmosphere had shot its way in to the maintenance corridors.

It would take the Nurail time to break into the access hatch beside the lift nexus and squeeze through the narrow laddered way. Maybe it would take the sappers enough time for Joslire's team to get through to the cannons before the Nurail did.

Shoot out the secures on foodstores forward door four, struggle through the half-opened door into the room. Joslire took refuge with Erish and Kaydence behind a shelf full of soup concentrate cartons. Toska piled up a hasty barricade of flour boxes to crouch behind and fired point-blank at the back wall.

There'd been no time to clear the shelves. Shattered bits

of storage containers flew like a sandstorm in the little room as Toska fired. Joslire grabbed a chip of something that imbedded itself firmly in the storage shelves behind them: dried sindal, for the mess's approximation of meat roast. Too bad. He had been hoping for a bite of dried fruit.

Toska was through the wall. Joslire joined Kaydence in clearing away the rubble till they could get at the smoking gap and through. If the Engineer fired the conversion furnaces to hasten the ship's progress, they were done for. The vacuum that the huge furnace would create would pull them into the engines, and they would become propulsion—not protection—for *Scylla*.

Joslire put the thought out of his mind. If they didn't stop these Nurail sappers, *Scylla* wouldn't go anywhere, ever again, except perhaps out in a three-sixty orb in fragments not exceeding seven eighties in size and five eighties in weight.

The wastechute hadn't been cleaned for a while. The handholds were full of debris and particulate matter. There were three sets of handholds spaced out around the tubular wastechute, and Joslire scooped and swept out each of them as he went, mindful of Kaydence waiting beneath him to follow him up the wastechute.

It was easier going here than the mechaccess at the lift nexus would be for the Nurail sappers, and they could only get one person up the mechaccess at a time, while three could fit at once in the wastechute.

The time it took to move up eighth by eighth was still maddening.

What would they find when they got there?

Toska popped the chute while Erish climbed up to hang opposite the opening, nursing his injured arm. When had Erish been injured? It didn't matter. They couldn't stop to think about it. They had to go on.

They were in corridor five, Kaydence running for the end of the corridor while Joslire was still helping Erish through from the wastechute. Sprinting after Kaydence and Toska, Joslire heard the voices, but Kaydence's voice was closer—

"We're behind. They're in third forward!"

They'd come too late. The enemy had already cleared the

lift nexus. The voices they heard were Nurail sappers on the way to Cannon Three.

They ran.

Corridor three wasn't a straight shot through; none of the corridors ran more than a few eighths without turning. There was a Nurail at the first turn waiting for them, and the round she fired stopped Erish in his tracks before Joslire's return shot separated the top half of her body from her legs.

The shower of gore and bits of flesh made it hard to keep their footing. But they had to catch up with the sappers before the sappers could get to the guns. There had only been eight Nurail to begin with, and they were down to three now—two once Kaydence killed the one waiting behind the next turn, taking him by surprise.

Two.

They didn't have time to take the turn carefully, whether or not waiting Death should stand behind the next wall. They had to stop the sappers. There were only two turnings left.

One turning.

No turnings.

They could see the sappers ahead of them in the corridor now, and the still-open door into Cannon Three's loading chamber further on. Joslire checked his weapon's charge one last time at a full run, steadied it as best he could—and fired. He didn't have much hope of aim, not running all out as he was.

He didn't need much aim.

It was a lucky shot, he got the furthest Nurail, and he fell against the wall to clear the field of fire for Kaydence and Toska behind him. Kaydence bolted past like a man in pursuit of his destiny, screaming, firing as he went—one shot, two shots going wild against the bulkhead at the far end of the corridor. The Nurail wasn't looking back, and from what Joslire could see the Nurail was gaining on the open door—

At last the door started to close, the engineers beyond overriding the system safes that prevented the load-doors from closing when the cannon was active. Closing the door wouldn't stop the sapper. But it would slow the sapper down.

Kaydence threw himself to his knees in a smooth skid and fired as the last of the Nurail sappers, turning, started to slide his body through the fast-closing door.

Joslire couldn't see at first what had happened. The Nurail he'd shot was beginning to stir, raising a weapon, which was trained on the back of Kaydence's head. Joslire had to shoot the man, and make sure he stayed shot this time, before he had any business trying to see through the mess of dust and smoke at the far end of the corridor.

It was quiet in the corridor now, no sound but for the subtle rain of pulverized metallic debris settling out of the air to the decking.

Picking himself up carefully, Joslire staggered over to where Kaydence sat slumped on his heels in the middle of the corridor. It was critically stupid to sit there like that. They'd be too easy a target to miss if there were any sappers left to shoot at them.

"Make the hit, Kay?"

His throat was rough and strained from running too hard, too fast, for too long. Manning the Wolnadi fighters was nothing like this. On the Wolnadis at least you sat down while you either chased down or ran from your enemy. Just their luck to have been on Ship's Security duty when the *Scylla* joined the Doxtap Fleet to help reduce the artillery platforms at Eild.

"Hard to say," Kaydence replied, hopelessly, staring at the ceiling with his head well back on his broad solid shoulders. "But we'll know in a bit. The ship will blow up. Or it won't. Then we'll know."

There was no help for it but to go and see, then.

Joslire limped forward—funny, he was bleeding, when had that happened?—toward the door at the end of the corridor, half-open, dimly visible now through the clearing dust. There was the door. There was the body on its belly facing toward the door, limp and ungraceful in abandonment—but what about beyond?

Stepping over the prone body of his enemy, Joslire Curran leaned into the doorway to find out.

The cannon.

He couldn't see the cannon for the face of Erling Miroah, standing in the doorway with a clearing-lever in his hand. As if you could stop a Nurail sapper with a clearing-lever. As if anything could stop a Nurail sapper within sight of his goal; these people were demented. And their insanity made them all but superhuman in what they had proved capable of doing . . .

"The cannon?" Joslire rasped.

Erling wasn't moving, calling back over his shoulder into the room beyond.

"No, it's Curran from Security. Send damage control. Send a medteam."

Why?

"The cannon," Joslire insisted, beginning to get annoyed. Why wouldn't they answer his question?

Erling moved to one side, working at the controls for the door. Joslire saw the cannon at the same instant that he realized why Erling hadn't bothered to answer his question. If the cannon had been hit, they wouldn't be here for him to ask. That was why. It must have seemed too obvious to Erling.

Joslire sat down between the bulkhead and the body of the Nurail sapper. It had been a fine effort. First Officer was going to have things to say about the fact that sappers had breached the maintenance hull in the first place. Kaydence came reeling drunkenly across the littered decking to sit down heavily at Joslire's side; together they watched Toska help Erish come up to join them. Erish's face was wet with tears of pain—or perhaps simply rage, and sheer frustration. Erish hated to be left out of the shooting. It was just Erish's bad luck to have been shot, but since he was walking it hadn't been too bad.

Joslire closed his eyes, exhausted.

Too much excitement.

At least things were quiet now.

He could hear ship's braid as if at a considerable remove, the Engineer dispatching damage control teams, First Officer reporting status to the Captain. He could hear ship's ventilators struggling to process all the chipped bulkhead and metal dust they'd just blown into suspension.

He could hear Kaydence's shaky breathing beside him, Toska catching his breath, Erish grunting softly with reluctant pain. He didn't hear the medteam coming up, even though they had probably been running. Well. Maybe he had had a short nap, then.

"Joslire, what's your status, here?"

"Sitting by, team leader." He couldn't rightly say "standing" by, could he? "It's Erish to go first. He's had the worst of it, I think."

"Right, move this one out to triage. Gala, Marms, on Erish. Joslire. You're hit. Robert, see what you can do about this, we'll have the next team up as soon as we can."

Joslire met Robert's level gaze and grinned. It was Robert's fifthweek in Infirmary, and he was working harder than any of them. They were all sitting down resting, after all.

"Oh, you're going to be in trouble," Robert warned. Joslire knew the joke. The officer didn't like them to let themselves be injured. The officer took it personally. "Extra duty for at least a month, Jos."

Right.

He'd worry about it when he faced the officer.

For now he thought that he'd just close his eyes.

Robert St. Clare wheeled the mover with Joslire on it into the next slot in the triage line. Infirmary was strange to look at on battle status; the clinic walls, the office dividers, the treatment room partitions were all pulled up into the ceiling or dropped down into the decking underfoot to clear as much space as possible.

The triage officer had already sent Erish on to Station Four. Their officer was at Station Four, though Robert couldn't see him, Infirmary being crowded, and the officer short.

One of the techs at the triage station cut open the fabric across Joslire's thigh, and the triage officer—Doctor Bokomoro, Degenerative Bone and Muscle—raised her eyebrows at the wound. "Five eighths' span of bulkhead, Joslire," she said, sounding impressed. "How did that happen?"

Like the rest of Infirmary staff, she called Joslire by his personal name. Joslire didn't care to be reminded of the Curran Detention Facility, where Joslire had been Bonded and given his Fleet name. Robert didn't care. He'd been assigned a name at random, like other Nurail bond-involuntaries, to destroy even so small a bit of information that they might have had about one another.

"It must have been in foodstores three, as the doctor

please. Because this troop can't quite remember. With respect.''

Still Joslire was formal with her. Formality was safety, for bond-involuntaries. It was all a part of their conditioning. Doctor Bokomoro palpated the ragged edges of the wound in Joslire's thigh with delicate care, frowning a bit. "Well. You'll do for Station Four when it clears. You're the last of it, are you?''

Her question was directed at Robert, who looked back over his shoulder down the length of the corridor, checking the triage line. They seemed to have hit a slack period.

"There aren't many in queue just now, Doctor, no, ma'am.'' So she could afford to set them aside, and let the officer perform what triage he liked. There would be time.

Doctor Bokomoro nodded. "Right. Take Joslire across, Robert, take these with you. Next?''

"These'' were Toska and Kaydence and Code, the rest of Security 5.4. All of them weary. None apparently injured. When Station Four cleared, Robert took the lead to their assigned slot, pushing Joslire on the mover before him.

The officer was leaning on the treatment table with both arms braced stiff-elbowed to the surface, frowning in evident anxiety.

"I am becoming bored with bleeding people,'' his Excellency was saying, his frustration clear in his tenor voice. "When is the Captain going to get to it, and take this ship out of harm's way?''

Shaking off wordless offers of assistance, Joslire slid awkwardly from the end of the mover to sit on the edge of the treatment table, facing the officer. Koscuisko scowled thunderously when he saw the exposed gash in Joslire's leg.

Sarse Duro, the senior medical technician teamed with Chief Medical, took one look and broke open a fresh gross-lacerations pack. "Shouldn't be too much longer now, sir. They said three eights to close.'' Noticing Robert, Sarse shut up to concentrate on Joslire's wound. It was out of respect for his feelings, Robert knew. He appreciated Sarse's delicacy.

Eild was Nurail.

He was Nurail, though he was from Marlebourne.

"Erish is to be uncomfortable, but has not too seriously

been injured. Joslire, you are bleeding, you had noticed."
His Excellency changed the subject without comment, putting a dose through at Joslire's thigh. Joslire steadied himself against the surface of the table, and Koscuisko put one hand out to Joslire's shoulder to help stop him from falling over. Muscle relaxant, maybe. Powerful pain medication, almost certainly.

"Kaydence. You are not moving as beautifully as usually you do." Their officer talked as he worked, Sarse Duro content to keep supplies coming. "I should make you all sit down, but then I would not be able to see you. Metal coming out, Joslire."

Along with a freshet of blood damped off almost immediately with a stopcloth. "Talk to me, gentles all, how do you go? I have seen none of the others, at least so far."

Well, he didn't have to answer this question, Robert told himself. He could just stand here and listen. That way he would find out before the almost-inevitable embroideries began. That could be useful for later.

"Kaydence did it," Joslire said, his head bent to watch Koscuisko clear the wound. "We were only there to wa—ouch." Something seemed to twinge unpleasantly; Joslire raised his head to meet Koscuisko's mirror-silver pale eyes, and Koscuisko smiled. Robert had always considered that Andrej Koscuisko had a very pretty smile, all those white teeth, and all of them in such an even line.

"You are a very great liar, Joslire, if I may hope to be forgiven for saying it. And you should be ashamed."

Grin answered grin, now. Joslire had known the officer for even longer than Robert had, and they had known him longer than anyone else—since Fleet Orientation Station Medical, before they'd been assigned to *Scylla*. But that had been three years ago.

And almost the first thing they had learned about Koscuisko was that they were clear to make jokes with him. Not that the others had been easy to convince that it was really safe; and that had depressed Robert at the time, because of what it indicated about the usual treatment bond-involuntaries expected to receive in Fleet.

"But it's true, your Excellency, I swear it by the officer's chin-beard," Joslire protested. There was no response from their officer to this impertinence; Andrej Koscuisko didn't have a chin-beard, smooth-skinned as any unmarried man. Koscuisko concentrated on smoothing the edges of the wound in Joslire's thigh flush with the layer of anaerobe that would protect the raw flesh while it healed.

After a moment Joslire spoke on. "Kaydence's shot was the only one that really mattered, when it comes to that. All the other ones do us no good if the last one doesn't go in." Serious now, Joslire was giving his report, which meant that the others were free to contribute.

"But it was Jos's idea to get through the wastechute behind foodstores forward. Or we wouldn't have gotten there in time." Toska Bederico, apparently no more than bruised and tired, was leaning against the stores table that would normally back against a wall that was now braced up in the bulkhead. "Can you get Jos to admit it, though? There's the question."

As a joke it was not a very fortunate one, in Robert's mind. Andrej Koscuisko could make anybody admit to anything, once he but got them down into Secured Medical and got started. Toska was tired, or he wouldn't have made so potentially ambiguous a remark. The officer didn't seem to have noticed anything; Koscuisko was tired, too.

Of course Koscuisko had been hard at work since the first casualties had started to trickle in. For Robert's own self he considered that he had the better part of the contract, since he only had to fetch and carry. That wasn't really work.

"Was that my idea?" Joslire sounded genuinely startled. "I don't remember it being my idea. I thought it was Erish. Are you sure? I'll take full credit, of course, Robert, write that down."

Joslire would do no such thing, needless to say. Joslire was scrupulous about credit where credit was due, sometimes too much so.

"Don't think so," Kaydence frowned. "I thought it was Toska. Whose idea was it? Because someone's got to go clean that up."

"Light duty, ten days." Their officer tagged Joslire's trouser-leg closed with a few strips of closing-tape to spare his blushes till he could change his trousers. Joslire blushed differently from people Robert had grown up with; he didn't pink from pale, he toasted from tan.

Of course there was the fact that Joslire was simply the color of mealcake to begin with. The officer put his hand to Joslire's shoulder for emphasis. "And keep your weight off your leg, you may walk if you must but no further than two turnings at a time. Now you must go to rest."

Joslire was subdued enough to let himself be moved by Robert and Code in tandem. Off of the treatment table. Back onto the mover. Koscuisko raised his voice and called for Kaydence, who was doing what he could to disappear; but there weren't any walls to hide behind just now.

"Kaydence, you are next. The shins of your boots look as though you had been using scourskin for bootblack." Koscuisko's desire to lighten the atmosphere a bit was clearly evident in his bantering tone; and it worked, too. Quite apart from the fact that Koscuisko was their officer, he was a personable man, whose determined cheerfulness communicated itself to his Bonds almost immediately. "Tell me about it."

Koscuisko was right, the front of Kaydence's boots were scratched and abraded across the shins. Kaydence actually did blush, and since Kaydence was the same generally clay-colored sort as the rest of them, it made him go all feverish in the cheeks. Well, clay-colored like Robert, at least. Their officer was so pale he was nearly blue in the face. And Toska was a little butter-colored, but Salom hominids were supposed to be that shade of sun.

"Sat down to make my shot, sir. Didn't stop moving. Probably just bruised, though, your Excellency—don't make me take off my boots, sir, please, there's a hole in my boot-sock—"

As if Kay thought pleading would do him the least bit of good.

Andrej Koscuisko merely tilted his head fractionally to one side with one of his most killing "Oh, but you know better than that" looks, and snapped his fingers.

Toska and Robert knew what was expected, and moved in to implement their officer's will and good pleasure.

There was no standing between Koscuisko and the welfare of his Security assigned, and whether or not said Security would rather not have an unmended undergarment exposed before all Infirmary had nothing to do with it whatever.

It could be worse.

Security Chief Warrant Officer Caleigh Samons could be here.

Their officer was only interested in the well-being of the skin beneath the stocking, not the condition of the bootsock itself, but let Caleigh Samons once find out that the officer had seen one of her troops out of uniform and there would be the very Devil to pay.

Command and Ship's Primes, Jurisdiction Fleet Ship *Scylla*, never met more informally than this—and in the Captain's office, rather than in meal-hall. There were allowances to be made for the state of exhaustion the officers shared with the rest of ship's assigned resources, but Andrej Koscuisko was too tired to make them, and he wished that his fellow Primes—and Ship's Command Branch officers, as well—would just go away and let him sleep.

"—carapace hull," Ship's Engineer was saying in between sips of hot shurla. "We lost most of the fiberloads. Secured Medical as well. Significant damage to the maintenance hull, but the atmosphere hasn't been compromised, we were lucky."

Wait, wasn't that good news, about Secured Medical being stove in? Andrej almost thought that meant something. Surely it would be significant once his brain started to function again, after he had slept perhaps five shifts. No, that was only forty hours. Perhaps six shifts, then.

Ship's Intelligence paused on his way to his lounger to offer Andrej a flask of rhyti, talking as he went. "Prelims from the rest of the Doxtap Fleet indicate that we actually did comparatively well. We only lost three flyers in action, Fleet's quite pleased. Goes without saying Eild is a little depressed about the whole thing."

Andrej accepted the flask of rhyti with a nod of thanks. Of course Eild was unhappy. The planetary population of Eild had lost its final bid to retain autonomy; and if recent history was anything to go by, they had only want, repression, and relocation to look forward to now. Relocation for selected portions of the population, at least, scattered, dispersed among sixty-four eights of Bench-integral worlds.

Not as though there was much left of the population of Eild by this time, and it had been an outpost world to start out with—like most Nurail worlds, with typically a hundred and twenty-eight grazing animals to every Nurail soul.

It was still a lot of people.

Even after starvation, plague, and war, there were surely sixteens of eighties of Eild Nurail to be moved. To be removed. To be raped from their native soil and abandoned in alien worlds where nobody would even speak their language.

"That's as may be." Captain Irshah Parmin's voice was dry and uninflected, clear indication of how he felt about the use to which his Command had been put. Irshah Parmin was a professional Fleet Captain whom Andrej had grown to respect deeply over these three years of assignment to *Scylla*. Irshah Parmin never let feelings interfere with his duty.

He didn't make too great a secret about the fact that he had feelings, all the same. "There's a relocation fleet standing off at Formiffer to take over. We'll go to admin refit, ourselves. Chief Medical, your report?"

The rhyti was very reviving; he was very tired. It didn't usually have so strong a stimulating effect on him. "Apart from First Officer's losses we have a mortality count of seventeen on wards, mostly due to the hit the carapace hull took at channel two. Of my other patients I list five as being in very uncertain condition, but upwards of ninety lacerations or wounds requiring bedrest or light duty, while the number of bumps and scrapes cannot be calculated."

There were seven hundred and thirty-five souls assigned to *Scylla*, and total fatalities rested at a mere twenty-nine so far. Even should they lose the five on close watch, they had gotten through this one with little scathe: though naturally enough the dead might think differently.

"Triage run the way you like it?"

That was delicately done. That was the Captain's way of asking whether Fleet had failed any of *Scylla*'s crew by failing to have the resources on site that would have saved their lives. Strictly speaking, triage was Medical's business; but Andrej could best honor his Captain's concern by answering the question.

"By our Lady's grace. Which is, I mean to say, yes, your

Excellency, we have been fortunate. We have not lacked for the beds we needed when we needed them."

He was more tired than he'd realized, but his lapse into idiom had amused—and not offended—his peers. Not as though he really was their peer, except for the formality of his rank. Irshah Parmin had in the past honored him by asserting that he might develop into a really top-class battle surgeon, some year. In Andrej Koscuisko's considered opinion he had quite a distance yet to go.

"Good to hear, Doctor. Thank you. First Officer. About that Security five-point-four. Precedent?"

What about Security 5.4? Andrej frowned. Security 5.4 were his people, bond-involuntaries, though 5.4 had been on Ship's Security during the engagement, rather than flying a Wolnadi. Precedent for what?

"I believe so, your Excellency. Bassin"—the Intelligence Officer's name was Bassin Emer—"has pulled the index cases. They call for evidence of innovative thinking in crisis making possible some success crucial to the survival of significant Fleet resources. Case is stronger the more significant the Fleet resources, and I think *Scylla* counts. I know Jik's angry about the wall—"

Now the Ship's Engineer, Jik Polis, grinned and nodded her long perfect oval head in confirmation; Andrej was more lost by the moment.

"—but I think we can document. That was clearheaded thinking under fire. It probably made the difference. And there's no question about the performance under extreme circumstances. I will file the request for Revocation next shift."

. "Does the officer of assignment know what we're talking about?" Irshah Parmin asked with evident amusement in his voice, clearly having noticed what Andrej could only assume was the transparent befuddlement on his face. "Never mind for now. We all need a rest-shift. Engineer, cut to minimum, administrative status in effect. We'll tell you all about it at staff firstshift, gentles, the usual time and place."

They were dismissed.

But Andrej didn't move.

"Captain, with respect." They were saying something about his people. He wanted to know what it was. "You were saying something about Security five-point-four."

First Officer Saligrep Linelly, rising to her feet, stretched to the full height of her sinewy body and yawned before she saluted to leave. The other officers followed as Sali left; they were alone. Captain Irshah Parmin stood from behind his desktable in turn, grinning as he twitched his left shoulder. Captain had never been quite right in his left shoulder. Something to do with an implosion round and some shelving, Andrej understood.

"What your people had to do to stop that sapper, Andrej. Those Nurail were so close to taking this entire ship out. First Officer thinks we have a case for revocation of Bond, if we can just get it through channels before they all die of old age."

Revocation of Bond?

Freedom?

Bond-involuntaries were slaves to Jurisdiction, condemned for crimes against the Judicial order to thirty years of dangerous duty in Security with a semi-organic artificial intelligence implanted in their brains to help guarantee their good behavior. Revocation of Bond would mean freedom here and now, retirement with honors and pension and accumulated pay as though they had somehow managed to live out the term of their servitude and seen "the Day" dawn at last.

"Revocation of Bond can only be granted by the First Judge at Fontailloe Judiciary." Andrej spoke slowly, thinking aloud. Trying to remember. "And endorsed by the majority of Judges Presiding on the Bench. That's five. Getting five Judges to agree on anything—"

Still, it was an administrative matter when all was written and read in. Not a point of Law or Judicial precedent. There was a chance. Captain Irshah Parmin nodded solemnly, then spoiled the effect by yawning in his own turn.

"Even so. That's what we mean to try for. Needless to say, no word outside this room, premature release too painful if eventually refused, and all that."

He should get up, Andrej knew. He should leave. He was going to fall asleep in the chair. And it wasn't even so comfortable a chair. "Of course, Captain. Anything I can do, naturally. It would be a great thing, if."

No, it was no good. He was hardly making sense even to himself. Captain Irshah Parmin waved off the incomprehensible jumble of words with an understanding gesture of his short square hand.

"Of course. We'll talk again. Now get out of here. Go to sleep, Andrej."

Of course.

Turning the wonderful possibility of a Revocation of Bond over in his mind, Andrej went only semiconscious to find his quarters, and fall into bed, and sleep the still unmoving sleep of the exhausted.

There was someone coming through the open door to his office, and Andrej Koscuisko let his stylus sag to one side in a loosened left-handed grip as he glanced up to see who it was. One of the staff physicians, almost certainly. Nobody else would walk into a senior officer's workspace without pausing to announce himself—not unless it was an officer even more senior, and the only officer senior to one of Ship's Primes was the Captain himself.

Oh.

It was the Captain, himself.

Andrej was almost too startled to remember to stand up. Three years on board of *Scylla*, and the number of times the Captain had come to Andrej's office—rather than calling Andrej to come to his—could be knotted on a short string. There was an uncommonly serious look to Irshah Parmin's otherwise quite pleasant round face; waving Andrej to sit back down, the Captain palmed the interlock on the desk surface to seal the office door before he sat down himself.

"As you were, Doctor. Only take an eighth. I've got good news, bad news, and news."

Being behind closed doors with the Captain was a very uncomfortable sort of thing; it only happened when Irshah Parmin had things to say he didn't mean to share, and in the past that had meant points on which Andrej's own behavior had failed to conform to expectation.

"Rhyti, your Excellency? Cavene?"

Andrej thought he sounded too serious by half, even to himself. What could this visit signify? He hadn't done anything he shouldn't have done, not recently.

"Neither, thanks, not staying. Which news do you want first? Never mind, I'll tell you. Good news, Secured Medical is out of order indefinitely, it won't be operational again until after we refit."

"Yes, Captain, good news. Bad news to follow?"

Something to do with the orders-packet that the Captain drew from the front of his uniform blouse, with a sigh of resignation. "This just in on courier. Since you're surplus, in a sense, with Secured Medical off line. Chilleau Judiciary's requisitioned you for the Domitt Prison until such time as we can demand you back to support the tactical mission as *Scylla*'s battle surgeon."

The Domitt Prison? Had he heard of that? The orders the Captain carried would tell him all about it, Andrej knew from experience. He had been detailed on temporary assignment before: always over the Captain's explicit objection.

"Prison duty, your Excellency. I don't believe I've done a prison tour yet." Prison duty didn't have to be too bad, as long as it was a standard Judicial correctional center, and not a processing center. The only thing the Bench needed Inquisitors for at correctional centers was to provide legal sanction for the exercise of prison discipline, and handle the occasional Accused. Not like processing centers at all.

Captain Irshah Parmin frowned. "It'll be weeks at best before we can call for you, Andrej. I haven't spoken to First Officer, but we're going to want to keep that Nurail of yours here on board, the Domitt Prison being in the middle of a Nurail displacement camp. Well, in a sense."

Oh, this was worse.

It was a processing center.

So what they wanted an Inquisitor for was to conduct Inquiry, exercise the Protocols, and perform his Judicial function exclusive of any other duties he might have had elsewhere; and for how long?

"I quite understand." Andrej could hear the strain in his own voice. "Quite impossible. Who is to accompany me, then?" Bond-involuntaries, that went without saying. The Bench's primary purpose for creating bond-involuntaries in the first place place had been to provide Inquisitors with helping hands. The bond-involuntaries' governors ensured that they couldn't decline to inflict whatever tortures their officer required of them simply because it was grotesquely indecent to do so.

He had eleven bond-involuntaries assigned to him here on *Scylla*, but that only made up two five-teams, with Vance as the only Bonded member on Security 5.1. So it had to be either 5.3 or 5.4. With Robert—and 5.3, by extension—held back, 5.4 would be assigned: Well, why not? If it was to be hard duty for them, there was at least the hope in Andrej's heart that it would be their last assignment before the Bench revoked their Bonds.

"You'll probably end up with 5.4. And Miss Samons hasn't been told, First Officer wants to keep things to herself to avoid rumors. It could take months to get the petition through."

Andrej could understand that. The possibility in itself was almost too much to keep to himself; it could only be worse for Chief Samons, who worked with Andrej's people much more intimately. "That's good news and bad news, then, your Excellency. What about news?"

"Ah. In quarters, actually, I didn't hold it, none of my business." Irshah Parmin's raised eyebrows gave him the look of a man suddenly realizing that he'd misplaced something or another. "Came in with the courier, letters for you from home. There's a packet of some sort. We're to turn you over to the Dramissoi Relocation Fleet when it arrives, Andrej, that's just three or four days out."

The Captain stood up as he spoke, and rubbed his face with his hands as though just waking up. "All I can do is promise to try to get you back as soon as possible. My hands are tied. I'd rather have you here."

Because his Captain felt that the Ship's Surgeon should be with the ship, regardless of how young and inexperienced he might be. And would have spared Andrej the ordeal that awaited him, if he could have; and yet Andrej had learned years ago that once he got started with the Protocols he had no difficulty at all implementing them.

"Thank you, your Excellency." The respect he owed his superior officer was offered freely, out of genuine appreciation. "I'll tell someone to pack."

Three or four days, well, he'd have plenty of prep time with as many as three days to reckon with. But what had the Captain said?

Letters from home?

From whom, at home?

From Marana, with pictures of his child, and news of how the son he'd yet to meet was growing?

Or from his father, grim and formal and imbued with decorous grief over the fact that Andrej—in violation of the very filial piety after whose Saint he had been named—refused to be reconciled to the duty his father had set him to, and still declined to beg forgiveness for having challenged his father's desire that he go to Fleet to be Inquisitor?

His father had no more idea of what Andrej's life was like in Secured Medical than Andrej himself had once had, before his training. Andrej had never tried to more than hint at the horrors that comprised Inquisition. His father would only take it as cowardice on his part, evidence of shameful reluctance to do his duty to the Bench and Jurisdiction.

"Security Chief Warrant Officer Caleigh Samons. For his Excellency, Chief Medical."

The calm clear voice that sounded from the talkalert provided a very welcome distraction for Andrej. Chief Samons. That was right. It was exercise period. She would be wondering where he was; or if not where he was, what excuse he might be thinking of to offer this time in his halfhearted but perpetual efforts to get out of the extra laps she would require of him.

"Coming directly, Chief. Koscuisko away, here."

Nothing was going to change his father's mind. Nothing was going to change the test to come, however many months at the Domitt Prison. Nothing could change the horror that he had of the hunger in his blood, but while he ran his laps he did not think about any of the things he could not change. He only thought of laps, while he was running.

That relief from mindfulness alone would have compelled him to seek exercise, were it not for the fact that Chief Samons put limits on his laps, to prevent injury.

Andrej went to join his Security and run his laps, and tried not to think too hard about the Domitt Prison.

◆ Two

It was five days after her early return from Worlibeg before Mergau Noycannir could get in to see First Secretary Sindha Verlaine, Chilleau Judiciary. She'd come back early on purpose to be sure that she was on site when the decision was made, only to discover that the decision had been made without her, the assignment she coveted given away to the last person in the world to whom she would wish it to go.

She'd waited five days for an explanation.

Admitted to the First Secretary's office, punctual to the eighth, Mergau stared at him as he sat behind his desk and did what she could to disguise her hunger. He was a thin reedy man, red-haired and pale-skinned, with watery eyes and a thin high-boned nose that made him look like a prey-animal flaring its nostrils anxiously into the wind to scent for hunters.

He looked small and rather insignificant, behind the great glaring expanse of his desktable. And yet he held the power she desired above all things.

"You have sent Andrej Koscuisko to the Domitt Prison instead of me." She had been Clerk of Court under Sindha Verlaine for only five years, but she was the one who had earned the Writ for him. She was entitled to speak to him directly. She was different from the others. "Why? I thought it was my assignment. Especially after what I did for you at Worlibeg, First Secretary."

He didn't look particularly receptive, his expression blank.

21

Perhaps she should have been more formal with him: But no, she was expressing her natural sense of outrage at being denied a privilege well-earned and well-deserved. To be mistress of the Domitt Prison . . .

Reaching for a stack of report-cubes, the First Secretary toppled them toward him, walking his fingers over the edges one by one. "Yes. Worlibeg. We're getting reports from Worlibeg, Mergau." He had a deep voice somewhat surprising to hear from a thin man. "They'll be talking about you for years. It's not exactly the kind of talk I'd hoped for, though."

He was avoiding the issue, and she wasn't about to let him. "I did as you instructed. I investigated and obtained confession, with collaterals. I executed the Protocols under my Writ, all as you desired."

Verlaine sighed, and kicked the stack of documents-cubes back with a decisive flick of his index finger. "Rather too much so. Mergau, I question your judgment sometimes: How likely was it that all of the Provost's family were plotting against the Bench? Five of them less than sixteen years of age, Standard."

"Confessed under speaksera and were remanded to the Bench, with a neutral observer on site at all times." She was surprised at his expressed discomfort. She knew how to handle children under the Protocols. Hadn't she been especially gentle with the youngest? "And there was no question that a message had to be sent. You said so yourself. To send a Fleet Inquisitor to the Domitt Prison sends a message too, and I believe I have a right to understand why I am being publicly disgraced in this manner."

She'd thought carefully beforehand about whether she should use the word "disgraced." The First Secretary didn't take well to manipulation; it was necessary to be subtler with him than with previous Patrons. But she had held his Writ for three years, the only person in the history of the Fleet to be admitted to Orientation Station Medical without a medical degree.

It was in his best interest to save her face. She was the visible symbol of his power and his influence.

Still, from his reaction she realized she should not have used so strong a word. " 'Disgraced.' " He spoke it as though it were not plain Standard, as though it were a word in a language unknown to him. "How are you disgraced because Koscuisko is to go to the Domitt Prison?"

Andrej Koscuisko to be master of the place, Andrej Koscuisko to enjoy the absolute power, but he would not. He didn't have the temperament to understand how to be master of the Domitt Prison. This was a man who would not discipline his slaves. The Domitt Prison would have as little respect for him as she did.

"It is a very significant. Highly visible. Politically critical job that needs to be done there. And you have chosen to send a borrowed Fleet resource rather than me. The message is clear enough."

Verlaine nodded. "Yes, indeed it is. Chilleau Judiciary elects an independent Inquisitor at the Domitt Prison because it is vital to our credibility that the evidence be perceived as sound. Andrej Koscuisko has acquired a bit of a reputation in Fleet circles over the years, Mergau. I've been keeping an eye on him."

She knew. And she needed to fix his attention on her, and not her hated rival. "I don't think it's unfair to say I earned that posting, First Secretary, and I had a right to expect it. Or at least to be privy to your decision before it became clear to all that I hadn't been so much as informed beforehand."

Verlaine reached for a dossier, looking bored. "You were in Worlibeg, Mergau. Or at least I thought you were in Worlibeg. I have an assignment for you of particular sensitivity, you may as well have this to begin review."

Mergau took a long slow breath, concentrating. All right. There was to be no discussion. It would only expose her to his irritation to press any further. She had to do what she could to salvage something from this interview: People were watching, listening, talking behind her back. She knew. She had informants.

So did he. He had more of them, and in more places. She was one of them, after all.

"Very good, First Secretary. The nature of the assignment, sir?"

He accepted her retreat into formality without any visible sign of having noticed it. "The Langsarik pirates. Bench specialists Ivers and Vogel have been working the problem. There are prisoners in transit to Chilleau Judiciary with what may amount to very pertinent information.''

Langsariks!

The Langsarik pirates had been the mercenary fleet employed by the world-family of Palaam against its neighbors until those neighbors had cried to Jurisdiction for admittance and protection. Since then the Langsariks had persisted as pirates, never quite stamped out, and of late their depredations had become increasingly savage and frequent.

The severity of the problem could be judged by the assignment of not one, but actually two, Bench intelligence specialists to find the Langsariks and their backers and put an end to them once and for all. Under most circumstances, one Bench intelligence specialist was considered more than adequate for any three given wars: one Judicial Irregularity, one Bench intelligence specialist.

If she was to have Langsariks to question . . .

''Are there any preliminaries?'' Mergau asked eagerly, reaching for the dossier. She could use Langsariks. With careful handling, the interrogation of some Langsariks could easily overbalance the snub the First Secretary had handed her over the Domitt Prison. ''And am I to work with the Bench specialists involved?''

Verlaine held on to the dossier for just long enough to cause her to lift her eyes to his face, startled, to see what was the matter. ''The usual statements.'' His expression was unusually severe. ''I want you to take every precaution with these people, Mergau. Full cooperation with Medical staff. I'll have someone detailed to cull the Controlled List for you. We must have information, not just confessions. This could mean the end of the Langsariks, if Ivers and Vogel are right about what these people should know.''

''Of course, First Secretary.'' Only now did Verlaine release the dossier into Mergau's anxious grasp. ''I'll get right on it. When do they arrive?''

If she could get the confessions, that would enable Fleet to put paid to the Langsarik pirates at last: She would be the crucial element in the Second Judge's triumph, a stunning achievement that would easily silence the critics who continued to question Chilleau Judiciary's handling of the Nurail problem.

"Twenty days out yet, Mergau. Plenty of time to start your preparations. And I want you to put everything else aside and concentrate on this. Information. Not just confessions. Information."

Twenty days.

Twenty days, and then she'd get what she needed to more than make up for the fact that Andrej Koscuisko, and not she, was to vindicate the Second Judge at the Domitt Prison.

Working their way through the displacement camp, row by dreary row . . . this was one of the most depressing places Joslire Curran had ever been in his life, the Curran Detention Center where he'd lost his name and taken his Bond not excepted. Most of the population of Port Eild was here. The city itself hadn't been badly damaged, but the Bench had determined that the population would be easier to handle if they were removed from their homes.

How many souls had there been in Port Eild?

How many souls were here in these shacks, huddled together in misery and distress?

Their Captain had seconded them on order to the Dramissoi Relocation Fleet, to serve with Bench Captain Sinjosi Vopalar's other medical resources and travel with the relocation fleet from Eild to Port Rudistal in the Sardish system, weeks away from this world. Where the officer would place his Writ at the disposal of the Domitt Prison.

The sky had been overcast since they'd got here, six Standard days of unrelieved mist and fog. Dirty yellow clouds, and the cloud cover no relief from the oppressive atmosphere, though it wasn't as cold as it could have been—and a good thing, too. The local stores were grievously inadequate to supply a population with sufficient clothing and bedding for cold weather.

He'd heard it said—by displaced Nurail, and more than once—that it had been deliberate, an artificial shortage to increase their suffering; but Joslire knew better. To imagine that the Bench spared a second thought for their suffering was to be misguided. The Bench simply didn't care.

It was Koscuisko's responsibility to work through the

holding areas, the ad hoc cells set aside to hold the Nurail identified as prisoners as well as deportees. There was a difference, and it could be a critically important difference—deportees were subject to privation and dehumanization, but they could not be put to the torture merely because they were no longer to be permitted to die on their own land.

All of the people his Excellency had examined in the past three days were prisoners detained for Inquiry, though no Charges had been filed absent a Writ—until now. When they got to the Domitt Prison, his Excellency would himself record Charges where appropriate, but for now the Relocation Fleet Captain wasn't pressing him. There was no question but that he had as much as he could manage, just working his way through these eights of sixteens of people, trying to decide whether they were fit for the trip and free from communicable diseases.

Finished in yet another overcrowded eight of cells, his Excellency came out of the dark low-ceilinged shed into the chill light again. Koscuisko had been working hard, he was tired; and if Joslire knew his officer, the prospect of having all these souls to be subject to his will at the Domitt Prison was beginning to eat away at him inside.

"I will for a moment in the air sit," his Excellency said to whoever was listening. "I would not mind a cup of rhyti. Very much would I like to smoke. But it would be more cruel than decent to those around, if I did that."

Lefrols stank, but they had their place. His Excellency was not an habitual smoker of lefrols: instead of being mildly addicted to them for the stimulus they provided, he had recourse to the herb when he needed distraction and could not get drunk. The relief from his cares the lefrols provided was moderate, to be sure; but at least afterwards he was not hung over.

Kay snapped the camp-stool he was carrying smartly into shape and set it down in the middle of the barren graveled patch that led between the long lines of temporary cells. Toska had the jug across his back, and broke the thermal seal to pour a steaming cup of rhyti as Koscuisko sat down wearily. Koscuisko took his cup of hot rhyti but didn't take a sip, not right away, resting the cup on his left knee, staring at the drink with an anxious frown on his usually tranquil face.

It wasn't easy for any of them to be here.

It was going to get a good deal worse before it got any better.

"How much further do we go today, gentlemen?" Koscuisko asked, squinting up into the sun with slumped shoulders. Code Pyatte flipped the status-leaves and squinted in turn, gazing down toward the end of the line.

"Says two more cellblocks in this section, sir. Eighty souls—no, sorry, hundred thirty. Doubling up a bit. It'll be just sundown, sir."

As difficult as it was to be here during the day, it only got worse at night. The whole camp was like one large, dark, cramped and overcrowded room at night. And then it started to get cold. It was a sharp depressing thing to know that he was warm and well-clothed, if a bond-involuntary Security slave, while there were children shivering in their parents' arms unable to sleep for the chill in the air.

Koscuisko drained his cup of rhyti and handed it back to Toska for safekeeping. "Better pick up, then. Thank you, Kaydence, I'll go on. Code?"

Koscuisko wanted the roster for the next cell-building; Code found it for him and passed it over. Koscuisko scanned the ticket and seemed to set his mouth against something unpleasant.

"All right. Joslire, if you would go ask for the keyman, please."

The keyman had been waiting, and propped the door wide open so that the officer would have as much natural light as possible. It was dark in the cells. Nobody in the cells had any grounds to insist on light—except that it wore upon the spirit to be kept in the dark like a chained animal.

These were Nurail, not animals.

But leave them alone in the dark for long enough and there would be no difference.

The first few cells were opened for the officer's inspection and closed again without incident, their occupants distressed and dispirited—hungry, cold, and thirsty, rations being adequate but on the frugal side—but hale and whole beyond that. It was only at the fourth cell at the back of the cell-building that the prisoner refused to move when spoken to, and Koscuisko tested the air as though he smelled something that he did not like. What was there to like in the smell of a temporary prison? None of these people had been permitted to wash for days. They weren't going to be here long enough to justify construction of facilities.

"Open here," Koscuisko suggested to the keyman. "Erish, if you would bring up the spare light. What can you tell me about your prisoner, keyman?"

The keyman looked anxious and weary himself. It couldn't be easy, Joslire decided, to have eight souls in care, with so little to do about basic problems of light and warmth. "I've had custody these four days past, your Excellency." The keyman was local, Joslire realized, with a bit of a start. Maybe he'd been a collaborator. Maybe he was thinking he'd backed the wrong side. "I can't get much out of him, he just lays there. He wasn't brought as sick, though, sir. I've let him be."

The keyman knew something was wrong, and was afraid he'd be blamed for it. So it seemed to Joslire. Koscuisko stood in front of the now-open cell as the portable beacon Erish had brought in lightened gradually to full illumination; it had to be brought up slowly, or else the sudden brilliance could be very painful to people who'd spent a week in a dim room.

"Has he eaten? Taken fluid? Voided body waste?"

Thoughtful and considering as the officer's voice was, Joslire could hear contempt and reproach there. The keyman as well, to judge from his response.

"I don't want anyone neglected under my care, your Excellency." Stiff, and offended, but more than that convinced that despite his best efforts he was going to be held responsible for something he hadn't done. "I've had the man in the next cell see to feeding him. And the rest. You could ask him."

If the prisoner was ill, the keyman would have known to report it right away, or risk an epidemic in camp. So what was going on?

"Thank you. Perhaps in a moment. Joslire."

The prisoner lay on one side with his back to the room, with a standard-issue blanket wrapped around his huddled body and his knees drawn up a little as if to try to conserve warmth. Still wearing Nurail foot-wraps, Joslire saw, but at least one of them was torn, or had been rewrapped by third parties who weren't familiar with native footgear. It was beginning to look ugly.

The cell was almost too small for both of them at once, but the closer he got to the prisoner the more convinced Joslire was that he knew what the officer smelled. The prisoner's tag said he was a young man, somewhere between twenty and twenty-five years of age Standard. Nurail could run short and slight for their age. Taken as a whole they tended to be underfed and undergrown, which only made a man wonder what they could have done against the Bench if they'd had adequate nutrition.

The Nurail in his blanket looked unnervingly like a child to Joslire, pale skin and cleanshaven cheeks and all. Nurail shaved till they were married. This one's beard clearly didn't grow quickly, if it grew at all, because there wasn't the usual several days' growth of stubble on that sweat-clammy face.

Koscuisko touched the backs of his fingers to the Nurail's forehead and waited, counting breaths. The prisoner was hot, Joslire could feel the radiation of body warmth clear through the blanket. Feverish. And there were other reasons a man would lose body heat at the back.

"I don't suppose you've got any transmit docs?" Koscuisko called over his shoulder, to the keyman. To Joslire in a quieter tone, he said, "Let's see about unwrapping him, carefully. Tell Toska I'm going to want my kit."

"No documentation," the keyman replied, sounding relieved. To be shown an out? That he couldn't be made to say where the prisoner had come from or who had brought him? "Some Fleet Security, I think, sir. Brought him, took the first available cell, left."

Oh, yes. Of course. Right.

Fleet Security.

And it could be. That was the hell of it.

Koscuisko worried the blanket free from the prisoner's nerveless fingers gently, and the man—or boy—opened his eyes suddenly, staring up at Koscuisko without moving his head. Terror, wild and anguished, and the white of the eye gleaming in the light reflecting off the back wall; terror and a good deal of pain, and Joslire beckoned for the officer's kit, where he kept his drugs—his anodynes.

"Shh," Koscuisko said. Not as if the prisoner had said anything. "We just need to have a look. We'll try not to hurt you." And drew the blanket back in careful folds, hissing through his teeth at the sight of the prisoner's exposed shoulders.

Raw meat.

And there was more of it, most of the prisoner's back had been laid bare, as though his back were all half-masticated flesh abandoned midmeal by a predator.

"Your Excellency—" Joslire started to say.

"It looks like a peony to me, Joslire. Open for me my kit, I want a strong dose of asinjetorix. Kaydence? No, don't come in, name of the Mother." The horror Koscuisko felt at the suffering those wounds represented resonated in his voice, muted though it was to avoid giving alarm to the tortured man. "Go order me a litter for emergency care. And tell them I want it now. And I will need a surgery, as soon as one can be opened for me."

Joslire found the dose and passed it to Koscuisko, who took it in his hand to show the prisoner.

"A pain relief drug," his Excellency explained, as quietly and soothingly as Joslire could imagine. Their officer had a gentle touch with patients. "Not any other kind. I'm not going to ask you what happened. The Bench has forfeited its right to ask you any questions, any more, ever, about anything."

No comprehension on the prisoner's face, but why would there be? Joslire wasn't quite sure he caught his officer's meaning himself.

The keyman's anxiety would not let him keep still and speak when spoken to, apparently. "Your Excellency, what is it?"

Pressing the dose home, Koscuisko waited for a moment, then stood up. "Fleet Security, you say? We will want a statement. It is abuse of prisoner outside of Protocol. He has been put to torture without authority of Writ, because there was no Writ at Eild until I got here, and if I had taken the peony to any man I would remember it."

The peony was the ugliest whip in the inventory, its multiple thongs heavy and barbed. Koscuisko never used the peony except to Execute. It could kill quickly; there was a species of mercy in a quick death—even when it had to be by torture.

Otherwise the peony was good for very little but to chew up flesh like warmed spreadable, and it was accordingly a proscribed weapon outside the custody of an Inquisitor. It was illegal for anyone but an Inquisitor to carry a peony, unless it was the bond-involuntary under orders.

"I don't understand, your Excellency. Peony?"

Maybe the keyman didn't know what it was. Maybe whoever it was who'd been responsible had been counting on just that; or didn't care whether they left clear evidence. Populations were subject to multiple abuses in the aftermath of a final defeat, and this was one of them. And no, Joslire was not in the least interested in what the prisoner's feet would look like once they got this anonymous victim to Infirmary.

"Take a message," Koscuisko suggested. "I am logging this prisoner as released without prejudice due to Judicial irregularity. I will not tolerate abuse of prisoners outside of Protocol. And I don't care who knows it."

And at the moment, here and now, it was because Koscuisko's better nature shuddered at the damning witness of the wounds on the prisoner's back. And not because Koscuisko was jealous of interference.

"If you say so, sir." The keyman sounded dubious. "I had no way of knowing."

Like hell he didn't.

How could any man keep a torture victim for four days and not know?

Still, the keyman got credit for letting one of the others nurse the prisoner, Joslire supposed.

He'd better get a word in to Chief Samons as soon as he could manage.

Something told him this was going to cause trouble for his Excellency. The funny thing was that it was precisely the better part of the officer that was constantly creating problems. The worse part—the appetite Koscuisko had for pain—won him praise and commendation: though not from Fleet Captain Irshah Parmin.

And Fleet Captain Irshah Parmin—the Bench Captain by

extension as well—would certainly have expected Koscuisko to raise this issue privately before taking the irrevocable step of logging release without prejudice.

Chief Warrant Officer Caleigh Samons, Chief of Security for Andrej Koscuisko, found her officer of assignment in a surgery within the temporary hospital that served the displacement camp. Having no brief to interrupt, she stood and watched him work through the sterile barrier that set the surgery apart.

The patient would logically be the Nurail who was responsible for Captain Vopalar's summons, the one Koscuisko had so summarily removed from the jealous grasp of the Dramissoi Relocation Fleet. Koscuisko worked with a look of absolute concentration on his face, salving the man's feet with exquisite care. From where Caleigh stood it looked like nasty burns on the soles of the apparently unconscious man's naked feet, a firepoint most likely; from Koscuisko's distressed expression he thought he knew exactly.

And he probably did.

What difference did it make?

People were tortured without benefit of Writ all the time. The fact that it wasn't supposed to happen was not material. There could have been information wanted, and no time to put in through formal channels for an Inquisitor's services. Things got out of hand when people were stressed, and being shot at tended to aggravate people.

Or maybe it had been something much simpler, someone taking advantage of the uncontrolled environment to express long-standing hatred for a personal enemy. Koscuisko could still be astonishingly naive, from time to time, for all the authority of his position.

He knew very well that such things were done. And still he let it surprise him.

"With you in just a moment, Miss Samons," Koscuisko said, finally noticing her waiting on the other side of the sterile barrier. "Very nearly finished here. Sweet Saints, it is ugly."

Laying one final gauzewrap carefully across the raw skin of his patient's foot, Koscuisko stepped back from the treatment table at last, nodding for the orderlies to come remove the patient. Pressing through the sterile barrier to join him now that the work was done, Caleigh handed him soap to lather up his bloodied hands, and stood by with the towel. This whole thing was off to an inauspicious start, but there was nothing to be done but make the best of it now.

"Bench Captain Vopalar would like to see you, sir. First Officer and Chief Medical as well. In the Captain's office."

It was well past sundown, cold and clammy with the fog. They'd been waiting for Koscuisko for more than two hours now. Her orders had been to find him and bring him when he was finished with whatever he was doing; that was a good sign, they weren't simply arresting the officer. But senior officers waiting on junior officers in Command offices well past thirdmeal never made for good hope of a forgiving mood.

Koscuisko had no comment as she helped him into his dutyblouse, finger-combing his hair and setting his cuffs to rights in silence. When he was ready to leave, though, he asked the obvious question.

"Am I in a very great deal of trouble, Miss Samons?"

It was funny of him to be so formal with her, when she knew very well that he found her physically attractive. Koscuisko was all the more formal and reserved with her for the fact that he would like to go fishing, to use the Dolgorukij metaphor, in her ocean. No. That wasn't right. It wasn't going fishing. It was that his masculine gender was a fish, and her ocean shores the place where it would very much have liked to frolic.

"I think it may be bad, sir." It could be all right. Irshah Parmin had been white-hot furious with Koscuisko on more than one occasion, and Koscuisko had come through without scathe. "Let's get it over with, one way or the other. Because your people are worried."

The Security that escorted them to the Captain's office were Dramissoi resources. Vopalar had Koscuisko's bond-involuntaries with her, a fact that could be construed as ominous. Caleigh didn't particularly care to mention that. Koscuisko would find out soon enough.

Command had administrative offices near the launchfield, in temporary buildings not much better furnished than the camp itself. Koscuisko was lodged in one of these, with his

Security housed all five in a room of equal size adjacent, and a closet for his chief of Security between the two rooms. The Captain's office was the size of Koscuisko's quarters and Caleigh's put together, but that didn't mean very large. There was no room for the bond-involuntaries, for instance, so they were all lined up at command-wait in the hall, and Koscuisko was so surprised to see them that he missed a step and nearly fell on his face before he recovered his footing.

Caleigh didn't want to give him time to wonder what they were doing here. She hurried him through to where Captain Vopalar was waiting, instead.

The orderly knocked at the door and opened it, and there they were, Captain Vopalar, the First Officer, and the Chief Medical Officer for the Dramissoi Relocation Fleet—Doctor Clontosh.

"All we know for sure is that we've still got the right number of bodies in Limited Secure, Captain," the First Officer was saying. Caleigh knew what he was talking about, and listened with keen curiosity.

Nurail displacement parties arrived day by day to swell the ranks of prisoners and detainees in camp. There had been some confusion a few days past surrounding one particular group of detainees and prisoners; a near riot, in fact, only barely contained—with commendable restraint, Caleigh thought—by Dramissoi Fleet Security.

She hadn't realized that a question still remained about whether or not the bodies had all got sorted into the correct categories when it was over. That seemed to be what was on First Officer's mind, though. "The numbers seem to add up. And if anyone ended up in the wrong part of camp, nobody's saying."

It stretched the imagination a little past its point of maximum flexibility to imagine anyone substituting themselves for a prisoner from Limited Secure. Those were political prisoners, and destined to stand the Question from the start. One way or another, though, Caleigh reminded herself, it was First Officer's problem, and not hers.

Captain Vopalar nodded to First Officer as Koscuisko entered, rising to her feet as the First Officer spoke. Once it was clear that First Officer had finished his thought, Koscuisko bowed, making his salute.

"Bench Captain Vopalar. I report, according to her Excellency's good pleasure."

Captain Vopalar received his salute with a curt inclination of her head, gesturing to Caleigh to follow Koscuisko in and shut the door behind her. Not a good sign, all in all.

"Yes, Koscuisko, I want to check with you about something, some misunderstanding, I'm sure. There's a rumor of some sort going around to the effect that you found a prisoner you felt to have been abused outside of Protocols, and that you summarily excused him without prejudice."

Koscuisko would probably have protested that there was no such rumor as such, that it was fact; but Vopalar didn't give him the opening.

"But that would be inconsistent. It's hard to imagine a ranking officer taking such a high-handed approach without at least thinking about how it was going to look. There could easily be an interpretation made that you felt our First Officer was a party to Judicial violations, at least passively. I can't imagine why you'd want to do any such thing without letting us know. I'd like an explanation of this rumor, Koscuisko."

So far, so good. Vopalar put her case strong and fairly, setting the issues out where even a very naive and thick-headed young officer would be able to see them all too clearly. On the other hand, there was absolutely nothing Koscuisko could say for himself unless he was going to prevaricate. Koscuisko would on occasion interpret the truth in a creative manner to get someone off the hook for some minor lapse or another, but Caleigh Samons had never known him to lie.

"I am. Surprised. That such an interpretation might be put on it, your Excellency," Koscuisko said. He sounded surprised, too. "But I must first confess myself, and then hope my actions may be leniently judged. There was a prisoner who had been abused outside of Protocol. The keyman had no information that would indicate any Dramissoi Fleet resource had anything to do with the matter. And I have logged release without prejudice for this prisoner, and spent these hours past addressing his wounds. Had I known you wished to see me, Captain, I would have come sooner."

She waved this off with casual goodwill, which Samons hoped would not disarm the officer. "No, no, Samons was told to find you and bring you when you were finished with whatever. But tell me. Doctor. What do you think having done what you did says to the world about the honor of the Dramissoi Relocation Fleet? You've accused us of abuse of prisoners, we're convicted without even a chance to make an investigation. I think I take that personally. You son of a bitch.''

Captain Vopalar sat down. For all the venom in her language her face was relatively clear; she seemed calm enough. She was willing to give Koscuisko a chance to recognize his mistake, and her officers—seated against the wall—would take their cue from her. Caleigh hoped that Koscuisko would make the right choice when he opened his mouth.

"To the contrary, Captain, with your permission. To have hesitated one moment would have been to suspect that the Dramissoi Fleet was corrupt in some way. To take immediate action was only possible because there was no danger of compromising any of the First Officer's people, your Excellency. The Dramissoi Fleet would not for a moment tolerate such abuse. Surely that is the message to be taken by its disposition of a prisoner found to have been improperly handled.''

Captain Vopalar stared at Koscuisko for a long moment, as if wondering whether he was being honest or insolent.

The moment stretched.

"And of a truth," Koscuisko added, slowly, reluctant to expose himself to rebuke but clearly aware that he'd better come clean. "Of a truth I did not for a moment consider the potential for the interpretation that you have suggested, Captain Vopalar. The man had been savaged. He had earned a full clearance. I thought no further.''

Vopalar glanced over to her officers, clearly soliciting reaction; the First Officer spoke. To Caleigh he sounded almost more exasperated than angry. Of course Koscuisko's action was more potentially compromising to Captain Vopalar than to the First Officer.

"So someone got knocked around a bit, Koscuisko. You know better than anyone that he was only going to get more of the same in Inquiry, what was the critical issue? Prisoners are abused outside of Protocol all the time, and no harm done to the Judicial order.''

Not where Andrej Koscuisko could do anything about it, they weren't. But Koscuisko prudently bit back the rejoinder Caleigh knew to have been on the tip of his tongue and answered the reproach mildly and reasonably.

"He was much more than merely knocked around, with respect, First Officer. Someone had laid him open from neck to thigh with a peony or something very like it, and burned his hands and feet and genitals as well. We are not talking any spontaneous roughhousing here, and it far exceeded what the Protocols prescribe for the Preliminary Levels."

Koscuisko turned his attention back to Captain Vopalar, who had sat back in her chair to listen as Koscuisko continued. This was new information, it seemed. Caleigh felt hopeful. "If my professional judgment were to be solicited, I would have no hesitation in calling it a solid start on a Ninth Level. Except that there were no Charges recorded. There is no excuse for it."

Koscuisko was getting a little emotional there, toward the end. A little too absolute. Caleigh frowned, willing her officer in her mind to be sensitive to the currents around him.

"Prisoners are the First Officer's responsibility, Koscuisko." All the same, Captain Vopalar seemed to have made up her mind in Koscuisko's favor. "I'm sorry it didn't occur to you to let the First Officer be the one to log your discovery. Makes us look bad, no matter how you choose to interpret it. I don't expect you to take things into your own hands this way. I require you to observe your chain of command, and if you just didn't think about the consequences, maybe you should be sure you think things through in the future. You understand?"

It was a fairly mild reprimand, considering. Koscuisko would have a hard time swallowing the idea of going through channels where a clear injustice was concerned; but Captain Vopalar had a right to demand he behave like a subordinate officer, since he was one. He'd know that. Caleigh hoped.

"As Command instruction I receive and comply with this direction, your Excellency." Stiff and stubborn. They'd know he was angry, but that wouldn't hurt. They would expect at least that much. "First Officer, that I exceeded my authority, I must to you apologize. There was no intent to create an unfortunate appearance. But I should perhaps have guessed that such might happen still.''

"Shouldn't happen again, Koscuisko," First Officer agreed, without rancor. "I'll detail an officer to accompany you on rounds from now on, just to be sure you can reach me at a moment's notice. I'm satisfied, your Excellency. No harm done."

They'd put a watch on Koscuisko, to be sure he didn't take it into his head to exercise his Bench authority without prior clearance again. But that was all right. In point of fact she liked Koscuisko, she respected his ability and his instinct, but his judgment was subject to occasional lapses. It wouldn't hurt to have someone there whose presence would remind him to stop and think things through a bit more thoroughly.

"Dismiss, then, First Officer. Doctor Clontosh, make sure that Koscuisko has no cause to complain of the treatment his patient gets in hospital, good-night. Koscuisko, stand by."

The First Officer and Doctor Clontosh left the room in silence, and Caleigh thought that both of them looked a little relieved. Koscuisko had not relaxed, however. Koscuisko knew better than that.

Once the door was closed again behind them, Captain Vopalar spoke.

"Koscuisko. There are five bond-involuntary Security troops in the corridor outside. You may have noticed them when you came in."

It would have been difficult not to. Koscuisko waited, without replying to this obvious statement.

"You're outside the scope of most forms of discipline, which is too bad, because you need discipline. Tell you what. You ever. Forget your place like that, again. And I'll find discipline that is within my scope, except it won't be your back, which needs it, but one of those Bonds outside. Because I can't have your hide, but I can have theirs. This is the way it's got to be, Koscuisko. Get used to it."

Captain Vopalar was right, too. She could invoke sanctions against Koscuisko's bond-involuntaries that would be unthinkable in the context of disciplining an officer. Koscuisko seemed to rock back on his heels, fractionally, in obvious shock at what she was suggesting.

"Captain Vopalar, they have no recourse, how can you think to punish them—"

"Not them, Koscuisko," the Captain interrupted. "You. Make no mistake, if I invoke six-and-sixty against any of those people it will be only because I think you need discipline. From your behavior today that's the only way I can be sure of getting your attention." She held his gaze for a long breath, as if to be sure that her statement received the appropriate emphasis.

And then she looked past Koscuisko to where Caleigh Samons stood at command-wait. "Miss Samons, why hasn't Fleet Captain Irshah Parmin killed this young officer yet?"

This was a clear attempt to lighten the atmosphere once the point had been made. It was also an interesting question. "It's not for me to say, your Excellency." Which was perfectly true. "With respect, he's never found it necessary to invoke sanctions. I'm sure you'll find no further fault with the officer's behavior, Captain Vopalar."

She didn't think Sinjosi Vopalar would take that approach with Koscuisko unless really pressed to it. Captain Vopalar sighed, and seemed to relax a little. "There's the problem with pretending people like you have any business exercising authority, Koscuisko. Fleet's given you the rank. But you don't have the authority. Because you clearly aren't competent to exercise it at this level, but we're stuck with you. Don't take any drastic actions. I don't want to flay your Security any more than you want them flayed. But I won't tolerate insubordination. And that includes taking actions without keeping your chain of command informed."

As deeply offended as Andrej Koscuisko was likely to be by this, Caleigh Samons thought Captain Vopalar had a point. Koscuisko had rank without having been promoted to it; he hadn't spent years in Fleet learning to watch out for pits of the sort he'd just fallen into. Maybe that was why Irshah Parmin hadn't killed him.

"Even as you say, Bench Captain." Yes, Koscuisko was offended and angry. But Koscuisko was capable of demonstrating sense and discretion. "If we may be excused."

Koscuisko didn't understand how much he *was* excused by Fleet, in respect for his difficult position. On the other hand, Koscuisko earned those indulgences every time he went to implement the Protocols.

"Get out," the Captain agreed, with no further anger in her voice. "And take those miserable Bonds of yours with you. I hope not to have to speak to you again, either of you."

For a moment Caleigh could hear Koscuisko's acid "The feeling is entirely mutual" so clearly that she was afraid he'd actually said it.

But the moment passed.

Koscuisko had got through this better than Caleigh had expected.

Now all she wanted to do was to get him and his bond-involuntaries back to quarters and lock them all safely behind doors till morning came.

◆ Three

The Domitt Prison stood on the rising ground above Port Rudistal, looking down on what had recently been a quiet Sentish port city distinguished only by its relative squalor and its Nurail population—which was redundant, in a way. Sentish had traded profitably with Nurail and Pyana alike for generations, true. Still, tolerating a Nurail population could only contribute to a progressive failure of civic hygiene.

The Domitt Prison stood apart.

Almost a year had passed since Administrator Geltoi had received his commission and arrived here in Port Rudistal with a Pyana construction crew and a line of credit against Chilleau Judiciary for the construction of a processing facility to serve the relocation camp that the Second Judge intended to establish on the other side of the river. There had been few Nurail available to him in Rudistal at that time; it had been before the refugee parties had begun to pick up, to be intercepted and shunted into his keeping.

Now that the last of the morning fog had finally burned off, Port Rudistal shone beneath the crisp cold rays of the autumnal sun, its peaked black rooftops glittering with dew. Administrator Geltoi—supreme authority under Jurisdiction at the Domitt Prison—looked out of his office windows over the city, toward the relocation camp across the river; and sang a bit of a traditional tune over to himself, absentmindedly.

"Your grazing animals are my meat, your children are my

41

cattle, you I spare to dung my fields, the Pyana triumphs over you."

It was an old song. Administrator Geltoi paid little attention to the actual words, lost in pleasant meditation on the general gist of it. Nurail and Pyana had clashed for generations, because Nurail did not know their place and would not learn it. The scorn of the Nurail had been directed against defeated Pyana in song after song, insolent tunes and contemptuous melodies; that was all over now.

A signal at the door to his office reminded Geltoi that he was expecting Merig Belan for a tour of the penthouse, to make sure for himself that everything was in order to receive the Writ. Turning from the windows, Geltoi touched the admit, not bothering to raise his voice for so inconsequential a person as Belan.

"Good-greeting, Administrator." The assistant administrator was Nurail, and grinned a good deal to demonstrate his approval and acceptance of the new situation in which he found himself. Geltoi bore no grudge against Belan for his blood, though it was true that Belan was a Sarci name, and the Sarci Nurail had been with the Wai during the successful defense of Port Mardisk—in which Geltoi's own family had met an undeserved and ignominious defeat.

That had been a long time ago, though the songs were still popular amongst the Nurail. Belan was a good Nurail, one of the decent Nurail. Belan knew how to behave in the presence of his betters.

"Good-greeting indeed, Merig. Is the car ready? Let's go."

He already knew the car was ready. He'd seen it approaching on the track between the containment wall and the administration building. It was a standard administrative official's touring car; passenger cabin, retractable roof, the driver's well separated by a privacy barrier, six Security posts alongside on the running boards. It had been an acceptable vehicle for his use for these past months.

His status had changed, though.

The prison was to be fully operational at last, with legal authority to produce admissible evidence—authority that resided in the Writ to Inquire, and the person who held it.

He wanted something new that would reflect his more ex-

alted position. Something to inspire the respect that he deserved: a senior officer's touring car, fully rated against
assault with incendiary and impact projectiles to three thousand impact units and the melting point of stalloy.

He'd had no unrest that slaughter or starvation had not
served to easily contain to date: But Geltoi took no chances.
His life was a valuable asset to Chilleau Judiciary and to the
Bench. His duty clearly called for him to protect that life as
best he could.

"Ready and waiting, Administrator," Belan said, but Geltoi was already halfway across the room. Belan hurried to
catch up; the sound of his heavy breathing amused Geltoi.
"There's a delivery coming, sir, seventeen ships cleared by
the Port Authority to your custody. Two hundred and thirty-
four souls."

Once the Dramissoi Fleet arrived his supply of replacement workers would logically start to diminish; the Port Authority would be forced to process them through the
displacement camp, rather than the Domitt Prison. He would
have to shepherd his resources wisely. Two hundred and
thirty-four souls? Excellent. He had plenty for them to do.

The lift at the far end of the corridor was waiting, properly
attended by the day-watchman, who bowed respectfully to
the Administrator as he stepped into the lift. The day-
watchman was Sentish, not Pyana, but he knew his place. It
was gratifying to receive such marks of submission from
Sentish now that the Pyana had triumphed at last—even if
they'd had to cry to Jurisdiction in order to do so.

Administrator Geltoi paused once he stepped out of the
building, taking a moment to savor the air and the beautiful
bright morning. The breeze from the river came up through
the town with news of the wealth of the water and the kinds
of things people ate for fastmeal here in Port Rudistal, and
swept any lingering unpleasantness that might still have
shadowed beneath his fortress walls safely away from any
conscious perception.

It had been nearly two months, now.

Within a few more weeks the accelerant would have done
its work, and there would be no hint of rotting flesh in the
air to disturb the senses; nor any distinguishing the bones

from those of Nurail who had died of quite natural causes years and years and years gone by, Standard.

"Administrator?" Belan prompted, sounding confused and a little uncomfortable. It amused Geltoi to note how nervous Belan still was of the filled-in pit where the construction crane had anchored, where they'd buried their mutineers. Belan had weak nerves.

Descending the steps without bothering to reply, Geltoi stepped into the passenger compartment of his touring car, settling himself against the deep blue cushions. Belan followed him meekly and pulled the door to; and the touring car swung away from the apron in front of the administration building for the prison proper.

It took long minutes to travel the distance.

The stark black walls of the Domitt Prison rose six stories high, and behind those walls—

Coming around the southeast corner for the main gate, the touring car turned in to the great central courtyard. To the left, the mess building, with the kitchen at the back with the laundry. To the right, administrative in-processing for new arrivals, and the prison's internal security detachment. There were only a few work-crews present, busy at sanding the pavement smooth.

The dispatch building that faced the great gate was quiet this time of day; the work-crews had already been dispatched to their day's labor. Only the replacement carts stood ready at the front, waiting for the word to carry fresh workers out to the land reclamation project as prisoners failed under the requirements of their task.

Geltoi took particular pride in maintaining strict accountability. The same number of workers that had left on work detail in the morning could be counted reliably to the soul returning in the evening. The fact that they were not the same workers was hardly material. What was important was that the numbers added up.

Pulling up at the back of the great square, the car halted to let Geltoi descend. This was prison internal administration, where the prison staff took their meals and guests could receive orientation before taking a tour. The day-warden was waiting.

"Good-greeting, Administrator Geltoi." It was his third

cousin at five removes, Delat Surcase; a poor relation, but a solid Pyana nonetheless. "To what do we owe this unexpected pleasure, sir?"

Surcase was a little nervous; Geltoi knew how to read his kinsman's resentful glance at Belan in the touring car beside him. It didn't hurt for Belan to know that he was resented on all sides. It helped to keep him honest, a difficult task with Nurail.

"Don't stir yourself, Warden, I'm just going to have a look at guest quarters. How are things going, by the way?"

Visibly relieved, Surcase nodded as if in agreement. "Nice quarters they are, too, Administrator. Quiet today, all work details hired out. Eight, maybe eleven replacements so far. No loss."

Quite so. Their hire more than covered their keep, true enough, but Nurail were vermin. The fewer of the malingering scum left in his prison by nightfall, the more room he'd have for the fresh shipment of Nurail livestock Belan had promised him.

When the Inquisitor arrived he would be brought in through here, and would use the main lift to travel up to the roof level. Administrator Geltoi kept a critical eye on his surroundings as the lift rose, thinking.

There was no reason for the Inquisitor to realize that this lift was normally locked off on the fifth level. The officer would have no reason to leave his penthouse at all—except to go to the Interrogations section that had been built beneath the penthouse, with its own lift for the Inquisitor's convenience.

Access was quite properly restricted between Interrogations and the rest of the prison. There were ways in and out of Interrogations apart from the penthouse lift, of course; there had to be communication between Interrogations and the rest of the prison for shift change, and prisoner transfer and feeding, and everything else. It was only reasonable for Geltoi to make sure that traffic was carefully controlled.

The lift rose to the roof and stopped there, locking into place on the receiving dock of the penthouse Geltoi had built for his Inquisitor's keep. Geltoi quit the lift, but not to go directly into the main portion of the penthouse; he went out the back of the receiving dock into the garden instead, to savor the full effect of the artificial reality that he had created.

They were on the roof of the Domitt Prison, six stories high; but with a climate-brake in place and warmth vented from the furnaces, it was as tranquil and quiet as any garden. Six stories high, but shielded from the weather so that a man could look out over the fields toward the river on one side and the land reclamation project on the other, and yet feel no urgent and ungentle wind in his face.

And on the roof, a garden, with a gracious penthouse to be their Inquisitor's quarters for the duration of his stay, and everything a man could need provided in abundance.

A kitchen, the cook already on station; bowing nervously as the Administrator passed through to check the pantry. The pantry well-stocked with liquor and delicacies.

Quarters provided for the Security an Inquisitor would bring with him to help him in his work, two domestics—decent Pyana, not Nurail, unlike the cook—to make sure that the officer's effects were properly maintained. Exercise facilities. A laundry.

Belan had done a good job. Associating with Pyana was improving him, so much was obvious. The living quarters were well-appointed, bathing facilities very inviting, the sleeping room itself positioned so that the penthouse's panoramic view of the town of Port Rudistal could be enjoyed at its very best; and yet there was something missing.

"Very well done, Merig." Geltoi's praise was sincere; Belan had truly exercised himself. It had to be that much harder for a Nurail scant years from savagery to comprehend what a civilized man required for his comfort, and Belan's achievement was all the more impressive for that. "My congratulations, in appreciation for a job well done. One last thing, though, minor perhaps, but important. He might want women. We should have someone from the service house to start him off, at least until we find out what he likes."

Something seemed to shadow Belan's face for just one instant; or perhaps it was just a wisp of cloud crossing the face of the sun. There was no shadow in Belan's voice as he answered, that was certain.

"Administrator. Absolutely correct. So obvious now that you mention it, and I hadn't even thought. I'll see to someone suitable myself, sir, that is—unless you'd like to make an inspection visit—''

Geltoi waved the idea off. ''No, Belan, you've done so well here, I want it to be all your accomplishment.'' And most of the women at the service house were Nurail, which meant one might as well have carnal relations with a beast of burden. Geltoi had rather too much respect for himself to do any such thing, though an Inquisitor's standards might be rather more flexible. ''I'm very pleased. Everything a man could reasonably want for his comfort and recreation. It's all right here.''

Once there were women on site this would truly be a self-sufficient installation.

Once Belan took care of that detail, Andrej Koscuisko would have no reason to leave his little piece of the Domitt Prison at all, until his Captain called him back to Fleet and *Scylla*.

The local planetary police fleet that had intercepted their fleeing ship—just off the Gelp shoals, so close to the Ninies vector and escape to Gonebeyond—had brought them here, to Port Rudistal. They were bound over as a group to the Domitt Prison, and the Domitt Prison held them at the landing site until night fell. They could see where the relocation camp was being built, across the river, the lights gradually brightening as the sun went down; but when the Domitt Prison came to move them, they were not urged in the direction of the river and the bridge to the relocation camp, no, they were marched through to the town instead.

First in one orderly group, at an easy pace, across the launchfield and into the dark streets beyond. It was the landing area, the warehouse section, no one there but night security, and that likely all automated; and the Domitt Prison began to move them a little more briskly as they went out until they were all crowded into a fast trot through the side streets.

Herded like cattle through the town, they were run all the way into the courtyard of the prison by men in transports with shockrods and other weapons. Some of the people stumbled in the streets; they were pulled into the transports by the Pyana, and once they were out of the town dropped out of the back of the moving cars once more, but on a rope this time. Dragged, if they couldn't find their footing.

Robis Darmon was one of the lucky ones; he could run as well as the next man, even older as he was. He did not lose his footing. They tried to help the ones being dragged up to get their footing and run, to avoid injury, but the Pyana would just as soon drag a Nurail in the dust as spit on them, and drove them away from the backs of the cars with the shockrods turned as high as they would go.

One of Darmon's companions, trying to get a young boy back on his feet, was struck by a shockrod, and he went down as well. They were out of the town by then. The Pyana didn't bother to tie his hands, they tied his feet, and dragged him headlong in the dirt all the way up to the Domitt Prison before they stopped to cut his body free.

He was not dead; Darmon saw him breathe. They threw him on a cart full of limp bodies, and the cart went away into the corner of the courtyard, and rising high above the wall in that corner were the steamvents of a furnace.

They couldn't burn the body.

The man wasn't dead yet.

Darmon raised his voice to protest, but was only clubbed for his pains; and began to understand.

They didn't care that the man wasn't dead.

They were more than willing to burn him alive.

They were Pyana; and Darmon and his fellow prisoners were in their power.

As beaten down as Darmon was by everything they had suffered, this final shock was too much to comprehend. He let himself be gathered with the rest and pushed into the darkness of the cellars beneath the wall, packed into storeroom spaces almost too many to a room to turn around. The bolts were shot, the locks engaged, the lights turned off; the jailers left.

It was as silent as a tomb.

He heard somebody start to shout or scream, as though one or two cells removed from this. He understood. They were hungry. They were thirsty. And they did not believe the Bench would treat them like animals, not even though the Bench was their enemy.

He heard the shouting, and the lights came back on in the

hall, he could see the thin edge of light shining in underneath the bottom of the cell door. The sound of heavy booted feet, Pyana jailers. Voices raised in angry obscenities, going away, as if into a room, coming out as though from a room, the sound of blows. And screams. And cries for help, and finally no cries, but only blows out in the corridor on the other side of the cell door.

Then the lights went off again.

And it was quiet.

Young Farnim beside Darmon began to weep, and Darmon put his arms around him to comfort him. And keep him quiet.

This was too horribly unreal.

As terrible as it was to have been taken, as terrible as it was to lose their freedom, they had thought that they were to be bound over to a Bench relocation camp. Not to Pyana.

Robis Darmon was a war-leader, though defeated; there was no dishonor in defeat against superior numbers with superior force of arms. If he had known that refugees were given to Pyana, he would have fought to the death. An honorable death in battle was to be preferred to a Pyana prison; but there had been no talk of the Domitt. They hadn't known.

He was too stunned to think.

He held to young Farnim beside him and stared into the darkness, trying to make sense of what was happening.

They stood there in the dark for untold eons before the lights came on and the door was flung open on its hinges. After so long in silence, the sound itself was almost like a blow. There were armed men outside, and some with shock-rods, and they were prodded with shockrods and threatened with blows until they filed meekly from the cell and down the hall. It was hard to see. The lights were blinding, after having been held so long in the dark.

There were toilets there, and a trestle-table, with food set out. They hadn't so much as smelled food since the Fleet had signed them over to the Domitt Prison and gone away; they found their places eagerly and fell upon the food, and it wasn't till Darmon had consumed the portion on his plate that he noticed that there were more prisoners than portions.

Limited space, well, he could understand that. He should

be sure to drink all that he could, thirst could be a worse enemy than hunger, but once he had drained his cup—and the one the man across from him had already abandoned, in his hurry to get to the toilet—Darmon stood up from his place so that the next man could sit down and have his portion.

They didn't put out any more portions.

The men who hadn't found a place were left to stand and stare, and were not fed, not even when the tables had been cleared of any food, not even when they had been pushed at the toilets one by one, not even when they were gathered up at the door to be taken back to the cell once again.

Not even then.

The rage among the prisoners was palpable, and there was a movement, a surge toward the Pyana who surrounded them. But there were too many Pyana. And they had the weapons; and one round served to stop more than one Nurail, fired at close range. Some were shot and some were clubbed, and one who seemed to have gained their attention was pinned to the floor by Pyana standing on his arms and legs and head and punished with shockrods until he stopped responding to the stimulus, bleeding at the mouth. And nose. And ears.

Then they were all run back into the cell.

There were fewer of them.

Would that mean more would be fed next time?

Or would the Pyana take away the food as their numbers dwindled, in order to maintain their suffering?

Darmon sought Farnim in the dark, whispering his name.

There was no answer.

Things couldn't go on this way, Darmon promised himself, fiercely. The Bench would demand an accounting. Surely.

He could not silence the dread in his heart.

And what about his family?

His son?

The survivors had all dispersed under assumed names, knowing the Bench was eager for blood and would destroy all of the fighting men that they could find. It was all the more important that his child escape. They had lost this war, here and now. There would be other wars. The Bench's cause was unjust. It would not prevail.

The verdict of history was on their side, but history would be silent unless the weaves survived to bring their story to the world. He had been the war-leader. His name was a rallying cry and a watchword to his people. To destroy the Darmon would be to destroy a piece of the Nurail identity forever.

Where was his son?

He had to survive this prison, if he could.

It was his duty to live and cry the crimes of the Pyana to the Bench.

It was a long time before anyone came for them again. They heard movement in the corridors as the other rooms full of Nurail were moved in and out for whatever reason; but once it was quiet it stayed quiet. It seemed to be forever.

It was only a matter of hours, Darmon knew that by the fact that he was hungry and not thirsty.

They took them to the feeding room again, and everybody ran to the tables as quickly as they could. Darmon held back until he could see that there were to be enough portions before he found a place, but his restraint was rewarded, because the place he found was by an empty place and he could share the extra ration with the others if they all ate quickly enough. There was only barely enough time to eat, and they were gathered up into a herd again, but not back to the cell this time—no, up the stairs, prodded by shockrods as they went. Up to the surface.

It was morning, but which morning? How long had they been here?

Morning, and the fog lay heavy in the courtyard. They were formed up into a company, four rows, with eight people in each, staring at the wall of a building in the courtyard. They could smell food. There were people all around, rows of people dimly glimpsed passing between buildings, shouts and curses and cries of pain and rage.

Things quieted down.

The sun cleared the wall of the Domitt Prison and burned off the fog.

They were in a great open central courtyard with the prison all around. One great building faced to the gate, three stories tall; and two other buildings faced each other from opposite sides of the courtyard, at right angles to the gate. They had their backs to the corner where the furnace's stacks were. Far above it all at the opposite wall Darmon could just barely see what seemed to be a roofhouse of some sort, perched atop a flattened place on the roof of the Domitt Prison, six levels high.

The day grew warmer, and the light and the warmth of the sun was welcome to Darmon after so long a period in the dark.

They stood there.

One of them fainted as they stood, and the Pyana guard dragged him out of formation and hit him with an oiled whip until he revived and struggled to his place.

It started to get hot.

A transport came around the corner of the building, headed for them, passing them. Darmon was on the end of the formation; he could see into the back of the transport as it slowed toward the back wall. There were limp bodies there. The transport went around behind them, and Darmon knew as certainly as though he had been told that they were taking the bodies to be burned. Nurail bodies. He prayed that they were dead.

The transport came around the other side of the formation, as though it had barely paused to offload its cargo. Dump the trash. A Pyana prison-guard hopped down from the tailgate and started to move Nurail from the formation into the back, where the bodies had been; two, three, five Nurail.

Then they left.

Their guards formed their company up into new rows. Darmon didn't see; maybe they brought replacements from the other cellar rooms.

They stood all day.

The transport came up two more times, and twice or three times one of the prison guards came down their rows with a pail of water and let them have two dippersfull each. It wasn't enough. But it was better than nothing.

The sun fell below the back wall of the Domitt Prison and work-crews began to return, Nurail work-crews, some on foot and some in transports. The people who had been taken out of formation during the day were not returned to formation. Where had they gone?

When they were taken back down to the cellar, Darmon concentrated on getting as much to drink as he could. There was enough food. Their jailers didn't seem to be too bothered by the existence of extra portions, but they got restless before there was time to eat all that there was, so Darmon and the others stuffed what they could into their clothing surreptitiously.

Back into the cell.

There was room to lie down, now, and Darmon even slept. When he woke up, the extra portion of bread he had hidden away was gone; but he didn't mind so much. Someone had been hungrier than he was. That was all.

He was to blame for all of this.

He had been the war-leader.

If he hadn't failed his people they would still be free to herd the grazing animals on home slopes, and argue about weaves. Free to kill each other over squabbles that ran uncounted generations back, without the interference of Pyana. It was his fault, and their right to demand whatever surplus he might have to offer any of them here.

But next time he would eat the food himself, before he slept.

On the second or third day, they came to him as he stood in formation and made him get into the transport with two others. So now at least he'd find out what had happened to the rest of the people who had been taken away.

He wasn't entirely certain that he wanted to know, but he was too tired to really care about what might be about to happen to him.

The transport took him out to a great earthwork; he was prodded into a line, to pick up a tool that lay where it had been dropped. By one of the bodies in the back of the transport?

They were packing dirt into buckets to be carried up the slope, and further along the earthwork he could see the foundation of a dike taking form in the ditch below them. The dirt was heavy with moisture, at the bottom of the ditch, and he could smell the river from time to time. Land reclamation. Some Pyana would profit from slave labor, clearly enough; but he couldn't spare the energy to think about it.

It took all the strength he could command to fill his bucket before it was jerked up and away by the conveyer and an empty one moved up to fill its place. People were beaten for not filling their buckets, he could see examples enough. But the overseers brought water.

No food, no, but water, and Darmon was grateful enough for the water after however many days of being kept dry that he was almost eager to work for a water reward. Survival meant doing whatever it took to conserve strength, to avoid punishment, to get as much to eat and drink as possible.

He filled bucket upon bucket with damp heavy earth as the sun crossed the sky and his hands blistered.

But when they were driven back to the prison, he didn't go back into the cellar. He stood in work formation instead, and the overseer called off names one by one, and people went forward into the mess building as their names were called.

Shelps. Finnie. Allo. Burice. Ettuck. Ban.

One by one the people to his right turned away and hurried to the mess building. When Darmon was next in line the overseer called a name, and Darmon went; and the overseer nodded at him with what might have been approval of the cleverness of an otherwise dumb animal.

From that time forward, Darmon was Marne Cittrops to the Domitt Prison.

And he understood.

He would be Marne Cittrops till it was his turn to drop his shovel in exhaustion and be hauled back to the furnaces, dead or alive.

Then the next in line from the cellar would become Marne Cittrops.

How many Marne Cittropses had there been?

Whoever Cittrops was, he had a sleep-rack in a cell with his work-mates assigned, and better rations, and enough to drink.

He would be Marne Cittrops.

Maybe he'd survive.

He could be grateful to Marne Cittrops for dying, for failing at his work, because this was a better chance at life than he had had shut up in the cellar, constantly short of food and sleeping with one eye open on the floor.

He slept better that night than he had since he'd been brought to the Domitt Prison.

In the morning they were roused well before dawn, but they were fed and watered, and a guard went down the line as they waited for transport with ointment that seemed to numb yesterday's blisters—toughening gel, perhaps. When the overseer called Marne Cittrops, Darmon ran meekly to his place in transport; and it was a long day, but he lived through it. He could do hard labor. He could beat this prison. He could survive this.

If he could only have word of his child, he could hope.

Now that he had finally gotten through all of the prisoners that the Dramissoi Relocation Fleet held in its displacement camp, Andrej Koscuisko walked standard rounds like any of the Fleet's assigned physicians. It had been three weeks since the Doxtap Fleet had destroyed the artillery platforms above Eild, and taken the world for the Jurisdiction. Some of these people were only now being seen.

Doctor Clontosh's staff had been double-shifting, triple-shifting, robbing themselves of rest and sleep to see that the minimum standards of patient care at least could be upheld; the Dramissoi took its responsibilities to its deportees with admirable seriousness.

Tent after tent-full of tense and resentful, desperate, or resigned and always suspicious people—was it because it had been this long before they'd had access to a physician? Or was it because they knew him by his uniform and his bond-involuntaries for an Inquisitor, and would as soon spit on as speak to him?

"Joslire, bring the satchel, please." The Bench Lieutenant, young Goslin Plugrath, had excused himself to see to an administrative problem that had surfaced in Andrej's tour of the last tent. Plugrath would be back: but not in a hurry. Andrej couldn't blame Plugrath for finding this tedious, still less for resenting being leashed to the heels of a senior officer like a watchdog.

"Gentles, stand by. And someone go for rhyti?" Toska would go; but the point was that he and Joslire would go into the next tent alone.

There were five people in the next tent, all adult males,

oddly enough. Or four adult males and one adolescent, but that was by the way. All of them very suspicious to see him. Oh, very tedious. With any luck, their mutual understanding of the fact that he was outnumbered would settle their nerves. It did nothing for his: But life was imperfect.

Two men seated, three on their feet, watching him warily. One with a soiled wound-dressing on his face, clearly more than a few days old; the best place to begin, clearly. Andrej beckoned for Joslire to bring his travel-kit.

"You, friend. If you would sit down here, where the light is better. I would like to change your dressing." There was no sense in asking what wound it was, where he had gotten it, how old it was. The fewer questions he asked, the more chance he had of gaining grudging cooperation. And it seemed clear enough to Andrej; something had sliced the man across the face possibly as long ago as would be consistent with Eild's last desperate struggle to retain its freedom. Carefully but crudely dressed, as though by persons with time but no resources—like persons in a displacement camp, sensibly reluctant to draw any attention to themselves if it could be avoided.

Working in silence, Andrej dressed the wound. It had been kept clean. There would be scarring, but there were no obvious signs of infection; and though it was quite obviously very painful, the Nurail bore his ministrations with quiet patience, unflinchingly. Clear across his face from above his right temple across the space between his eyes at the top of his nose, traveling the full distance of his cheek to terminate at the jawline—almost too precise to be accidental or inflicted in the heat of battle.

But it was none of Andrej's business.

"It's healing well." Two of the other Nurail had come to stand to one side where they could watch, being commendably careful not to alarm the Security outside by stepping between Andrej and the open door. "I do not envy you the sting of it. Are you able to sleep? No matter, here. Accept these, to be taken if the wound should begin to trouble you, three at a time but only twice a day. You have access to drinking water? Good. And if your temperature should start to rise, present yourself on emergency report. Any infection in tissue so close to your brain must be treated with absolute seriousness.''

If Robert were here there would be an unspoken joke on this issue, communicated in its entirety with one quick glance—how could it be that there should be an issue, when he had been so many times instructed that there was not enough Nurail brain to begin with for damage to be detectable? It would be a joke, if it were Robert, but Robert was not here. Andrej missed him.

It had been Robert St. Clare at Fleet Orientation Station Medical, all that time gone, who had shown him how he was to carry himself to survive the use to which Fleet meant to put him; Robert, and Joslire, of course. And Robert had been sent with him to *Scylla* as part of the bargain that he had made with the Station Administration for Robert's life. But Joslire had elected to follow him of his own free will.

Joslire—

As Andrej's thought traveled from Nurail to Robert to Joslire he glanced around to find Joslire, just to see him there. Joslire stood at the ready with the travel-kit; but something was a little peculiar, almost wrong.

Joslire was upset about—what?

"Thank you, sir." The wounded Nurail's voice startled Andrej back into focus. "It has been a little wearing. But all's well here aside."

It had to be painful to speak, with his face cut in that manner. Andrej appreciated the courtesy all the more; thanks were something he almost never got to hear, any more, not since he'd been seconded to Dramissoi. Andrej nodded, smiling in appreciation but unable to quite take one man's word for it even so. "That is good to learn. All is well with you, then?" he asked the nearest Nurail, a short and stocky bearded man who seemed to be frowning, by the lines of his forehead.

"As well as can be hoped for, in such a state as you find us—"

Then he bit the phrase off short, leaving Andrej to wonder if it had been all he'd meant to say. But it wasn't up to him to press it. If the Nurail said he was all right, he was all right. Andrej had no brief to force examination upon these people without good and evident reason to do so.

Therefore he merely took the statement as complete, and did a quick scan of the other faces in the tent. The second Nurail beside the bearded one, also bearded, but tall and well built like Robert rather than being short and more or less square in shape. Two others sitting on a sleep-rack together, the younger wearing a blanket across his shoulders as if he were cold, meeting his eyes gravely as Andrej looked at him.

Something . . .

The younger man had unusual eyes. Andrej couldn't decide what it was he noticed, from where he stood, but if he went over to look—to satisfy his curiosity—he would probably give the wrong idea. Something peculiar. The blanket across the young man's shoulders was lapped over his knees, falling in concealing folds over arms clearly folded across his chest—

Joslire.

Joslire had noticed something.

And suddenly Andrej knew exactly what it had been.

His mind racing, Andrej stared at the young Nurail on the sleep-rack, trying to consider—judge—evaluate—balance, and decide as many of the questions in his mind as he could manage in an instant. Joslire had noticed, but Joslire had said nothing. Joslire said nothing now, only bowing in acknowledgment when Andrej looked back over his shoulder at Joslire standing by the door.

Lieutenant Plugrath was off with the quartermaster and did not care to pay too much attention one way or the other. But he had his clear duty, how could he not cry this to the First Officer at once?

Because the blanket folded so carefully across that young Nurail's shoulders and across his knees did not conceal arms that were folded across his chest.

The angle of the curve of the upper arm was wrong; it was a little thing, and he never would have snagged on it but for his unusually rich experience—especially recently— of dealing with people whose arms had been shackled behind their backs.

He had been quiet for too long. The Nurail had all noticed; and although Andrej was careful not to notice in turn, there was a savagely repressed sense of desperation in the eyes of the Nurail in the tent, all fixed on him. All except the youngest, who had turned his face away with a fine air of casual unconcern. It was very well done. It was valiantly done. It was a splendid effort.

It didn't work.

"That is a nasty scrape, across your throat," Andrej said to the young man. "If you don't mind, I mean to have a look at it." And there was a scrape, visible now that the Nurail had turned his head. Had there not been one Andrej would have been forced to invent it.

"It's nothing to trouble the officer's self over, really, no need—"

"There is no use in arguing with physicians." The tension levels within the tent were mounting moment by moment; and he had to have control of the situation, for Joslire's sake as well as for his own. Uncomfortably aware that the odds of being jumped out of sheer helpless rage and frustration were increasing to a dangerous degree, Andrej forged ahead.

He couldn't walk out on this now. One way or the other he had to resolve it. "Especially not physicians with rank, we expect to be allowed to make up our own minds about things, regardless of appearances. Howsoever obvious they might seem." Maybe that would be a hint. Maybe.

Andrej crossed the small space in the tent past the seated Nurail with the wounded face, willing himself to display in his posture and his pace a confidence that he did not feel.

A rope burn, that was what Andrej had seen on the young man's neck, and it only convinced Andrej that he did in fact know what was going on. What had happened.

"If you would shift," he suggested to the Nurail who sat on the sleep-rack next to the younger man, glaring up at him with affront and savage hatred. "I'd like to sit down and look at this welt."

What should he do?

Clearly the young man had been somebody's prisoner.

Clearly it was his duty to report it.

Yet he had heard First Officer say that there were no prisoners unaccounted for, and that Nurail who had been half-flayed with the peony had also been somebody's prisoner—and unlawfully misused by them. What did he care if somebody had meant to send the young man to the torture, so long as the Dramissoi Relocation Fleet had overlooked him?

There were so many prisoners already.

He was tired and angry, tired of tent after tent full of frightened people held in straitened circumstances, angry at the casual abuse so many of them had suffered prior to their arrival here.

Could he rationalize taking the Law into his own hands, to aid and abet a fugitive from justice?

That was the point exactly, though, at least in a sense.

This young man was not a fugitive from justice.

He was a fugitive from a vengeful Bench, and that was something else entirely.

Slowly, as if almost despite himself, the Nurail shifted to one side, making room for Andrej to sit down. The young Nurail himself was watching Andrej carefully, and the expression on his face looked to Andrej to be at least as much challenge and curiosity as fear.

Andrej sat down beside him and lifted the blanket carefully from behind the young man's back, draping it to the front over the young man's shoulders to preserve the illusion. Yes, chained at the wrists behind his back, and the hands themselves swollen—it had been days, perhaps, with no way to get to a tool intelligent enough to decipher the Bench-standard manacles or sturdy enough to hammer the bonds through by main force.

Just as well.

Hammering through the bonds would have damaged the wrists badly. The Bench was very careful about its security encoders; the likelihood of finding a key sophisticated enough to do the job was not good. Keys for manacles were restricted issue, much more tightly controlled all in all than the manacles themselves.

These Nurail probably would not be able to find a key at all, still less before the damning fact of the matter would be revealed—as it would surely be during in-processing at Rudistal, if not before.

Few Judicial officers were assigned master keys.

But he had one in his travel-kit.

He was Andrej Ulexeievitch Koscuisko, Ship's Inquisitor, Jurisdiction Fleet Ship *Scylla*.

He was expected to have lawful need to loose a prisoner's

manacles, even it was only to be in order to bind them over into some other form of restraint.

"I'll want a salve, Joslire." It was dim at the side of the tent where he sat, but Andrej didn't need more light to know what he was looking at. The skin would have suffered the effect of those manacles, especially over a period of days. But that wasn't so much the point as that his salves were in his travel-kit. "Bring me my bag, if you would, it's the shorris ointment, I'm not certain how to tell you exactly where to find it."

Shorris ointment would go for the welt at the young man's throat as well. Someone had dragged the young man by a halter, perhaps. There were marks from a beating, blood soaked through clothing and dried, but that would wait. First things first. The Nurail were confused, and anxiety could make a man irrational.

He had to keep talking. "Have you other hurts, that I should be told of?" Joslire brought his kit, but had not handed it to him; Joslire knelt down in front of where Andrej sat, instead, searching through the contents of the kit he opened on the floor. Andrej noted that Joslire had his back to the door. No one standing in the brighter light of day outside the tent would be able to see quite what Joslire was doing.

"Shorris ointment," Joslire said, pulling something out of the bag at last to pass it to Andrej in both hands. "I think that this was what his Excellency wanted?"

The right ointment, too, all of these years of fifth-week duty in Infirmary had served Joslire well. He knew what he was doing.

There was more.

There was something underneath the ointment pot as Joslire passed it to him, something familiar to his touch.

His master-key.

"Precisely so." Over the years Andrej had learned that he could do sometimes quite irregular things in Inquiry without causing his Security distress. The governor that ruled a bond-involuntary's life apparently recognized that by the Bench instruction only mutiny and treason were forbidden to Inquisitors.

This was significantly different.

This was active commission of a near-criminal act, could the fact that Joslire knew what Andrej meant to do truly keep Joslire's governor at bay?

It had to wait. Whatever the explanation, it was clear that Joslire was at peace with his governor here and now; Joslire suffered no pain. Unlike this young Nurail, who was due for a sharp discomfort as the manacles came off—

"Thank you, Joslire." He kept his voice casual, business-like. "You, there. This may sting a bit. You might want to come and hold your friend still in one place, for me."

One of the men came to stand in front of the young Nurail, taking him by the front part of his shoulders carefully. The expression on the man's face almost gave Andrej pause; this seemed more intense even than the care a man had of a young relation, and if this boy had escaped from Limited Secure, he could be of political importance.

Almost Andrej wanted to think twice: But no, any man with a cousin or nephew or son would be desperate to see his kinsman safe from torture, free from threat. Andrej saw all of the confusion and wild hope that the young man declined to share with him in his expression, gazing up at his older companion.

Three small adjustments. Feeling with his fingers in the dim light, Andrej fit the master key to the secure that locked the wristpieces of the manacles. The mechanism unlatched, and the shackle's locks cleared; but as Andrej had feared, they'd been in place for too long. The flesh had swollen around the wristpieces and held them in place.

"This will not be pleasant," Andrej warned whoever was listening. A quick dose of something generally soothing was what he wanted, but to call for such a dose or to be seen to press one through would be inconsistent with the handling of any given welt, and might raise an unwelcome question in somebody's mind. If not now, perhaps later. "Joslire, top-ical anesthetic. Please."

He had to expose skin before he could anesthetize it. He peeled one wristpiece open carefully, first one half-ring, then the other, and the greedy manacles carried bits of torn skin with them as they came away.

"Not too much longer, now. Try to breathe." *That's one*, he'd almost said. He couldn't say that. One what?

Daubing the topical anesthetic around the livid bracelet of scored skin, Andrej waited for the numbing to take effect before he tried the wristcuff on the other hand. The other wrist was worse, because it had been uppermost of the crossed arms, and had more trauma accordingly. Andrej did what he could to make the prying bearable, but it was hard on the young man to suffer the pulling apart of the manacle's wristpiece.

Andrej salved the wound in silence while the Nurail muffled his cries against the jacket of the older man, who stood and held him, stroking his hair with grim tenderness. Circulation would increase almost immediately, and that could be even more difficult for the young Nurail than the removal of the manacles had been.

With help from the men who were clustered now around him, Andrej shifted his patient's arms gently to the front to lay forearm across thigh, careful to keep the blanket folded to conceal the wounded wrists. The wrists would heal. The livid welts would stay hidden by the cuffs of his shirt until they healed. It would be all right.

"Well, there need be no permanent damage." Now that that was taken care of, Andrej laid ointment on a sterile pad, which he applied to the rope weal across his patient's neck with a delicate touch. That had been his excuse, after all. "Sometimes massage can be helpful, improved circulation speeds the healing. Carefully done to avoid breaking the skin open, of course."

He couldn't be too obvious. He didn't know whether Lieutenant Plugrath had returned yet, and might be waiting outside, listening to what he had to say. "Are there other hurts that I should know about? This is the time to speak, to tell me them."

The older Nurail who had been holding Andrej's patient stepped back a fraction now, unfastening the young man's shirt to open the garment and uncover his back. Andrej revised his assessment of the young man's age, studying the bruised shoulders and the muscles that showed beneath the skin. Not yet a man. Not a boy either, but in the borderland between them. Perhaps so many as seventeen years old, Standard, but that was stretching it.

It had not been a bad beating, Andrej could see that as the

fabric fell down from the patient's shoulders to his waist. The beating was not the problem. The problem was the burns beneath the young man's arm, long stripes, precisely spaced, in the tender skin at the underside of the upper arm and on the side of the torso beneath the armpit.

Torture.

Torture, again, abuse of prisoners outside of Protocol, and Andrej was glad to see it, because it removed any nagging questions in his mind over whether he should not really report this to First Officer.

"Let me have a burn-dressing, Joslire." If he spoke quietly enough, no one would hear from outside, or at least not enough to make them think twice. "And some sampers cream."

If this ever came out, it would be Joslire to suffer for it, Joslire or another of his Bonds. He was hazarding their pain against his whim. He had no right. Yet Joslire clearly seemed intent on putting the gamble forward.

Andrej stood up.

"Shorris ointment, five days, three times a day applied to broken skin with clean hands, carefully." Holding the salve-pot out to the older Nurail standing beside the sleep-rack, Andrej counted off instructions and indications one by one.

"Sampers cream for burns, lift the dressing and apply the cream, then lay the dressing back down. I'll bring a fresh dressing the next time I see you." If he ever saw them again; and he didn't expect to. Regardless of whether he was going to reveal their secret, they knew that he knew the secret, now. They would do whatever it took to disappear into the metaphorical woodwork—changing places with other Nurail who would pass during meals or sanitation breaks, perhaps.

"That's it, then?" One last chance for any further requirements. He could feel the weight of the manacles in his pocket; he'd transfer them to his case in the next tent. Chief Samons didn't go into his case, and Security wouldn't ask questions. If he put them in one of the backslits, he could always pretend they had been there all the time.

"If his Excellency would care to give his name," the man with the scarred face said. "It may be possible to exclude you, from the general curse the Bench has earned."

As thanks it was more than gracious, really. "My name

is Andrej Koscuisko, and I have earned my share of the blame well and truly.'' They would know why. They could read his rank as well as any of the others. ''But I am grateful for the thought regardless. Good-greeting to you all.''

Nodding his head in general salute to the room at large, Andrej quit the tent with Joslire at his back, and paused just outside the doorway. Down one long graveled lane he could see Bench Lieutenant Plugrath, on his way back from his errand to rejoin them and resume his nursemaid duty. Closer to them, but coming from the opposite direction, Toska with rhyti; Andrej moved down to the front of the next tent to wait, just to make it clear the last tent was finished. Nothing interesting there.

''Joslire. You amaze me.''

Quietly spoken. And tried to express his confusion, concern, appreciation, anxious inquiry in four short words that would send no message to any casual eavesdropper.

''I know your mind,'' Joslire answered, as quietly. Clearly convinced that they weren't in danger of being overheard or the conversation remarked upon, for the next few breaths; because Joslire spoke as a free man, not as a bondslave. ''The officer is the rule of Law to me. My trust in thee is absolute.''

Now Toska was here with the rhyti jug. Andrej sat down on the camp-stool that one of the others brought up for him, finally, covering his confusion with attention to his rhyti. He'd learned that trust could give a bond-involuntary back a measure of freedom; he'd learned that from Joslire, in fact, early on. Joslire's utter conviction frightened Andrej a bit: What if Andrej should fail, and betray him?

He could not fail a man who knew him so well—and who trusted him anyway.

The realization steadied Andrej, and comforted him.

Handing his empty rhyti flask back to Toska, Andrej nodded to the newly returned Plugrath as though nothing had happened; and turned in serene self-confidence to go into the next tent full of Nurail.

There was work to do.

No time like the present to be back at it.

◆ Four

The days passed one like that before and after, and day by day Robis Darmon began to lose hope of ever leaving the Domitt Prison.

There was no alteration of the schedule, and no lack of bodies to replace those who failed beneath the task. Many failed. It wasn't that which disheartened Darmon, or Cittrops. He was not losing strength, not too quickly; he was holding his own.

He saw too much.

Day after day, as people fell, to be dragged off still twitching to the furnaces.

People who slipped into the deep trenches being dug for the foundation of the dike, and who were left there, screaming in pain or calling out half-delirious for help, until they stopped crying. To be buried in gravel, whether still or not, as the work of the foundation went forward.

Gradually day by day he realized that men who saw such things would never be released to speak of them, because it was a crime by Bench precedent to murder men in such an offhand fashion. Even if they were only Nurail. Slave labor could be levied by a prison, there were rules, but work-crews had to be treated like laborers and not like cattle, and when they left the prison they had to be paid off for their work.

Not killed and replaced, killed and replaced, killed and replaced again day after day.

The prison administration had no intention of permitting them to live.

There was no hope, no future, and no sense of time or purpose. He had almost forgotten that he was not Marne Cittrops. He didn't know who Marne Cittrops was. It didn't matter.

All he really remembered was a son.

He hadn't seen his child here, not yet; he hadn't heard the overseers gloat that the only surviving child of the Darmon had been taken or killed. They didn't know they had the Darmon himself, yet; he had been taken prisoner under an assumed name for self-defense. Now it was even better. There was no connection between Marne Cittrops and Robis Darmon: and no word that would indicate that his child was a prisoner.

He could keep breathing as long as his child was free.

He would not leave the Domitt, not alive.

But Chonniskot was free.

And there was hope.

He labored next to the second man he'd come to know as Shopes Ban. The sun was coming later, leaving sooner; he had no way to tell the time as such, but anyone could see that the sun rose less completely opposed to where it set day by day. Tracking south, by Standard convention, which meant winter, which meant shorter days; but it was still brutally hot and dry work at the bottom of the great ditch, and he was still as grateful for water when it came.

Five days after the new face had come to be named Shopes Ban, the overseer came with troops in the middle of the day, searching the line, looking for someone. Robis kept his head down, kept his eyes down, looked as stupid as he could. Shopes looked at him out of the corner of his eye, but Robis forced himself to look ahead, sending his warning low-voiced through half-parted lips so that the sound would not betray them.

"Keep working. You're nobody. Concentrate."

He knew who Shopes had been in a previous life; he thought Shopes had recognized him, though it had been a day or two before he'd noticed that the searching confused gaze Shopes would turn on him had been replaced by despair and fathomless sorrow. Shopes had been a junior officer. His name was Shopes for now, though, and Robis fixed that firmly in his mind.

He had forgotten everybody's name.

He had made it his business to bury all the names he used to know beneath the gravel that came down the slope to line the bottom of the foundation ditch. He buried a name every time a Nurail fell and was kicked beneath the huge stalloy rollers of the loader to be ground into dust with the refuse from the work. The fewer names he could remember, the fewer names he could be made to say if they found him; but they hadn't found him. They seized Shopes Ban instead, and carried him away to special transport. Up the slope.

When the overseer came with dippersfull of water, Robis begged the extra from him and was allowed to gain the gift by groveling. He didn't mind. It was nothing to do with him, and everything to do with just survival. He had to do whatever he could do to get enough to eat, to drink, to survive. No matter how it burned within him to beg of a Pyana what would be granted any dog in simple good husbandry. It was too late to die with honor and go to glory. His duty was to survive as long as possible, because the longer he survived the greater were his chances of somehow getting through. Some way. No matter how hopeless it might seem to be.

Twenty-plus days in vector transit from Eild to Rudistal with the Dramissoi Relocation Fleet, with little to do but play cards and accompany Koscuisko and his young shadow Plugrath as he did his rounds through the transports. Koscuisko would much rather be with the rest of the fleet's medical staff even now.

Caleigh knew the thought that was in Koscuisko's mind as he stood at the top of the steps in front of the dockmaster's Administration building, gazing over the river to the relocation camp beyond. But he hadn't been sent here to help keep the relocation camp healthy. And soon he would no longer be the Dramissoi Relocation Fleet's concern at all.

Bench Lieutenant Goslin Plugrath stood one or two steps lower than the more senior officer, with his hands clasped loosely behind his back, looking bored. Taller than Koscuisko, bigger than Koscuisko, dancing attendance on Koscuisko had all too clearly not been Plugrath's idea of a good

time. Caleigh gave him good marks for professionalism all
the same: He'd been polite and respectful throughout.

"That's done the last of it, Chief," Toska said, wiping the
dust from his hands with his whitesquare. "Loaded and
ready."

The Dramissoi Relocation Fleet had put a car at their disposal, and a Security escort under Plugrath's command.
There wasn't all that much luggage to stow; bond-
involuntaries traveled light, partially because they had no
personal possessions to account for. Caleigh nodded.

"Be at ease, then, Toska. Stand by, we should be getting
out of here."

The sun was setting over the hills west of Port Rudistal,
the brilliant glare of its long rays throwing the low tents of
the relocation camp into high relief against the lowering
clouds to the east. It was cool and damp on the loading field
already. Once the sun went down it was going to get cold.

Lieutenant Plugrath shifted his weight where he stood,
turning his head on his short neck to the officer. "I'll just
go send a reconfirm, your Excellency." Plugrath didn't believe senior officers should be kept waiting any more than
Caleigh did. Koscuisko was willing to wait, in this instance,
but unwilling to make a fuss about it; he just nodded gravely.

As Plugrath turned to go up into the building, however,
Caleigh saw something coming from between the towering
hulks of the launchfield loaders, weaving its way toward
them through the canyons between the close-packed warehouses.

"Bench Lieutenant." Calling him down to the loading
level with her, Caleigh gestured, pointing with her chin.
"Our escort, sir?"

As the car cleared the maze of warehouses and picked up
speed along the launchfield perimeter, Caleigh could see that
it was a touring car, luxurious and expensive, with a carload
of what was probably Security behind it.

"So it would seem, Chief. And about time."

Once Koscuisko set foot in that transport he would be
halfway between the Dramissoi Fleet and the Domitt Prison,
properly assigned to neither. Caleigh wondered whether Koscuisko had fantasies of hijacking the transport, and making
for—for where?

There was nowhere for him to go.

He couldn't go back to *Scylla* without clearance from Vopalar and the Domitt.

She was being silly.

The touring car and its escort pulled up in front of the landing with a fine flourish of kicked-up gravel; and the Security troops, hurrying out of their transport, formed up to receive the officer. Caleigh was not impressed: But they were merely Bench resources, not Fleet, and only prison security at that. She was privileged to work with bond-involuntaries. The standards could not be compared.

Now the touring car's passenger cabin door opened, and a man stepped forth from the open-roofed interior. Looked vaguely familiar, in some way. He shifted his gaze uncertainly between Caleigh and Lieutenant Plugrath, as if not quite sure who he should address; and settled on Plugrath at last. Very properly.

"His Excellency?"

He didn't take Plugrath for Andrej Koscuisko, no, clearly not. He wanted to verify Koscuisko's identity.

"Waiting," Plugrath affirmed, not very helpfully. "And you, sir?"

"Assistant Administrator Merig Belan, from the Domitt Prison. Come to carry his Excellency's party to quarters on site. If you'd present me, Bench Lieutenant."

So he'd studied the rank-markings, even if he'd had to concentrate on the rank Plugrath wore for a moment before deciding on the appropriate mode of address. Plugrath gestured for Belan to precede him up the stairs to where Koscuisko stood patiently, secure in his knowledge that they'd come for him when he was wanted.

"The Domitt Prison's assistant administrator, your Excellency. Merig Belan. Administrator Belan, his Excellency, Andrej Koscuisko."

On the one hand, technically speaking, the assistant administrator might rank equally with Koscuisko in the prison chain of command; or perhaps higher. On the other hand, Belan had asked to be presented, which clearly indicated his expectation of assuming the subordinate role.

There was the fact of the Writ to consider. When his Excellency was not in the presence of his administrative superior, he was a functionally autonomous power in Port.

"Administrator Belan. Are we to go to quarters, now?"

Belan bowed. "The Administrator's profound respects, your Excellency, and I'm to tell you that he's indulged himself so far as to prepare a small reception in your honor on site. It's not too long a drive, if your people would care to load?"

Koscuisko was looking to Lieutenant Plugrath instead of responding directly; Plugrath answered in Koscuisko's stead.

"Administrator Belan, with your permission, I'll see his Excellency to greet Administrator Geltoi personally. Because if I failed to escort the officer to the threshold of the Domitt Prison, Captain Vopalar would have some very unpleasant things to say to me about lack of respect and neglect of military courtesy."

Well, they'd be a little bit of a traveling-party, then. Because Belan had brought Security, and Plugrath had quite naturally had Security, even if Belan's Security seemed a little on the ceremonial side of an officer's escort and Plugrath's Security looked a little to the assault-ready side of an honor-guard.

For a moment Caleigh hesitated, looking down at the open roof of the touring car at the foot of the stairs; surely Koscuisko's blond head would make too good a target against the dark plush fabric of the interior?

It wasn't for her to say.

Nor was Rudistal a hostile Port. It was a Bench protectorate, and there hadn't been any trouble at Rudistal, or Vopalar's First Officer would have let her know. Surely.

"Follow us, then, by all means." Administrator Belan's hearty agreement was a little forced, but not insincere. Caleigh decided it was just that Plugrath's presence hadn't been anticipated. "And now. Sir. The light will be going."

Was it her imagination, or did Lieutenant Plugrath frown as he caught sight of the touring car?

The officer was beside her, at her elbow. "Miss Samons. We don't want to keep these gentles from their thirdmeal." He sounded a little amused about something; the careful dance taking place between Plugrath and Belan, perhaps. "A reception, perhaps there will be dancing girls. I beg your pardon, Miss Samons, that would be of limited interest to you, please excuse me.''

If she was tense enough for the officer to feel a need to tease her in so formal a fashion—she was too tense by half; and for what?

Caleigh Samons knew the answer to that one.

''Life is full of surprises, your Excellency. Who knows. Maybe dancing boys provided specially for Chief Warrant Officers.''

It was up to Plugrath and Belan to be tense just now. Especially Belan; it was his Port, after all. Oh, perhaps not his Port, but certainly his prison.

Caleigh squelched her errant thoughts firmly into decent self-respecting silence, following Koscuisko down the stairs.

The touring car that the Domitt Prison had sent for him had positions for three Security to stand on the running boards on each side, which meant that Chief Samons insisted on her place at the leftmost, rearmost post, and very tiresome of her, too. But there he was.

There Miss Samons was, more to the point, with Code and Toska on his left, Kaydence and Joslire and Erish on his right, and no one for him to talk to except Lieutenant Plugrath and his assistant administrator, neither of whom were anything close to as stunningly seductive as Caleigh Samons even on a bad day.

Perhaps it was just as well she was on the running boards behind him. Well out of arm's reach. He was tired and he was very depressed, and in the mood he was in just at present he might very likely have suggested some activity to take his mind off his troubles that would be inappropriate. As well as just as likely to be politely rebuffed, which would only make his mood even more black and hopeless than it was already.

''His Excellency had a good transit, one hopes?''

Their cargo was loaded and the three-car convoy was under way, and Belan was trying to make conversation. Andrej had not had a good transit, unhappy about the souls entrusted to the Dramissoi Relocation Fleet and apprehensive about what awaited him at the Domitt Prison. But there was no sense in being gratuitously unpleasant to Administrator Belan even so.

"Thank you, Administrator. Twenty-one, twenty-two days, almost restful, really. Rounds, of course."

The car traveled on through the dark streets, one long block of narrow buildings after another to either side and rather too close for Andrej's comfort. A man could get claustrophobic in streets such as this, which was more than ridiculous on the face of it—that a man should have grown accustomed to live in *Scylla*'s narrow corridors and yet feel closed in upon and prisoned in the open air just because the warehouses in Port Rudistal had been built close and high. There had been an open area between Rudistal and the Domitt Prison, if Andrej remembered aright of what he'd seen from the launchfield. That would be a welcome break: But then they would be at the prison. That was not to be welcome.

"Quarters are actually on site, then, Administrator?" He'd gathered as much, but he might as well have it confirmed, Andrej decided. That way he could get started on a truly world-class case of self-pity now, rather than wait a moment longer.

Of course he had been preparing to immerse himself in self-pity ever since Captain Irshah Parmin had first told him that he was to be sent on this assignment. Still, truly professional results depended on thorough groundwork and advance preparation. There was no time like the present to finish off the foundations, and lay the first course of a monumental attitude problem.

"There's a penthouse suite prepared for his Excellency and his party," the Administrator confirmed. "Every convenience. We hope you'll be very comfortable, sir. And if there should be anything lacking you have only to let us know."

The car was slowing, but they were nowhere near the Domitt Prison; no, they were still deep within the cavernous bowels of the warehouse district, for all Andrej could tell. The car was slowing to avoid running into the car in front of it, the lead car with Belan's Security from the Domitt Prison.

Lieutenant Plugrath seemed to become a little agitated, all of a sudden.

"Administrator, why are they slowing down, tell them to drive on. It's not a good idea to idle in the streets with rank like this on board."

Behind him Andrej could hear the canopy rising to meet over his head and form a roof for the car. Who had decided to close the car he didn't know. Maybe Chief Samons thought it would make the Bench Lieutenant feel better.

"Of course, Lieutenant," the Administrator agreed, his eagerness to please as evident as his confidence in the innocuous nature of the slowdown. "Bad in principle, though no cause for alarm, I assure you."

The car had almost stopped. Through the now-enclosed windows Andrej could see Plugrath's Security detachment pass at the double, six men to the front car to see what the slowdown might be. His own Security would stay with him, naturally.

The Administrator, frowning unhappily, keyed the car's com-braid for transmit. "Sami, this is Belan. What seems to be—"

Then Andrej saw the car in front of them explode into a black fury of dust and scrap, with a huge furious roar that struck him like a blow and deafened him.

An explosion, yes, he knew it had to have been an explosion, he knew what an explosion looked like, but still he only sat and stared without comprehension at the ruin of shards and fragments against the windows at the front of the car while the Administrator struggled frantically with the handle of the car door. Trying to get out. Yes, that was right, they should get out of the car, a car stopped in the street was a sitting target, but who in the name of all Saints could they be shooting at?

Lieutenant Plugrath was shouting something, but Andrej couldn't hear a word, deafened by the blast. He'd better get out of the car before the Lieutenant was hit by accident. Not that he was interested in being shot at. He'd been shot at before; it had made him angry, the first time it had happened, it still made him angry. Were they shooting at him?

Were they, indeed?

Administrator Belan got the door open at last; the door

was pulled open from outside, and frantic hands seized him on his way through the door to hurry him out. Security. Andrej started out of the car in turn, but they wouldn't let him step foot to pavement.

They grabbed him and threw him headlong to the street, and themselves down on top of him to half-drag his body bruisingly away from the car—toward the nearest wall, Andrej supposed, stupid with the shock of it. People were being shot at, Andrej could hear the impact of rounds against the pavement and the sharp report of Security's weapons returning fire. Carbines. Mortars. Flame-throwers. Thorough of them, Andrej had to admit it.

The ground lifted beneath him and struck him in the face with a bone-shattering blow that flattened his entire body and took his breath away.

Shocked body and soul by the force of the blow, Andrej lay for long moments open-eyed, open-mouthed, before he could think to try and catch a breath.

And then it hurt so much to breathe that he didn't want to, and he stilled himself out of fear of the pain to come until his body made him gasp for air—which only hurt even worse.

Years passed.

Andrej fought for breath, and fought with the unwillingness of his own body to breathe, and tried not to notice the pain that came in to fill up the empty spaces as shock ebbed away and left him vulnerable.

His heart began to beat again.

He was lying on his belly on the pavement, the stink of rock-dust and overheated metal was in his nose, his cheek scraped raw against the rough pavement. There was something heavy and hot on top of him, covering him, pressing down on him—was he buried under an avalanche?

Something told him no.

Something told him he knew what had happened.

If only he could put his finger on what that was—

Then the weight shifted. Kaydence Psimas and Caleigh Samons alike rolled away from him carefully, and Andrej could turn over onto his back.

"Excellency." It was Toska, who should know better. "Excellency, are you all right, sir?"

When it should be Kaydence and Chief Samons who should be asked, they had been more at risk than he had been. He had been protected by their bodies. If anybody was not all right, it would be them.

The sudden shock of stunning pain ebbed rapidly, now. He was sore, yes, but not more than bruised from what little he could tell. He had to get up. He had people to see to. Kaydence, how was he? Toska? Chief Samons? The others?

"Miss Samons," Andrej croaked. His voice had got jarred loose in the explosion, as it seemed. He cleared his throat and tried again as Toska and Kaydence lifted him carefully to a seated position. Oh, holy Mother, he hurt. He was going to truly regret this, in the morning. "Miss Samons. Kaydence. Are you all right? What has happened? Where is everybody?"

Now that he was sitting up, Andrej's mind cleared moment by moment. He could see Kaydence, crouched down at his side. He could see Toska, whose face looked to be somewhat blackened with blown ash, but not burnt. Testing himself, arms and legs and knees and joints, Andrej took inventory, listening to Kaydence's report.

"No harm, your Excellency. Chief Samons and I had something to cushion the fall." Andrej himself, that was to say, and if Andrej considered that his body was not near so pleasant a pillow as Chief Samons's might be, the point remained that he was somewhat more yielding than the pavement to land upon. "Two explosions, your Excellency, probably mines. Buried in the street. Casualties mainly the prison Security in the lead car, and some of the Lieutenant's people. Some shots fired, but none after the second explosion, and they seem to have run off the ambush pretty well."

"Where is Chief Samons? Toska, your face is dirty, have you been burned?" A man couldn't help asking. A person got anxious.

Toska pulled his whitesquare out of the front plaquet of his dutyblouse and moistened a corner with his tongue before scrubbing at his cheek with experimental fervor. The whitesquare came away black; Toska's skin was the color it was supposed to be, beneath—a little reddened from the chafing, but otherwise unburned. "Seems to be just soot, sir. Are you sure you want to stand up? Already?"

Yes. He was sure. He knew he was alive; Kaydence and Toska appeared to be all right. Chief Samons had left his side as he'd sat up, and had not yet reappeared to make her report. There were Code and Erish and Joslire yet unaccounted for.

Supported by Kaydence and Toska to either side, Andrej found his footing in the rubble and stood for a moment, grateful for the steadying hands of his Security. Looking around.

To his right, the rearmost car, emptied now but apparently undamaged. That was the way they'd come, then.

To his left, the wreck of the lead car, and the pavement torn up in chunks and heaps of rubble. Bodies, some half-buried in the debris, some apparently caught up in the twisted carcass of the lead car itself. Lieutenant Plugrath and the Administrator, talking to one of Plugrath's people; hurrying over, once Plugrath noticed Andrej on his feet, making what haste they could over the chewed-up pavement.

"Field-expedient ambush, sir, probably recognized the touring car on its way in. Two mines, apparently laid in maintenance traps beneath the pavement. Expected two cars, with the Administrator in the lead rather than second place. Lucky for us."

Not so lucky for the lead car. That went without saying. Andrej eyed the wreck of the touring car in front of them with grim distaste. If he had been in the car when the second mine had gone off . . . and the driver probably had been.

"Casualties?"

"Rough count, fourteen, sir. Six out of eight in the lead car. Five of mine who'd come up to investigate. Driver in the touring car, one of mine shot in firefight. Your man's not quite dead yet, help's on the way."

His man?

Caleigh Samons stood up from her place of concealment on the other side of the wreck of the touring car. She didn't do anything as rude as beckon, as vulgar as whistling. She didn't need to. The expression of grief and distress on her face spoke more clearly than words, and carried its meaning with persuasive force.

Andrej started for her, carrying Kaydence and Toska along with him in his wake.

Erish Muat was seated on a curved wheel-housing blown clear of the touring car, his face clean and white, blood soaking his trouserleg from thigh to calf. Code was cutting the fabric away from Erish's knee as Andrej made his way toward them; oh, lovely, a furious laceration across the top of Erish's knee, and splintered bone glistening with sickening brilliance under the emergency flares that Plugrath's people had set up. And it was the same leg that Erish had injured chasing those Nurail sappers down the corridors of *Scylla*, in a race for the main guns.

It was a nasty injury, but it was well short of threatening Erish's life; and that left only—

Andrej put his two hands to either side of Erish's neck and kissed his forehead, briefly. "You are hurt, my dear." Which Erish had doubtless noticed. "Kaydence. Have we any hope. Of finding my travel-kit, in all of this."

But in the turmoil of his mind, beneath his immediate focus on Erish's pain, the calculation raced toward its grim conclusion. Here were Erish and Code. Here were Kaydence and Toska. He had seen Chief Samons. And that left only . . .

"Sir. Joslire's down, sir. You've got to see to Joslire. Your Excellency."

Erish knew the fear in Andrej's heart as well as he did. Andrej didn't want to slight Erish's pain, just because of the terror that he felt—but as long as Erish understood, perhaps it would be all right, the Lieutenant had said that help would be arriving—

Stumbling over the uneven surface in the street, Andrej struggled to where he had seen Chief Samons last.

There was blood everywhere.

As Andrej neared, Chief Samons rose to her feet from where she knelt beside Joslire, and almost despite himself Andrej took note of the way Joslire's body lay upon the ground. He didn't want to see. He knew what it meant. He couldn't not see, couldn't not understand; he was a doctor.

It was Joslire.

But he was still a doctor. He couldn't turn the analysis off in his mind. He knew almost before he saw that there would be concussive injury to the body cavity. Trouble in breathing. Slow drowning in his own blood, as the lungs filled with fluid.

Joslire.

Kneeling down in the rubble at Joslire's side, Andrej took Joslire's right hand, rubbing the knuckles with his thumb as though to work some feeling back into a hand numbed with cold.

"Joslire."

Oh, it was frightful, it was bad. Joslire lay facing up in the debris in the street with his head cradled back into a hollow of some sort, blood pooling at the hollow of his shoulder, his uniform black with it. Pooling, not overflowing, so there had been some traumatic cauterization; Joslire was not bleeding to death quickly. Slowly, yes, that, but it was the fluid in his lungs that would do for him. He had to be raised, no matter how it hurt: Because the pain in his lungs would only get worse until they did.

"S-sir." Joslire stuttered in his pain, but as he spoke his voice got stronger. Shock was good. Shock was useful. Shock could help to insulate Joslire from his agony; if only help would come before shock killed him. "Sir. Is it. Morning. Yet. I pray it may be."

Morning?

It wouldn't be morning for nearly two shifts. They had come out at sundown, and it was the time of year when nights began to run long in Rudistal. It would be getting cold. What could Joslire mean by "morning"?

"Come and help me, Chief. Have Kay and Toska found my travel-kit? Yes, we need to lift, now, Joslire. This is going to hurt—"

Did hurt.

Joslire cried out short and sharp, a sudden shout of pain that seemed to echo against the far wall and shake Andrej to the pit of his stomach. Joslire cried out, but then fell silent; and there was no telling they were hurting him but for the shaky shattered sound of his rough breathing. Andrej held Joslire in his arms, and Chief Samons searched for material to make a support of some kind. Joslire settled his head against Andrej's shoulder, breathing hard.

"Please. Your Excellency. Is it morning, come. I've waited for it. For so long."

Chief Samons found some cushions from the passenger cabin of the touring car, some all but destroyed and good for padding, one or two almost intact to make a back support. Kaydence and Code helped them settle Joslire in Andrej's arms so that he could breathe. Toska was helping Erish across the short stretch of street between where Andrej had left them and where Joslire lay; that was good. They would all be together.

"What is he saying?" Andrej half-whispered, to Chief Samons. "About it being morning?"

Kaydence heard the question, and Kaydence paled, seven degrees whiter than he had been before.

Then Andrej understood.

The morning of the Day.

The text scrolled through his mind unwelcome and unbidden, but he could not make it stop.

A bond-involuntary with sufficiently serious an injury sustained in the line of duty may elect to terminate his Bond under honorable circumstances rather than incur the expense to the Bench required to return him to duty status. Termination of Bond under such circumstances is equivalent to successful completion of the full Term for purposes of nullification of Bench issues outstanding.

Joslire meant to claim the Day.

He meant to die.

The Bench was willing to forgive the balance of Joslire's debt as a matter of economic practicality. If it would cost more to heal than to replace him, the Bench was willing to let Joslire die: And that was the question that Joslire was asking him.

Furious denial rose up into Andrej's throat; he swallowed back angry words of rebuke with difficulty. Claim the Day? Whoever heard of such a thing? What could Joslire mean by trying to do this to him?

"Oh, no," Andrej murmured, almost to himself, horror-stricken. "Oh, please, Joslire, thou can'st not—"

He heard himself speaking, and choked his words back down into his heart, where they burned horribly. It wasn't fair for him to try to keep Joslire, not if Joslire wanted to go. He had no right to so much as ask it.

Joslire was waiting for him to continue, watching him, as though all of Joslire's soul were focused in his eyes on Andrej's face. Joslire was in pain. But Joslire was not worried.

Shouldn't he be worried? It was a bond-involuntary's right to claim the Day, but Andrej held the Writ. He could do anything to his bond-involuntaries he wanted. He could deny Joslire the Day; it was for him to decide whether Joslire was to be permitted to go.

Joslire could be healed, with time.

But to live on as a bondslave would be torture.

And after all that Joslire had given him, and done for him, and taught him, to betray Joslire would be worse than simple ingratitude; because for Joslire to live enslaved—and betrayed as well, by a man in whom he had placed his trust—would be ceaseless anguish upon torment.

As much as Andrej wished, he could not do it.

"It is true." It was Joslire's right: Joslire had earned his freedom too many times to count, and could not be challenged on the manner in which he chose to elect it. There was nothing left. Andrej looked around, Erish, Kaydence, Code, Toska; Chief Samons. Cradling Joslire in his arms, Andrej laid his cheek against Joslire's forehead, speaking the words in dread and misery.

"It is true, Joslire, the Day is yours, to claim as you wish it." The faith, the trust that Joslire had in him, how could he grudge it to Joslire to find his freedom here and now—when Andrej would leave Fleet at the end of eight years, while Joslire would be bound for twice as long yet?

"Oh." Joslire had closed his eyes, apparently overcome—with emotion or with pain, there was no telling. "It is well come. You'll give me my pass, then, your Excellency."

He should not hold Joslire so close to him. It could not make breathing easier. And breathing was hard already, and would only get more and more difficult, where was his kit, where were the drugs that would ease Joslire's dying?

Joslire didn't want any painease.

Joslire only wanted to die, and embraced his pain as the glad proof that he was to be free.

"Stand all apart." If this was Joslire's will, it would be so. But Andrej couldn't help but try one last thing; Joslire had a right to the information, so he could make his decision in full knowledge of all of the facts that Andrej had at his command. "Joslire. Our Captain has petitioned to revoke thy

Bond. It may be that thou art to be free, and yet alive. Oh, reconsider.''

Reconsider, Joslire. For my sake, if for no other reason.

But Andrej knew he had no right to say it.

He knew Joslire had heard him; he could tell that Joslire understood. It made no difference. "No better way for me to die than here and now. And by thy hand." Shock was steadying Joslire's words; there was to be no chance of pretending that Joslire was not in full command of all his faculties. "Even if. I've waited for this. Whether or not."

No mercy.

No yielding; and no hope.

"Come, then." Andrej raised his voice and beckoned to Code, who stood nearest to him at a few paces remove. "We must all say good-bye to Joslire whom we love, because he is to leave our company very soon. It is your moment, gentlemen, only someone must kiss Joslire for Robert, who will be sure to fault me that he was not here to cheer Joslire's parting."

Pain made a man selfish. Andrej could hardly stand the thought of Joslire dead, but there were others here, and who was to say they did not love Joslire as much or more than he did? They had been closer to Joslire, in a sense. They had lived together, trained together, worked together, fought together—and even taken comfort in one another, when comfort was needed.

Stumbling awkwardly to his feet, Andrej struggled over the chunks of street and pavement to find a place where he could be alone, to try to gain some mastery over himself. He knew what Joslire meant for him to do. He could think of no token that would show more love and gratitude.

And at the same time Andrej could not believe that he could do it, that he would be able to do it, that he would not falter and fail at the last.

Standing in a daze like a man about to crumple, Andrej stared out into the street without comprehending the scene he saw there. Support had arrived; the street was full of people, ambulance crews, Security. Wreckers. The Port Authority. Lieutenant Plugrath came up behind Andrej where he stood and spoke to him, but it was a moment before Andrej began to understand what Plugrath was saying.

"They'll take Curran to hospital, sir. There's the life-litter just now coming up, had to clear the wreckage on the other side. If we're not too late, sir. It'll only be—"

Once he could grasp Plugrath's meaning Andrej started to shake his head, struggling to keep his voice steady while he wept in desperate sorrow. "No. Lieutenant. Joslire is not to go to hospital. Erish, but in a moment or so, not before."

He hadn't said the important words. Plugrath was confused, and Andrej didn't blame him. "Sir, surely it's Curran worse wounded, we'll get him to hospital, there's time for your other man once the emergency is safely in transit."

No.

The emergency was safely in transit now, to a refuge more secure than any hospital. Plugrath could not know that.

"Joslire will not be with us much longer, Lieutenant, he has claimed the Day, as is his right. I would have you keep these people clear of us. It is bad enough that he elects to die in the street in this manner without there being arguments in his last breaths over whether he is to be allowed to go."

Yes, Andrej told himself, sternly.

No arguments.

No matter how bitterly Andrej wished to dispute Joslire's decision.

"Sir." Plugrath had been startled into silence, more or less; but at least Andrej had made his point. "I beg your pardon, sir. No idea. Excuse me. I'll see to it directly."

Plugrath went away; and the noise and bustle seemed to abate, somewhat, but whether it was because the cordon of Security that formed between them and the world shut out the noise—or whether he was in shock, and could no longer quite hear—Andrej didn't know.

Too soon, too soon, here was Code at his back, tear-streaked of face but resolute of voice. "Sir. We're ready for you, sir. We're all ready. Joslire most of all."

He couldn't face it. He needed more time. But every moment more was another anguished breath in Joslire's ruined lungs, another gross insult to Joslire's shattered body. Andrej went back, and knelt down at Joslire's side once more, taking Joslire's hand into his own.

Joslire was smiling, and it wasn't a grimace of pain, it wasn't a rictus of agony, it wasn't the hysteria of shock.

Joslire was smiling because Joslire was free, or as good as, and the pain Joslire was in was as nothing to Joslire compared to his honor, and the reclamation of his name.

The sound of Joslire's breathing hurt to listen to, because Andrej knew how much each ragged breath hurt Joslire, and the smell of raw flesh and drying blood was heavy and oppressive in the chill air.

"Joslire." He knew what Joslire meant to have, of him. He wanted it to be soon for Joslire's sake, even while he wanted it never for his own. Desperate to deny Joslire his freedom in order to have the comfort of his company, Andrej only asked one final question, knowing that he would not betray his man. His friend. The support of long black hours, and his unfailing bulwark in the adversity that was his life. "Joslire. Thy knives. What is to become of them, when thou art dead."

Emandisan five-knives had profound religious meaning to Emandisan, though the knives themselves looked almost exactly like Fleet-issue to Andrej. Once Joslire was dead, there would be no one to drill him in his technique in throwing-knives, technique Joslire had taught him; and yet the knives Joslire had taught him were a part of him, now, how could he put a part of him aside?

Joslire's smile widened, even as his hand tightened in Andrej's grasp. The pain. Joslire reached up his free hand to the back of Andrej's neck; what did Joslire want? A kiss to speed his parting? That was the Dolgorukij way of it, when taking leave. Andrej bent his neck to Joslire's purpose, but Joslire did not want a caress, Joslire wanted the knife sheathed at the back of Andrej's neck between his shoulder blades, the mother-knife that had been the very first Joslire had taught him to wear.

"They have been here all along," Joslire said. It became difficult to understand him; it was harder work for Joslire to catch his breath moment by moment, and the fluid in his lungs followed his breath up into his throat to garble his voice horribly. Joslire spoke slowly. "Since the first. That I came. To understand your nature."

Joslire could not hold the knife at eye level, his hand sinking slowly to his chest. Twitching his hand impatiently for pain, Joslire settled the knife that he held loosely in his grasp so that the point of it pricked at the back of Andrej's hand as he held to Joslire. Joslire's hand in Andrej's grip tightened yet again, with a sharp spasm of pain crossing Joslire's face. *Who was holding whom?* Andrej wondered.

"Thy knives," Joslire said, and his body convulsed in ferocious agony, his grip like iron. The knife Joslire held bit deep into the back of Andrej's hand, and with an effort almost superhuman in its terrific concentration, Joslire drove the knife clear through between the bones, pinning his hand and Andrej's hand together.

The pain was very sharp, very surprising.

But Andrej was too startled to cry out.

"Thy knives and my knives. One and the same. Give those on my body back to Fleet, they're nothing to do with me. My knives are thy knives, now and forever. To the end with thee, my master. And beyond."

Pinned together, palm to palm, blood flowed and mingled. Joslire was staring at him with uttermost intensity, as if to will him to understand something Joslire had no words to communicate.

Oh, had it indeed been so, for all this time?

How could he have been so blind, as not to see?

"Give me my life. And let me go, Andrej."

But whether Joslire actually spoke the words—or Andrej only imagined that he had—Andrej could not begin to say. Joslire lost his grip on the hilt of the mother-knife, his hand falling like a dead weight to one side.

"Chief." He could not move. He was tied to Joslire, pinned to Joslire, sewn into Joslire's life. "If you would, please. I require some assistance."

She hardly knew quite how to approach it; Andrej could imagine she felt awkward. She pulled the knife out through the back of Andrej's hand, and the blood ran hot down his forearm. Andrej cherished his pain to himself to fix his last moments with Joslire in memory.

"Thank you." He held his bleeding hand out for the return of the blade, and she reversed the knife to pass it to him hilt-first, out of habit. It was time. It was almost too late. Joslire meant to die by his own blade. It would be cheating him, to let him die of loss of blood or dry-land drowning. No matter how much it hurt, both physically and emotionally. In a way, the physical pain was bracing to him; it helped to deaden the agony in his heart, and see him through to do right by Joslire.

Andrej put the point to Joslire's throat.

"It is the Day." Joslire's gaze was unwavering; and grateful. "Thou hast been good to me, Joslire, and I have loved thee. Go now, and may the holy Mother grant thy spirit easy passage to thy place."

He knew how hard to push, and at what angle, and to what exact depth.

One final breath, as Joslire gasped, as if in surprise or in ecstatic pleasure.

Andrej kissed Joslire's staring eyes for love, and Joslire's mouth for parting.

But even as Andrej kissed him, Joslire died.

Vanished from his body; dissolved into the air.

Even as Andrej kissed him Joslire's spirit fled; and it was only a dead body, now, only an abandoned piece of damaged flesh, only something inanimate and unimportant that had once housed a man that he had loved.

Andrej rocked the empty shell in his arms and cried aloud to the uncaring night, blind with grief and deaf to any sound in the reverberation of the emptiness in his heart. Alone. Joslire had gone away. He was alone.

Never to have the comfort of Joslire's companionship, ever again—

◆ Five

He was alone, abandoned, and bereft; but he was still Andrej Koscuisko. He had responsibilities that he had to see to.

It was cold in the street. The icy air caught in his throat, rough as it was with weeping. Every bone in Andrej's body seemed to ache, but whether it was because he had been kneeling for too long on rocks and gravel holding to a corpse as though there was some trace of Joslire there, Andrej didn't know.

It was only a corpse.

There was no one there.

But other Bonds were with him still, and though he took no comfort in their presence he could not in fairness overlook them. He was still responsible for them. He had been selfish in his grief for Joslire. They had loved Joslire, too.

And—what was more to the point—not only would they grieve, but they might fear that he would be resentful of them for being here when Joslire was dead. Erish had to go to hospital. Someone should probably see to the new wound in his hand. There was a body to be disposed of. The Domitt Prison was still waiting for his Writ.

He had to get a hold over himself, and be an officer, not some ordinary bereft soul who had the freedom and the luxury to grieve for his dead without a thought for what effect his behavior had on those around him.

"Miss Samons. If I could see you for a moment. Please."

There was a good deal of activity around him, as it

seemed. The sounds of movement and of people talking seemed to increase gradually in volume, as though the information they contained was coming into focus, in some way.

Chief Samons knelt opposite him, wiping her face. "Sir."

"Erish and our others, how do they go?"

He had got stiff, holding the stiffening corpse. Frowning, Chief Samons reached out for his hand to help him to his feet. "They've given Erish good drugs. Code's in pieces. Kaydence is with him. So far, so good."

"Call Plugrath to me, then." He must have been holding Joslire very tightly, from how his muscles ached. "What's happening?"

"Plugrath's got the street locked down. The Port Authority would like to murder that administrator, Belan." Raising her voice, Chief Samons called back over her shoulder. "Bench Lieutenant. His Excellency is asking for you, sir."

He wanted to go see his Security, but he had to get this out of the way first. Lieutenant Plugrath had brought Belan with him; Belan was very pale. Plugrath hardly less so.

Lieutenant Plugrath spoke. "What's to be done, sir?"

Yes, with the body. People who died on duty were cremated, the remains returned to point of origin by special courier. That was the common fate for anyone who died in service; Fleet could not afford to handle bodies, still less concern itself with the myriad different rituals and rites required by all the souls under Jurisdiction. They would need facilities to burn the body. Hospitals would have them. Erish had to go to hospital, because even if Andrej had not taken a cut through his palm he was not an orthopedic specialist. Erish needed to be seen by bones-and-joints, not neurosurgery. It all fell into place.

"We'll go to hospital, Lieutenant." There could well be a wake-room at the hospital. It was Standard procedure to provide one. "There is a rated facility in Rudistal? There must be. Administrator, I am sure you can for us your senior's pardon obtain, and say that we will be a little late."

They were already late. How late were they? He had no idea what time it was. He didn't care.

"Yes, sir. Of course, sir." Belan almost stuttered in his nervousness. Andrej could empathize; it was a hard thing to be shot at in the first place, and a senior officer's being ambushed while in one's company was probably the stuff of nightmare from an Administrative point of view. "There is Infirmary at the prison, sir. Shouldn't your party rather proceed now to your station, rather than make a side trip to the civil facility?"

"No, we should not." Prison infirmaries were not hospitals. Erish needed a hospital. He deserved a specialist. And more than that, the body was to burn, but it was not to be considered for a moment that Joslire's corpse should be put to the fire in a prison—as though still the Bench's prisoner, a slave, a bond-involuntary. Joslire was free. He would be decently cremated with all due respect. And at a hospital, since as far as Andrej knew there were no Emandisan churches.

It was too much to hope that Belan would understand, and so Andrej didn't try to explain it at all. "Take us to emergency receiving, if you please. At hospital. We will once the sun has risen see to the body. Lieutenant, you must arrange for handling after that." They had not been at the Domitt Prison when the attack had taken place; formally they were still the Dramissoi Fleet's concern. Perhaps. One thing was for certain; they were bound to go to the Domitt Prison, but what remained in the world of Joslire Curran should not.

"As you say, sir. I'll tell the Administrator." Belan was confused and a little resentful; he hadn't given Belan any good reasons for his apparently high-handed behavior, Andrej realized. His insistence must seem arbitrary to Belan. He didn't care. He didn't have the energy.

"Tell also your service house. I will want a suite. And sufficient professional assistance, for my gentlemen. For tomorrow morning. I am sure the Domitt Prison will not grudge us a day for mourning. We have lost somebody that we loved."

As had some of Plugrath's Security, but it was different. None of them were Bonds. Or perhaps it was the same, but his own people were all Andrej could be expected to keep in his mind, surely.

Belan nodded, unhappily, but went away.

Andrej hoped he wasn't in trouble with the prison administration even before he'd gotten to the prison. But if he was there was no help for it.

"They're ready to load you for the hospital, sir. You can all ride together, if you'd like."

All ride together?

Did Plugrath mean with Joslire in the car?

The street had been swept clean, debris cleared away. Far above in the black sky Andrej could see the brightest of the stars over Port Rudistal shining in the night. This was the street that had taken Joslire away; Andrej took one final look at it, convinced that he would remember every detail for as long as he should live.

But Erish had to go to hospital.

Turning away, Andrej climbed into the transport-cabin to go to hospital, and put the street behind him.

Their baggage had been packed in the rearmost car, recovered more or less undamaged after the firefight. Once they got to the hospital's wake-room, the first thing that the officer did was wash and change his uniform. The one he had been wearing was soaked with Joslire's life's-blood, clear through to the skin; and while they'd dealt with such issues with their officer before—on other assignments, mostly—it had always been the blood of someone else, someone they didn't know.

Code almost thought Koscuisko didn't want to wash the blood away, because it was Joslire's blood, and rinsing himself clean of it was letting go of some small piece of Joslire. But it couldn't be helped. Joslire was dead. The officer had to change, because he couldn't go into treatment rooms with his uniform so heavily contaminated with blood and dust.

Once he had changed, it seemed to Code that the attitudes of the hospital staff changed, as well. As if they only just realized that Andrej Koscuisko was a ranking officer, rather than just one step up from Bench Lieutenant Plugrath.

They'd all trooped up to check on Erish, and by that time the bone man was just finishing glazing the last chips of patella back into place preparatory to closing up Erish's knee. Koscuisko lectured Erish about the brace he had to wear, too, which was a joke on their officer, because the bone man noticed the field bandage wrapped around the officer's hand while he was gesturing to make his point, and called a soft-tissue specialist.

Having just made so strong a point to Erish about obeying medical instruction, their officer had no choice at all but to sit and let them do things to his hand. It was funny. Almost it was funny. If it hadn't been for what had happened to them it would have been funny.

Then it was two hours before sunrise, and they had all gone back down to the wake-room adjacent to the bodymill. Joslire's body was there, and Joslire's kit. The officer claimed it was important that the body be dressed in clean clothing when it was burned, and Code didn't see where that made any sense at all, but as long as it made the officer feel better they would all go along with it.

It wasn't as if they'd never lost a member of a team before, though this was the first time it had happened to Code since Koscuisko had been assigned to *Scylla*. With Joslire and Robert St. Clare, who was bound to be hard hit by this event; Robert was sentimental.

So they all took off their dutyblouses and rolled back the sleeves of their underblouses and undressed the body that had been Joslire, and washed the wound that had once been his chest as best they could, and dressed him once again in clean undamaged clothing. Code wondered whether Koscuisko wasn't right in some sense about it being important.

Handling the body helped to separate his sense of sorrow from his here-and-now, in some way. There was so clearly nothing left of Joslire there, not even when he knew it was Joslire's body, and Joslire's clothing.

One thing was more than obvious: Joslire was gone from there. There was no sense in grieving for Joslire. Joslire was feeling no pain. For himself, yes. But later.

The officer took away the knives and gave them to Chief Samons. The knife that had killed Joslire had been cleaned, and Koscuisko was wearing it once more in its harness between his shoulder blades. To think that Koscuisko's knives had been Emandisan, and all this time they'd all assumed that they were so much better than Fleet-issue because Fleet issued better to officers. To think. All of this time. Emandisan steel. Joslire's own five-knives.

Erish could not do much, because he was drunk on the

drugs they'd given him; but Erish cut the braid away from Joslire's sleeves once he was dressed in his clean uniform. Joslire was free. He should not wear a slave-uniform, not even to be burned in.

Code could envy Joslire, being dead, because though he was dead Joslire was free.

It was almost time.

The sun would rise within the eighth.

It was important to the officer that the body not go into the fire before the sun came up. It made no sense to Code, and there was a question in his mind about whether the officer had a reason or was simply carrying a childhood pattern forward because he was in shock.

Scant moments before sunrise. Koscuisko had called for the precise time from the Port Authority and marked it by the clock in local reckoning. The furnace was ready: square and white and featureless, the door standing open, the interior gleaming in reflected light.

The corpse for burning on a narrow gurney, ready to wheel up to the mouth of the furnace, when the body would be slipped onto the high gridded floor of the furnace on a plank.

The officer, waiting, and the rest of them with him, exhausted and addle-headed with grief and the medication that they had all been made to take, and waiting for the next part to be done.

Now the time had come.

The sun cleared Port Rudistal's horizon, though there was no telling from inside this room. It would be sending its first long feelers across the relocation camp, across the black cold sullen river, into the Port, up to the foot of the Domitt Prison that had caused them all so much grief already—and before they'd so much as even arrived there yet.

Koscuisko spoke.

"Oh, holy Mother," the officer said, and just for once it wasn't an oath or a profanity. Code realized that the officer was praying; and it sent a shudder through him to hear it.

"This is Joslire, your child, the child of your body, who you love. Whom we have loved. Now it has pleased you to take him back, and we bitterly regret it, though I am grateful that you took only one of their lives."

Koscuisko was not religious, though he kept the icon with

its ever-burning lamp tucked into the corner of his sleeping-room. So much was merely habit; Koscuisko had never paid the slightest bit of attention to his patron saint—of Filial Piety, as he'd once told Code—in all this time.

"Send therefore guides and adequate equipage, and see your child safely home to shelter beneath the Canopy. And extend your hand over me and mine, Chief Samons not excluded, for you have bereft us all to your own purpose, which we are not empowered to understand. Holy Mother. So prays to you with all his heart your child Andrej, unfilial and unreconciled, but your child yet."

A gesture of his hand for them to move the body into the furnace let them know that he had said what he felt needful.

Koscuisko stood and watched while they put Joslire in the furnace. Chief Samons secured the door.

She touched the switch, and the safeties engaged, and then the telltales on the wall began to move as the temperature within the furnace started rising.

Long moments, and Koscuisko watched the telltales, and Koscuisko wept, but to himself this time—not like before.

Code wept as well. He didn't notice what the others were doing. He and Joslire had had a rocky start in the beginning, because of some forgotten issue with Robert, and Joslire trying to keep Code out of trouble with Koscuisko while Code had thought Joslire was trying to cover for Robert. Who had annoyed him.

The index on unreduced organic matter within the furnace started to fall off, first bit by bit, then in a smooth slow curve. Flesh did not long remain in such temperatures. Bone was more resistant: But the furnace had been built to serve the dead.

When the index fell below its breakpoint, the officer straightened his shoulders and wiped his face with his white-square.

"It's done," Koscuisko said. "As done as done." Though it would be a while before the furnace could be opened. It took time, to vent such heat. "And we have nothing left. Oh, holy Mother. Gentles, let us go away from here."

Nothing except each other.

Kaydence in the lead, and Erish limping, they left the room.

Left Joslire behind.
Joslire was gone.

Koscuisko had cleared it with Plugrath and with the Domitt Prison—Administrator Geltoi, if Caleigh remembered the
name correctly. The prison was treating the issue very carefully. Bond-involuntaries were much more exotic than ordinary mortals, and common report embroidered upon a special
relationship between them and the Inquisitors in token of the
unusually absolute power a Ship's Inquisitor had over their
lives.

No one who had witnessed the death of Joslire Curran—
howsoever indirectly—could doubt that the relationship between Koscuisko and his dead Emandisan bond-involuntary
had been intense and highly personal. At this point Koscuisko could probably have told the Domitt that he was going
into retreat for two weeks, and taking his people with him;
and no questions would have been asked. At least not right
away.

As it was, he was simply going to Rudistal's service
house, and for a day. More than reasonable. Really.

They left the hospital in the bright morning; it amused
Caleigh to see how many more Security posts there seemed
to be, suddenly. Ship's Inquisitors were even more rare a
commodity than bond-involuntaries. To have hazarded the
life of one created a huge embarrassment for Dramissoi and
the Domitt alike, even if it had most likely been the Domitt
that the ambushers thought they were striking at. Well, they
had. Indirectly, maybe. But no less effectively for that.

An uneventful transit to the service house, uniformed
troops at every turn. It wasn't the most luxurious facility
Caleigh had ever been to in Koscuisko's company, but it
would do. Koscuisko made a point of visiting service houses
at every opportunity; it was for the benefit of his bond-
involuntaries assigned as much as anything else, from what
little Caleigh could tell.

Koscuisko's bond-involuntaries had few opportunities to
develop social bonds for recreation on board *Scylla*, though
Robert St. Clare was a great favorite amongst the ladies in
both Security and Medical. For what that was worth. So Koscuisko went to service houses so that his people could enjoy

what transient pleasure could be lawfully obtained in the embrace of the professional partner of their choice.

Caleigh hoped there were free women at this service house. As far as she knew, St. Clare was the only one of Koscuisko's people with a sister that had taken a Service Bond, but the other bond-involuntaries were sensitive about the issue as well.

When it came down to it, though, it wasn't an issue of recreation as such that brought them to the service house this morning. Nobody had slept. And they were all in shock. And the officer was in no condition to stand an inbriefing with prison administration.

Koscuisko went up to the senior officer's suite while Caleigh made arrangements for his people. A suite of rooms beneath the one Koscuisko would be using, with direct access in case of emergencies, per standard operating procedure. Food and drink and sexual contact ad lib: but these were all just comfort items.

It was as important for the bond-involuntaries to be left to themselves to share their common grief and observe what forms of mourning they might choose. There were ad hoc rituals that bond-involuntaries shared, ways of coping that they had developed over the years; and that was strictly their own business.

Once she had assured herself that her people were to be properly seen to, Caleigh went up to the senior officer's suite to give the officer a status report, wondering whether she should bother.

The senior officer's suite was as large as the troops' gather room taken all together. Caleigh identified herself to the doorkeeper and sought out the suite's exercise area, where she expected to find her officer.

She had to cross the front room to get there. They were laying the table for his meal; and she could see through to the bedroom with the bed made up and waiting, the bedclothes arranged invitingly. It made her want to cry. And she hadn't cried since she could remember. Wept, perhaps.

She was perhaps a little bit hysterical. She'd valued Joslire Curran as much as the next man; he'd been as genuine an asset as a Chief Warrant could wish. She'd learned early on to rely on him and St. Clare to manage the officer on those

occasions when Koscuisko—for whatever good and sufficient reason of his own—had had too much to drink, and
got the terrors.

Being in Security meant that people that you knew and
relied upon were frequently killed, and usually traumatically
so. It wasn't that. She'd never seen a Bond claim the Day.
She'd never dreamed of seeing Koscuisko so naked in his
grief, on his knees in the street in front of everyone, the
deepest—most private—secrets of his heart on display for
anyone who cared to notice.

There was no reason for the sight of a waiting bed to make
her want to cry.

She went through to the exercise area, where she could
count on finding Koscuisko having a massage.

Right first time, Caleigh congratulated herself, stepping
into the warm dark room. Koscuisko lay facedown on the
padded bench-table with the house masseur frowning over
his upper back and a towel draped discreetly across the middle part of his body. He wouldn't be surprised to hear from
her; she cleared her throat, to put him on notice that she was
here. All right, she was intruding, but Koscuisko liked to
know. Sometimes the masseur took it a little personally,
however.

"H'm. Sir. I've seen to arrangements made for your people, sir. As you would wish it."

Her interruption earned her a glare from the masseur. Koscuisko intervened to head off a confrontation.

"Thank you, Fishweir. I am very much obliged to you."

Fishweir sounded Chigan to Caleigh. Impressive. The best
masseurs in known Space were Chigan. A group of fellow
Security had taken up a collection to buy her a massage for
a promotion gift, years gone, when she'd made her first rat-
ing. She could remember it as though it had been yesterday.
Wheatfields. The masseur had been of Wheatfields, not of
Fishweir. Chigan was Chigan. Caleigh wondered, suddenly,
whether she had just worked her way out of any chance of
a massage herself by offending the man.

"I don't like to prescribe, your Excellency." Fishweir,
whomever of Fishweir, shrugged it off, wiping excess oil
from his hands on a clean towel. "But your whole body's

in knots. I think the only thing for it is a glass of caraminson wine. I'll send up a flask.''

Yes, Chigan by the accent. Koscuisko made as if to rise; Fishweir placed a hand firmly in the middle of Koscuisko's back and pushed. Koscuisko subsided, capitulating.

''You are very kind. It is generous of you to offer.'' Koscuisko had the authority to prescribe whatever he liked for himself to ease his pain; many Ship's Inquisitors took that way out, and became addicted to mood-altering substances. Koscuisko's mood-altering substance of choice remained alcohol.

That didn't change the fact that for most people a flask of caraminson wine was a once-in-a-lifetime experience, worth every bit of the cost. And only licensed professionals could provide it. ''Here is my Chief of Security, Fishweir, her name is Samons. She knows that I am worried about my bond-involuntaries. One wonders whether massage might be made available for her benefit as well.''

Of course it might. That wasn't what Koscuisko was asking. Professionals at a Chigan's level were to be approached as carefully as if they were—well, Ship's Surgeons, for example. Koscuisko was asking whether Fishweir would condescend to favor Caleigh herself with the skillful medication of his educated hands.

Fishweir shook his head with polite regret. ''Sir, I'm Unreform. I'm sorry. No offense, Chief.'' And while most Chigan offworld simply treated women as though they were female men and dealt with Chigan cultural taboos in that manner, ''unreformed'' Chigan were prohibited by their creed from any form of physical contact with the sex of hominid that carried young in utero. Caleigh didn't mind Unreform Chigan. It was nothing personal. Fishweir was clearly well intentioned as he spoke on.

''I'll tell you both something, though, and you can take it for what you feel it may be worth. The nature of grief is heavy, wet, and cold. It settles in your stomach. You need fire to drive it off or it'll make you sick.''

Fishweir had been stroking Koscuisko's body as he spoke, as if restlessly. Now he stilled his hands, one at the small of Koscuisko's back, one at the back of Koscuisko's neck, and rested himself there. Caleigh wondered that Koscuisko would submit to being touched at the back of his neck, when he was so selective about who he would touch in that manner, and when. Perhaps it was to do with surrendering himself into the capable hands of a professional.

The thought ambushed Caleigh Samons, and took her breath away.

Surrender herself.

Into the hands of someone who could take care of her.

She shook herself to clear her mind. She was a senior Security warrant officer. She could take care of herself. She had been taking care of herself—and her officer, and her troops assigned—for years.

But the shaking didn't work to clear her mind and rid her of the alien thought. Someone who could take care of her, even if only for a few hours, even if only in a sense.

Someone like her officer.

She knew the strength of his body from combat drill, she knew the strength of his will. She knew the strength of his passion from these few hours past, watching him grieve for Joslire Curran. She knew the quality of his mind from what she had heard of gossip from Infirmary, surprise at his skill level, appreciation for his ability, finally gratitude for the healing in his hands.

Oh, someone to be responsible for the next few hours, someone to see to her needs—

The very idea was so foreign that it turned her stomach.

At least there was a sudden strange sensation there, in her belly. And surely it was revulsion at the very idea.

Unless it was desire for comfort, after what they had suffered last night?

"There, now." Fishweir stroked up the length of Koscuisko's body one last time and turned away, his voice low and calm and caressing. "You're to lie still for at least four eighths. Miss Samons, time him. I'll have the kitchen send up some warming, drying food. Good-greeting, your Excellency."

Professional courtesy was all very well.

But Fishweir was Chigan.

And Koscuisko was beautiful, in a masculine sense, his body maybe a little white but smooth and sleek with the lithe lines of his Dolgorukij musculature. It wasn't the bulk of the muscle but how the muscle tied in to the bone that made the difference with Dolgorukij. Koscuisko was much stronger than he looked, and if he took her into his embrace—

She shouldn't be having these thoughts. He was her officer. Granted that Koscuisko desired her; most men did. She didn't want him.

She only wanted comfort.

And that desperately.

All of her life spent taking care of things, seeing to the well-being of her troops—

"Slow count, Chief," Fishweir reminded her, on his way out.

Was it her imagination?

Or did that damned Chigan know exactly what was going on in her clearly stress-addled mind?

"Have you made plans, Miss Samons?" Koscuisko asked, casually, after a moment had passed. "They could lay two places. Unless you've found something of interest here."

Did he mean that he hadn't?

"Haven't had a chance to check, sir. Settling the others." Hadn't been particularly interested. She was tired, and she just wanted to sleep. She'd thought. And hiring a man wasn't the same as surrendering an hour to someone she could trust, and there she went again, and she was going to have to concentrate. And take a nice cold shower. Which would not be relaxing.

"It is said that grief likes company. But only aggrieved company. I would be glad of your companionship, I do not feel like talking with a stranger."

"That would be nice. Thank you." It was an effort to keep her voice calm and casual; when she was hungry. "I should probably get a wash in before we eat, though."

"Plenty of time." Koscuisko's voice was muffled against the pillow on the bench-table. "Perhaps so much as an eight, but I hope not. I'm hungry. We didn't get our thirdmeals in, last night, and fastmeal gone begging as well. Tell the kitchen, Miss Samons, and we will sit down together. That will be comforting. I will enjoy that."

Leaving her officer to lie quietly in the serene calm of the exercise room, Caleigh called the kitchen to arrange for doubled portions. And had them send up a second wrap-robe as well. If Koscuisko thought it was just too odd of her, she could cover for it somehow. But it didn't need to mean anything. Fatigue could explain it. And she didn't care. She was reckless with weariness and hunger to be the one taken care of, just this once.

She went through the officer's bedroom into the washroom beyond, and stripped, and lay in a tub full of hot water until she knew by the quiet sounds outside the bath-enclosure itself that the house staff had carried away her clothing to be cleaned, and left her a wrap-robe.

Clean white toweling, sweet with a fragrance of sun. It was probably a perfume. Caleigh didn't care. The warmth of the robe was comforting, and the silk slippers for her feet were very caressing as well. They had put out a sleepshift for her, much like the sleep-shirt that had been waiting for Koscuisko in the exercise room, hanging on a hook. Koscuisko had already had his wash. It was the first thing Koscuisko always did when he came to a service house, regardless of whether or not he anticipated seeking entertainment.

She was as dressed as he was, and had seen him naked, what was there to think twice about? Caleigh tied her long blond hair up in a loose damp knot and went out to find the meal-table.

Koscuisko would have known she had gone into the washroom; he would have heard her. He seemed a little surprised at it, but took her reappearance in stride. Maybe he wasn't taking it in stride. Maybe he was too beaten down by everything they had been through to be surprised at anything.

Their meal was ready for them, one way or the other, and that took care of having to talk about much of anything for a while. Dinner? Supper? Fastmeal? She'd lost track. It was midmeal by local reckoning, and she didn't usually take much of a midmeal, but she found herself to her surprise accounting for her fair share of the meat-dish.

Some of the bread.

Quite a bit of the side-vegetable.

And one of the two glasses of caraminson wine, no more than two mouthfuls of fluid really, but a powerful soother and muscle relaxant that would ensure they both slept well and deeply, to the effective healing of their bodies—when they slept.

She couldn't talk to the officer.

She kept getting distracted.

It was not precisely comfortable, but it wasn't awkward, either; she couldn't say quite how she felt about it.

The servers took away the dirty dishes and laid out fruit and cheese and sweets, and went away. Koscuisko crossed his forearms on the table's edge and leaned forward, regarding her with a very inquiring look in his mirror-silver eyes.

"Tell me what is in your mind, Chief," he suggested. "It may be that I should know, and if I have offended I can only ask for consideration. But I am very stupid just at the moment. And I am not accustomed to the sight of your shoulders—"

The sleepshift was a little loose, and the wrap-robe was not snug. The collar lay open across her shoulders; it might even have slipped to one side or another during the course of the meal without her taking much note of it.

"—and it becomes very difficult to remember that you are Chief Warrant Officer Caleigh Samons. Rather than a woman whose body I desire very much."

Well, that was nothing new. Was it? He'd never told her, not in so many words. She'd never needed to be told. It had always been obvious enough.

She was making a mistake.

She shouldn't be considering it, only—only she couldn't shake the thought. One eight, two eights, that was all she would ever ask. Two eights to lie in the arms of a man who could take care of her. She was more than Koscuisko's match in combat drill; it wasn't that.

Joslire had trusted him.

Joslire was dead.

"That's two of us tired. Your Excellency." To gloss things over and go away would be best. It would be safer. Koscuisko did not have to do with subordinate troops; and had apparently set that between them in his mind from the beginning. She had always appreciated his respect for her professional skill. She didn't want to lose that. "I should go see about a room. I'm glad to have had company, though. After what's happened."

Stupid Koscuisko might be, and she might be in shock. He looked at her directly, no defenses, no pretense. He was not the Chief Medical Officer, nor the Ship's Inquisitor. He was Andrej Koscuisko. Just at this moment that was all he was.

"It is not strictly speaking necessary for you to go out to an empty bed. There is in the next room one which is very suitable, and already made up to welcome you. We will be Caleigh and Andrej just this once, perhaps. I could take comfort from your body, Caleigh. And it could be that you would have some comfort from mine."

Oh, yes, precisely. The idea exactly. Yes.

She didn't know exactly how to say it, so she didn't say anything. She only stood up slowly, debating moment by moment about the wisdom of this course of action.

She walked uncertainly in slippered feet toward the bedroom and stopped in the doorway.

Now or never. Point of decision. Make or break.

Koscuisko took her carefully around the waist from behind, and kissed the side of her neck with contemplative deliberation; and she knew that at that moment she was the center of Koscuisko's universe.

He had the power of complete absorption, absolute concentration on whatever had caught his interest at the moment.

Right now he was centered on her; and raised his bandaged hand to stroke the opposite side of her throat as he kissed her.

She was drunk with arousal, but whether it was the pleasure his caress gave her or her enjoyment of the intensity of his attention—or even the caraminson wine—Caleigh didn't know.

She didn't think it mattered.

He had said that he admired her shoulders, of all things?

She shrugged the wrap-robe down around her elbows, and leaned back against Koscuisko's welcome strength.

To affirm life honored life, and to honor life was to respect the dead.

Koscuisko kissed her throat, and Caleigh shivered with the pure pleasure of it, and ceased to think about anything at all in the world except Koscuisko's touch and Koscuisko's kisses.

*   *   *

Andrej awoke to a restrained bustle of activity in the other room and blinked his eyes at the ceiling, trying to make sense of the confused memories that jumbled in his mind in the disorder of an uncompleted dream. It was not a familiar bed. There was a warmth to it that was more than of his body, and a fragrance that was familiar, but out of place. What was going on?

Someone was speaking low-voiced in the outer room. Kaydence. "Packed and ready, Chief. There's word with the house-master from Lieutenant Plugrath. Wants to inspect the officer's escort before we're to leave. Something like that."

"I'm not going to ask you how you know, Kay."

There, that was Chief Samons's voice, quiet and serene and even affectionate. Kaydence had an insatiable appetite for information that he was not supposed to have, and was always fraying braids in which he had no business just to see whether it could be done. Within limits. Kaydence's governor kept him from too much meddling.

It had been meddling with Bench systems that had gotten Kaydence his Bond in the first place, after all. "Chief." Kaydence sounded aggrieved. "I came by the information honestly. Courier delivery, voice confirm. You slander me."

It was like an addiction of sorts with Kaydence, and in the years Andrej had known him he had fallen foul of his governor more than once when enthusiasm outran prudence. There was something else, though. Andrej frowned, thinking hard.

"I don't know if that's possible, Kay. You'd be twice as offended if I implied you couldn't find out."

Chief Samons.

It was the fragrance of her body, in the bed.

Sitting up suddenly, Andrej stared at the still-dimpled pillow to his right.

Chief Samons?

It had been Caleigh, and there was one of her long blond hairs on the pillow.

Caleigh, and she had called him by his name, and he had numbered all the secrets in his mind that he had ever wanted to know about her body and solved them one by one with self-indulgent thoroughness.

His fish rose up amidst the bedclothes and crested at the very thought of it, but Andrej could not be bothered with the importunities of his masculine gender. Let his fish breach. There were people in the next room. He had to get dressed. It was morning. The clockpanel in the headboard of the bed made that quite clear.

"How's the officer?" Kaydence asked.

Andrej had turned to get up and find his underlinen, but the question froze him in midpivot with a handful of bedclothes half-raised in the air.

"He slept well, I think. There's a Chigan masseur. And he prescribed caraminson, I'd tip him twice if I could."

Nothing.

No hint of hesitation, no vague suspicion of a concealed truth, no stutter. Nothing. Freed from his paralysis, Andrej set foot to carpeted floor to find his clothing. It was to be their secret, then.

"I don't know how well Code slept, Chief, not even with all the help he had." Kaydence's voice sounded thoughtful. "What about our Chief, how is she doing?"

It wasn't the sort of question a bond-involuntary would normally ask a superior. It was a little too personal; and that could mean impertinent. But Kaydence asked it quite naturally and calmly, taking care of Chief Samons as though she were one of them—one of the Bonds. In a strictly limited sense.

Kaydence's artless question brought home the full enormity of Andrej's loss with renewed force. They had all taken care of each other. Now one of them was dead; and if they weren't careful, Code might follow where Joslire had gone. A bond-involuntary who couldn't work his way through survivor's guilt could force his governor into overload. It was one of the ways in which a bond-involuntary could commit suicide: a particularly self-punitive way, to brood on one's own failings until one's governor took over the task of self-flagellation and carried it to its ultimate extreme. Very horrible.

But not as horrible as what he meant to do to the people who had stolen Joslire away from them. A governor on overload meant death in agony, but without the proper drugs that death could take mere hours to conclude. He would execute a masterpiece, a Tenth Level Command Termination that would last eight days and more before it was concluded. Joslire would be avenged.

He had to get to the Domitt Prison, because he had experiments to perform before the Port Authority found his prey.

That meant getting dressed.

His uniform was waiting in the bedroom for him, but his boots were not; Andrej went out in slippered feet to see how he was to speak to Chief Samons, and get his boots at the same time. Kaydence had gone. Chief Samons sat at the meal-table having some cavene; and stood up as he entered the room, bowing her salute.

"His Excellency slept well?"

Only a very subtle hint of the joke, there. And no mockery. But no trace of the woman who had welcomed his embrace, either. Just as well that his fish had got tired of being ignored, and tucked its head back sullenly into his hipwrap, where it belonged.

"Thank you, Miss Samons. Excellently well. And you?"

"Just what the doctor ordered. With respect."

No awkwardness, and no denial. This was not so difficult as Andrej had feared. It was not to be necessary to pretend that nothing had happened; it was not to be expected that it would happen again.

Fair was fair.

"I'm glad to hear it. Did I hear Kaydence telling you about a word from Plugrath?"

He was better off without the distraction she would represent, had she hinted that he might again embrace her.

He wanted nothing to interfere with his vengeance for Joslire.

Administrator Geltoi watched the small convoy approach, frowning into the early morning sun. To have waited so long for a Writ, only to be delayed at the last moment by this unfortunate accident—really, he had suffered reversals before, but this was a bitter one.

That wasn't even all.

Koscuisko had injured his hand during the attack, and would doubtless need some days yet of recovery time.

Couldn't he just direct his Bonds to the work, wasn't that what they were for? Yet a wounded man had a right to expect light duty in respect for an injury. Try as he did, Geltoi couldn't make out the execution of the Writ to be "light duty" no matter how he approached the problem in his mind.

The little convoy was closer by the moment, and would soon be hidden behind the compound wall that circled the administration building and the prison alike. Geltoi got out his conning-glasses; he could tell which one was Koscuisko from Belan's description—seated in the senior officer's place, wearing duty black in token of his station as one of *Scylla*'s Ship's Primes, short and fair-headed, no beard.

Geltoi frowned.

From where he stood, Koscuisko almost looked Nurail.

A trick of the light, surely, and there was no cause to suspect any such thing. The officer's brief said his system of origin was the Dolgorukij Combine. There were no Nurail in the Dolgorukij Combine that Geltoi had ever heard of, still less any Nurail contaminating the blood of one of the Combine's oldest and most influential—if not richest—noble houses. It was an accident of nature, a freak of genetics. Yes.

The convoy didn't swing wide at the crossroads to make for the gate outside the prison's entrance, though. Instead the convoy took the branch that led toward the administration building.

This was interesting. For Koscuisko to come to him straightaway—and it would be Koscuisko's own idea, Belan had his instructions—was the behavior appropriate to a subordinate officer; and very gracious of Koscuisko to have made the public gesture. Geltoi smiled.

Yes.

Not Nurail at all.

The convoy cleared the perimeter gate and pulled up in front of the administration building, out of Geltoi's line of sight beneath the second-story overhang. Geltoi sat down behind his desktable to wait.

After a moment's time Belan signaled. "Administrator. Your pardon, sir. The Judicial officer has asked for a short meeting."

Yes, very nice. It was an interesting sensation, to receive such public tokens of respect from a ranking Fleet officer.

Making up his mind to forgive Koscuisko in advance for the days he would surely be less than productive, Geltoi keyed his respond.

"A surprise. Of course. Immediately, Belan." If he'd been able to foresee this, he might have laid a small welcome out in his office, some pastry, something to drink. But that might indicate that he'd expected Koscuisko's courtesy as his right, rather than being pleasantly surprised, not at all intending on asserting his technically superior rank as Koscuisko's administrative commander, and so forth. So perhaps it was just as well this way after all.

When the door to Geltoi's office opened it was both wings of the double doors at once, two people opening the door, two people coming through it—and behind them, Andrej Koscuisko. With his surviving Bonds, yes, the green piping on the sleeves of their uniform set them apart as bond-involuntary. The woman behind Koscuisko in turn would logically be the Chief of Security who would accompany a senior officer: And a stunning Chief of Security she was, too.

Koscuisko stopped four paces in front of Geltoi's desktable and bowed with formal and unforced respect. "Administrator." Well, he could still be taken for Nurail, Geltoi supposed; tear his clothing, soil his face, let his hair grow unkempt and greasy, and perhaps some confusion might exist. But for the rest of it Koscuisko was clearly too intelligent and too well-educated to be taken for Nurail. He had manners.

"I am Andrej Koscuisko. I present myself with apologies for the delay. We are obliged to you for your kind understanding." In the matter of a day for mourning, clearly. "That the Domitt Prison has also some loss suffered, our condolences. I have brought the Writ to Inquire to support the Judicial function at the Domitt Prison, Administrator, and to that end I am at your disposal and command."

Very prettily done. And sensitive, too, to remark on the loss of the personnel assigned to the Domitt Prison. Two of the dead Security had been Pyana.

Geltoi raised his hands in a gesture of acceptance and dismissal. "Not at all." Was he to call Koscuisko by his name? Was he to call him "your Excellency"? He was senior. Perhaps he should use Koscuisko's professional title, that would do the trick. "We're off to a rocky start with you, I'm afraid, Doctor. You're injured. I expect you'll need—how long? Before you're fit to work?"

Koscuisko looked a little confused, frowning slightly, turning his head fractionally to one side as if avoiding an unexpected draft of some sort. "I had not anticipated delaying further, Administrator. I had expected to make the orientation inspection today. And review cases waiting through tomorrow, to be started the day following."

This was a surprise. But not an unpleasant one. They were as ready as he could have wanted to be for an inspection; Geltoi had directed that the replacement bodies on standby be moved back into the cellars, just for today, in order to spare Koscuisko the sight of them.

It was a little odd, though. Everything that he had heard about Koscuisko from Chilleau Judiciary had prepared him for a man who would be taking advantage of any opportunity to put off his duty. Not that anyone could fault an Inquisitor for the quite natural impulse to delay unpleasantness.

"Excuse me, Doctor. Of course. I had misunderstood. Has the Port Authority any news for us on those who attacked you?"

The one issue resolved, Geltoi turned his attention to testing Koscuisko's attitude on the only other issue of concern before them. There was probably some way for Koscuisko to make the assault the Domitt Prison's fault. The Port Authority was certainly taking a critical approach, and the Port Authority should know better, too, than to scorn the source of good patronage.

Administrator Geltoi himself would not have gone into Port Rudistal without more Security than they had sent for Koscuisko, but that was exactly the reason fewer Security had seemed called for to escort the officer's party. Administrator Geltoi needed protection: The locals knew who he was, and didn't care for his no-nonsense approach to prison management. Koscuisko looked nothing like him. Koscuisko had not been at risk of being mistaken for Administrator Geltoi. It had been sheer vandalism, really.

"I have this morning spoken with Lieutenant Plugrath from the Dramissoi Relocation Fleet." Who had made an unflattering report to his superiors about the manner in which

Koscuisko had been escorted; but that was by the way. Plugrath was a very junior Lieutenant. And the only reason there was any to-do at all was that a Fleet officer had been inconvenienced by-the-by. Koscuisko was unhurt, for all the fuss the Port Authority was making.

"He tells me there is not yet anything definite. I have asked him to come and see me from time to time to make report. I hope that he can be cleared to do so, Administrator."

Geltoi rather liked the idea of the Lieutenant dancing attendance on Koscuisko until they came up with satisfactory results. Perhaps it would teach Plugrath to amend his attitude and his behavior. Perhaps.

"And gladly. Doctor. I won't keep you, you'll want to get settled in to quarters. I've scheduled a small welcome for dinner, how would it be said in Fleet, thirdmeal. I will anticipate with pleasure making your acquaintance then. In the meantime please pace yourself, Doctor, you are willing to work I see, but you have been wounded. You must not strain yourself."

Inquisitors as a class were vulnerable to stress. That was one of the reasons it was important to provide a secure place for Koscuisko, a safe haven, insulated from the sordid environment in which he was required to work.

"With respect, Administrator, you mistake the situation, to an extent." Koscuisko bowed with formal grace; it was clear he only wished to clarify an issue. "It is very good of you. But I have no desire to put anything off, quite the contrary. When Lieutenant Plugrath for me finds those who have murdered Joslire I have promised myself a suitable execution. I shall be needing the practice, while I wait."

More and more interesting.

"Commendable, Doctor. And very understandable. Belan will see you settled, and we will meet again for dinner."

Hadn't the report said that Koscuisko himself had actually killed his bond-involuntary?

But the Nurail who had ambushed them would still be responsible. Yes. Geltoi had no problem with that.

He had plenty of Nurail for Koscuisko to practice on.

✦ Six

Bored for two days, and now right terrified: Ailynn had heard that to be characteristic of the life that Security bond-involuntaries led, but up till now she'd never had the experience herself.

Bored for two days: She'd been ordered for the day before yesterday, midshift, to have her briefing and meet her betters in the place they meant to keep their Inquisitor. Terrified right now: Because finally the Inquisitor had arrived. And she to be available to him for his use, whatever that might suit his fancy to be.

She'd never met an officer with so much rank. She'd never met one of Fleet's torturers, though she had known her share of Pyana ones. And even the Pyana in this place spoke with respect and fear of an Inquisitor.

They would enjoy her suffering.

Or perhaps not enjoy it, the housekeepers had not been aggressively cruel to her these two days past; there was no particular reason to expect they would delight in her bruises. But they were Pyana. Pyana didn't think Nurail even had souls, not really, though they used the common phrase. "Nurail souls" was just as much to say "Nurail beasts" or "Nurail chattels."

Ailynn stood waiting in the front room beside the officer's bedroom doorway in the gracious roofhouse that enslaved Nurail hands had built for him, listening to voices as they approached. The housekeepers had greeted the officer at the loading dock where the main lift came to rest. Cook had waited to be introduced in the kitchen, his proper place. Ailynn had been hired for the officer's use for relaxation: and had been placed next to the bedroom accordingly, to meet the officer.

"Belan, this is astonishing."

It was a clear voice, a cold voice, and it spoke without much inflection, even though the language was emphatic. Ailynn suppressed a shiver.

"On the roof. One might as well be in the country. And so extensive a plant, as well, it will be difficult to return to *Scylla* after such luxury as this."

The officer. Ailynn told the data over in her mind, counting the beads in her fretting-cord one by one as she went with her hands decently concealed beneath her apron. Aznir Dolgorukij. An aristocrat, at least in his home system. Surgeon, and Inquisitor, Jurisdiction Fleet Ship *Scylla*. Five bond-involuntary troops, except that there were only four to come here now, and nobody had bothered with the names. A Chief of Security, a Warrant Officer. Miss Samons.

Andrej Koscuisko.

"His Excellency is very kind. We hope you'll be comfortable here, sir. Your personal quarters are in through the sitting-room, this way."

Belan. More Pyana than Nurail, and fed at the enemy's table rather than be penned with his family. She didn't think she blamed him for the choices he had made, because it was only common sense to elect to be safe and respectable if such was offered. But he forgot his family and his kind. That was more difficult to decline from blaming.

Here they were.

Coming into the beautiful front room, with its great windows and its well-padded furnishings, its polished wooden tables and its bright clear lights. Its Service bond-involuntary.

She knew the officer by his uniform, the Bonds by the piping on their sleeves, Belan by sight, Chief Samons by her sex.

Ailynn bowed as the officer scanned the room. He might not even see her. He might not notice her. She was only part of the furniture, as one with the toweling or the linen that had been provided for him to soil as he liked.

Only when she had made her bow and straightened up she

found that the officer was looking right at her. Not tall. Very
elegant, in his black uniform; and his black uniform made
her afraid, because only senior officers wore that color, and
senior officers frightened her. Frowning. And no color in his
eyes. Like ice. Like the cold moonlight glittering on the water.

"And this?" the officer asked Belan.

Belan seemed to hesitate, almost to blush. He was the one
who had come to hire her. The house-master knew that she
was scarred, and would suffer less damage if the officer used
force. Belan had wanted a Service bond-involuntary rather
than another woman, because no one knew what an Inquisitor might like for recreation, and it was not to be considered
that he should be answered back. Belan had wanted her particularly, a slave, who could not raise her voice regardless
of what Koscuisko might put her to.

"This woman is from the service house, your Excellency.
For your convenience. Though if you'd prefer some other
accommodation—you've only to state your preference, sir,
the Administration means to spare no expense."

Koscuisko crossed the floor toward her, and Ailynn
watched him come in an agony of humiliation. Would he
reject her as below his standard? Or would he accept her,
inferior though she was, because the less worth she had in
his eyes the more easily he could use her?

She'd thought that she'd become inured to the degrading
treatment to which the Bench had condemned her.

She was wrong.

He stopped too close to her. He had no right. She had no
right to step away from him. Looking her up and down.
Leaning more close yet, to speak into her ear.

"You would perhaps tell me, if you are from Marlebourne?"

What had he said? She couldn't grasp his meaning, so
different was the question from the suggestive sneer she'd
more than half expected. He waited for her answer for a
moment, but she could not answer; he explained.

"Because I could not bear to keep you, if you were from
Marlebourne. My Robert St. Clare was Bonded there. He
once said that his mother's people held the slippery slope,
no, I misspeak myself, he said the Ice Traverse."

It still made no sense at all to her. "I have no threads in that weave. Sir. Your Excellency." She answered to him as low-voiced as he'd spoken, out of involuntary response to his tone. "As it please the officer."

"His" Robert St. Clare. As though the man were his possession. None of the Bonds he had brought with him looked Nurail: just as well. This was a fearful place to be Nurail, the Domitt Prison, built on Nurail bones by Pyana slave-masters, a prison for her people with the enemy of their kind to hold the key.

"We will not dispute with the Administration that they have brought you here like a commodity, in that case. Be at ease. We will try not to make things difficult for you."

Koscuisko was still speaking very close to her, but stepped away, raising his voice as though he were just finishing his thought. "And we shall sort well enough together. Very well. Now. Administrator Belan. There must be office space, where I can the briefs of prisoners review. Jurisdiction procedure requires I perform an inspection tour, I understand, and this we could accomplish here and now?"

They would all assume he had been laying down his law to her. Ailynn felt the heat rush into her face; but it was only what they would expect. Why had he concealed his question, in that way?

"Office space on the next level down, your Excellency, and the work area as well. A separate lift, though. Shall we get started?"

There were ways up onto the roof, but few ways down. Did Koscuisko understand yet that he was to be a prisoner, here? Administrator Geltoi controlled traffic within his prison very carefully. It was the only thing that had saved him from the hatred of the prisoners who toiled beneath his damned Pyana oversight: But the less she knew about what had gone on here, she reminded herself, the more easily she would be able to rest.

If rest at all, in the presence of a torturer.

A torturer for whose personal satisfaction she had been procured, she, scarred and damaged goods, and Nurail, no loss if she should take an injury, and no one to intervene for her in this man's sleeping-room.

"Perhaps Miss Samons will see to settling in. Code, come

with me, we will with the Administrator go exploring.''

The officer drew one of his Security with him and left the room with Administrator Belan.

Ailynn stood as still as the others. Waiting.

Once the officer had left, the Chief Warrant Officer broke from her polite position of attention, starting toward Ailynn, beckoning for the Bonds.

''Right. My name is Caleigh Samons, I'm Chief of Security. These are Kaydence Psimas, Erish Muat—'' the one who limped stiffly, one leg bound straight in a walking-brace—''and Toska Bederico, the officer has taken Code Pyatte with him, we can introduce you later. And your name?''

They were strange to her. But they were all bond-involuntaries, the same as she was. Ailynn felt oddly comfortable, surrounded by their friendly curiosity.

''Called Ailynn.'' She all but croaked it, her voice so stiff in her own throat. ''Ailynn Stoup, Chief, sorry.''

''You would prefer to be called which? The officer generally uses first names. By and large.''

''Ailynn, then, Chief.'' The Chief Warrant Officer was as tall as she was, but seemed a little thinner, if more muscular, and the Chief Warrant Officer had rank. They didn't see too many women with rank in the service house, for one reason or another. Ailynn found the Chief intimidating: It made her a little annoyed, to be so awed. She was only afraid of the officer, and projecting. Yes.

''Ailynn, we'll talk. After we're settled in. You should know some things about the officer. I wish I could tell you not to worry.''

They were on her side.

The unspoken message was communicated clearly in the Chief's reluctant candor. On her side, and with an issue in common, the officer. That wasn't an issue. That was a man. Ailynn felt a little better all the same.

''Kay will bring you the officer's personal luggage, and you and he can get things put away. Come on, Toska, let's go make sure nothing else gets lost, those boots took me a month to break in. Erish. Sit down. Critique Kaydence's folding of his Excellency's boot-stockings.''

She had been isolated and afraid for two days in this prison place. Now suddenly she was part of a group, accepted without question, gracefully included, one of them. If only in a sense.

The relief she felt was almost as unnerving as the tension itself had been.

There would still be the officer to face.

But she would not be as alone as she had feared.

"Folding socks is an issue?" she asked the one called Kaydence, timidly. Kaydence was big and broad-shouldered, with a huge grin full of white teeth and dark black glossy curls that fell a little long on the back of his collar. They were all big. Only the officer himself was sized for her.

"We'll make it one before we're through, Cousin Ailynn. Come on, Erish, you can't critique from here, come through to the bedroom with us."

Cousin Ailynn.

Bond-involuntary code.

You are not my sister, but you could be my sister, and I mean to treat you as though you were.

It was Kaydence's statement that he would not be taking advantage of her availability in the officer's absence.

Much encouraged, Ailynn followed the bond-involuntary Security with the officer's luggage into the bedroom to get things put properly in their place.

Andrej Koscuisko walked with Administrator Belan across the garden with Code at his back. At the far end of the garden there was a lift let into the peaked black slate roof of the Domitt Prison, which would provide them access to office and working levels.

Belan didn't seem to have much to say, so Andrej amused himself with his own thoughts. Belan looked more Nurail than Pyana. Administrator Geltoi was emphatically Pyana by his ruddy complexion and the characteristically haughty expression that typically resulted from the notoriously bad teeth of the Pyana as a race.

The woman from the service house was Nurail, both by the astonishing beauty of her complexion and by the color of her auburn hair. Maybe Belan suspected that it was in poor taste to have called for a woman on site, but would not say so. Naturally.

It was a very pleasant garden, warmer than Andrej would have guessed a roof-garden could be in a place as near the cooler extreme of this world's temperate zone as Port Rudistal was. Fruit trees, and bearing ripening fruit at that. Fountains, and graveled paths on which Chief Samons would doubtless insist he run his laps.

Which he and Code and the rest of them would run alone, without Joslire, for as familiar as Chief Samons had become to him—as sincerely as Andrej cherished his surviving gentlemen—it could not be denied that Joslire had been much closer to him.

Joslire's unspoken sympathy and unwavering support had seen Andrej safely through his orientation; he had hoped to see Joslire go free, his Bond revoked. And now some Nurail terrorist had murdered a man who was better than any sixteen of them could possibly be, with their families figured in—

Oh, he had to concentrate, there would be time. He would have his revenge.

The lift opened to a signal of the hand, and tracked so smoothly down to the next floor that Andrej was only vaguely aware of being moved at all. He almost expected to see the garden again, when the lift door slid apart.

"We'll stop on this floor first, your Excellency." Belan sounded as though he were apologizing; but for what? "Your office, sir, if you'd care to have a look. To your left."

Apologizing for being a Nurail in a prison run by Pyana, perhaps. The office conformed to the penthouse for luxury, the furnishings rich and well-appointed. There was a beverager beside the door and a meal-area, but what caught Andrej's attention first and foremost were the windows that stretched the length of the office.

The view was spectacular.

He could look down from here at the roof of the Administration building to his left, if he liked; but it was the view out over the city to the river that held the most interest. The city, and the camp beyond, stretching twice as far as the city itself to either side of the pontoon bridges that crossed the river from the landing site.

"Secured comaccess." Belan's remark rather startled Andrej; turning around, he saw that Belan was standing at one side of the desk, where the holocube stood. "From here his

Excellency has access to the visuals from the next floor, or the Record, or the prison administrative offices or Security, as the officer please. This bank pertains to the penthouse suite."

So he could let people know if he was going to be late without the tedious necessity of sending Security all the way up one floor and across the garden to tell them so. Well, of course.

"I'm sure I shall find everything perfectly satisfactory. What about the next floor?"

Nodding, Belan started for the lift as Code stepped hastily out of his way. "Yes, sir. This way."

The Interrogations area.

Sixteen cells, eight to a side; from the lift he could either walk through the restricted cell block or bypass it if he cared to go around. Andrej went through; sixteen cells occupied. He'd seen these people before. Their faces were unfamiliar; but their expressions were not—suspicion, fear, hatred. He knew these people very well indeed. And before their acquaintance was concluded they would come to know him; nor were they likely to take any benefit from that.

Through the restricted cell block to another area of closed doors, with a pair of prison guards who jumped to surprised attention as Andrej opened the communicating door. His work-rooms. Belan hurried past to open one, a middle room to Andrej's right. Code posted himself to one side of the door in obedience to Andrej's gesture, to wait while Andrej and Belan went in.

The room was clean and sweet-smelling; it had never been used—nor could it have been, in the absence of a Writ assigned. Standing in the middle of the room, looking around him, Andrej could not tell if he was more apprehensive or eager to be back here when the time came. He hated what he did, and he hated himself for doing it, but there was no denying the soul-shattering fact that while he was at it he could hardly get enough.

And, oh, Joslire was dead . . .

He was to be master in this place, the undisputed and absolute authority from working-floor to penthouse, with no check or requirement but that he gain confession from those criminals referred for his Interrogation.

He would gain confession.

He was good at this.

There was no question in Andrej's mind but that he could perform his Inquisitorial function in such wise as to uphold his Writ in an exemplary manner. And someone had taken Joslire away; and would suffer for it. He couldn't bring Joslire back, not even as the autocrat of the Domitt Prison with the Writ on site. No skill in surgery, no degree of rank, no amount of money could bring Joslire back into the world.

Since he couldn't change the fact, it was clearly the idea to concentrate on changing how he felt about it. He knew that he would derive pleasure from the exercise of his lawful authority, pleasure more intense and addictive than that to be taken in the embrace of a woman.

Perhaps it wouldn't make him feel any better, but he'd feel good, and that would be a welcome change from the state of anxious stress he'd been in since Captain Irshah Parmin had first told him that he was to come to the Domitt Prison and be Inquisitor here.

"Quite as it should be," Andrej assured Belan. "Let's go on."

He would be back here soon enough, to practice his revenge.

The officer's briefing had stated that the Domitt Prison had been built on time, under budget, and its Administrator recognized by an impressed Bench for his good management accordingly. Code knew what to make of that: slave labor, and plenty of it.

The prison didn't have to pay prisoners more than a token amount for the labor it could lawfully demand that they perform while they were awaiting trial. It was supposed to offset the charges to the Bench for lodging, clothing, food. And if prisoners were convicted—whether executed or not—the prison didn't have to pay them at all.

"You have many work details, it seems, Administrator. One wonders what work there might be for so many, that they don't run out of jobs."

Code could read the question in the officer's voice. They were sitting on a tracked-mover, touring cell blocks from the middle of the long side of the prison, where the lift through the far doors of the Interrogations section had placed them, three floors down, to the corner, where they would take another lift to the ground level.

And there weren't more than four in eight of the cells occupied at all, let alone fully occupied.

Four-soul cells, and how many of them on a side, how many floors, how many sides, how many souls?

"No worry about that, your Excellency," Belan replied. Code's place was at the back of the mover; looking down the length of the corridor, he tried to calculate the numbers. The officer's briefing had said maximum occupancy was three times eight hundred souls. "We have enough to keep us busy for quite some time. There's to be a new industrial complex built up on reclaimed land, the Domitt has title to the acreage."

Almost too great a temptation to exploit prison labor to its fullest, then. But the Bench would just as soon recycle Nurail into something useful, like public works, as stand the expense of relocating them. Code didn't like the idea.

"How long have you been receiving prisoners?"

Yes.

The prison had been a collection site until the displacement camp had started up; and not all of the souls it had collected had been prisoners per se, but refugees of one sort or another. Bodies the prison could put to good use on construction.

"We've been authorized to process only for six months, your Excellency." And did the Assistant Administrator sound a little uncomfortable? "Unfortunately we had a bad outbreak of parlic fever. Just two months ago. We lost nearly half of the prison population."

As an explanation it was a reasonable one, Code supposed. Being condemned to the Bond carried with it some benefits, after all; Code knew more about epidemiology than he'd ever thought to learn.

Associating with medical staff for the fifteen years he'd been a bond-involuntary, Code knew that there were any number of prison illnesses that could create a problem if they once got out of control. And they could spread particularly rapidly on work-crews because of the contact and redistri-

bution of souls between exposed and unexposed work-crews
from day to day.

Two months ago?

The relocation camp had been established two months ago.

Was it just that fraction too convenient that there'd been
an epidemic, mass death, mass burial, just at the point at
which the Domitt Prison was faced with accounting for the
people that it held?

But if he didn't like it, that meant the officer was four laps
ahead of him already. Code knew he could rely upon the
officer's judgment.

Down a lift at the elbow of the building to a ground-floor
corridor, mover and all. Thence to the exit, halfway down
the length of that corridor, administrative offices by the looks
of them; and out into the courtyard. Across to the nearest
building, and the mover carried them to the entrance on the
short side nearest to the dispatch building that faced the gate.

Mess hall.

The serving lines were empty now, sterile and featureless
between meals; there were five in all, and once Code had
followed his officer through one of them, he could see row
upon row of ledges set at elbow-height that stretched nearly
to the back of the building. People didn't sit down to take
their meals, then, but stood with their dishes on a serving-
ledge and ate as best they could. Efficient, Code supposed.

Downstairs to the kitchen to admire the lifts that carried
food up to the serving lines in series.

It was warm in the kitchen. It hadn't been very warm
outside. But the furnaces were running, they'd all seen the
thick plumes of smoke from the smokestacks, both on the
roof and from the ground level. So the kitchen was harvesting some of the heat from the incinerators to use to cook the
prisoners' daily rations.

That made sense. There were a lot of prisoners. Every day
was baking-day at the Domitt Prison, obviously, too obviously to have to comment on it, except that Code didn't smell
any baking. Not that he was hungry. He'd had enough to eat
at fastmeal just this morning to last him well into the week
to follow, if need should be.

Baking day or no, the officer was satisfied with the preparations under way for the evening meal, the long rows of

cold loaves set out, the ranks of soup-vats with their broths simmering. Code shrugged it off, following his officer and Belan through the kitchen to the back of the building where the wash-house was.

The officer wandered through the great cavernous vault of the communal showers, turning every ninth or fifteenth spigot on to test the temperature of the water. Not scalding, no, and it was not supposed to be. But adequately warm, to judge by the temperature of the mist and steam that the officer kicked up in passing.

The furnaces must be heating water for the communal showers as well, Code decided. He was glad that there was at least plenty of good hot water in the showers. Prisoners on work detail deserved a little comfort at the end of their day.

Pausing at the far end of the showers, the officer took a bit of toweling from the nearest stack of linen on the shelves to dab at his boots. Code appreciated the gesture on Koscuisko's part, even though it wasn't his week to see to that detail of the officer's uniform. Water spots on bootleather were to be avoided.

Looking around for the soiled linen hamper, Koscuisko caught Code's eye, and smiled, a quick grin that demonstrated Koscuisko's appreciation of just that fact. Code bowed, the only response expected or allowed in so public an environment. Which was to say, in the presence of another soul, beside Koscuisko and bond-involuntaries assigned.

Yet all the while he knew that there would be worse things to clean from Koscuisko's uniform than mere water-spotting, in the days to come.

By the time they were finished touring the mess building there was a formation drawn up and waiting in the empty space behind the dispatch building, between the mess building to one side and the prison's internal Security building on the other.

Approaching on foot, Andrej suffered himself to be led through the ranks and have shift and section leaders introduced to him. Standard procedure, of a sort; and very proper, too. It was in everyone's best interest that prison staff know what ranking officers looked like.

Once through the formation, Belan, joined by the prison's senior Security officers, escorted him to the Security building for a tour of the prison's receiving area. This was where statements were taken and decisions made about release to the general prison population or referral to the Inquisitor for questioning.

There was a smell here that Andrej knew, the familiar stink of blood and terror, agony and abuse. But it was no longer fresh. If there had been violations committed it had been days since the last of them, and now that the prison had a Writ on site there would be no need for prison security to overstep their bounds. No sense in making any fuss about something that was no longer an issue.

At the back of the building Andrej found the holding area, where breaches of internal discipline could be evaluated and corrected.

Punishment block.

When people were in prison it was difficult to get their attention, because simply locking them up wasn't much different from not disciplining them at all. Cells were shared, though, and the need for companionship was powerful; isolation could be an effective form of punishment. That was why there were blind confinement cells in punishment block.

Andrej looked into an empty cell, because it seemed to be expected of him. There were as many cells occupied as unoccupied; and at the end of the row of isolation cells he could see three or four square latched hatches cut at floor-level, not very high, and a screened opening above each one near to the ceiling.

"Whatever are these for?" he asked Belan, who stood with the shift supervisor in charge of conducting this portion of the tour. They might be storage hoppers of some sort, he supposed. But what would storage hoppers be doing in punishment block?

"Er. Ahem. Lockboxes, your Excellency." The shift supervisor sounded a little diffident. Perhaps a little uncomfortable. "For prisoners with self-discipline problems, sir. They go in through there."

Lockboxes?

People crawled in, through those latched hatches in the wall?

"I'd like to see one." Something in the idea tickled Andrej's fancy. Crawling, through a confined space. "They don't seem to open, or am I mistaken?" If a man had a fear of enclosed spaces, it would be difficult to do.

Part of him liked it to be difficult.

"Indeed not, your Excellency," the shift supervisor— Thamis—confirmed, readily. "If you'd care to have a look, though. We'll fetch a stool. Only one occupied at present, sir."

Someone was in one of those?

Oh, better and better.

One short moment, and someone came running with a stool to place it in front of a particular grate on Thamis's direction. Andrej stepped up onto the stool to peer through the grate, realizing after a moment that he had to open a blinder-shutter in order to do so. The moment that he did, however, someone inside screamed; and did not stop.

"Please, please, don't. I won't. Not ever, not again. Ever. Please. I can't bear it, oh, oh, please."

Andrej stepped down.

It was hard to get a good look into the box with someone in it taking up space, soaking up the light. He could move the stool and look in another room, an empty room.

Or he could gratify a growing curiosity.

"Shall I?" he asked Belan, with a nod toward the trap near the floor. "I must admit. I would like to see how it is done, to get in and out of such a place."

Belan and Thamis exchanged glances; then Thamis shrugged, good-naturedly. "I'm sure our Lerriback has learned his lesson, Administrator," Thamis said. "We'll let him out for your inspection, sir. Just don't expect the prisoner to show due respect. This is the third time this week he's been confined, he won't learn manners on work-detail."

Thamis came forward as he spoke to unbar the catch securing the little hatch at floor-level, and pull it open with the toe of his boot. "Come along, you dirty little Nurail beggar," Thamis called; his voice was more genial than his words, perhaps out of respect for Andrej's presence. "Out."

Wriggling with convulsive spasms that might have been funny, the man named Lerriback scrambled out, sliding on his rump into the corridor to huddle against the far wall and lie there trembling.

Andrej stepped up on the stool once more to look in; and Thamis crouched down to shine a torch up from below obligingly. The lockbox seemed impossibly shallow to Andrej, too shallow for a man to so much as put his arm out to the opposite wall without being forced to bend it at the elbow. Square. He had just seen how difficult it was for Lerriback to get out; it would be as difficult to get in, and once one had stood up there would surely be no way in which a man could hope to lie down and rest himself.

To be faced to the wall for hours on end was a petty torment, common enough because it was not sanctioned under Protocols and therefore not forbidden as an ad hoc exercise in bullying. It was difficult to condone such insidious torment.

But at the same time it could not be condemned out of hand; there were no rules against it. He, himself, had used the trefold shackles—officially recognized only as restraint, and not as punishment—to wear down the resistance and erode the spirit of a stubborn prisoner; and that was not much different.

Gesturing for Code to come to him, Andrej leaned one hand against Code's shoulder to steady himself as he got down off the stool again. He knew why he was trembling, within himself. Joslire had loved him despite it all; and Joslire was dead.

"You, what is your name?" Andrej asked. "Lerriback?"

The Nurail had been trying to make himself as small as possible. He reached out, clutching blindly for Andrej's ankle as Andrej spoke to him. There was no threat; he clearly only wanted to show his submission.

But Andrej had already made work for Toska by letting his boots get water-spotted. He was not inclined to suffer smudging hands, and moved away from the Nurail, who stared at Andrej's feet as he stepped back with an expression in which desperate hope was replaced by helpless fear.

Andrej could follow the progress of the emotions in Lerriback's face. That he was not allowed to show abject self-abasement could only mean that there would be more punishment. Lerriback gathered himself up into a fetal curl of misery and wept, covering his face with shaking fingers.

"Lerriback, I have spoken to you," Andrej warned. He shouldn't be doing this. He knew it. The anguished fear the Nurail had of the lockbox ate away at the better part of Andrej's nature and exposed the beastly passion that lay at the foundation of his being. His interest had already been aroused by the idea of such close confinement. And now arousal began to touch his appetite as well.

"Sir. Beg pardon. Yes, sir, as you please, sir."

It was shameful to see a grown man so reduced. More shameful still to enjoy the sight of it. "You do not like your lockbox, Lerriback?"

"No, sir—or—yes—"

It was a cruel question, taunting and unfair. If Lerriback was afraid of the lockbox, he would not want to go back. He would not want to do anything that would get him sent back. He would not want to be disagreeable. He would not be able to guess whether he was supposed to tell the truth; or pretend that he had enjoyed his own punishment, so as to avoid an implicit criticism of those who had punished him by characterizing the punishment as disagreeable.

What would it be like, if he said that Lerriback was to be shut up again?

Lerriback raised his eyes to Andrej's face; but could not seem to quite make eye contact, glancing away to one side in repeated twitches as though it was painful for him to look at his tormentor. And he'd never even seen Andrej before. Andrej was impressed; Lerriback was very much afraid of the lockbox.

His knowledge only made Andrej desire the test more passionately; and he knew that he was wrong. Wrong to desire that Lerriback be afraid. Wrong to anticipate the pleasure he would have in it.

"Mister Thamis. I cannot deny the obvious effectiveness of this for discipline."

He had to raise his voice, and speak out against what was in his own mind. Or he would shame himself in front of all these people; when usually it was only a prisoner, and his Security, who were witness to his moral degradation. And prisoners were almost always as good as dead.

"And still, though I am not the one who should say this,

we should not rely upon such methods for good discipline. This Lerriback, is he under Charges?"

"Prisoner awaiting disposition, your Excellency." Thamis betrayed no sign of confusion in his voice. Polite. Never hint to an officer that you think his behavior may be contradictory. "Disciplined for disruption in work-crew. Attempted assault on crew supervision. A chronic offender."

"The Domitt is a new installation, we should guard against the appearance of irregularity. Prisoners should be punished after evaluation of offense, and according to the Protocols." Thus-and-such a range of punishments for thus-and-such a range of offenses. The Levels for investigation of the offense, and the restrictions.

If the suspected offense is misappropriation of Judicial stores to a value not in excess of two million Standard and confession cannot be obtained at the Sixth Level you must find that no cause can be proven and release your prisoner . . .

"It would be prudent if we were to restrict ourselves to the Standard range of adjudicated punishments. Forgive for me this Lerriback the balance of his offense, Mister Thamis. If he offends again he must be punished under Protocol."

"He has been a very persistent offender," Thamis warned. "With his Excellency's permission. If his Excellency is certain that it is the right thing to do."

No, he wanted to stay away from "right," he didn't want to begin his association with the Domitt Prison by implying criticism of its Administration. Captain Vopalar's reaction to his release of that one prisoner was too fresh in his mind, even at some weeks' remove.

The thought distracted him.

Joslire had been with him when they had discovered that savaged Nurail prisoner. Joslire had handed him the key when they had found the escaped prisoner. Joslire had trusted him. Joslire was dead: Nurail had murdered him.

Did Andrej really care whether some Nurail suffered in excess of what was decent or deserved, when a Nurail had taken Joslire away from him?

"Only that it would present a better appearance to be seen to observe the letter of the Law, Mister Thamis. And it might

cause embarrassment for honest prison Security if there
should be tales told in some manner.''

Maybe Thamis thought Andrej only wanted to have six-
and-sixty from Lerriback sometime. It didn't matter what
Thamis thought. And he'd have as many six-and-sixties as
he wanted, starting soon.

''We yield to your professional judgment, your Excellency. Styper. Take Lerriback back to the cells. Oh, he can
have a day off work-detail, just because, in honor of the
officer. And full rations besides.''

Whether Thamis was merely indulging him didn't matter
either. Lerriback would be excused the balance of the torment he was to have suffered; and he—Andrej told himself,
firmly—had better get on with his orientation. There was
doubtless a great deal more of the prison to cover. ''Mister
Thamis, I deeply appreciate your flexibility in this matter.
Administrator Belan. Shall we continue our tour?''

''Infirmary next, your Excellency.'' Belan sounded as
though he were just as glad to be away from here. He'd made
Belan uncomfortable, then. That was too bad. Belan could
have no idea what Andrej's Security went through.

What he would begin to put them through, and all too
soon.

All too soon? Or not quite soon enough?

Code was waiting. Code's presence steadied him.

Andrej nodded, and followed Belan out of the punishment
block, to complete his tour of the Domitt Prison.

''We've never been in a situation quite like this, Ailynn,''
Caleigh said. ''We don't know exactly what to expect from
it. But there are some things we may be able to predict.''

Unpacking completed. Facility secured; the penthouse,
servant's quarters, gardens. Supplies delivered twice daily or
as needed via the same route they'd come up on. No need
to worry about unexpected visitors; there appeared to be only
the two ways up onto the roof, not counting the fire-stairs.

The Service bond-involuntary Ailynn sat calmly waiting
opposite Caleigh at the common table in the dining room.
She seemed a sensible woman; one of the auburn-headed run
of Nurail, deep red-brown hair, blue eyes with the matte-
grey sheen of stalloy to them just at present. Like any sen-

sible bond-involuntary she had the self-discipline to speak when she was spoken to, but not otherwise.

Koscuisko's people got spoiled.

Would it recoil on them, when Koscuisko was gone?

"Now. We've been assigned to the officer for more than three years gone past. We think we know a little bit about him. Such as, he's a good doctor." It was a little hard to approach the issue that was on her mind; but it needed to be done. With Joslire dead, their need for allies to help deal with Koscuisko was even more pressing than it would have been otherwise. She had to level with Ailynn. No matter how reluctant she might be to say things that could be sensationalized to the detriment of Koscuisko's dignity.

"He's also a very effective Inquisitor. Something to do with empathy. Hands-on practitioner. He can't do the work unless he does it personally. When he tries to get by with just using drugs he can't get into it and follow through."

This was the most delicate part, and Caleigh chose her words as carefully as possible. "Although the officer is under normal circumstances a compassionate man, he suffers an alteration of behavior when he's asked to implement the Protocols. He doesn't like to hurt people until he starts hurting them. But once he starts hurting them he enjoys it a great deal, can you understand what I'm saying?"

Now Ailynn bestirred herself, having been asked the question direct. "I'd guess your point is that he's to be savage, Miss Samons."

A little sharp for a bond-involuntary, but Caleigh had been speaking as frankly as she knew how, and had asked for a response in as blunt language.

"Well, yes. More or less. He tries not to take it out on us, though. Tries. It's very hard on him, sometimes, he'll be so involved with what he has been doing. And then has to interrupt for a night's sleep."

Involved was not the right word. Or it was, but not applied in quite that sense. Impassioned. Absorbed. All right, aroused, and if the source of his arousal was not directly sexual in nature, its expression quite naturally was.

"What is it to do with me, Miss Samons?"

Caleigh sighed. Oh, what, indeed. What it came down to was that this could be hard on Ailynn, because Koscuisko at loose ends—with days spent at Inquiry behind him and days yet to come—was going to be very much in his own world. It wasn't the world in which Koscuisko usually lived, which was full of other people that Koscuisko cared for. It was much more exclusive than that, and comprised almost solely of Koscuisko himself and prisoners who existed to give him pleasure. And incidentally information.

Caleigh took a deep breath. "We don't know how he's going to react to being here, Ailynn. But I want you to be ready for whatever. I mean muscle relaxants. Lubricants. He might not stop to think, not with his head full of his day's work."

What it came down to was rape, even if that was not the word the prison administration would use to describe it. Ailynn was here for Koscuisko's use, and whatever use he made of her would be considered lawful and unremarkable.

Whether Koscuisko would take advantage of her presence was something they wouldn't know until it happened, but if it happened it was likely to be sudden, quick, and brutal. Not because he meant to be cruel to her. Simply because all that was in Koscuisko's world at such times were people who existed for his gratification.

"It wouldn't be the first time. Even the third, or fifth." Caleigh thought Ailynn's response pertained more to what she'd thought than to what she'd actually said. "But I'll be guided by what you can tell me, Miss Samons. I'll do what I can to preserve the Bench resource."

Did she mean Koscuisko?

Or that she had no more value for her own body than to avoid damage, if she could, because she was to "preserve the Bench resource"?

"And if he frightens you. Or if you're hurt. Don't keep it to yourself. We're all in this together. All of us. You can help us. We'd like to be able to help you. I am asking for your trust, Ailynn. It's your decision whether or not to extend it."

She couldn't put too much emphasis on that word, "asking." Too much weight and it would come out a demand, and a bond-involuntary was required to submit to a demand. That wasn't what she wanted. Not at all.

Ailynn simply nodded, and stood up, apparently comfortable enough that the interview was over. Or willing to trust that she would not be reprimanded if she was mistaken.

Was that an answer?

"Thank you, Miss Samons. It's kind of you."

The woman was not giving anything away. On the other hand, to have survived she had to have learned to protect herself. Caleigh rose to her feet in turn.

"Let's check on the others, then. The officer should be back from his inspection shortly. You haven't met Code yet."

Time would tell.

She'd done what she could.

When she had been to bed with Koscuisko, he'd been careful. He'd engaged her with a female-superior position, minimizing the impact of the strength in his body. And still she'd known that she'd been to bed with a Dolgorukij, even after hours of sleep and a glass of caraminson wine to speed the recovery.

She didn't like to think of how it would feel for a woman if the officer was distracted, absorbed in the urgency of his need, not paying attention. If Koscuisko injured the woman, it would only add to his burden of cares.

They all had cares enough already.

Ailynn stood aside for her to pass, yielding precedence to rank.

Having her here could make things much easier on the officer.

But if Koscuisko hurt her, it would be worse.

◆ Seven

His third day at the Domitt Prison, the first day of his first Inquiry here. Andrej Koscuisko had set his documentation in order yesterday; and had made his choice.

He knew what was about to happen. He would have some soul into work-room. He would hurt some soul who was to be helpless against him. He would gain evidence and put a confession on Record, for the use of the Second Judge at Chilleau Judiciary; and he would enjoy it.

"Cell Twelve, gentlemen." Standing at the entrance to the restricted block, Andrej made his announcement in a clear voice. Cell Twelve would know that he was to go to torture. But the other prisoners would know that their doom was to be delayed, at least for a day. "Through to work area, if you please."

Cell Twelve hadn't been here as long as some of the others, might be a little more resilient than people who'd been shut up in the dark for too long. Well, not in the dark, but in holding cell, where the food and the exercise both made available were not calculated to sustain good health.

The prisoner didn't struggle much against Code and Toska—what would be the point?—but suffered himself to be bound and taken out from his cell, staring at Andrej white-faced with a sort of keen hunger. Curiosity. Dread, mixed with challenge. The experience of the prison had not worn him down yet. There was to be some friction there. That would make it easier, in a sense.

They took the prisoner through to the work area. Andrej

stayed behind in company of two of Geltoi's turnkeys, standing in the holding block, looking around. Some of the prisoners would meet his eyes. Some of them would not come to the front of the cells, not even when bidden; why should they?

There was no question about who he was, or why they were there. He would be getting to each one in time. They would give satisfaction, and then they would die, and the sooner he got a good start on Cell Twelve, the sooner his people would come for the next he would select.

The door to the work-room that his gentlemen had prepared for him was standing open, Toska and Code waiting on either side of the open doorway. The prisoner, within, waiting for him. Andrej paused on the threshold to assess the situation.

His chair and his lamp, on a bit of carpeting with the table convenient to his hand.

A rhyti-service waiting for him, a thin wisp of steam curling off the surface of the cup that had been poured out to be ready. Sintermayer leaf, by the smell of it, a good enough grade of rhyti, if not top quality. Not that the prison administration could be expected to know. For most rhyti drinkers, a brew from sintermayer would be more than satisfactory.

The prisoner, half-stripped and faced to the wall, his wrists bound behind his head with a stalloy bar threaded between neck and elbow to keep his arms well back and prevent his folding them around his face to protect it from the blows that would come.

Starting his prisoners only half-stripped was conservative, though it meant calling Security in later on to finish the job. Sometimes he found other hands that were willing to do the work—

Unbidden in his mind's eye, the image rose up white and red in all of its pitiful horror, the shock of total nakedness, and the brutal surprise of an assault . . .

He shook himself clear of it, bidding his beast to heel. "Quite in order, gentlemen." Code and Toska bowed from their posts, their faces clear of any trace of what they might be feeling. His praise was carefully couched in neutral terms, and intended to address their professionalism pure and simple. This was the job to which the Bench had condemned them for crimes against the Judicial order. It was not necessary to require them to pretend that they enjoyed it.

Stepping through into the room, Andrej closed the door. It seemed his prisoner winced or recoiled as the latching mechanism engaged; but there wasn't much the prisoner could do about it.

Crossing the room to sit down in his chair, Andrej took up the controller. The tether that leashed the prisoner began to move, tracking up and across the ceiling, dragging the prisoner with it into the middle of the room. The length of the leash from anchor-point to the prisoner was a little short once in that position.

The prisoner arched his body as if in pain and rose up on the balls of his feet, trying to relieve the pressure on his throat from the leash, turning about slowly to face Andrej where he sat. Andrej adjusted the controller to let some slack into the tether. There was no sense in rushing things.

He drank a cup of rhyti, thinking about how hard it had been for him—once upon a time—to start an Interrogation. A long time ago; three years, nearly four years, at Fleet Orientation Station Medical.

The prisoner was watching him, his whole body stiff with apprehension. There was a part of Andrej's spirit that shared that apprehension; he knew what was going to happen to him—had already begun to happen—and what it would mean for both of them.

Andrej let some more slack out at the tether, and the prisoner lost his balance, falling down heavily to his knees. Yes, precisely. Andrej took up a length of chain and fastened it around the prisoner's knees, hooking it to the anchor in the floor. He didn't want to have to deal with watching out for stray kicks. The prisoner had been decently hobbled, right enough, but a man could not be faulted for striking out on an instinct when he was being tortured. It was best to deal with such potential problems up front.

"My name is Andrej Koscuisko." Finally he spoke to his prisoner, who stared tight-lipped and resolute at him. White in the face. "I hold the Writ to which you must answer, by the Bench instruction. And the information I must have from you requires that you betray your friends, and cause, and family."

His blunt speech startled the prisoner, a little. Andrej spoke on. "You know you are accused at the Intermediate Levels, and this means that you may win your liberty by resisting all temptation to betray your secrets to me, because the Bench will not accept use of speaksera under these conditions."

Not to coerce confession, no, and it was not quite honest of him to make such an assertion when he was clear to use another drug—by accident, of course—which would betray the prisoner to himself, without Bench invalidation of the evidence. Without reproach or reprimand, even though the Bench would surely know that he had cheated, and condemned the man out of his own mouth by means of a dirty and underhanded trick.

Bright pain and glittering blood were clean and wholesome, when compared to such despicable ruses—

"Here we are about to begin, and I can almost promise you that you will submit to me in time. It is nothing to do with you, and everything to do with pain. If you are willing to confess to me right here, right now, I have it in my authority to accept your confession and verify it with a truthteller, and the Bench will grant you simple execution in consideration of your cooperation."

Was he making sense? He was speaking to a prisoner, a Nurail taken captive and locked up in prison waiting for torture. How could he know whether the prisoner understood what he was saying? "Speak now, and die a swift and easy death. Or defy me and be tortured till you speak, because you will not die until you speak, if I can help it."

There, that was much better. That made sense. Andrej could see it in the prisoner's face.

"I'll not."

The prisoner's voice was strained and hoarse, but determined. "It may be as you say, torturer. But not if I can help it. And I hope to God and free space to defeat your purpose, you and your Bench with you."

It was well said, and honestly. No vainglorious boast of endurance or resistance. The prisoner would know better than to think that endurance and resistance had anything to do with Protocols. If he could, Andrej would deal honestly with his prisoner, and give him a fair chance to go to death without betraying his secrets. There was little indeed that could be called honest or fair about torture. But he would do his best.

Not even in the black depths of his passion was he so depraved as to cheat on the Protocols.

He'd never needed to.

The Protocols themselves provided everything a man could ever want, and more—

Andrej put his two hands to either side of the prisoner's face, for emphasis. "I know a great deal more about this than you do." It was fair warning. "Please be sure of what you choose."

No answer.

No sense wasting energy repeating oneself, Andrej supposed. A prudent choice. He went to the instruments-rack against the wall, and chose a whip. He would need one that he could control in his right hand, his left hand was still healing. The prisoner had made his choice. Somebody had to suffer for the fact that Joslire was gone; and though it couldn't be said to be the prisoner's fault, this prisoner was all he had right here, right now.

He unloosed the bar that clipped the prisoner's arms behind his neck and drew the chain up to stretch the man's wrists overhead. Stepped back a pace, and struck from behind, watching the welt start to ooze blood as he gathered the whip back into his hand. The prisoner cried out, when he was struck, but as much startled as hurt; it was all right. There would be time. It would develop.

Again.

He was just warming up.

The prisoner flinched away from the blows; but there was nowhere to flinch to, he was alone in the middle of the room, pinned knee and wrist to floor and ceiling. Nowhere to go. No way out. No escape, except confession.

It did feel better to be hitting someone.

Or at least it felt good, and any good was better than the icy agony in Andrej's heart where his friend Joslire had been.

The officer was late to supper, as he had been these two days past since he had started processing his prisoners. That was what the housekeeper said, processing, as though that could cover the fact that people were being put to torture. But they were only Nurail to the housekeeper: not really people.

The officer did not try to pretend differently.

He sat slumped on the edge of the bed unfastening his underblouse while Erish Muat pulled his boots off one by one to take them away. A freshly polished pair of boots was already waiting for the officer's use in the morning; there were three pairs, they rotated. And carried the Emandisan knives from pair to pair as need should be, because the officer would not be parted from his knives except in bed.

Erish went out with the boots, and the officer sat in the dim warmth of his bedroom with his clothing half-undone, silent. Ailynn stood at the open door to his washroom and waited. There was clean linen laid out, and warmed toweling, but she dared not speak to urge him to his bathing. She was afraid of him. She couldn't help it.

His people were afraid of him, and trusted him at the same time; she didn't understand it. She didn't need to understand to know that she was frightened of him, coming up from torture-room with the blood of his work staining his uniform and a serene expression on his face that made her shudder to look at it.

After a moment the officer ran his fingers through his fine blond hair, and stood up wearily. He had been working all day. It was physical labor. She was sure he would accept a massage; but was it permitted to her to suggest one?

Or had she not better just keep her mouth shut and mind her own business? Physical labor; yes; but it still meant torture. Perhaps it was more appropriate if his body ached from it.

"I am not sure that it is good for you to be here, Ailynn," he said. "Would it not be better for you to sleep in your own place?"

She didn't have a place. They hadn't provided one. She had a pallet behind the screen to go to when the officer was done with her, if he declined to suffer a whore to sleep with him in his bed. Koscuisko had not scorned her from his bed. But he had made no use of her, either.

"According to his Excellency's good pleasure." As in all

things. "Would the officer prefer one of the men to help him wash?"

Raising his head slowly, he looked back over his shoulder at her, eyebrows raised. "I am not sure that I myself express well, Ailynn. I mean that I begin to fear for you. I am so much beguiled, by this work, and it may be that I forget myself. Should you not go?"

Well, one thing was certain, she could agree. He didn't express himself well, at least not so she could understand him. She could hardly guess at his meaning.

But there was nowhere for her to go.

"I have been procured for your comfort, sir. The rate schedule puts no limitation on what form of recreation the patron may wish to elect." He knew that, surely. "You are the officer. I am under Bond. If I am unacceptable, more suitable entertainment can be provided, as the officer please."

Koscuisko put his hand to the back of his neck, arching his spine as though a pulled muscle troubled him. "No, it is not that. And I do not wish it. There would be fault found, and then a beating."

He moved as he spoke, so that he stood beside her when he asked, leaning against the doorjamb. Very close. Facing into the washroom. Looking at her. She didn't know quite how to respond; and he continued.

"It is only this, Ailynn, I am a man like any other, which means that my fish desires thy ocean." Whatever that was supposed to mean. "It is in my work force and violence, all through the day. And I do not want to hurt you, should I forget how to respect the privilege of your body."

It was hard for her to tell the threads in his weave, but Ailynn thought she began to grasp his pattern. "His Excellency should not concern himself. I have no feeling, sir." Nor was it "fish" which had damaged her, and left her so badly scarred that they could send her to any given rapist without concern that she would lose her economic value at his hands.

Koscuisko stared, and she couldn't read his face, his eyes too pale in the uncertain light for her to even know for certain if he was looking at her. "Oh, is it so indeed, Ailynn?" She couldn't interpret his tone of voice, whether sorrowful or relieved. "And still the thing is that if you were not here neither of us would have cause for concern. Surely you could share with Kaydence or with Code, Erish is a little stiff yet, or there's the divan in the front room. Out there."

"If his Excellency is pleased to direct me to entertain his Security—"

They had called her "cousin." But that wouldn't make any difference. They would all do what the officer wanted. If the officer wanted that.

"No, not at all. Oh, this is going nowhere." Whatever it was that was on Koscuisko's mind, she clearly wasn't catching at his meaning. He wasn't angry at her for her stupidity, and that helped. She wasn't stupid. She didn't understand him. "We will forget I ever raised the thought, Ailynn, I can find no solution to this trap, and you are in it."

Chief Samons had said he could be violent, but why would he try to shield her from that? She had been leased to service his desires. She couldn't imagine that he didn't understand that.

"Does his Excellency bathe tonight or shower?"

If it wouldn't come together then it wouldn't, and she was safer to retreat into routine either way.

"Run the bath, please, Ailynn. I'll have a soak." He started to strip slowly, and she slipped past him to run the bath before collecting his soiled clothing for the housekeeper to see to in the morning.

"Beg for me Cook's indulgence, and ask for some of his good casserole. I will want cortac and some cards, have you to play the game of relki ever learned?"

It was his custom in the evenings, so far. He bathed before he ate, and played card games with his Security, drinking quantities of cortac brandy that staggered her—without setting him to staggering. And interfered with her as little as though he had been stinking drunk, which was to say not at all.

She could deal easily enough with this, if Koscuisko were to turn out to be a mere drunkard; drunk men posed few threats, unless it was a beating.

All of this concern for her, lest she should suffer violence at his hands—did they think she didn't know what it was like already?

But as long as she could avoid it, she would take their care for her and be grateful to be treated like a human being.

Instead of a Nurail.

Bench Lieutenant Plugrath came escorted by Chief Samons, and did not look to be in a happy state of mind. Toska could appreciate that. It had been five days, here at the Domitt Prison, and nobody in a happy state of mind except the Administration, who were coming to understand what the officer could do with captive souls when time and inclination both permitted.

"Lieutenant Plugrath reports to wait upon his Excellency's pleasure," Chief Samons said to him. Chief was bearing up all right. Koscuisko did what he could to insulate them.

Toska bowed to signal his receipt of her instruction. "Yes, Chief, I'll just go tell the officer. The Lieutenant may wish to wait here—"

No, the door to the torture cell opened, and here was the officer himself. "Toska, I want—" Two hours into his morning's work, lost to the appetite within him, Koscuisko was flushed of cheek and glittering of eye. Smoking a lefrol.

Toska cringed in his heart from the sight and smell of the officer's lefrol, and not because he objected to the stink of it so much as that he knew Koscuisko's mind. A smouldering lefrol was an honest stink. The officer was as likely to find a dual use for it, inside.

"Your Excellency," Lieutenant Plugrath saluted. Very formally. "You've asked for a report. Shall we go to your office, sir?"

Because Lieutenant Plugrath had never been in torture cell before, so much was clear. Koscuisko only smiled.

"Not necessary, Lieutenant, come on in. Toska. Come with me. I've a small task for you. Lieutenant?"

There was no graceful way for a junior officer to refuse a senior officer's instruction. Toska had even less choice in the matter. Reluctantly, as if making up his mind only as he went whether he was going to object or not, Plugrath followed the officer into the torture-room. Toska stepped across the threshold and secured the door.

"Your Excellency." Plugrath's formality was one way of insulating himself; Toska knew that. Formality was one of his own best defenses. "You've asked for a report on our investigation. There's been a concerted effort on the part of the Port Authority—"

But Koscuisko held up his hand. "One moment." Gloved hands. The officer wore his gloves when he was working to save the tearing of the skin over his knuckles when he struck someone. Toska supposed it protected the bandage on the officer's left hand as well. "Toska, you are to strip the rest of this clothing, leave the hipwrap for the present. Then I will have you to set up the wheel. Go to it."

Their officer was sensitive to the constraints imposed upon them by the governor. Koscuisko was usually careful to suggest, advise, request, rather than put his orders in so short a form. It helped them preserve some dignity, howsoever artificial, to comply with instruction because they had been asked politely; rather than because the requests were actually orders which they had no choice but to obey.

In the middle of a torture-room Koscuisko took the opposite approach, but it had its source in the same consideration. Koscuisko gave orders to his Bonds in torture-room, short, blunt, unambiguous. In order to keep clear the understanding that they had between them: None of the Bonds would do any such thing of their own free will, if given the choice. Koscuisko took pains to emphasize the fact that for a Bond there was no choice.

Toska had wondered why Koscuisko had taken the Writ to Inquire, when the officer had first been assigned; bond-involuntaries had no choice, but Koscuisko was not under Bond. Since then Toska had learned that not all such coercive "bonds" relied upon a governor. Koscuisko was under Bond to his father's will, and for Koscuisko at least that was enough to hold him to the work he feared and hated.

Koscuisko had started on this one yesterday at about mid-meal, and there was little difficulty managing the prisoner accordingly. Difficult to handle, yes, because the body had been cruelly marked already, and it hurt the man to move him even as little as was required to strip what was left of the prisoner's trousers and footgear from off that misused flesh. Toska cut fabric away with a utility knife swiftly, with practiced skill. The officer did not like to be kept waiting.

And the sooner he was done, the sooner the officer would let him leave the room.

"You will give me just a moment, Lieutenant, I should not like to lose momentum. Momentum is very important in maintaining interest in a conversation, don't you think? H'mm?"

Standing at his prisoner's head while Toska worked, Koscuisko nudged the man's cheek with the toe of his boot. The prisoner groaned, but with more fear than pain. Koscuisko smiled.

"Yes, I think so, too. Continuity. You are only one part finished with your story, and it is interesting, I am eager for more details."

Toska bundled the rags of clothing into a wad and set it aside, hastily. The wheel, the officer had said. Slipping the catch, Toska raised the framework from its storage space in the floor-slot, locking the axle into the lifts. The officer preferred the wheel to the more traditional stretcher because the wheel was only chest-high, and could be adjusted. The officer liked to be close to his work. He liked to be able to concentrate on the expression on a prisoner's face without straining his neck.

Toska couldn't spare a moment to look at Lieutenant Plugrath, but the subtle desperation in Plugrath's voice as he protested was as expressive as anyone could have wished. "Excellency, really, it will take just a moment to update you, shouldn't we step outside while these—preparations are going forward?"

The prisoner couldn't move himself to help or to hinder them. Toska took the man by the naked ankles to move him to the wheel; Koscuisko had clamped his lefrol between his teeth and taken the prisoner by the bleeding shoulders. Helping out.

It was another of the things Koscuisko was careful about, he didn't call them in unless he needed them, and when he did Koscuisko did his best to minimize the extent to which they had to do things that would actually hurt.

So Toska got the ankles, which had been bruised through the foot-wraps by the occasional blow but which were otherwise undamaged. The officer himself handled the raw skin of the prisoner's shoulders, lifting with Toska to arrange the body on the narrow stalloy rim of the wheel.

Chest-high.

Just as his Excellency liked it.

Toska fastened the prisoner's newly bared ankles to the anchor in the floor. While the officer chained the prisoner's wrists at the other end, Toska leaned down to fetch the cross-braces up from the storage well. Cross-bracing fixed behind the prisoner's knees and elbows along the curve of the wheel was called for in order to provide the required stretching effect.

"Quite impossible," Koscuisko insisted. "Toska needs my help. My client needs to be decently settled here before we can go on, isn't that right?"

Talking to his prisoner, talking to Lieutenant Plugrath. The prisoner's head hung down against the wheel's rim, the sweat of his pain shining in the bright lights overhead. Koscuisko gave the floor-pedal a few experimental taps, and the wheel rose by a few eighths. Toska got the elbows fixed just in time.

"You were telling me, Lieutenant?"

Toska stood away and waited. Koscuisko would send him out when Koscuisko noticed him. But Koscuisko would have to notice him first. And it could be that Koscuisko wanted him for something else; there was no telling what the officer would come up with next, during his exercises.

Toska hoped it wouldn't be very long before Koscuisko noticed him.

None of what Koscuisko had in hand to deploy against a prisoner could be said to be pleasant: But the wheel was terrible. Koscuisko had no idea. If Koscuisko had known how frightened Toska was of the wheel, he would have had Kaydence in to help instead. Toska was as certain of that as he was sure that the sun would rise over Port Rudistal in the morning.

"You asked for a status report."

Now Plugrath was furious; he knew that he was being manipulated, now, and as deliberately as the officer tipped hot ash from his lefrol into his prisoner's eyes to make him cry out.

"Concerted effort on the part of the Port Authority has

failed to disclose significant information to date. Investigation is ongoing. Findings include confirmation that the Domitt Prison—Administrators Geltoi or Belan, preferably both—were the intended targets of plotted ambush activity in Port Rudistal. We're on to a few strands, but the braid is fraying fast, the trail's running cold already. Captain Vopalar has authorized resources not needed to secure the relocation camp to assist in the legwork. That is all I have to report at this time. Your Excellency.''

Koscuisko had leaned his elbows up on his prisoner's naked chest, and smoked his lefrol thoughtfully with his forearms crossed in front of him. Nudging the wheel's level fractions higher from time to time, to make the prisoner whimper. Toska knew that Lieutenant Plugrath couldn't want out of this any more badly than he did: yet was constrained by Koscuisko's superior rank almost as effectively as a bond-involuntary under orders was constrained by a governor.

Neither one of them could flee until the officer was graciously pleased to let them go.

''It is not good enough, Bench Lieutenant,'' Koscuisko said. Touching the fat coal end of his lefrol to a bloody welt across the prisoner's belly. Making him choke back a shout of protest and of pain. ''I don't care who they thought they were attacking. I don't care why. Someone has bereft me of one of my Security. It is bad practice to permit one's Security to be shot down around one. I want better news than this the next time I see you, Lieutenant. Would it inspire the search to greater effort if I asked your subordinates to me also, to express my sense of urgency in person?''

Burnt flesh stank, and the knowledge that it was living flesh seemed to make it even more nauseating. Plugrath was as white in the face as Toska imagined he could ever get. ''Sir. With respect. This is beneath you. And to bring hard-working troops in here—I resist that notion, sir, as strenuously as I possibly can, and will do so to my Captain if necessary.''

''Lieutenant.'' Koscuisko only sounded entertained. The Lieutenant didn't know how Koscuisko was, during times like this. The Lieutenant had only seen the better part of the officer up till now. ''Your threats amuse me. It will be even more amusing to receive you at my workplace should you try to avoid the reports you have promised. I want results, and if I need your squad leaders' attention I will have it, and if I want reports every day I will have them too. Do we understand each other?''

He stepped on the floorpedal, and the wheel moved, and the prisoner shrieked out loud. ''Oh, please, oh, please, I can't tell you, I don't know—''

Plugrath ignored the prisoner as best he could, but Toska couldn't help but understand. There was no defiance there, at least not up front. Koscuisko was tormenting the man for Plugrath's benefit. Of course it was up to the officer who he tormented, and how; how long, and to what end. But it was a bad sign.

This was only going to get worse, as time wore on.

''His Excellency makes himself transparently clear.'' Plugrath was at least as much angry as disgusted. Toska granted the Bench Lieutenant good marks for a strong stomach: It wasn't that he lacked grit. ''I will wait upon his Excellency in two days' time to make report. It will not be necessary to invite the shift supervisors. Sir.''

Koscuisko eased off the wheel by a few marks, and the prisoner caught his breath in surprised gratitude. Terrified and surprised gratitude. Toska could empathize. He didn't want to.

''I will to myself reserve the pleasure of being judge of that, Lieutenant. But am content to wait for the decision. That is all there is for you, Toska, show the Lieutenant out, and don't come back. Oh, except to bring some rhyti, have Kaydence do it.''

Toska hoped his own gratitude was not too obvious; it would be a breach of etiquette to imply that he wanted out of there, howsoever indirectly. Their officer valued their professionalism. They valued his selfishness in Inquiry.

''According to his Excellency's good pleasure. Your midmeal, sir?''

Koscuisko waved him off; Plugrath was already at the door. Koscuisko wouldn't talk to them with the door open. ''I will call for midmeal when I feel the want of it, Toska, rhyti for now. And leave me.''

Koscuisko would be anxious to be on with it.

Toska made his salute and opened the cell door for the

Bench Lieutenant, following him out quickly and closing it up once more.

What Plugrath might have to say to Chief Samons, if anything, was nothing of his business.

"Officer wants rhyti, Kaydence, says to send you."

If he stilled himself at post and blanked his mind, the image of the tortured Nurail would not torment him for long.

Ceelie Porlich could no longer see, and breathing was so difficult that he longed to be done with it. It had been so long. It had been so hard. And as much as he tried, he could neither make it stop nor make an end of himself, out of what they did to him—

"You're holding out on me. Nurail scum. When will you learn?"

Sneering words, and brutal blows. Ceelie tried to shield his body; but he was bound. He didn't understand it. When they had taken him from the work-crew they had told him he was to stand Inquiry, under Charges.

"Please."

He could barely speak, his mouth too badly torn by blows. Someone squeezed a spongeful of cold water out close to his face, quite close, he could feel the moisture on his cheek; but he could not get more than a drop or two of the water. And he was so thirsty. "Told you. Everything."

There had been no Charges. There had been no Inquiry. There had only been this fearful room in the detention block, forever. If he was to be tortured, why was there no Record? Why was there no Inquisitor?

"But not everything you know. You're holding out. Tell, you filthy piece of—"

Frantically, convulsively, Ceelie tried to flee away from the pain that possessed him. It was no use. It held him, white-hot and ferocious, for three thousand years. And when it finally stopped, Ceelie could hear the voice speak on as though only a moment had passed.

". . . until you tell me what you're hiding. Well?"

Hiding. Oh, for someplace to hide, someplace to get away from here. Why wasn't he dead by now?

Or—great God—was he dead already?

"What about 'the war-leader'?" the voice demanded, suddenly much closer. And the beating had stopped. War-leader? The war-leader was safe. He had not betrayed the war-leader. No, he had kept silent, all of this time; he had not so much as spoken the Darmon's name.

He wanted to die.

Once he was dead the torture would have to cease.

There was a new pain, now, and it was as sharp as acid, as heavy in his chest as monuments. He couldn't breathe. He couldn't hear. Oh, was this it at last, was he to die?

It faded.

It faded, and there was something in his mouth. Real water. Cool and sweet. He drank it gratefully, not minding how hard it was to swallow for the slaking of the worst part of his thirst.

"War-leader Darmon, on your work-crew." The voice; but this time it had to be his imagination. Because he hadn't said it. "Which one of your work-crew is the war-leader?"

Right beside him, to his left. And he hadn't even recognized him at first, although he'd been one of the Darmon's lieutenants for the raid on Moltipat. That had been a wonder, that raid. They had given the Bench something to think about.

"Pay attention," the voice said, and there was pressure that Ceelie didn't like against the pulpy shattered mess that they had made out of his foot. Oh. Centuries ago. "Never mind Moltipat. What was his name?"

Someone was crying, very close. Some other man put to the torture, that was it, and Ceelie hoped he'd die soon, who-ever he was. Ceelie hoped for his death breath by breath, because that was his only way out of this. But the war-leader was safe. Nobody even knew he was the war-leader. Cittrops had no thread in the Darmon's weave, whoever Marne Cittrops had been. No, the war-leader was safe from these men with their cudgels and whips and irons and—and—

"Good little bootlicker, yes," someone said, approvingly. "Extra water, for that. And how would you like a little—extra—current, to go with it?"

Agony in waves, torment in gusts that felled his spirit lower than it had ever been. Ceelie lay in his suffering and trembled, waiting for his death.

Unless he was already dead.

Unless he was dead, and being punished, what could he have done in his life that would have earned him such monstrous torture to balance it out?

"Pick him up," the voice said. "Another for the furnaces, but whack him good first, he's earned out. Going by the name of Marne Cittrops, same work-detail. There should be a bounty, for that one."

He could have betrayed the war-leader—

No.

He could never have betrayed the Darmon. Never.

It was the last thing in Ceelie's mind as someone hit him across the back of his battered head with a stout cudgel, and set him free from torment.

The things they'd done to him, the torture he'd endured, it had been more than Ceelie's mind could grasp.

But he had not betrayed War-leader Darmon.

It was cold in the mornings, now, and a man looked forward to being set to work. Not for the work itself, though that work seemed to have a good enough goal. But for the warming of it. The cells were cold, and the blankets thin.

There was misery in the cells, misery in the work-crew, misery going in, misery going out. The only things that made a bit of relief in the hard cold relentless grind of his life were the few moments they were given in a week to have a hot wash, and the time it took to stand at the high tables in the warm mess building for the evening meal, and the moments on the work-crew when the mindless routine of the body took over from the ever-anxious working of the mind to suspend time and transcend reality with the simple physical act of work.

Marne hammered at his bit of hardened ground and lifted his shovels full of heavy earth and did what could be done to cover for those around him when they began to fail. The foundation ditch for the dike got deeper, wider, longer day by day. But every morning it was full of water, to be pumped out by Nurail on the most primitive of manned pumps Marne had ever thought to see being used for work—rather than a museum—in his life.

He wondered, from time to time, what they would do when the weather started to freeze overnight; none of the

Nurail on the work-crew had winter clothing, and it didn't seem to be something to expect the prison administration to make up. He supposed they would find out when it got colder whether they would be given clothing—because they were needed for work—or not, because the Pyana had too many Nurail prisoners at their disposal to be bothered over preserving their health. Their lives.

There had been no protective clothing up till now. When a Nurail injured a foot with a pickax, the overseers simply rolled him down the slope into the ditch, to either drown or die beneath the next avalanche of gravel. When a Nurail was struck in the head by a beam or a bucket being hoisted it was the same story.

Marne worked in his place on the line, knowing he could not afford to admit the horror of their situation into his mind if he hoped to survive. Concentrating on making it from one round of water carried down the line to the next round. From water to the end of day. From end of day to the mess building. From the mess building to his cell. From his cell to the morning call.

He was getting so good at concentrating that he didn't notice the guards arriving on site, paid no attention to whatever was happening upslope. The guards had come for Shopes Ban days ago, Marne couldn't remember. They had come for one other in the work-crew since then. It was better not to think too hard about it, since there was nothing he could do.

They were for him, this time.

The guards came down the slope with the overseer, but they didn't pass him to go down the line.

They stopped.

Marne kept working. Showing that he could. Demonstrating the only skills the Pyana valued in this place, ability to shovel heavy earth and keep shoveling.

"This one," the overseer said, and it could no longer be ignored, they were looking at him. "Marne Cittrops. Who did you say?"

The guards came up around him. "War-leader Darmon," the squad leader said. "He doesn't look like a war-leader to me."

Marne kept working. Maybe it was the next man. But they surrounded him, and they were staring.

"He looks more like a Nurail mule, to me. But the order tag says war-leader. No roughness, now, friends, he's for the Inquisitor, and the Inquisitor doesn't hold to 'abuse of prisoners outside of Protocol.'."

That was good for a laugh. Marne took his chance, swinging with the shovel at the nearest guard, jumping at the man who stood downslope from him. He could make them angry. Any defiance was brutally dealt with on the work-crew, with shockrods and with clubs. If he could make them angry enough, they would not be able to take him back to the Domitt Prison, they would be forced to let his body roll into the ditch and cry an accident.

It didn't work.

The one guard dodged the shovel, and though he went down in the gravel he didn't seem to take much hurt.

The second put his fist to Marne's stomach, as Marne charged, and Marne went headlong into the dust himself, with two Pyana dragging at his heels before he'd even landed.

"Careful," the squad leader reminded them. "Like I said. No unnecessary roughness. We wouldn't want to interfere with the exercise of the Writ. No punishment he might earn here and now can compare with what the Inquisitor is going to do to him."

All too true.

All right.

He was for it.

Marne kicked out at the hands at his ankles and stood up, climbing the steep slope with Pyana all around him to where the car was waiting. He would have liked to get a drink of water before they left, but there was no hope of that.

Poor Ceelie.

What he must have suffered, before he died.

But at least that meant that Robis Darmon was free to confess whatever he liked of Ceelie's role in their struggle; Ceelie was dead, and could no longer be made to suffer for what the Bench had decided were his crimes against the Judicial order.

*   *   *

"At Kosova. Your Excellency. Yes, I was there, and—oh—I threw a bottle-rocket through the window of the Bench Administrative building there, yes, that was me, I confess it—"

Andrej shut off the firepoint with a disgusted snap, turning his back on the prisoner. Young Nurail. Quite young, actually, but a man by his beard still, unless he'd been in prison longer than possible had he truly been part of the street-fighting in Kosova. Which Andrej did not for one moment believe.

"Be still. I am in no mood to be played with. You were nowhere near the Ailleran system when it happened. You are making it up."

Inventing it. Confabulating. Spinning a story. Faking a weave.

Lying to him.

Perhaps lying was too strong a word, it had been two days. There had been a confession to a lesser offense early on, and then confession in form to the Recorded offense just after midmeal today; but nothing since then except for garbage. Could he blame this prisoner, this Kerag Darveck, for making things up to try to satisfy the Bench requirement?

Andrej was expected to develop leads, pursue issues, obtain proof of collateral involvement and cross-accusation where he could. He had no need to reproach himself on that subject: What he had done to Darveck, these long hours past, had been squarely within the Bench requirement, and all well within the Protocols.

But there was nothing there.

He'd thought that there might be, at first, and that Darveck was grasping at clearly implausible straws in order to put him off the scent of some true thread. He'd tested for it, and ingenious cruelty had never failed him yet; nor had failed now.

Andrej knew.

Darveck was guilty of a crime to which he'd been brought to confess in due form: But no more than that. He had been part of the defense of Meritz. He had quite probably been taken there, or not long afterward. And that was all the Bench could in justice lay against Darveck's account.

It was a problem.

How could Darveck have been referred on the much more serious charges that were on Record, when he'd been nowhere near the system—and all too possibly even in custody, already—before the troubles at Kosova were well started?

Darveck lay shaking on the floor, in fierce torment from the vise and clamps. He clearly could in honor have no more of young Darveck. No more at all. True enough that "honor" was not the word to speak in torture cell; it was also true that in order to be able to put the Protocols forward it was absolutely necessary for Andrej to be able to pretend that he was bound by them.

To be bound by the Protocols meant sending this one away.

"Please, sir." Weeping in pain, and in fear of more pain. It was lovely. It was perfect. He wanted more: And he could not have it. Or rather, he could have all he wanted, but he should not take it, because Darveck had done only so much wrong as he had already suffered for in overabundant measure. "Please, sir, it's true, it's true, oh. I'll tell you what you want, take it away, my foot . . ."

Had told Andrej everything he knew; and a very great deal more besides. There was simply nothing there. And no help for it. The sound of the Nurail's weeping was a constant stimulation to Andrej's nerves, the fear Darveck had of him as exciting as the weight of a woman's braided hair sliding undone between his fingers. More so. Differently. But to the same effect; and still he could not countenance making Darveck suffer any longer.

He had to relieve and remand.

There was no help for it.

"I don't want to hear it." Calculating doses, Andrej loaded an osmo, then another. Something quite strong to start off with, because as keen and sharp and merciless as the pressure of the vise was against the bone, it was only going to get worse as the vise came off. "I do not in fact believe a word that you are saying."

There was no use pretending to practice here for vengeance upon Joslire's murderers when Andrej knew quite well what Joslire himself would have trusted him to do. All the more reason why he had to do the right thing for Darveck: who stared in wide-eyed terror at the dose in Andrej's hand, the white of his eyes brilliant and grotesque in the light from the overheads. "Please not the List, oh, please, your Excellency. I can't—"

Trying to reassure Darveck would do no good; Andrej knew that. The best thing was to simply go ahead, and let the action of the drug speak its own truth. "There is nothing here to be afraid of," he promised, pressing the dose through at the prisoner's throat.

After a breath or two young Darveck blinked once or twice, in clear astonishment. "Yr'Excellency?"

"This is going to hurt. I'm sorry. Here we go." Loosening the vice, pulling the needle-pins whose job it was to find the nerves within the joint and wear on them. Pain receptors within a joint produced a signal that did not decay in the same way as those nearer the skin. For fierce white-hot bright pain that would not abate there was nothing like prying a joint apart fiber by fiber; and certainly nothing like that now. He had finished with this one interrogation. That was all.

Finished, but had had no resolution for the thirst within him—

Not an issue. The vice came away from the ankle joint, the skin beneath livid with bruises and insult. There would be a matter of days before Darveck would be able to put weight on that leg without danger of an injury. The drug did good work, Darveck did not scream.

By the look on Darveck's face—the relaxed muscle of the cheek and jaw, the eyes traveling with slow deliberation from object to object in the room—the drug had taken hold, now. Andrej pressed the second dose through, just to be sure, because he wanted to assure himself that Darveck would not succumb to shock and die.

It was late.

Too late to start with a fresh prisoner.

The gentlemen had been on their feet for hours and hours on end, on either side of the door outside.

Andrej went to the door, toggling the switch. "Kaydence." Security could sleep standing up with their eyes open, that was true. That was no excuse for keeping them on watch without a break simply because his body ached with the pleasure of the torment he'd put Darveck to and the fierce consuming desire to have more.

"Kaydence. Yes. Call to Infirmary. This one is to be dismissed to the civil authority, but he'll need a few days in hospital, Infirmary must stabilize before we can in decency refer."

It wasn't the best idea to send torture victims to civilian hospitals. The infirmary at the Domitt Prison would logically be both equipped to address the injury and more inured to the sight of it. Kaydence bowed low with a calm serene face and stepped away from the doorway to the common call; Andrej leaned up against the doorjamb and rubbed his eyes. Oh. He should remember. It was prudent to remove one's work-gloves before one rubbed one's eyes.

Infirmary was perhaps not much occupied, this time of day—this time of night. There was a litter and a team with a physician before too much time had passed. Andrej waited to let the staff physician make preliminary examination; then the doctor came to him and saluted.

"His Excellency intends us to release this prisoner, sir?"

Sounding a little dubious. Well, it was a prison, and one of the reasons Andrej had particularly wanted to be here when the doctor came was in order to be very clear about his intention.

"Precisely so, Doctor—Forlop, yes, thank you. You have the documentation with you brought? You will need this."

The Infirmary staff would be responsible for developing the medical record, but Andrej was the only one who could sign disposition of prisoner. He, and Administrator Geltoi.

He had not satisfied himself—

Doctor Forlop bowed in polite acceptance. "As his Excellency says, sir. Thank you. I'll send a report to your office. Shall we be going?"

A hint. Straightening up—he had been slumped against the wall, trying not to think about tension—Andrej gave the nod.

The party left.

He was alone with his Security.

They needed to be sent to bed; and he needed to wash.

The penthouse was warm and quiet. Andrej sent his gentlemen through to the kitchen. He couldn't remember if they'd eaten.

He couldn't remember if he'd eaten; but he didn't want to

eat, his hunger was for screaming, not for food. The sooner morning came the sooner he could satisfy his need. He had to go to sleep, so that it would be morning when he woke.

His bedroom was quiet and dark, familiar with the smell of his favorite soap and comforting with the fragrance of a woman's hair. Ailynn. There was a thought. Perhaps he could lull the beast to sleep in Ailynn's arms.

She only slept beside him in the bed because he liked the companionable warmth; waiting for him, she was not in the bed now, but napping on a low cot behind the screen in the corner. He knew she had a pallet there, and he didn't like it; but that seemed to be the only allowance for her privacy in this place. He hadn't told her to put it away. He could hear her breathing, calm and regular. Soothing. Could he not take comfort in her embrace, and be at peace, even if only for a few hours?

He had to wash.

She had been ready for him, there was his nightshirt on the warmer with the bath-towel, and the other things that he might want for grooming laid out ready in a tidy array. A comb. A nailbrush. A jar of fragrant lotion to take the stink of sweat and blood and terror from the forefront of his senses.

He started the shower to run, to get the temperature of the water right. Ailynn usually took care of that small chore, she'd learned the precise mix he liked almost immediately— people learned quickly, when their safety depended upon avoiding aggravating some slavemaster. And he was one. At the very least he was to Ailynn a slavemaster, and if there was to be no help for it why should he not at least make use of her body?

Scarred, she had said.

Stripping, he left his clothing on the floor and unfastened the sheathing of Joslire's five-knives with fatigue-clumsy fingers. He wondered whether he should be wearing Joslire's knives in torture-room; wasn't it a little like making Joslire come in there, with him? There was something unusual about the backsheath knife, as well, though he didn't think he could tell anybody and have them take him seriously.

The knife had gotten heavier, since Joslire's death.

Andrej set the knives and the sheathing up on a shelf apart

and stepped into the shower. There was a little draft that lasted for a moment; that would logically be Ailynn, Andrej knew, awakened by the sound of water running, creeping into the washroom carefully to carry away his soiled clothing.

Lathering up the soap, Andrej started washing, rubbing hard at the dried blood that had soaked through his clothing to his skin. His fish was half-tumescent, irritable in his hand, half-ready to raise its head and rage against the world: At such times his fish was no friend to him, but a quarrelsome member of his household for whom he was responsible but whose behavior he was powerless to amend for the better.

His fish had been stroked by the anguish of tortured souls all day. Now it resented being rubbed down with soap and warm water and bidden to sleep, and grumbled at him while his belly ached with unresolved tension.

His body was as clean as he could wash it. More or less.

Andrej dried himself, grateful for the small luxuries of warm clean toweling and a quiet room. Slipping his sleep-shirt over his head, he went back out into his bedroom, knotting half the ties absentmindedly and ignoring the rest.

He liked Ailynn; he didn't want to distress her.

But he was on fire with the remembered sound of that Nurail's weeping. If he could not find some way to ground the tension, he would not be able to sleep.

Ailynn was sitting very straight-backed on the edge of the bed with her hands resting on either side of her, flat against the coverlet.

Waiting for him.

The bedclothes turned back, and she herself in her bed-dress, which meant that the contour of her shoulders was clearly visible beneath the thin white fabric even in the dim light of the night-glows. Her hair was drawn back in a thick heavy braid, tied neatly in a knot for sleeping. Andrej sat down beside her, taking her braid into his hands to undo the ribbon-loop that kept it from coming undone in the night.

Her braid came loose and lay against his palms, heavy and silky. He laced his fingers in between the plaits, remembering Marana. The joy he'd had in taking down her hair, knowing she would welcome his fish within her ocean.

Ailynn didn't speak.

That was fine, too.

He unraveled her braid twist by twist until he'd worked his hands up to the base of her skull, and paused, cupping the heat of her skull against his palms, feeling the seductive caress of her hair against his fingers.

Oh, he wanted.

And he couldn't have.

But he could have Ailynn, and maybe that would do the trick.

She put her hand out to the back of his neck, very sweetly indeed, and drew him down to lie with her across the bed. There was no reason she should know what a Dolgorukij would have meant by such a gesture. Andrej took no offense; and teased her little tongue out of her mouth with kisses, so that he could suckle at her while he reveled in the sensation of her unbound hair against his arms wrapped around her back.

It was a very pretty little tongue, a cunning tongue, a sweet and tempting tongue, and would it be very wrong—Andrej asked himself, half-drunk once more with passion and with need—if he pretended to himself that she was willing?

Her body was soft beneath his hands as a woman's body properly was, as he had learned to define and appreciate what was desirable about women's bodies when he had been young. He had learned to appreciate the desirability of other sorts of women's bodies since, and that of Chief Warrant Officer Caleigh Samons—as an example—exemplified one of those other sorts neatly indeed.

But there was no arguing with one's fish.

And his fish felt that the woman in his arms was just exactly what a woman ought to be; and wished to crest the breakers of her surf and gain her ocean now, right now, immediately.

And still there was the thing that she had said to him, days ago, what had it been?

Scarred.

Andrej kissed her parted lips a few more times for friendship's sake and went exploring down the lines of her throat. Her shoulders . . . but he was not going to be distracted, because there was a natural limit to how long he could demand that his fish wait before it disgraced him by breaching the dikes and expiring of exhaustion on dry land.

Soft and fragrant, and open to sensation, too, as far as that went, willing to admit pleasure when it came—Andrej mapped out the soft womanflesh of Ailynn's breast and shoulders, and all the while set his right hand to find out about her scars.

She stiffened, when his fingers slid gently between her thighs; stiffened in fear, and opened to him in duty. Which was not of course the best reason, but it would suit his purpose here and now.

Whether the warm moisture he sought out was arousal or simply the sensible precaution of a professional woman made while he was in the shower, Andrej didn't know. There was an easy way to find out, but he didn't care to know. It would be awkward. He stroked her carefully instead, making up his mind to where it was that she was scarred and whether she could be enticed to take any delight at all from his caress. Imposed on her or no.

The fish that complicated the lives of men was a stout and very self-respecting thing that did not hesitate to breach and put its head up to see what might be going on around it. That which was private to women was a more modest and reticent little minnow, though sweet to the taste; unlike other fish, which were stronger in flavor and indelicate in their appreciation of an affectionate salute.

Ailynn's little minnow was of brave heart, willing to be coaxed out of its safe place beneath the shelf by the seashore to permit itself to be admired and stroked. She had been scarred by rape, then, and not otherwise mutilated by design. That was something.

But his fish was urgent with him to let it seek the ocean.

She would have been within her rights to suffer his embrace in stoic silence, or return only what caress or endearment he might instruct her to employ. That was the privilege of paid women. One could purchase the hire of their bodies: But it was in poor taste to demand that they pretend that they enjoyed it.

Ailynn was more generous and charitable with him than that.

The shaking of her breath was unfeigned, the flush of sweat that made her sweet breast taste salt was not cosmetically created, the eager stiffening of her nipples did not result from surreptitious pinching or a light touch of astringent. She consented without words, without being asked, to trust her body into his hands to be gently used by him, and the frank honesty of her arousal served to keep him focused on what a man was to do with a woman in bed.

Seek the ocean, yes, that was what it was all about. But carefully. Mindful that too great a splash at once could lay bare rock. Ensuring that the wake of his fish's passing washed well over her minnow in the shallows, to rock it to its ultimate delight as his fish pleasured itself in the salt deeps of her secret ocean.

He tried.

But there had been too much.

He'd spent long hours keyed up to a keen-edged anticipation, only to have denied himself gratification at the last. The flesh was intent on being recompensed for being made to wait so long, with such persuasive provocation to his lust.

His fish went all the more furiously to work because it was half-mad with being denied, determined to have its pleasure before its opportunity was withdrawn.

He worked the angry tension of his body out within hers, caught up and consumed by the day's pent-up frustration, desperate to find physical release.

He didn't want to hurt her.

But he had to have an end to the thirst that tormented him.

And when the crisis of his body's need resolved itself at last, he was too grateful for the grant of two breaths of time spent without thought to want to drop back into conscious awareness before he absolutely had to.

Gathering Ailynn up into his arms, Andrej laid her properly in the bed and pulled the covers up over them both.

Oh, for just one hour, to exist without awareness—

His mind was stilled and emptied in the aftermath of all-conquering sensation.

Andrej slept.

◆ Eight

Be still, Ailynn admonished herself, fiercely. Be still, be quiet, breathe as evenly as possible. Don't hold your breath. Slow. Shallow. Even breaths. The officer will go to sleep, but not if he knows. Be very quiet. Relax. Pretend.

The physical effects of fear diminished in her body, her breathing slowed, her heart began to beat more regularly. Clipped close in the arms of the sleeping officer, Ailynn focused on being in her body, deep inside her body, making her body an insulation to shield and protect her against panic. She was far, far away, inside her head. No one could touch her here. And what they did to her body, if they hurt her body, it was so far away it would be centuries before she realized that she was in pain.

Yes.

Better.

The officer stirred in his sleep and stroked her back, settling his cheek against her forehead. Calm. Her body was calm. Her breathing was regular. Her body was asleep; the officer would not wake.

Her mind raced, circling a familiar track and accelerating on every curve. Her little kitchen in her apartment in Ogis. The Bench order to evacuate for relocation; the men who came to hurry her along. Or leave her there, so long as she was dead, but since she wasn't dead—after two hours, three hours of sport—rape her from her home and natal place to bend her neck to Jurisdiction bitterly against her will.

The ambush of the relocation party, her escape, those bitter

159

cold and fear-filled months of underground resistance, the wounds so slow to heal. Her capture. No trial; the rules of Evidence were satisfied in the facts of where and how she had been taken. No trial, and no execution by torture or otherwise; something far worse instead.

The Bond.

The Bench had made the Bonds to serve Inquisitors, because free men could not be forced to implement torture. Service Bonds were a quite different category, it was pure punishment with no excuse of Bench utility except to serve as deterrent.

We will take you and those of yours who are fit enough, and we will make them bond-involuntary, and if we will not torture them in obvious ways we will make sure they suffer— we will require them to assist in the torment of others like themselves. And if they are fit for Service and not Security, we will harvest the use of their bodies in a more traditional fashion.

Service Bonds.

To be put to the rapists, night after night, and the fees collected by the Bench that owned her—by its own enactment, that had by superior force of brutal arms taken her for a chattel slave for crimes committed against the Judicial order . . .

It had only been four years.

How was she to hope to last thirty?

The officer had treated her with unusual courtesy, not— as far as she could tell—because she was a woman so much as because that was the way he treated all his Bonds. And the officer had not come to her in anger or in mockery to confront her with her helplessness or demand the forms of self-abasement frequently invoked by other rapists.

She had not minded opening to him, though she would have rather been left to herself. And still he had reminded her that she was a slave, not intentionally, but only in the fact that she was not permitted to grant or withhold her consent.

And she was afraid of Andrej Koscuisko.

He had come to her as gently as he could, she was sure of it. And still he had lost himself in the act. The pitiless strength of his arms still around her was terrifying.

If he should use her as strictly as he had just now when he approached her with good will, how was it to come with her when he should be annoyed?

She was trapped and prisoned in Koscuisko's sleeping embrace.

She had no hope of escape or of protection.

Service Bonds had to get used to that, but could she ever?

Ailynn had little pain from the passage, having been put on notice more than once that he might be abrupt with her. Little physical pain, and even a small echoing reverberation of the pleasure he had given her with his touch; but in her heart Ailynn was desolate.

She wept.

She couldn't bite her grief back down into her heart, betrayed to grief, ambushed by it here in the warm quiet dreaming dark with the officer asleep beside her. Ailynn wept to be reminded that she was a slave, and though Koscuisko might be a good "maister"—to use the Nurail of it—it was still as a man who owned her that he came to bed.

She grieved; and the worst possible thing happened, the officer woke up, stilling her cries gently with his hand put to her mouth as he rose up in the bed to lean upon his elbow.

"Ailynn. Oh, hush, please, Ailynn, my gentlemen will be distressed for you, do you have pain?"

Folding her close, as though that could make it better. Rather than worse. She put her face against the crumpled warmth of his half-laced sleep-shirt and wailed in desperate anguish as quietly as possible.

He pet her and rocked her, and she wept because she could not know from day to day whether the next five men to whom the Bench sold her would be decent men or brutes, and whether Koscuisko kissed or clouted her was up to him entirely. Nothing for her to choose.

She cried herself out and clung to him, exhausted. He had a cool damp cloth in his hand, now, and patted at her flushed cheeks and swollen eyes with a delicate concern; she had waked one of her cousins, then, because she knew Koscuisko hadn't gotten out of bed.

Ailynn caught her breath.

"One trembles to ask whether it is something in particular one has done," Koscuisko said. "Because of two problems.

And one is that politeness interferes, and people under Bond are not permitted to accuse or upbraid officers without suffering the reproach of their governor. And the other problem is that it must be, and therefore there's no sense in even asking. Ailynn, I have grieved you, I am sorry.''

It wasn't exactly that.

It was.

She had no words to explain herself to him: And yet he did not deserve to suffer because the Bench had put her beneath him. It wasn't Koscuisko's fault. And he had tried to be careful, even as caught up as he'd been in his own body's need; and her body was grateful for the small pleasure that it had of him, because there was so little pleasure else for her body in her life.

She was embarrassed to caress him in the presence of some possible other, since she did not know who else might be in the room. But she should try to explain. Trembling in fear of her own temerity, Ailynn put her face up to the officer's, and kissed his mouth with hesitant care.

"It's not what you might think, sir." And it wasn't. "I'm heartily sorry to have wakened you. Nothing of what the officer has done. Or almost nothing."

That was true, and her governor didn't bridle at her candor, even though it came a little close to a reproach of sorts. That was the trick of living with a governor, to learn to speak truth in such a way as to avoid conflicts in her mind.

"I will want to make examination, later." Whether or not Koscuisko believed her was difficult to say; she couldn't tell one way or the other, from the sound of his voice. The officer was accustomed to living with bond-involuntaries. He might suspect that what she said was at least so much what she was trained to say as how she felt. "But now I want you to lie quiet and rest, Ailynn. Erish, comfort your cousin as you like, or as she likes rather. I am going downstairs to my office."

And since Koscuisko was familiar with dealing with Bonds, Koscuisko would know that what she said to him in unsolicited physical contact was from her heart, unedited and unforced. It had been a risk to offer a kiss; some men did not want intimacies with whores beyond those that they themselves demanded. But perhaps he would think about the statement that she had tried to make to him with the gesture.

She had instruction and direction from Koscuisko, to lie quietly and rest.

Tucking the covers close against her back, he rose to dress, giving the damp cloth to Erish to continue the work of patting the hectic flush of desperate sorrow gently from the skin of cheek and forehead.

Ailynn knew how to do as she was told, she was a slave under Jurisdiction. And it was very nice, Erish's tending of her. So she closed her eyes and invoked her memory, not of before or after, but only the time during that Koscuisko had brought joy to her body; and went to sleep.

Andrej pulled on his rest-dress rather than wake anybody. He was only going to his office. Rest-dress meant very full trousers that belted around the waist, with a soft wrap-tunic to cover; it looked almost like skirts, to Andrej, and it had taken him a little while to get used to that, but it was only part of an officer's wardrobe. Not a calculated affront to the holy Mother, an attempt to claim the superior status of femininity by dressing as a woman. There was no apron, after all.

He could wear padding-socks with rest-dress, he didn't have to put on his boots, and that was another significant thing about rest-dress. Collecting Code on his way out toward the office access lift, Andrej stepped carefully from flagstone to flagstone in his padding-socks; the night was cool, the ground damp with dew, and padding-socks were not moisture-impervious.

The lift was waiting, of course, and his office was dark in the night. Andrej could see the lights from Port Rudistal and from the displacement camp beyond from the corridor as he approached. Would they be able to see him, he wondered?

Code started the rhyti while Andrej sat down to stare at the surface of his desktable, brooding. He had frightened Ailynn, or hurt her. Perhaps both. He could send her back to the service house, and she would be in no further danger from him; but the problem with that was twofold.

He had forgotten who and where he was, in her embrace; and it seemed to Andrej that he had to have that avenue of escape, or else he would not survive until he was called back to *Scylla*. The distraction was short-lived, perhaps, but it had been genuine. He wanted to know that it would be available again.

Two, of course, was that if he sent her back they'd think that she had displeased in some way, and things would be made unpleasant for her. And also she would simply be put back to work accommodating multiple patrons instead of one, howsoever moody and difficult that one might be.

Poor Ailynn.

What was a woman's hire, for a night?

Senior officers weren't charged at service houses, though Andrej always made a point to tip well. The expenses they incurred were all charged back to Fleet as preventive medicine. He didn't know how much Ailynn's time cost.

He could find out.

Pulling a piece of notepaper toward himself, Andrej picked up a stylus to start calculating.

When he had been in school at Mayon Surgical College, the charges for recreation had been standardized by the school administration. Students paid out twenty Standard for two hours of company, eighty to be accompanied all night. Mayon's Service professionals had been an elite of sorts, because the standards set by the school administration had been aggressively strict in terms of the benefits packages enjoyed by the staff.

If he figured eighty a night for Ailynn's company, and the prison was providing lodging, linen, and her meals—it had been four weeks, that was thirty-two days.

Nearly a month.

Had it really been a month?

Had it been so long since Joslire claimed the Day?

He'd dressed by himself in the dark, and not retrieved his knives from the washroom. He hadn't thought about it. But once he realized that he was without Joslire's knives, the place between his shoulders where the mother-knife should have been started to ache.

A month.

A month, bereft of Joslire, and trying to soothe the hurt with poultices made up of the atrocious torment of his prisoners . . .

It could not have been a month.

Eighty a night for Ailynn's company, unless there were allowances made for livery and maintenance; that was thirty-three thousand—and some—for a year, and the term of the Bond was thirty years, so that was something in the neighborhood of one million. Standard.

If he were to rent her from the Bench until the Day came for Ailynn, because the Bench would not accept a forfeit for her crime.

Still, what were salary monies for, if not to buy things that he wanted? It wasn't as though his living expenses were burdensome. And more than enough money for his needs in rents and other income from his holdings in the Koscuisko familial corporation. He was its prince inheritor, after all. By any Standard measure he was rich.

Nor had the Koscuisko familial corporation gotten rich by throwing away money on self-indulgences that could profit them nothing—

Joslire was dead.

Joslire had been his man, and had died in his service.

It was the right of household retainers who gave up their lives to defend their masters to be remembered in the family chapels as house benefactors, with prayers and litanies, and inclusion in the family's Catalog for pious observance.

Could he not justify it to himself if he hired Ailynn to be Joslire's nun? Religious professionals came more dear than those who provided personal services of a sexual nature. Ailynn would even be cost-effective, considered in that light.

It was an absolutely idiotic idea, and the more Andrej thought about it, the better he liked it. There were funds set aside for the maintenance of religious professionals and the support of religious establishments. Joslire had died in Port Rudistal, he should be remembered here. He would hire Ailynn to be Joslire's nun, and buy a house to be a nunnery.

Uncle Radu might question Andrej's choice of abbess, but it was in Andrej's right to build and maintain chapels from dedicated funds so long as a rule of devotion was established and maintained. Ailynn was not Dolgorukij, but neither had Joslire been; why should he not?

He would have to think about it seriously.

Once he was awake.

Setting the sheet aside, Andrej pulled the nearest stack of

documents toward him. He hadn't spent much time in his office over the past few days. Technically speaking he was the senior medical officer at the Domitt Prison, though nothing to do with Infirmary; it was up to him to review and countersign mortality and incident reports.

There were a lot of administrative reports; he was backlogged to a significant extent. Had it really been so long since he'd reviewed the mortality roster?

The newest one was dated just yesterday, that explained it. But the one from three weeks ago was still sitting open, waiting for disposition.

This was odd.

He had four weeks' worth of mortality reports before him. He could track the numbers from week to week.

When he'd got here, the Domitt Prison had been losing more than one in sixteen a month to preexisting injury or illness, and Andrej had been suspicious about trailing mortality due to the epidemic Administrator Belan had mentioned to him.

To be losing one in sixteen was high mortality. But Andrej could think of many reasonable explanations. It made sense that prisoners taken in the aftermath of one Bench campaign or another might not have had enough to eat in the days before their capture and imprisonment.

The Nurail that the Dramissoi Relocation Fleet had taken in had been badly stressed, and not all collectors of refugees could be counted on to treat their wards with as scrupulous care as Captain Sinjosi Vopalar. Andrej had expected the mortality rate to decline, though, as the prison population stabilized.

Mortality rates had gone down.

But not by enough.

He'd been here nearly one month, Standard, since this was one of the short six-week months. Any prisoners referred by the Dramissoi Relocation Fleet had been here for as long. But there were more admissions on the mortality report than there had been prisoners with the Dramissoi Fleet: Andrej was in a position to be confident of that.

Where were the new admissions coming from?

Were they some exhausted and half-dead survivors of yet another Bench campaign against the Nurail?

Hadn't Eild been supposed to be the last?

There were disquieting indications that something was wrong, here. Too many dead. Prisoners referred on accusation of things they could have had no part in, and more and more of the prisoners seemed to have been physically stressed as he worked through the cells and they filled the cells back up behind him. Physically stressed as though they had been overworked and underfed, and for how long?

He could request a kitchen audit, ensure that the kitchen served decent rations on a decent schedule. Work-details were entitled to increased rations to support the physical labor they were asked to perform. Maybe the Administration didn't know.

He saw Bench Lieutenant Plugrath twice a week, in his office, in the morning. There had been no real news for this past while: And in his heart Andrej knew that they would never find the people who had bereft him of his friend. Not now. Too much time had passed. A kitchen audit, and he'd ask Plugrath for an admissions report, just to set his mind at rest about who all those Nurail on mortality report were and where they were coming from. It would be a simple enough task.

In light of the high mortality rates at the Domitt Prison, he would take steps to assure himself that there was an explanation beyond the Administration's control. That would protect them all from possible reproach. Once he had but reviewed the kitchen audit and gotten an admissions reconciliation from Lieutenant Plugrath, he could sign off on these documents with a good conscience.

He was hungry himself, now, thinking of those stressed starved prisoners. He was going to wake his poor Code yet again.

Maybe if Cook could be persuaded to make Code's favorite fastmeal, Andrej could be forgiven for the unsettled nightwalking of the sleepshift now all but past.

Administrator Geltoi signed off on the daily transmit to Chilleau Judiciary with a very satisfied flourish as Belan watched. "Another sound day's work from our Inquisitor," Geltoi announced. Unnecessarily; but Belan enjoyed hearing it regardless.

Countersealing the secures, Geltoi tossed the completed documents-cube into his transmit stack as he continued. "The First Secretary will be pleased, there should be no further questions about our prisoner handling. This will have shut the mouths of any critics, by now. Were it not for our effort, the Second Judge would still be exposed to reproach in the public eye from others on the Bench."

As long as Geltoi was content Belan was happy. Geltoi was Pyana, and if there was anything Pyana were good at, it was administration. Geltoi knew how to take care of things.

"It needed only that you be provided with appropriate resources, Administrator," Belan assured his superior. "Once you but had what tools were needed. That was all. They'll know better than to make you wait next time, sir."

So much was only understood. Geltoi wasn't really listening, picking up a piece of documentation with a frown. "At the same time, however. And only his job, true, I grant you that ungrudgingly, Belan."

Grant what? Belan had no idea what that document contained. He waited, humbly, for the Administrator to explain, knowing all would be made clear to him. And that if he didn't understand, it was because he was mere Nurail, not Pyana.

Geltoi spoke on. "But at the same time one wonders if a more—shall we say—mature officer would have made quite this same choice. There is a time and a place for everything."

Something Koscuisko had asked for, Belan grasped that much. Something Koscuisko wanted to do, or to have done. He'd had his inspection tour his first day on site, and he'd been satisfied—at least he hadn't said anything to the contrary. So it couldn't be that.

"What is it, Administrator?" Belan asked, waiting to hear something quite obvious and innocuous. Something he could laugh at himself for being concerned about. Something Geltoi would certainly laugh at him for being concerned about, though the Administrator seemed to be setting up the joke to be on him. It was Pyana humor, at the expense of a dumb Nurail. Belan supposed he was lucky Geltoi didn't indulge in more of it in public.

"Our young Inquisitor. A question about 'mortality rates,'" Geltoi said dismissively, flourishing the document.

This wasn't what Belan wanted to hear. He was concerned about the mortality rates. He knew Geltoi had everything under control, Geltoi was smart, Geltoi had told him so. He hadn't been able to quite cure himself of worry, though. He didn't understand Geltoi's brilliant management plan, whatever it was. "And requests the preparation of a kitchen audit, to be used to validate his endorsement. It's awkward, that's all. A waste of time, complying with a mere formality."

Belan wasn't sure what that even meant. "A kitchen audit, sir?" He was free to ask questions, though, when he didn't understand something. Geltoi was always willing to explain. Sometimes the explanation didn't make any sense.

"Number of measures, Standard, of flours number this and that ordered daily to be used in the preparation of thus and such a number of baked goods of whatever sort and fed to so many at what times with thus much wastage and that much returned. A kitchen audit. Easy enough to prepare, Belan, don't get me wrong. But a bother."

Belan wanted to frown, concerned. He didn't want to give Geltoi any cause to wonder about his loyalty, though. And Geltoi would figure out a way to make it right. "I'm surprised, Administrator. The requirement almost presents the appearance of questioning administrative practices. Have you spoken to the Writ, sir? Perhaps he'd like to withdraw the request."

How could Geltoi allow a kitchen audit? The kitchen staff was Pyana, and there were no records kept as a Nurail understood them. Geltoi had assured him that none were necessary, and Belan knew better than to question Geltoi's judgment. It was probably true that Pyana didn't need to keep records to know exactly how much of what had been fed to whom and when.

That the kitchen had been selling food back to the local markets surreptitiously—through Pyana contacts—Belan knew; Geltoi had been up front with him from the start, and he had his cut. Geltoi had promised him it couldn't be traced back.

Belan had sometimes wondered.

Geltoi was looking at him, considering; as though he thought Belan had actually had a good idea and was wondering whether to endorse it or not. As a Nurail idea it was obviously crude and unformed, probably flawed in several important senses that Belan could not hope to begin to guess at. Maybe with some adjustment Geltoi could find it useful: But after a moment Geltoi seemed to make up his mind, shaking his head.

"I agree, Belan, thank you for your delicacy. I'm sure he would have done it differently if he'd stopped to think how it might look. But now that he's made a request, it's best just to respond in good form. I'll make your point with him when we discuss his findings."

The Administrator would rather Koscuisko had not asked.

The realization chilled Belan to the bottom of his stomach.

"How can I best support you, Administrator?" he asked, just a hint of the anxiety he felt showing in his voice. It wouldn't do to show too much anxiety. That might call his confidence in Geltoi into question.

Geltoi set the document down, pushing it away from him, turning in his chair to look out of the window. "Oh, nothing for you in this one, Merig." Geltoi was clearly dismissing him; and Belan was just as glad. "Just put in a word to the kitchen-master, ask him to get on my scheduler. Sometime soon. Today. Tomorrow. It wouldn't do to make our Inquisitor wait. And on the other hand we mustn't act precipitously."

This Belan understood almost too well.

"Thank you, Administrator. I'll see to it directly. Myself."

Geltoi wanted to be careful about this audit.

In all the time Belan had worked for Geltoi, all of the long months it had taken to build the Domitt Prison, he had never known Geltoi to hesitate. The Administrator's fearless decisiveness in the face of unknown factors had first impressed, then won Belan over to the Administrator's service; he had come to realize that Geltoi knew what he was doing with such assurance, such a grasp of cause and effect and time and place, that Belan could only watch in awed wonder.

All of this time he had supported Geltoi, certain that Geltoi was in complete control.

This kitchen audit, though it worried him, was going to come out all right. It had to.

If Geltoi had been wrong, and all of the things that Belan had done in his service should come to light after all—

It was unthinkable.

Belan shut the idea off.

The sooner he saw the kitchen-master, the sooner all of this would be resolved.

The officer came up for his supper in good time, today, perhaps because of his early morning. Ailynn helped him into the bath as she had done all of these days gone past, and the officer would not look at her. She thought she knew what was in his mind. She thought she understood.

She didn't know if she had the nerve to make her stand, after last night.

She carried his soiled uniform away, careful as she always was to clear his pockets and set his hand-manuscript aside on the bedtable. She was an honest woman, though she was a slave, Ailynn reminded herself. She had a right to speak to him.

She'd been thinking about it all day.

The officer came out of the washroom with his rest-dress trousers on, but she had his upper garment. He was not in uniform. He could not go out of his bedroom like that.

"Ailynn, I cannot find my, have you seen—"

She held the garment up in both hands, before her; seeing what she held, he started for her quite naturally and easily to receive it from her.

She put her hands behind her back, and his wraptunic with them. The skin of his uncovered body was very white, in the dim calm of the bedroom. Fair-haired men were frequently very pale, Koscuisko almost unnervingly so.

"If I could have a word, sir."

Koscuisko stopped in his tracks and stared, and Ailynn struggled on.

"I. Want to talk to you. There are things that we should be clear on, you and I. Your Excellency."

She had a chance.

She hadn't understood, until last night.

It was too wonderful a chance to let pass just because she was afraid of him.

"Give me my clothing, Ailynn, I am cold. Please. We will abide and talk."

Oh, yes, her heart said to her, and she all but lost her

balance in relief. And with the sudden tears of fear relieved that burned in her eyes, but she kept her voice calm as she answered, handing him his wraptunic. "You hurt me, last night. But—"

He had stopped in putting on his wraptunic almost before he'd started; she knew she had to speak quickly if she was to hope to avoid misunderstanding.

"But not so much that it should stand between us. How can I do my job, if you won't have me, until you need so badly that you. Well."

His Security were Bonded, as she was. He let them take care of him, and he took care of them in turn as best he could. In a month she had seen enough to understand that what was between Koscuisko and his Bonds was more than duty. They were more free than Ailynn could imagine, and she wanted some of that liberty for herself, even if it could only be for a little while.

Koscuisko belted his wraptunic thoughtfully. Thinking. It took him a moment to answer her; because he was listening. Paying attention. Taking her seriously.

Showing respect, for all that she was a slave.

"It is an offense to make you whore for Jurisdiction, Ailynn. I say it, and I do not expect to hear any denial." Because she would assert that she was repaying her debt to the Bench that had spared her life, if he asked her. That was the formula she'd been taught. She also knew that what he said was true. "It is also a sin to have to do with people who are not permitted to decline. It is in a sense as much as to exploit children, O holy Mother."

How careful he was in what he said. And how he said it. It only made her more determined.

"The officer would not wish to deny me my dignity." The word was almost ridiculously incongruous, applied to herself; but Koscuisko gave his other Bonds their dignity. She saw no reason why she should not have at least equal respect from him. "I have a purpose and a function, though it is defined by Jurisdiction. I have come to envy your Security, you let them do their job, and you respect them for it. Let me then do mine, and have your respect also."

It was hard, so hard. She was afraid. She knew Koscuisko didn't want to hurt her, but she couldn't help the fear. She had to go on through it: because knowing Koscuisko didn't want to hurt her was no longer enough.

Gazing at her in something like horror, Koscuisko shook his head. "There is nothing to envy my gentlemen, Ailynn, Joslire dead and Erish still limping, and all of them to be called into the torture-rooms with me—"

Closing the small distance between them, Ailynn put her fingers to his lips to stop his speech. Hardly believing that she found the nerve. Sensing the uncertainty of her governor. "Their job to protect and support you. You let them. You give them respect. You permit them their own judgment."

Not in torture-room, no, she didn't know about that. But here in quarters, where they shared in partnership to cope with where they were and what they had to do. All six of them. The trust they had in him, and he in them, was astonishing. She wanted in. "I only ask so much as that, your Excellency. It is my job to ease you with my body. Let me help."

She could watch and wait in passive silence, do as she was told, hope for the best and fear for the worst. Or she could pretend that she had a job as real and as important, in its way, as the job Security performed: if Koscuisko would permit her that privilege. "I don't want to be pitied for my Bond. I want to be granted self-respect. Pretend you value what I have to offer. Condescend to let me comfort you."

She wanted to belong.

And it was her job.

The Bench had condemned her to the Bond for punishment and deterrent example, but the Bench had done so equally to his Security. It was worse for them. All she had to do was suffer abuse. They could be required to inflict it.

"I will be frank," Koscuisko said, at last. "This is the problem. The problem is that it is not you I want, Ailynn. It is nothing to do with your desirability. It is because of that which is monstrous and unholy in my nature."

As if she didn't know that already.

"I will trust you, as my cousins outside this room trust you. And say what is on my mind." It got easier as she went along. "His Excellency found relief for the lack he felt, last night. Was it not so, sir?"

He only nodded, his eyes fixed on her face. She couldn't

tell whether he was getting angry at her or not; in the dim light there was no separating rage in his face from concentration, for Ailynn. She didn't know him well enough. She'd been sleeping in his bed for a month; and still she hardly knew him, but that was only the way of her life.

"Take comfort then in a way which is not monstrous or unholy, and it may make it easier for you." And would let her be truly one with the others, part of the group, someone who belonged. "I will not pretend. That I don't desire comfort as well, sir. And have had little pleasure of the sort you shared with me last night, for a long time."

She was sure he would know what she meant.

But would he accept her argument, weak though it was?

Whores were never to solicit pleasure for themselves, not unless it was the patron's pleasure to assign them that role in advance and pretend to be subordinate.

And still Koscuisko did not let his people lack for food, or rest, or medicine, or anything at all that could be got to comfort them. She would be grateful to have a caress, even purchased with the use of her body. It would be profit the Bench could not keep from her . . . if Koscuisko consented.

"You do not mean to ask to be misused," the officer insisted. The tone of his voice was still unbelieving; but he had not rejected her offer. Or not yet.

"If only the officer did not let frustration build within for overlong." She put her two hands flat against his chest, feeling the warmth of his body through the wraptunic. "It will go easier with me if you come more often to embrace me, sir."

He would admit the sense of this.

He almost had to.

"I have heard you," Koscuisko said. "Is this what there was to discuss, Ailynn?"

Her heart turned to stone and sank within her bosom. He would be cold to her. He would not accept. He would not let her in.

"You have not answered me, your Excellency."

What had she asked him?

"It could be said to be owing," Koscuisko murmured, as if to himself. "One does not know if one dares risk it, Ailynn. Kaydence will be very severe with me should there be tears. He is your champion, did you know that?"

"Either that or simply has a weakness." She had heard the good-natured teasing. "And a question apparently exists over the exact location of it."

Koscuisko had a beautiful smile, when he was caught off guard and smiled with all his teeth. They were small, even, and regular, but it wasn't that, it was that being surprised into a smile took layers of weight of care from off his face and made him look much younger.

"Listening to Code, and should'st not, has weaknesses of his own, Code does."

She had been standing very close to him. Now he put his hand around her waist to turn her toward the door, in perfect friendship and amity. But spoke to her quite seriously, for all that. "It is your right to claim consideration from me, Ailynn, according to the rules that I was raised to."

Ailynn couldn't tell if that meant he was agreeing.

It demonstrated well enough that he was listening to her.

She wondered if Koscuisko understood how strange and rare that was.

Just short of the still-closed door he stopped. "You wanted to talk, Ailynn. Have you for now had satisfaction from me?"

His meal would be getting cold; his liquor warm. "I will tell you in the morning," she teased, daringly.

Koscuisko laughed, and gave her a quick kiss that had none of the torturer about it.

It might work.

One way or the other she would work in partnership with his people; and belong, belong by choice, for the first time since she had been sentenced to her Bond.

Taken from work-crew as War-leader Darmon, locked into a place to wait for torture. He wondered at the luxury of these cells; the sleep-rack was almost a bed, the bedding itself warm and clean and comfortable, water for washing that was sweet enough that a man could drink it at his will. Perhaps this torturer was of dainty sensibilities and only wanted fresh clean healthy prisoners. He hadn't eaten so well since he'd come to the Domitt Prison.

And it looked as though he was to have his chance to find

out about the torturer himself, little interest though he had in
the question.

The holding cells were open all along one wall so that
there could be no hiding at the blind angle of a room while
a door opened. That was probably why it was warm in here;
it wouldn't do for prison staff to take a chill. Darmon was
amused by the insight.

There was a trade-off of sorts between closing people off
and holding them in solitude to fret and fume until their
nerves were raw; or letting them watch their fellows go away
one after another and never come back. The Domitt had
clearly opted for the latter means of increasing the torment
of the condemned.

It was an advantage, to Robis Darmon.

The more he could learn of who and what he faced, the
better prepared he could be for his turn when it came.

And it would come.

He watched this young Inquisitor come through the holding area, twice a day, sometimes more often. Bond-
involuntary Security troops at the officer's back, and Pyana
turnkeys to open and close doors. A slim but solidly built
young officer, an alien name, Anders Koscuisko—no, Aanderi, he had heard. Aanderi Koscuisko. The Writ in residence
at the Domitt Prison, and had his mother guessed at the look
on Koscuisko's face when he came out from torture in the
evening she would have drowned herself rather than deliver
a son who could take such pleasure in the pain of suffering
captives. Darmon was sure of it. And Koscuisko not even
Pyana.

Morning of the fifth day since he'd been taken from the
work-crew, and probably two eights after fastmeal. They
were fed three times a day, in holding cell. The torturer
wanted them strong and able to answer all of his questions.
*What would the torturer do with answers that would com-
promise the Domitt Prison?* Darmon wondered. Because as
satisfying as Koscuisko clearly found his work in and of
itself, he was as clearly unhappy with the Administration.

"See you this man, Administrator." Koscuisko had
brought Belan with him this morning. Belan. Fat and well-
fed, sleek and stout and fattening on the flesh of his own
kind. There was a special place in Hell for such as Belan.

He would look much more than merely just uncomfortable there. "As I have warned you. You can read as well as I, this Brief says Lerriback, and says that this is the man we saw in punishment block. Has it been seven weeks? Or eight, now?"

There were only sixteen holding cells; though Darmon couldn't see everything, the sound carried as clearly as anyone could wish. Koscuisko stood in front of the cell two souls down, with his back to Darmon. And Belan beside him, and the Security, green-sleeved bond-involuntary Security slaves. Darmon wondered what it must be for them to be put to such work as Koscuisko could demand. Bond-involuntaries were not the enemy. The enemy was Koscuisko; and Belan.

"His Excellency has been eight weeks in Port Rudistal." Belan's answer had a sound of grasping for a wisp of reed in a current that was sweeping him to destruction too fast for recognition of the danger. "Not quite so long here. You were tired, and I can't say I remember, sir. It looks like the same man to me, and of course the documentation—"

"My point exactly." Koscuisko sounded upset, even angry. "The documentation gives the name, and even could be made to describe the man we saw during my tour. But not this man. You cannot have neglected to notice, this man has no gray, and the Lerriback we met looked nothing like so young. I would expect experience of a prison to age a man. Rather than the reverse."

Oh, if Koscuisko was confused at seeing two men named Lerriback, how would it be if he should start to count up how many Lerribacks there were. How many Cittropses. Maybe he'd suggest it to the man, when it was his turn to go to die by torture.

"With respect, sir." Belan was polite, but not beyond standing on his dignity as the Assistant Administrator of the Domitt Prison. A true Pyana under the skin, no doubt, Darmon told himself. No, he did not believe that, Belan was Nurail, no matter how depraved. "I wonder you don't note the obvious. Almost every one of your Interrogations to date has proved to yield some assumed name. This prisoner was masquerading as Lerriback, or as someone else named Lerriback. That's all. I'm sure."

This was too good to want to miss a word. Didn't Belan watch where he was going?

"Prisoners coming in under assumed names one expects," Koscuisko agreed, easily and freely. "And identified by the face, and their also-called. The war-leader you have brought for me, for instance. Taken for us not as Marne Cittrops, though, but as War-leader Robis Darmon, lately so called. And this is different."

"Sir?"

Darmon couldn't decide if Belan sounded confused and resentful because he didn't follow Koscuisko's reasoning, or was simply not playing along. Pretending it wasn't perfectly obvious where the argument was headed.

"So here is described a prisoner on Charges, and very pertinent Charges they are too. Named Lerriback. It is the man we saw, this description sorts with what I remember, see you here? There are notes in the file. Confined in lockbox for fractiousness. I was looking forward to Lerriback, Administrator Belan, and this is not the man, nor is he the same man under the name of another. Who can this be, and how can the Protocols be lawfully exercised against whomever Lerriback, when this is not the man?"

Just as well he was a prisoner here, Darmon told himself, and confined behind security grid in cell. Elsewise he might have kissed the Domitt's torturer; and the gesture would almost certainly have been misinterpreted.

"Maybe the other wasn't really Lerriback—"

"The documentation describes the man I wished to make go back into the lockbox," Koscuisko insisted. "And prisoners are referred on documentation. Take me away this not-Lerriback, Administrator Belan. And either bring me Charges against him—whoever he is, but him, charges I can match to the man by more than name—or find for me my Lerriback. Wherever he is. I will have nothing to do with prisoners referred on insufficient documentation. And to do otherwise would be dangerously close to a failure of Writ."

So either Koscuisko was a raging hypocrite, or the prison administration had made an error. Perhaps both. Darmon knew it wasn't likely that the last, or next, or original Marne Cittrops had looked anything like him, except by accident. Would they waste valuable Inquisitorial time on prisoners with no secrets, just because a man could be made to say anything?

No, it had to be that when they referred it was for who the prisoner actually was. Not who the prison administration called them on work-crew. War-leader Darmon, and not Marne Cittrops at all. Someone had something on the prisoner in the cell. The Administration had used that prisoner to fill a place on work-crew vacated by somebody named Lerriback. They hadn't got the details all updated. The bodies didn't match.

"Doctor Koscuisko. I protest, in the strongest possible terms. Throwing around language like that."

That had got Belan's attention. Failure of Writ. It meant that there were too many procedural or other faults within the system to lawfully support the Judicial function; and therefore the exercise of the Judicial function was not lawful. And therefore the people who had exercised the Judicial function were guilty of violations of Law and Judicial procedure to the extent that they had executed functions lawful only in support of the Judicial Order in the absence of true justification.

It was worth dreaming about.

If the Writ failed at the Domitt Prison, all of the murders would be recorded as such. All of the murderers treated as murderers, not good Bench officers upholding the Judicial order.

It was a lovely fantasy.

And it would never happen, because the only person who could invoke failure of Writ was the torturer who held the Writ to Inquire; and that meant Andrej Koscuisko here and now. The last thing Darmon could imagine Koscuisko doing was putting an end to his own recreation.

Not having seen him come from his daily work, these five days past, with that drunk drugged look of utter satiation on his face, and still always ever eager for some more.

"I beg your pardon if I have offended you." Koscuisko was doing nothing of the sort. He didn't care. "It is only out of respect for your Administration. We must tolerate no such discrepancies. I want this one remanded to Dramissoi today, Administrator, if there are no charges against *him*."

And, oh, wasn't Koscuisko rubbing Belan's face in the

dirty little problem he'd uncovered. A torturer through and through. If it hadn't been Belan, Darmon almost might have wanted to feel sorry for him.

"Of course, your Excellency." Belan wasn't happy, but there was next to nothing that Belan could do about it. "I'll launch an investigation into how this might have happened, and report back to you. Was that to be all for today, Doctor Koscuisko?"

Darmon didn't envy Belan his position; it had to be uncomfortable, Pyana on one side of him, Koscuisko on the other, family ties and friends cut off from behind him by the choices he had made for his life and nothing to look forward to. It couldn't be enjoyable. And Belan deserved every bit of it.

"Thank you, Administrator Belan. I know that you could not but be as shocked as I that such a thing could happen. We're just lucky in this case that we caught it before things went too much further."

How many people had this torturer murdered asking questions that they couldn't answer about crimes that they had not committed?

Koscuisko walked down the row of holding cells, and stopped in front of him. Darmon stepped back from the security grid. He had no desire to be struck with a shockrod for the crime of standing too close to the front of his cell in the presence of an officer.

"I will with this war-leader start while we are waiting," Koscuisko said to his green-sleeves, looking at Darmon with a measuring eye. "War-leader Robis Darmon, I understand. Or are you to claim to be Marne Cittrops, instead? It will delay the progress of the exercise. I will not disguise that fact, from you."

Now the torturer was talking to him. Darmon knew that he was afraid, because he had no illusions about the sort of pain that he was going to suffer. The more he could control the interchange, the better off he'd be. Even the illusion of control could help a man cope—

Darmon filled his face with as stupid a look as he could muster. "Excellency, there must be some mistake." If he looked at the Pyana standing with Koscuisko's Bonds it was easy enough. "My name is Lerriback."

The Pyana guards started forward to pull him out of his cell and beat him for his insolence. Darmon wondered whether it might not be worth it even so, for the look on Koscuisko's face.

Koscuisko held up his hand, and the guards came to attention.

"Oh, indeed you must be," Koscuisko said. "I can see the family resemblance. How you have managed to grow back your hair in such short order is a wonder to me, Lerriback. And taller as well? There must be some unusual healthful effect in the water here."

Darmon knew a moment's grim panic. Family resemblance—there was a family resemblance, for people who knew how to look. His son was beardless yet, but Chonniskot was his son. He had his father's greengold eyes, and that not usual among Nurail.

Was the torturer playing with him?

"Take for me this prisoner to work-room, gentles, if you please. You know what to do."

No, the torturer was just playing.

Why not?

The Domitt Prison was his own resort, in a sense. A private recreation field for those that could find recreation in such work as a torturer performed.

Koscuisko might not know that the war-leader of Darmon had even had a son, or that Chonniskot had escaped with Farlan and Sender. If Koscuisko knew and Chonni had been taken—taken or killed, identified, one way or the other—Koscuisko would surely let him know about it, to increase his despair, to impress upon him that he had nothing further to lose.

There were worse ways to be taken to torture than with good hope for his child's freedom, by an Inquisitor who seemed at least as interested in scoring off the Domitt Prison's Administration as paying attention to his work.

And still Darmon was afraid, because he knew that he was being taken to torture.

This was a torture cell, then, and would be his final battleground. Darmon looked around him as the torturer's green-sleeves stripped off his shirt and shoon and everything that had been in between, cutting away his boots, binding his wrists with chains.

It didn't look like much.

But it smelled.

He'd always thought of torture cells as dark, and this one wasn't, every corner was clearly illuminated. He didn't understand most of what he saw, though: a large square block in the middle of the room, coming waist-high. Some sort of a raised pan set against the wall, but not the obvious, because there were no coals, no smoking irons.

The grid on the wall and the hooks in the ceiling he could understand altogether too well.

The torturer said nothing, looking at the beverage-server on the table next to the armchair that waited there for the officer's comfort. Darmon suppressed a shudder: It was cold, and he was afraid. Naked he could urinate on his torturer in contempt, though that would probably not be worth the pleasure he would derive from it. He wasn't sure he had the water to urinate with. He was that frightened.

Fear was shame to nobody.

No war-leader worthy to send other souls to death could have illusions, though it was important sometimes to pretend. People had fear. It was a natural response. Courage lay in going forward with fear, not in the absence of fear.

Once they had finished stripping him, they uncoupled the chain between his wrists and hooked the manacles to tethers in the ceiling, drawing his arms well out in two different directions. Shackled his ankles, he was disappointed to note, and anchored them to the floor. No kicking, then. He would have had to get in a lucky hit to do the torturer any damage, barefoot as he was, but it was still a shame to have the fantasy taken from him.

"That will suffice for now," the torturer said. Oh, good. Then he could go back to his cell. No, of course not, it was the Security that the torturer addressed, and Darmon knew better than that. It was a lame joke, if a private one. Jokes helped. "I will call you when I want you. Go away."

Now they were alone together.

Darmon considered blowing a kiss, but restrained himself. There was no sense in being provoking.

At least not yet.

He would save his provoking till later, when things were far enough along that if the torturer lost his temper for one moment he might make the critical mistake that would let Darmon out of this.

Seating himself in the armchair, the torturer looked Darmon up and down; then spoke.

"I am Andrej Ulexeievitch Koscuisko, and I hold the Writ to which you must answer. State for me your name, and your identification."

"My name is Marne Cittrops. But my mother's people—"

Wait.

He didn't know what Cittrops's weaves had been.

The torturer had taken a little book from out of the front plaquet of his uniform, and opened it, sitting there with a stylus in his left hand, waiting. Smirking. Darmon thought hard and fast.

"—would not share so much as the name of their weave with any damned Pyana. Or their pet torturer."

The torturer would know very well what was going on; or he would guess. Koscuisko smiled more broadly.

"I am a Judicial officer, War-leader, and the Bench transcends all of your petty ethnic differences. I am particularly anxious to hear your weave, Darmon. I am collecting. See?"

Koscuisko said "petty ethnic differences," but without much pretense at conviction. It occurred to Darmon that Koscuisko was an odd sort of a torturer: but the book that he held up, what could that be?

"I can't see from here. Sir. Why don't we trade places, and you can swing on these ropes for a while, and I'll sit down and admire your work close up."

Koscuisko was collecting weaves?

"It would mean nothing to you unless you read church music. It is an Aznir script. You are evading. I have asked you for your weave, for posterity's sake. If you are Marne Cittrops, you will give me—one. If you are not, well, all to the good, I will obtain another."

Nurail had been murdered here by this man, but if the weaves were passed—the tune and the telling, or even the telling alone—the knowledge they contained would not be lost. The people that had been killed on the work-crews, crushed to death or in some other manner, had not been given time to pass their weaves before they died. How many had they lost?

"If I was not Marne Cittrops I would have the same answer."

No. Perhaps not.

It was true that some of the weave-lore was outdated. The hill-people had started to sing the weaves as a way to preserve technical knowledge about land navigation; and their importance as maps had gradually become outdated as the Nurail had spread throughout their worlds.

By then the weaves had collected much more than just land-lore. Words and music, the telling and the tune of it, there was history in them, genealogy, contractual and family relationships centuries deep and as much a part of a Nurail as his very skin. Nurail were passionate for a start, and the emotion that invested the war-weaves could inspire fighting men to awesome feats.

They were defeated and dispersed in this generation, but there would be Nurail in the next, and the weaves their only inheritance now. The music. The knowledge of the Nurail collective unconsciousness preserved in old lyrics and older tunes, the voices of the dead speaking to the living yet with words of advice and of admonishment. The power.

He was the war-leader of Darmon, and his mother's people had held the most powerful war-weave of them all; but his daughters—to whom he would normally pass his mother's weave—were dead. If Koscuisko wrote down weaves it would be there, and if someone should find it later—if Koscuisko were telling him the truth, and not making a joke at his expense, and the document did not simply get lost—

Koscuisko closed his book and put it away. "I'm sorry to hear that. I was looking forward to it. Well, then, which is it to be? Marne Cittrops? Or War-leader Darmon?"

This was too obvious to be allowed to pass, even if he was bound naked in chains while the other man sat at his ease in an armchair. "Why don't you tell me? What possible profit could there be in being a war-leader, of all things? Rather than the harmless innocuous little slave-laborer that I am."

The torturer looked him up and down with insolent amusement in his eyes. "I would not have said 'little.' And it is of course your choice to remain Cittrops as long as you can support the pretense. You are here on good suspicion of being the war-leader, though, and therefore I have it at command to put you to the Question until you confess to being the war-leader, whether you are or not. It is only a question of time.''

"Oh, well, in that case, yes. I'm the war-leader. The one that rogered your mother at her mam's knee. If you kept your mouth shut and looked stupid you could pass for Nurail, did you know that?''

The chains that stretched his wrists out to the ceiling rubbed uncomfortably. Darmon tried to resist the temptation to worry at them. He wasn't going to get any more comfortable than he was right now. That was a given. "Then you could be the war-leader. We'll trade places.''

Now Koscuisko was on his feet, plucking a record up from his side table. He carried the document over to where Darmon stood half-stretched to the ceiling, turning so that Darmon could read the text on the clear assumption that Darmon could read plain Standard; or was it part of the trick to get him to admit to his identity?

"War-leader Robis Darmon. Your family is dead, it says here, you have no one to protect any longer. If you will not provide the Bench with a confession you know what will come of it. The exiles will cherish your memory and those left on site will romanticize you until the whole thing starts over in the next generation but one. Confess, and it will help in the integration of the Nurail into Jurisdiction, with a better life for what hypothetical grandchildren you might have.''

He could read plain Standard, come to that. His family was dead, the record listed them out—and well it should be so, because if the record said his daughters were killed no Nurail could be tortured to death for the crime of being heir to the war-leader.

But there was no mention there of Chonniskot.

"You already said that you can make me confess to being whomever. And I believe you. What's the point?''

"Collaterals,'' the torturer said, and he sounded a little surprised. "In order to restore the Judicial order, the Bench needs to assure itself of war-leaders, generals, lieutenants. I want your evidence, and what you know of other persons of authority hiding under assumed names, as you were.''

Poor Ceelie. Darmon kept his face as blank as he could. He'd known as soon as they'd come for him that Ceelie had been pressed beyond the limit of his endurance. He could not afford to exhibit any grief for someone he could not admit to having known; and still it burned. It was his fault Ceelie had suffered, and Ceelie had died, because he had failed against Jurisdiction. Ceelie and so many others . . .

"So you torture a man till he names a name, and then you torture the next. That's not good evidence. That whoever you took away from work-crew, that Shopes Ban, he may have called me out as the First Judge for all I know, why should you believe him?'' The shackles cut against his wrists. Already his elbows began to ache; but then he was not a young man, any more.

The torturer frowned. "I have had no Shopes Ban, I'm sorry. You're unraveling the wrong plait.''

All that Ceelie must have endured before his death, and the torturer would not so much as admit to knowing of him. Robis's voice was a little sharper than he'd expected, when he spoke. "No doubt you've had too many of us, torturer. I wonder you can keep any apart.'' Sharper than was prudent for use by a chained man, for a fact. Koscuisko just stared.

"I would that you were right, Darmon or Cittrops.'' It was a peculiar tone of voice; and a peculiar expression on the torturer's face, as well. "But when they visit me at night I know each one of them, and all too well. But never a Shopes Ban among them. Believe me. I would know.''

People were taken from work-crew all the time; and always it was assumed that they'd been taken to the torture. If Koscuisko was telling the truth, it was someone else who had tortured Ceelie Porlich. Darmon had been a good judge of character, in his time. He believed that Koscuisko was telling him the truth.

"They took Shopes Ban away,'' he insisted. There was something gone wrong here, and he hadn't quite caught it by the mane. "Eleven, twelve days ago. Who took him away? Where did he go?''

"And why does it matter?'' Koscuisko mocked at him; but there was a serious question beneath Koscuisko's belittling jeer. "Because he was the only one who could have identified you as War-leader Darmon?"

For a moment sheer outrage and disgust possessed Darmon entirely. "Listen, someone took Ban. If he was killed it was by you or by prison security. If he wasn't killed he'd be back on work-crew till he died. And you're the Writ here, don't tell me you don't know what's going on. You killed him. Or he was murdered—"

Wait, that was almost funny. To be tortured to death by Koscuisko was different from being murdered? Well, in the eyes of the Bench it was, for a fact.

But Koscuisko had gone to an instruments-case that he let down from the wall to reveal an array of whips, with a flail, and a knout, and divers other lashes. Thinking about what Darmon was saying, perhaps. But more likely just deciding which of his toys he wanted to play with, just now.

"Take care before you make such accusations," Koscuisko warned, turning toward him with a whip in his hand. Darmon knew the sort of whip it was; it was the same sort that had killed his uncle Lijon, years ago. "I will not suffer my Writ to be dishonored. Not more than in its exercise itself. You are the war-leader of Darmon, and you have information that I require. Let us begin to controvert together."

Controvert.

That was a funny word for torture.

Darmon felt the first burning caress of the whip, and closed his eyes, and wondered.

Who had murdered Ceelie?

Could he convince Koscuisko someone had?

If Koscuisko knew that referrals were being obtained unlawfully, by prison guards and torture outside Koscuisko's Writ—would Koscuisko take steps to avenge that poor young man?

The impact of the whip was a steady insult, and the fiery lines of aching torment it laid down with every stroke were maddening.

Darmon fixed his mind on Ceelie Porlich as a touchstone. Shopes Ban.

He had to remember Ceelie was Shopes Ban.

And if he could concentrate on something extraneous to him, perhaps he would keep the torturer from the victory, this time.

◆ Nine

Administrator Geltoi was interviewing the Pyana housekeeper Eps Murey when Belan arrived with the kitchen-master. Letting himself in quietly, he gestured for the kitchen-master to step through before he closed the door again behind them.

"What's changed up there recently, Murey? Anything?" Geltoi asked. He sounded angry; but it was just his way of interacting with subordinates. Belan had long since stopped feeling that it was personally directed.

"Well. There's the woman. The bedlinen to change more often. Seems to have taken an interest in her, with the Administrator's permission."

Belan winced. What a thing to say, a crude reference to Koscuisko's personal relations with the woman from the service house. It could have been worse, of course. Murey could have been Nurail: Then the Administrator would have been disgusted at his forwardness, as well as his crudeness of speech.

As it was, Geltoi splayed his fingers wide with a gesture as if deflecting a noisome insect. "Oh, very good indeed, Murey. I need different information from you. Has Koscuisko said anything in your hearing? Any gossip amongst his Security? Anything you've heard from that Chief Warrant?"

They'd considered putting in snoopsensors when they'd built the penthouse, and only refrained at the end because it would be difficult to justify should the Inquisitor find out they were there. Geltoi was obviously feeling the lack, now.

"I'm sorry, sir, there's nothing. The officer complains of the documentation he has to process. The Chief Warrant Officer ensures that Muat completes his physical therapy, Muat protests that the officer is not completing his. They play relki. The officer would rather not put in his laps and the Warrant Officer sees to it that he does. I've heard nothing to report to you, Administrator."

So either Koscuisko didn't have a hidden agenda, or he was keeping it to himself. Why should he share his concerns with his Security? One might as well ask a Pyana to unburden himself to a Nurail. It wasn't done.

"Complains of documentation, you say." Administrator Geltoi did not seem to have come to the same conclusion. "Anything specific? Think, Murey. I'm half convinced Koscuisko is out to cause trouble for all of us."

"Only about having a backlog on his desk, sir. I'd have spoken to Administrator Belan direct if I had heard anything that might point to a problem."

Koscuisko's documentation was backlogged because Koscuisko didn't spend much time in his office. He got up, got his laps in, had his fastmeal, went to work; then up to bed late, usually after having his midmeal at least and sometimes his thirdmeal as well in the cells with his clients. Prisoners.

Victims; but that was a Nurail thought. The Pyana word was better, clients. It helped disguise the precise nature of the services Koscuisko provided. And glossed over the helpless suffering of the prisoners entirely.

Geltoi drew a dish of vellme closer to him across the surface of the desktable, glaring irritably at the light reflected in the milky liquid. "Very well, Murey, but I rather hoped for a more complete report. See if you can't get something out of the woman. And maybe you'll report to Belan every day or so whether there's news or not. I don't want any surprises like the kitchen audit."

Murey hadn't known about the kitchen audit, from his reaction. And would have loved to have had the details, exactly what Koscuisko wanted; but had been dismissed in a fairly obvious manner. Murey bowed with reluctance and went out of the room, eyeing Belan with a mixture of curious greed and hostile resentment as he passed.

Belan was used to it. There wasn't a single Pyana in all
of the Domitt Prison who wasn't convinced that they had
more right than he did to stand next to Administrator Geltoi
in the order of things.

"The kitchen audit, Administrator. We have an appoint-
ment to review it with you before we submit it to the Writ."

It was hard to tell if Geltoi was listening. Dabbing a fore-
finger into the dish of vellme in a contemplative manner,
now, Geltoi sucked the drops of fluid from the wet fingertip
thoroughly before he spoke.

"Absolutely, Merig. I'm not taking any chances. Koscuisko hasn't shared any concerns with me, if he has any,
and that would have been the normal thing to do. Still, I may
be overreacting. Let's have a look at the audit, then."

Belan agreed, if only within his own private thoughts. Geltoi was overreacting. Belan had read up on the formal relationship between a Writ on site and the prison administration.
The Writ was responsible to the Bench for reasonable and
prudent measures to ensure that prisoners were housed and
fed, and the Protocols respected. The kitchen audit was just
another item on the list of things an Inquisitor might do to
fulfill his formal responsibilities.

Also Geltoi was not overreacting a bit. If Koscuisko realized that prisoners were not being fed full rations even
when they were on work-crew, Koscuisko could cry failure
of Writ at the Domitt Prison.

The kitchen-master laid the six required reports out on the
Administrator's desktable in careful array. "Stores and dis-
bursements, showing rations received, Administrator. The
audit standard says on average an underrun of two in eighty
up to a cumulative overrun of eleven in eighty is acceptable
variation. It was hard to decide how to determine what population figure to use, though."

The Domitt Prison was at its full lawful capacity with the
new arrivals from Eild's collections and the aftermath of that
siege. Belan knew that it had been at more than full legal
capacity for longer than that. It hadn't been an issue earlier,
when the prison was being built; they'd received prisoners
without manifest, and that meant nobody really knew how
many of them there were.

That one riot had taken a lot of the pressure off, as well,

one hundred and seventy-four killed trying to reach the gate, surely as many again wounded, and the offending parties gathered—living and dead—and buried all at once in the pit that had anchored one of the materials-cranes that they'd been using to hoist heavy items up to the upper floors of the prison.

Dead and alive together.

Belan kept his eyes focused on the audit report by an act of will. Outside the Administration Building, beside the outer wall of the Domitt Prison, safely shielded from any curious eye in Port Rudistal by the containment wall, and the pit already there and ready to be filled in. He could still hear the screaming as the accelerant was broadcast onto living flesh, screaming that muted only gradually as earthmovers pushed the excavated dirt back into the pit.

It didn't matter.

They were dead.

He was Assistant Administrator Belan. He had a position of privilege and influence, even amongst these Pyana.

Pyana had done so well as they had over the years in just such a manner, why should he have nightmares? It was the Pyana way. Feeling guilty only indulged his own inferior Nurail nature.

"You've gotten the traffic reports from the landing field, Belan?" Geltoi asked. His tone of voice hinted to Belan that his inattention had been remarked upon, and he hastened to reclaim his fault by providing reassurance that all had been done as Administrator Geltoi would wish it.

"Together with best-estimates from the relocation camp, and tied in with reports on blockade intercepts, Administrator." He was proud of how thorough he'd been. None of his figures stood out by itself. He had support for everything, and convincing reasons why the Domitt claimed so many fewer souls on its admissions than the remanding parties might have thought they were transferring.

Geltoi had been completely correct on that issue. Nobody could ever tell the difference. There had been too much confusion, and records not well kept, and sometimes lost for a very small fee.

The population statistics were valid.

"As long as you're satisfied, Merig." Administrator Geltoi leaned back in his chair with the dish of vellme in one hand. "All right. Go ahead and sign for me. And get it delivered right away, and be sure that if Koscuisko has any questions he knows to ask us first."

For a moment Belan stared, confused. Him to sign? It was for the Administrator to sign the audit . . . but when understanding came it was complete and comprehensive. Of course. The Administrator was delegating. That way if there should be a problem further on . . .

Wait.

If there was a problem further on, it would be Belan, not Geltoi, to answer for any discrepancies in the kitchen audit.

What was there to worry about?

Geltoi was Pyana. Pyana were sharp. Administrator Geltoi was smarter than anyone Belan had ever met. There weren't going to be any problems.

And if there were . . .

Geltoi was watching him closely, clearly searching for signs of disloyalty or rebellion. Belan swallowed his reservations and stepped up to the desktable, pulling out his idiostamp to sign the documents.

If there was a problem he was damned.

He had no hope of outwitting a Pyana.

His only chance was to keep being useful, and hope that Geltoi would protect him.

He had been forever at the Domitt Prison, now. Not even Ailynn's graciously extended efforts to help him through the night were quite effective; which meant Andrej became more and more irritable day by day. There were so many screaming trembling bodies in this place. And he was so careful with each one of them.

The body that half-lay across the block was neither trembling nor screaming; Andrej knew what was required, but there was a problem, he had no more of the drug that he desired in the set of doses that he carried with him. No more within the cell. He would have to requisition wakekeepers from Infirmary, but for the present he would just borrow from stores in the next cell.

"Kaydence."

Going to the door, Andrej keyed the admit, blocking the

interior of the room from view by standing well within the doorway. Kaydence saluted, bowing toward the center of the room without turning to face Andrej, knowing that Andrej didn't want him to look. "Kaydence, into the second cell to the dose-rack go, and for me the doseunit store of midipar bring out. You are to come through with it, when you come back."

He needed the wakekeeper in a hurry, or he was going to lose this prisoner. And there were still just one or two more questions before this particular prisoner could die, and leave Andrej to concentrate on the other projects he had going in other cells even now.

So many.

And so hard, to keep himself to the rule of conscience every time. He had not abused a prisoner outside of Protocol. He'd never needed to violate the Protocols in order to gain dominion.

The prisoner who was accused of being War-leader Darmon, with whom he had spent the morning, was an unusual experience for Andrej in that respect; and by now—four days into that exercise—Andrej really rather hoped that he would lose, that Darmon would go to his death unconfessed. Andrej admired him.

But it was more difficult all the time to do the decent thing and let them go, when he was finished. There was so much. He'd thought the surfeit of suffering would slake his appetite; it didn't, it only seemed to sharpen it. The war-leader's resistance, admirable though it was, made Andrej the more savage with other prisoners—Tarcey, here, for instance. And day by day the unholy accumulation of the suffering of helpless captives scraped away new layers of raw nerve like a flensing-knife, until his resolve was frayed to the snapping point.

Kaydence came into the cell with the drug Andrej wanted and stood waiting, patiently, to see if the dose was right. Andrej put the dose through at the throat of his prisoner, fresh meat to the bestial hunger in his soul; the prisoner stirred, with a grinding groaning sound of fathomless despair, and Andrej forgot all about Kaydence being present.

So many, and so much, and not enough. Never enough. His sharp keen agonizing knowledge of how wrong it was to embrace such a thirst only heightened his thirst, and he had kept himself from the slaking of it with a stern effort time and again, determined not to take advantage beyond what measures served the Judicial purpose.

Fetching a glass of water from the potable-water spigot at the back of the cell, Andrej touched his prisoner's face to get his attention, offering the glass. For a moment he wondered if the prisoner had escaped after all: There was madness in the look of that dark eye, glittering feverishly under the lights from the ceiling. The moment passed. The prisoner closed his eyes, exhausted and submissive to Andrej's will; and drank from the glass of water gratefully.

"Now let us talk," Andrej suggested.

He had a camp-stool that he could pull close, to sit upon and be at a good level to watch his prisoner's face. The man tried to flinch away from him on instinct, but his wrists were chained to the side of the block on which he half-lay, sprawling. There was no "away" for him to flinch to.

"Yes. Your-ex. Len. Sie."

Wrists pegged to the sides of the cube, arms stretched to either side of the near corner, and the prisoner's body across the block so that most of his torso lay atop it on his belly while his legs fell unsupported off the opposite corner. A very awkward position to be in, really. One in which it would be almost impossible to rest.

"The Tanner's raid on Port Preyling, who planned it?" Andrej asked gently. At this point a man needed very little by way of persuasion to speak out. It was deciding if he was telling the truth—

"Don't know." It was a protest from the heart, one pregnant with fear and horror. "Told you. Please. Don't know. Please."

Yet it was in Andrej's power to hold this man and torture him until he accused someone, anyone, just to make it stop, just to win his death. Then there would be another soul to torment, and good cause and justification to invoke the Advanced Levels, and as little chance that whomever was accused had real guilt to confess as that this man was lying. It was a seductive concept.

"All right. I'm sorry. Just making certain. Can you tell

me why Haren Morguiss went over to the Darmon, at Fidenbanks.''

Four days of torture, and this the fifth. The prisoner swallowed hard. Andrej gave him another drink of water.

''Not sure. Heard. Assault on family. Bench in Pyana pockets.''

The prisoner's face was dirty, under the bright lights; dirty, and pale. Bruised, and altogether disreputable to look at. Why would anyone think twice about spurning a piece of such human trash under his foot, and taking what pleasure there was to be had in the death-throes of human vermin?

Why should he torture himself, day in, day out, precise to Protocol and strictly to the Judicial standard, when any of these prisoners confessed could be lawfully tortured until they died for crimes against the Judicial order?

''What came of it?'' The defection of Haren Morguiss had been a matter of much debate in recent months, debate about whether Nurail were inherently treacherous because of their savage animal nature or were simply incapable of understanding more complex concepts of loyalty and fidelity. Andrej knew better than to imagine that Nurail were incapable of loyalty. He had firsthand experience: much of it here.

''Family was compromised, children sold. Disrespect of Bench. Pyana treachery.''

The Domitt Prison had been built by Pyana with imprisoned Nurail slave-labor, was staffed almost exclusively by Pyana as far as Andrej had seen—

''It's illegal to sell children under Jurisdiction, Tarcey. Watch what you say,'' Andrej warned. But not because he meant it. He wanted more information; and also Tarcey was fearfully sensitive, by now, to any criticism from his torturer.

''No disrespect—sir—please—no disrespect—''

So sensitive that his fear of punishment was almost as strict and terrible to him as the punishment itself. Almost. Andrej knew that he should reassure Tarcey, and pose the question in a form that Tarcey could understand; and yet why should he?

Why shouldn't he take one, just one, of all these souls, and instead of keeping constant guard over himself to prevent the commission of some cruelty in excess of the gross cruelties that the Bench required of him, put his conscience aside, misgivings away, shut up the voice of decency and pity, and revel in the rich wide field of horror that the Bench had granted him?

So many souls in torment, why should he not take one, just one, and see if he could satisfy his lust once and for all by indulging it to its fullest extent?

"Sent to prison for civil offenses by Pyana torturers, one of the daughters indentured I—I think, oh please. Your Excellency. No disrespect."

"It's all right." His voice was soothing and reassuring. The prisoner lapsed into silence with his eyes shut tight against the bright lights and remembered horrors, weeping. Andrej rose unsteadily to his feet, half-sick with conflict, desire, and self-loathing; and went to put the extra doses Kaydence had brought away in the shelf-rack.

Wakekeepers.

Pain-maintenance drugs.

Put them together and a man went to Hell, and lived there, abiding in ferocious torment for eternities before the body finally failed or the dose wore off. Or the torturer took pity. Whichever came first.

And Tarcey was so frightened, of the mask.

Just next to the dose-rack, cleaned and returned to storage. Waiting. Promising.

Andrej slipped the catch, and opened the equipment rack, reaching out a waiting hand to touch the cold heavy surface of the thing.

It had worked for him in Tarcey's case, right enough; but Tarcey had confessed, and had no more to say that Andrej was interested in hearing. And would be put to death. Lethal injection.

What if . . .

He was the rule of Law at the Domitt Prison. He could do anything he liked.

Staring at the equipment rack, one hand to the cheekpiece of the mask, Andrej stared at the wall unseeing for long moments. Struggling.

Realizing only gradually that someone was speaking to him.

". . . for thirdmeal."

What?

''If you would care to take it in your office, sir. Or perhaps go up to quarters now?''

Kaydence. That was right. He'd had Kaydence run an errand for him. He'd forgotten to send him away.

What had gotten into Kaydence, though? Bond-involuntaries were not to speak unless they had been spoken to first. Andrej didn't want thirdmeal. He wanted to take the mask to show Tarcey, just to show him. Tarcey was so afraid of the mask. Andrej wanted to enjoy that helpless terror.

''Oh, go away, Kaydence.'' Kaydence wasn't being insubordinate, not really. Kaydence was trying to help out. It was so hard to close an equipment rack up and walk away, sometimes. It got harder and harder as he went along. ''I don't want my supper. Go and wait outside. I will come when I am ready.''

Kaydence's intervention was grounded in genuine care and enabled by trust; was it best in the long run—Andrej asked himself—to have given his people the idea that they could trust any officer?

Because Kaydence was not doing as he was told.

''Yes, sir. Going immediately, sir, except that the officer should come away as well. If the officer please.''

Or, in plain language, *you are not in command of yourself and should be removed from this environment before you do something you'll regret later.* Andrej wondered at Kaydence finding the nerve to speak to him like that, issues of trust aside. This was far from the strict standard of careful respect and formality that bond-involuntaries were expected to exemplify—for their own protection.

He stroked the mask, distracted, his fingers feeling their way from the cheekpiece to the eyepiece almost without conscious volition. The eyepiece. The earpiece. The—

Kaydence was nearer to Andrej, now, standing very close behind him. Moving slowly, moving deliberately, Kaydence reached around from behind Andrej to take his hand at the wrist, plucking it away from the seductive surface of the mask with careful but unapologetic firmness.

''There's a nice bit of savory for the officer's thirdmeal,'' Kaydence said. Coming around from behind Andrej now to close up the equipment rack and lock it into place, putting his back to it, placing himself between Andrej and the temptation that tormented him. "Baked apple for aftersweet. The officer will wish to wash. Please. Sir. Come away from here."

Kaydence's voice had begun to tremble, just a bit. As though he were beginning to realize how flagrantly he was violating all that he'd been taught. Backing up toward his chair, staring in astonishment, Andrej sat down, trying to understand how he felt about this.

Insubordination.

Clear and repeated failure to comply with lawful and received instruction, utterly contrary to conditioning.

His Security had learned to take liberties, over the years. As long as Andrej himself was careful to take no notice, Security weren't forced to evaluate their actions against their codes of conduct. Without the internal stress state resulting from having done something one knew one should not have done—or having not done something that one should have—the governor did not engage.

The governor.

Hard-wired into pain centers in the brain, and calibrated to respond to specific internal stress states by providing a corrective noxious stimulus direct—

Like the most merciless torturer imaginable, literal-minded and absolute, and one that was immune to appeals to conscience or affection, one that Kaydence himself had invoked and surrendered to . . . one that would continue to execute a fearful penalty, defined on a predetermined scale and measured against the extremity of Kaydence's distress, for as long as Kaydence believed that he had earned punishment—

Oh.

It was an astonishing idea.

And Kaydence knew that he had been insubordinate. No, worse than insubordinate, he had actively interfered, Kaydence had committed an intervention. Bond-involuntaries were never to handle instruments of torture without explicit instructions, though of course they were expected to tidy up from time to time in due course. Still less were they to use coercive force against their officers, preventing or compelling in any way—

Kaydence knew, because Kaydence was white in the face and breathing a little shakily, standing at attention now but with his eyes fixed desperately on Andrej's face.

Andrej smiled.

It was too perfect; he couldn't help it.

Kaydence knew that he'd earned punishment.

And Andrej didn't even have to touch him to make him suffer.

"I am surprised at you," Andrej observed, and kept his voice careful and level. To give no hint. To provide no hope of indulgence or forgiveness. "How do you mean to explain yourself to me, Mister Psimas?"

Kaydence was tall and powerfully built, broad-shouldered and as steady as an oak.

Now Kaydence staggered under the ferocious force of Andrej's cold rebuke, and crashed down to his knees as though he had been struck by lightning.

"You'd only. Hate yourself." Kaydence's words were heavy with a burden of fathomless grief and dreadful fear. "Even more. And there's so little we can do."

Kaydence couldn't keep to his knees. He fell onto his face on the floor, crawling forward awkwardly to crouch trembling at Andrej's feet. The governor. It didn't know Kaydence had acted from love. It didn't care. It only knew that Kaydence had taken a chance, and was to be disciplined for insubordination strictly enough to put teeth into the mildest of rebukes from his officer.

Leaning his forehead against the edge of the chair just to one side of Andrej's knee, Kaydence clutched at Andrej's wrist, seeking reassurance, forgiveness. His voice staggered and halted like a drunken man, so brokenly that Andrej could hardly make sense of his words.

"Only. Touch me, if you're going to. Punish me. I could still pretend—I mattered to you, then—"

Time stopped, and the instant shimmered in Andrej's mind too full of conflict and promise for comprehension.

Kaydence.

Suffering.

Loved him and trusted him, how much more would Kaydence suffer to be punished—

Andrej blinked once, and time was, once again. Oh, no. Not Kaydence. Holy Mother, in the name of all Saints. Not Kaydence.

Paralyzed with horror, Andrej could not move.

Kaydence had reached up for Andrej's hand, petitioning for some small comfort in his pain. But Andrej could not move to clasp Kaydence's trembling fingers. Kaydence's hand slipped slowly down to cover his face, instead; curling his other hand around Andrej's ankle, Kaydence started to shake, shuddering with pain and weeping with desolate grief.

Andrej knew how to translate that language in Kaydence's body. Kaydence's governor had not stopped, when time had stopped. Kaydence believed that Andrej was angry with him, and meant for him to suffer. Kaydence's governor was equal to the task of punishment.

Not Kaydence.

Oh, holy Mother, in the name of all Saints, not Kaydence.

Out of his chair in a spasm of ferocious anxiety, Andrej cradled Kaydence to lie on the floor, desperately trying to get through. "Please, Kaydence, you've done nothing wrong, you were quite right to mention my supper, Kaydence, don't—''

It was too late.

Kaydence was lost, his governor hell-bent on performing its function. Punishing Kaydence. Putting him to torture for his crime of trying to take care of his officer, trying to protect his officer, trying to do right.

Kaydence's eyes were open and staring, fixed on some point in space that had to be more horrifying than anything Andrej had ever seen. To judge from Kaydence's expression.

The governor had engaged. And the governor punished out of all proportion with the severity of the offense, because bond-involuntaries were criminals after all; and had to be strictly disciplined, to ensure they took their lessons to heart. There was nothing that could be done but put Kaydence out, interrupt the pain response with induced unconsciousness so that the governor could complete its punishment sequence without Kaydence quite feeling it.

No time to kiss Kaydence's staring eyes and beg forgiveness.

Andrej put his thumbs to either side of Kaydence's neck and pressed until the body relaxed, limp and unconscious.

It wouldn't last.

Kaydence would wake again to agony within too short a

time. But Andrej could get him to Infirmary by then, and get the drug he needed. He didn't have it with him. Kaydence wasn't Nurail, Kaydence was Class-One, an entirely different category of hominid. The drugs Andrej had brought for Nurail patients and Nurail prisoners would do no good for Kaydence.

He had to get to Infirmary.

And what punishment a man might merit who had been for even that one instant willing to consider torturing an enslaved soul who trusted and believed in him—

Later.

Andrej sprinted for the door to fetch Toska, leaving his prisoner to fall asleep and die.

His overriding need to shut off Kaydence's pain canceled all others.

The Domitt Prison's Infirmary was as bleak and depressing as everything else about a prison was. Erish envied Code his familiarity with the place: Code had been here before. He'd been the officer's escort on his tour of the prison.

Nine weeks ago, now? Ten?

Maybe as long as that. Erish didn't remember, exactly, and he didn't want to think about it. He had been Bonded in a prison. The operation had been done in a prison surgery, although one considerably more sophisticated than this. He could remember the terror as he woke as clearly as though it had been yesterday, rather than seven years ago.

The operation. The implantation of his governor. And how vulnerable it had made him feel, how difficult it had been for the Infirmary staff not to take advantage, just that little bit, of the fact that he was helpless and terrified, and could only comply with whatever instruction as quickly as he could and hope to avoid punishment.

Kaydence's governor—

Erish didn't know what was going on; nobody did. Chief Samons had got the call from Toska, they'd arrived just in time to hear the officer tell the guards to take them to Infirmary. Right away. Immediately.

Kaydence laid out on a carry-plank, guards as guides, Koscuisko had hurried them all through to Infirmary to transfer Kaydence to a treatment-table, calling for sixteen units of one of the most powerful anodynes in the entire Inventory.

Chief Samons waited until Koscuisko had put the dose through before she asked the question.

"Your Excellency. If you'd care to say what happened, sir."

Joslire dead, Kaydence in agony . . .

"He said only three words to me," Koscuisko replied, in a voice full of anguished self-reproach. "And I let him believe that I had taken offense. Oh, Kaydence."

Erish thought he understood.

It was hard on them all being here, but no question existed in Erish's mind that it was hardest on Koscuisko himself. Koscuisko got lost. Joslire had been able to call Koscuisko back when he was in danger of wandering; Kay had misjudged his moment.

Kaydence trembled on the treatment-table as though he heard Koscuisko's voice; Koscuisko frowned at him, in horror. "No, it is not to be imagined. Kaydence must be unconscious, there was enough vixit in that dose—"

Setting his fingers to the pulse of Kaydence's throat, Koscuisko shook his head, clearly unwilling to accept the evidence he read. "Where is the staff physician. This is wrong."

And took Kaydence's head between his hands at the back of Kaydence's neck to shut Kay's mind down with the pressure of his thumbs. "I cannot afford to repeat the simple approach too many times, it is reduction of blood flow, there can be no chances taken. The staff surgeon!" Koscuisko snarled at the Infirmary aide standing nervously at the door to the treatment room. "The staff surgeon at once, the need is critical, why are you standing there?"

The Infirmary aide bolted. Koscuisko drew a dose from the same vial he'd drawn on for Kaydence's medication and discharged it over the palm of his hand, sniffing at it, tasting it, finally breathing the fluid in three short sharp sniffs. Then Koscuisko swore, and went to the stores shelf in a furious and furiously controlled rage.

Searching the shelves.

Striking through the secures with a savage blow of the heavy bowl of a powder-crusher. Scattering medication as he went, talking to himself while Erish stood with Code and

Toska and wondered. Chief Samons opened Kaydence's cuffs and collar, beckoning for Toska to take off Kaydence's boots as Koscuisko muttered.

"Exhausted the dose, maybe the lot was old, shouldn't be old, and someone had used some of it. Where's another. Should have more dissiter, here, prison full of Nurail. Yes, I need some vondilong, running short. Pink-tinged, bad sign. Chief."

Koscuisko tossed a vial over his shoulder in Samons's direction, not pausing in his search, not looking around. Chief Samons caught it: vondilong, a standard stimulant for Nurail, but what had Koscuisko meant by its pink tinge being a bad sign?

Chief Samons tucked it away and opened Kay's over-blouse. Erish was glad to see that Kaydence's boot-stockings were beyond reproach, for once.

The officer blamed himself for Kaydence's suffering, and might well have good reason. But they were all in this to-gether: and the officer blamed himself for entirely too much already.

Should they risk a grouping? Erish wondered. The officer needed balance. It had gone better with him once he and Cousin Ailynn had come to an agreement. A grouping . . . it had never been done.

And had it been anyone other than Andrej Koscuisko Erish couldn't imagine even entertaining the idea for a moment.

There was activity outside the room; a senior medical man came hurrying in. With a vial of something in his hand. The staff surgeon? Or as good as, Erish guessed, not envying the man his position in light of the ferocious face the officer turned on him.

"Your Excellency. Your pardon, sir, no word, what seems—"

The officer wouldn't listen, not for a moment. "Your stores are outdated and your vixit doesn't work, when was the last time you ran an assay on these drugs? I require nar-cotics, and I require them now. My man Kaydence. Is in pain. And the dose I got from emergency stores, it may as well have been sterile solution, bring me vixit. Now."

The staff surgeon offered the vial he carried, in a hesitant sort of way. "I took the liberty, Cabrello said . . ."

Koscuisko snatched the vial out of the staff surgeon's hand. "And pray to the holy Mother that your stores are merely outdated, and not adulterated, if I should lose my Kaydence after all that we have been through I will not rest till I have taken reparations. In coin of my own choosing."

The officer knew what he was doing. The officer had never made a mistake in his medical practice, not in the years he had been on *Scylla*—not one that had cost life or suffering, that was to say.

No man was perfect.

That wasn't the point.

The point was that the officer was absolutely confident that what he'd given Kaydence had not been any sort of medication. The last thing Koscuisko was going to do just at this moment was hazard Kaydence's life against an overdose.

So Koscuisko was convinced.

The Domitt Prison had lost control over its pharmacy stores.

Did Koscuisko think that the staff was in on it?

Some of the staff almost had to be, by definition, but how far did the corruption extend?

The officer put the dose through.

Kaydence's body lost some of its tension.

Koscuisko stood with his head bent close over Kaydence's face, listening to Kaydence breathe as he rested his fingertips lightly against Kaydence's throat.

Finally Koscuisko straightened up, and fixed the staff surgeon—who did not look like he knew whether he was more anxious or annoyed—with a sharp querying gaze that Erish would have found very uncomfortable, had it been directed against him.

"And it was truly *vixit*, this time, I trust," Koscuisko stated flatly. "I am concerned about the state of this emergency stores area, Doctor."

The staff surgeon blushed. "Ah, only a senior technician, sir. Our senior physician hasn't quite reported on shift yet. If we'd only known you were coming. Sir."

But that was too clearly compromising a statement. If they'd only known Koscuisko was coming, they would have shown him into the treatment room reserved for prison staff, instead of prisoners. Where the real narcotics were. Instead of outdated or adulterated ones. Erish could decode that well enough; and if he could do it, the officer could obviously do it that much more quickly.

"We'll take a monitor back up to quarters. You do have monitors?"

The officer had clearly elected not to follow up—not now. There was Kaydence to consider. Still, the question was a little pointed, and the staff surgeon—or senior technician—scowled briefly before he smoothed his expression out.

"Yes, sir. Medical monitors available for issue at his Excellency's pleasure."

Because once Kaydence had been drugged deeply enough to deal with his pain, he was drugged deeply enough to need to be on monitor. Just in case. That meant a grouping was right out for now, Erish realized. Someone would need to sit with Kaydence. Two someones, if one of them was the officer, because the officer would be drinking.

Also Kaydence had to be a part of any grouping. It wouldn't be a true grouping without him.

So much for that idea.

"Thank you, senior technician. And I'll take the rest of this vixit with me for if I need it."

Removing restricted drugs from Infirmary?

His Excellency was a Chief Medical Officer. He knew better.

His Excellency held the Writ at the Domitt Prison, and could do anything he liked.

"According to his Excellency's good pleasure," the senior technician agreed, a little sourly.

Kaydence had the best of this, Erish decided. Kaydence was unconscious.

It would be up to the rest of them to deal with Koscuisko for the next few hours, and Erish for one was not looking forward to it.

◆ Ten

Andrej Koscuisko lay on the tiled floor of the washroom singing quietly to himself and thinking about alcohol. Wodac. There had been cortac brandy, at one point; but cortac wasn't strong enough to answer to his need. It didn't matter. As long as there was enough of it, Andrej didn't really care what kind of alcohol it was.

Singing in the washroom had several advantages when a person was drunk. One of them was the classic acoustics of the tiled room, something he'd only discovered as a student at Mayon. At home, washrooms were wood and stone like the rest of the house. Wood rather dampened the reverberation of one's voice.

There were stacks of toweling and a carpet in this washroom, which had the same dampening effect, but the carpet had been rolled up and taken away. Andrej suspected that it might have become soiled, in some way, but he could not be sure.

He took a drink.

Someone had wrapped him in a blanket, because the tiling was cold and he was only half-dressed. It had been a gesture of concern, Andrej was sure; but one with an unexpected side effect. He'd rolled over onto his side facing the wall. Now he couldn't seem to get himself unrolled.

His drinking arm was free, and the bottle was half-full, so that did not present an immediate problem. It could create difficulties further down the line. Andrej could only hope that someone was keeping an eye on his wodac bottle. It would never do to run low on wodac, he could not stay as drunk as he was without a fairly steady infusion of fresh wodac, and the last thing Andrej wanted to be was not-drunk.

There were reasons.

He was certain that they were very good reasons.

He didn't even want to know what those reasons were. That was the whole point of getting drunk, after all. He couldn't have called those reasons into his mind if he'd wanted to, except that he had an idea it was something to do with—

Almost a glimmer of a thought. Andrej swallowed several mouthfuls of wodac hastily. That had been close. He had to pay attention.

Lying on his side facing the tiled washroom wall, drinking wodac and singing to himself. The odds were good that these washroom tiles had never been exposed to the saga of Dasidar and Dyraine, so it was a public service he was providing, really, cultural enrichment of naive tiles.

Dyraine was the mistress of meadowlands, she had six spinners for each weaver and four weavers for every loom in her long weaving-house by the flax-fields.

The tiles echoed pleasantly, so close to his face that he could hear the vibration in sympathy with the catalog of Dyraine's wealth. It was an interesting effect. There was a word for it, vibrato, Andrej thought, but the whole point of drinking was not to think.

He sang instead.

Six flax-fields for every spinner, six fat ewes and six times sixteen pretty lambs, and all for the looms of dark-eyed Dyraine.

Settling his head in a softer place on the floor—he'd got a corner of the blanket beneath his head at the temple, it wasn't comfortable, it annoyed him—Andrej closed his eyes and concentrated on the words to the old song. It was good to sing about Dasidar and Dyraine. It was safe. They had had misunderstandings too, but it had all come out right in the end. Well, eventually.

Each of her looms twelve spans high, and each of her looms three spans wide, no skill of any on the Lake's broad shore could be compared to the weaving-women of dark-eyed Dyraine.

H'mm.

Something was wrong.

He didn't hear the buzz of the vibration.

Maybe he'd forgotten to open his mouth?

She dyed her fine wool with the sapin-flower on the white shores of the Lake, and took the tiny currit-shell to make her lustrous purple.

No, he could hear his voice, but no vibration. What was wrong? Andrej moved his head a little to stretch his throat. Maybe he wasn't singing loudly enough. He didn't want to sing loudly, there were people he didn't want to disturb. But he was focused now on finding out. The song sounded so much more poignant, somehow, with the buzz of the vibration of his voice in the tiling. Like the background drone of the lap-lute that traditionally accompanied the singer.

Perfumed with rare Myelosin and patterned with swallows in flight, the tapestries of wide renown came from the looms in the weave-house of the dark-eyed Dyraine.

Well, there was the vibration, right enough. Andrej sang on; but twisted his body a little as he went. He was lying on his side, and one elbow lay beneath him. It was beginning to go to sleep.

Needlewomen of astounding skill put linen thread to woolen weave and woolen thread to fine spun flax to glorify the house-mistress and praise the pride and management of the dark-eyed Dyraine—

Halfway through the phrase, though, the vibration stopped. Andrej stopped and opened his eyes, scowling. What was happening, here?

He'd moved.

Were there faulty tiles here in the washroom?

That would be a discrepancy. Everything else in this fine house was perfect. The tiles in the washroom could not be allowed to destroy the overall perfection of the house.

Which one was it?

Now, he had to keep his eyes open for this, Andrej admonished himself. It was difficult, because he was having trouble focusing. He took a drink. Well. Better.

Flax shining like the stars, like the sun on summer waters, flax that shone like milk or cream, such was the flax spun for the linen that was cut and sewn into the apron with long

strings that tied around the linden waist of dark-eyed Dy-
raine, of the weavers . . .

Four tiles up. Four tiles down. The tiles were as square as
his hand was broad. And they all sang back to him as he
chanted out the old story, giving him their approval by providing background music. All of them but one.

Dyraine's wicked brother-in-law, clearly.

Or maybe Dasidar's pledged sacred-wife?

Snowy flax as pure as light, shining flax like running wa-
ter, flax as fair as morning bells was cut and hemmed and
trimmed in braid to overlay the bird-wing arms, the fir-
branch shoulders, the sweetapple bosom of dark-eyed Dy-
raine.

Second tile from the floor. Just by his nose. Defective.

It would have to be replaced.

It seemed a little out of true, as well, not quite as much
in line with the others. Perhaps it could be set right, and then
it would not be the brother-in-law or the pledged sacred-wife
at all, but could represent Sarce of the mountains instead.

That was a much more sympathetic role.

The tile would thank him for setting it right, for saving it
from the eternity of hatred and contempt that was the self-
elected destiny of Dyraine's spiteful brother-in-law and Das-
dar's uncharitable pledged sacred-wife. No tile in its right
mind would prefer to be Kotsuda or Hoyfragen when it could
be Sarce of the mountains.

Andrej tapped at the corner of the tile that was out of true
with the mouth of the bottle of wodac, pausing thoughtfully
to refresh himself as he did so. It was a thick bottle. He
tended to break bottles, when he was drunk. His people did
their best to give him his drink in a stout flask.

He wasn't doing this right.

The corner wouldn't be tapped down to true.

The tapping only jarred the other corners out of true as
well, cracking a thin outline in the tiled wall.

Oh, how aggravating.

All right, if that was the way of it, the tile would simply
have to go, and make way for some more worthy tile. A tile
that would appreciate its place and understand its role in the
greater scheme of the washroom wall. The wife of the
wicked brother-in-law, who refused to sleep in the bed fur-

nished with unseamed linen for as long as Dyraine was in exile . . .

Scratching at the tile with impatient fingers, Andrej concentrated on prying the wretched villain out of the wall. He had never liked the wicked brother-in-law, not even at the wedding when he'd brought the golden skeps with their heavy hives of pure black honey from the blooms of each of the four mountain berries. Never. The brother-in-law had only gotten what he deserved, and not enough of it.

The tile came away from the wall and clattered softly to the floor.

Andrej saw what the problem had been immediately.

It hadn't been the tile's fault at all.

There was a scrap of cloth there, between the tilebed and the wall, dampening the vibration, muffling the sound.

Seized with a sudden spasm of keen remorse, Andrej picked up the poor scorned tile from the floor and kissed it for an apology. Poor Elko. It hadn't been Elko's fault.

He'd had no choice but to take the lambs, since that wretched Simar was his mother's brother's daughter. Oh, how remorseful he had been, and how sweetly Dyraine had forgiven him, and how nobly Dasidar had requited the tender impulse that had led him to hide the one rimeno yowe. It was too poignant.

Andrej wept, and pulled the bit of cloth away so that the tile could be restored to its proper place. Oh, only one, only one little rimeno yowe, but all that Dyraine had been left with to comfort her—no, it was too much.

Pieces of the wall came with the cloth tag.

Pulling something behind it.

Someone had come in to comfort him in his grief; or had they been there all along? Someone was here now, one way or the other. Maybe they didn't know about Elko. There was more than one of them; they moved him over onto his back, away from the wall, but Andrej kept a firm grip on the bit of cloth.

Lying on his back was a mistake.

The pain in his stomach was astonishing.

Someone offered him the bottle of wodac, but just for once Andrej wasn't interested.

Rolling onto his side again away from the wall, Andrej

curled his knees to his belly in a ferocious spasm of retching, clutching the cloth tag and the packet that had come out of the wall with it in his hand.

Oh, he was drunk, and it would be hours before he could see straight, and hours longer still before he would want to.

But that was what happened when a man got drunk.

Oddly enough it never seemed to stop him.

Now it was morning come.

Ailynn went as softly as she could with a chilled cloth for the officer's head, wondering how he managed to sit up at table. She'd tended her share of drunks at the service house; she'd even been drunk herself, once of a time.

And what she remembered most particularly was that she hadn't been able to tolerate so much as the smell of food for at least three days after. What the officer had been last night had not been drunk: He had been right stupefied. And still wanted his rhyti, in the morning; or if he didn't want it, he still asked for it, and drank it when it came.

Chief Samons had brought medication from the officer's kit that seemed to help. Koscuisko's people knew how to manage Koscuisko drunk and then hung over; it was a hint, to her, that it had happened before upon occasion. It was perfectly true that the officer drank every night. But nothing like this. She could not have come to know his body as well as she had, otherwise. Koscuisko drank, but he didn't come to her drunk; or not in any way that she could recognize as interfering with his concentration or impairing bodily function. She was in a position to know.

"I woke up with a wad of cloth in my hand," the officer said to Chief Samons, with a grateful glance at Ailynn in return for the chilled compress. "What on earth was I up to? I am afraid to ask."

A good question. Chief Samons smiled not so much in mockery as in chagrined recognition of the situation Koscuisko found himself in. "Singing in the bathroom, sir. One of the tiles seems to have offended you. You pulled this out of the wall with it."

The wad of cloth. Or something wrapped in cloth. What had it been doing in the wall? Chief Samons set it down in front of the officer, and Cook came in with a glass and a tray. Flat unseasoned crackers. What was in the glass was anyone's guess.

Koscuisko nodded his thanks politely, sniffing at the contents with an expression of hesitation and doubt. Seeming to take his courage into his hands, Koscuisko drank from the glass; hesitantly at first, then with renewed confidence.

"What. Is this," Koscuisko asked the cook, who had hung back waiting for a response. And grinned.

"As it please the officer. I'm Nurail. If anyone knows about bodywrack, it's Nurail, sir. Or so they tell me."

Hangover remedy. Nurail folklore held that cooks were magicians second only to weavers in their occult powers. Koscuisko was staring at the empty glass in awe.

"Go to the school at Mayon when you can, and your future is made," Koscuisko said. "From the pockets of grateful students, if not from medical research. You are a phenomenon. And I am in your debt for this exceedingly."

The cook made a small bow of gracious acceptance, still grinning, and went back to the kitchen while the officer tipped the glass back to get at the last drops of the potion.

"I am a new man," the officer said. "I am reborn. I am renewed. I am—going to eat a cracker. Ailynn, if you would, open, here. But. Chief. Kaydence, how does he go?"

It was that short a moment between the opening of a window out of the house of Koscuisko's pain and the flying wide of the great doors to readmit the anguish that had set the officer on his drunk in the first place.

"He's been up to have a drink of water and wash his hands. He made it back to his bed just in time. Sleeping off the meds, sir, no apparent complications."

Not in pain, that was to say. Ailynn pricked open the knot of cloth that secured the outer layer of the wad, concentrating on her task as Koscuisko mused aloud.

"The hell of it is. I cannot swear. That I didn't mean. To hurt him."

It was difficult for the officer to come out with the damning self-accusation. Ailynn smoothed the cover-layer of fabric flat on the table's surface. It was none of her business.

"That's to work out with Kaydence, sir." Chief Samons wasn't offering much reassurance. But she wasn't blaming. She was right, after all; whatever had happened, it was between Koscuisko and his man. That was the tally of it.

"Ailynn, what have you got?" the officer asked in wonder. Distracted from his private pain. There was to be nothing he could do about that until he could speak to Kaydence.

Ailynn folded back the protective layers of cloth to reveal the secret that had been hidden behind the tile in the washroom. A book. Sixteen, twenty-four leaves of paper, not much more than the size of her hand, and rolled back upon itself twice to make a compact cylinder. A book.

Ailynn stared at it, in horror of what it might reveal.

The officer laid tableware down on either side to hold the edges flat. It hadn't been in the wall for all that very long. It couldn't have been. The Domitt Prison was less than a year old, Standard. The paper was as crisp and square-edged as it had probably been when the book went into the wall. But it hadn't been very good quality paper to start out with.

"Standard script," Chief Samons noted, looking over the officer's shoulder. "But I'm not sure I can make any sense of it."

Ailynn could.

Standard script, but it was a Nurail dialect.

The words spoke all too clearly to her Nurail heart.

"Ailynn?"

The officer had noticed a change in her expression; or the officer had guessed.

" 'My name is Morse Wab, from the port at Cluse. My mother's people hold the Time-Smoothed Stones.' " Ailynn read the cramped script off in dread of each next sentence, translating as she went. " 'In order that the weave of our suffering should not be lost. This record I have made. Look for others, we are all dead men.' "

She didn't want to read any more.

But she was the only person here who could read it.

"This prison was built by Nurail work-crews." The officer's tone of voice was neutral. Careful. "I remember Belan told me so—"

"Slave labor," Ailynn interrupted, in terror of her own temerity. Dread of the document's secrets outweighed her natural sense of self-preservation. "Sir, it should be kept close. At least until you know what it says."

Nobody was surprised at the suggestion. Ailynn blushed, suddenly, and sat down.

"There are, how many pages here? Ailynn. Let me to know what the document says. I need for you to translate it, and write it down for me, but do not under any circumstances set the document down and go away. I will set Toska to watch at your back, to see that what you do keeps secret still."

She'd been afraid of that.

There were stories, fragments of stories, rumors, pieces of horrible suggestions whispered in the night . . . some of them probably real. Some just imagined.

Yet if the officer had not had questions of his own already about what had happened here, would he be as anxious as he seemed to know what this dead Morse Wab had to tell him?

"According to his Excellency's good pleasure."

Of course.

Koscuisko put his hand out to her shoulder, in apparent sympathy with her feelings for the task that he had set her to.

Took up a handful of the crackers, and rose to go complete his morning grooming and set out to work.

So then would she.

She didn't want to know what Wab had seen, but the dead had a right to be heard out.

Kaydence's sleepshift wasn't scheduled to end before first-shift, and here it was only a few eights into fourth; but he was awake and rested, looking for something to do.

He was excused from exercise period because the officer had said he was to rest for at least three days.

He was excused from having to spend much time on his uniform, as they all were. The housekeepers that the Domitt Prison administration had installed here did laundry, linen, pressing, and a very tidy job they did, too—every pleat perfect, razor-sharp, crisp as anything. He tried not to wonder whether prison labor was responsible.

Being excused from exercise period, and not having boot-stockings to mend or bootleather to dress, Kaydence Psimas was at loose ends; but he knew what to do about that. If he was at loose ends, there were plenty of other people here strung taut as a reverb string. The best thing to do with his extra time was go and donate it to someone with use for it: so Kaydence went to find who had the night-watch duty with the officer, to send him to supper and early to bed.

The officer was below in his office.

Erish stood in the dim corridor outside the door to Koscuisko's office. Erish was weary; they all were, because the longer they stayed here in the Domitt Prison, the less sleep anyone got for dreaming. Erish was tired.

And Kaydence hadn't had a chance to speak to the officer since he'd disgraced himself, two days gone by now, trying to step into Joslire's place—and failing to do what Joslire could have done.

He hadn't quite understood how deep their loss was.

Part of him was terrified of Koscuisko, as well.

Frightened of the officer all of them were, at least in a sense; it couldn't be helped. A man who was capable of what Koscuisko could do was a force to be feared, quite apart from the pain that he had at command. Frightened of the officer: but trusting him, as well.

One of the things that happened to bond-involuntaries was that the power their officer had over their lives made them unusually vulnerable to their officers. Now Kaydence realized how much of his self-worth he'd placed in Koscuisko's hands, serene and confident that Koscuisko would handle his sense of self-definition as gently as possible.

He wished more than anything he hadn't said what he thought he remembered saying. He wasn't going to ask. He could remember the words in his mind all too clearly: *if you want to hurt me, it's up to you, but at least let me know you take pleasure from it. That way I know that it means something to me.*

Passion was extreme, and extremes were dangerous, but he couldn't stay out of Koscuisko's way forever. And he didn't want to.

Coming up on Erish in the corridor, Kaydence gestured with his head for Erish to leave. Erish looked a little skeptical; Kaydence nodded, to reassure Erish that he meant to relieve him. Once Erish was sure that it was what Kaydence wanted, he didn't hesitate longer. Sensible man, Erish. It was one of the many reasons Kaydence liked him.

The officer was at his desk within, concentrating on the document he'd pulled from the wall together with the prose-scan Ailynn had prepared. Kaydence slid smoothly into his post and let his mind blank, standing content on watch.

There was no sound except for the hushed murmer of the ventilators, the subtle sounds of the beverager on the other side of the door talking to itself, the rustling of papers, the turning of pages. For a long time.

Then the officer raised his voice and called for his Security.

"Erish. I want you to go and fetch Kaydence for me."

From the sound of it, Koscuisko was speaking as he moved, rising from his desk—to fetch a flask of rhyti from the beverager, perhaps. Kaydence stepped into the doorway, making his salute, glad of the moment to steel himself before he was to look upon the face of his officer.

"Here, sir." He heard only a little of his own discomfort in his voice. He wondered how much more Koscuisko was reading; the officer could do that. Joslire had said that Andrej Koscuisko smelled what you were thinking. "In what way. Can I render assistance. Sir."

No, he was still calling Koscuisko "sir" rather than the more oblique "the officer," and he had clearly heard himself refer to one Kaydence Psimas in the first person. As "I," not as "this troop." Frightened of Koscuisko he might be; humiliated over what he might have said to Koscuisko in the torture-room. But in some basic way nothing had changed. He still trusted the officer.

So could he get Koscuisko to believe that?

Koscuisko blushed, staring at Kaydence with an expression of surprise.

"Oh, Kaydence." It was a cry full of grief and guilt, and yet it was muted. Koscuisko had already convinced himself that there was nothing he could say to make things right between them: That was so like the officer. "I cannot say how ashamed I am, to have caused you to suffer. And at the same time I need information. I want you to try to find some of these Nurail for me."

Kaydence couldn't think about it; his mind shied away from the memory every time. He knew what his governor

could be like. He started forward with a confidence he did
not feel; pausing at the beverager to draw a flask of rhyti for
Koscuisko, as sweet and milky as Koscuisko liked.

"No man as full of such good drugs as I got could possibly complain, sir. On a buzz for three days still. Can't be
had for money." The cheerful cover-up sounded almost natural to Kaydence. Almost like normal. "With respect, your
Excellency. Which Nurail?"

Koscuisko looked at him for a moment longer yet, as
though suspicious that his blithe demeanor masked residual
pain—which in a sense it did. But that was Kaydence's business. And as long as Koscuisko believed that Kaydence suffered no physical distress, Koscuisko would leave it that way,
out of respect for Kaydence's privacy.

"There is first a person called Shopes Ban whom I wish
to see in the morning, if he can be located. But then the man
who has written this narrative, this Morse Wab. I want to
know what happened to him, and to the people he calls out
by name. Something is not right here, Kaydence, we all know
it, and yet I cannot yet grasp how wrong it may be."

The narrative would certainly so indicate. Kaydence had
helped Ailynn with parsing her translation out, so he had
read the translation—in a sense.

Allegations of murder by overwork and underfeeding and
neglect were serious even by the Judicial standard. Prisoners
could expect to suffer privation, without people like the officer to insist on their welfare. But prisoners were not supposed to be put to death prior to the processing of specific
charges; let alone by torture.

Offering the rhyti to his officer with a bow, Kaydence
went past Koscuisko where he stood to sit at the comaccess
on the officer's desktable. It felt very odd to be sitting in the
officer's chair. But the sense of being out of place faded fast
as Kaydence concentrated on his task.

Shopes Ban was first; no difficulty. Kaydence tagged the
officer's referral for the morning and went on.

Morse Wab was a Nurail name, and Ailynn had given it
translated flat without any hints about its Standard spelling.
He didn't need to have worried, though; he found his man
within moments.

Morse Wab was in the system, on remand.

According to the prison records, Morse Wab had arrived at the prison six months ago; and was still here, prisoner pending development of Charges. Assigned to a work-crew on the land reclamation project.

"Not dead?" the officer asked, surprised, looking over Kaydence's shoulder. Kaydence surfaced out of his concentration.

"Not according to this, sir." Kaydence pointed out the status blocks confidently. "In pretty good health, actually. On the work detail."

"Because a person has to be fit to do heavy labor, yes, of course," Koscuisko agreed, thoughtfully.

Koscuisko standing at his shoulder; Koscuisko at his back. There was a token Kaydence wanted: Suddenly he wanted it more than anything. And he could not ask. "The other names, sir?"

"Here, I have a list for myself made. What status can you find for them?"

It was a simple thing with ties as deeply braided into the fabric of Koscuisko's being and ancestry as the rest of his genetic structure was. Time-honored. Traditional. Something that belonged to a quite different sort of relationship than that in which the Fleet had bound them over to Andrej Koscuisko. The words were not very different in plain Standard: Fleet saw officer and bond-slave; Koscuisko thought of it as master and man, in a context in which both terms meant something quite particular to him.

"Skein in braid, sir. There's Mannie Bellose. Also alive. Also on work-crew."

Kaydence read the names off from Koscuisko's list, keying as he went. Several names. The spelling betrayed them on some, the prison would yield no record. But they got good hits on more than half of them, and all of the hits they got were listed as on the prison rolls and working.

"What is a man to make of it," Koscuisko mused, leaning forward over Kaydence's shoulder. Kaydence tried hard not to tense.

"Four possibilities, sir. On the off chance that the officer was asking."

"H'mm." Koscuisko was focused on the stats Kaydence had called up for him, his attention apparently absorbed by the problem. "I will speculate, and you will correct me in my recitation, Kay."

Koscuisko would only touch people at all if he liked them. Bond-involuntaries only if he trusted them to interpret the intimacy as affection, not as any of the other things it could be to a bond-involuntary—starting with casual violation of personal space, and ending all too often in physical bullying or demands for sexual services.

Did Koscuisko trust him still?

"One, that the name is wrong, simply like enough to another. But you have checked twice eight names, Kaydence, and here are ten replies. And no prisoner so named is found here dead."

Kaydence nodded. Happy to be working on developing this problem with the officer, one on one, and on an equal footing. Miserable with longing for a sign.

"Two, that these living prisoners simply share the name by coincidence. They're different people. But we should see multiple hits on single names if that happened. One dead, one living."

"Three," Koscuisko said eagerly, as though enjoying their shared understanding of the problem. "They are the named prisoners. Morse Wab, or someone representing himself as Morse Wab, simply lied, to cause embarrassment to the prison. There are speaksera. A man could ask."

Especially his Excellency could ask. Only his Excellency could lawfully ask, with a speakserum. Koscuisko held the Writ.

"Or there have been prisoners who have died without a record made, and the question of how they died and why it was not recorded is something the officer will want to investigate."

Those were the four ideas Kaydence had in mind, at any rate.

After a moment Koscuisko decided. "Order me up these people, Kaydence, we need not tell anyone why we wish to speak to them. Let the Administration believe they were named in Inquiry as collaterals. We cannot ignore the narrative. But it will be prudent to keep quiet about it."

Because there were only two out of those four ideas that seemed likely to be true; and if Morse Wab had not been lying, it meant that the Administration was committing systematic murder in full knowledge that its conduct was criminal. And under a Bench authorization, at that.

"Directly. Your Excellency."

He knew what to do.

But as he moved to invoke the prisoner calls, Koscuisko leaned over Kaydence's shoulder to peer at the comaccess, putting his hand to the back of Kaydence's neck so that his thumb lay at the base of Kaydence's skull and his fingers rested naturally and comfortably around the side of Kaydence's throat.

"How could such a thing be managed?" Koscuisko seemed to be talking to himself, puzzling out a problem. "But there is money to be made, and the staff is Pyana. I do not know what to think of it. I tremble, that it could go further than this prison alone."

The muscles of Kaydence's neck, the muscles of his shoulders, the muscles of his upper back surrendered up their tension gratefully at the touch of Koscuisko's hand. The officer was not going to stand off from him. He was still Andrej Koscuisko's man, though he was a bond-involuntary.

Relief and gratitude betrayed Kaydence to himself. He had always suffered the embarrassment of having a sentimental nature. Kaydence caught his breath and bowed his head; Koscuisko, startled, started to move, started to take his hand away. Kaydence didn't want Koscuisko to take his hand away. He couldn't ask. He couldn't explain. Had he been able to explain, he wasn't sure but that misplaced pride might have prevented him from speaking anyway.

Kaydence raised his right hand to cover Koscuisko's hand instead and hold it to him, claiming his status without words in terms Koscuisko himself had taught him meaning to.

Turning the chair on its seat-pivot, Koscuisko folded his arms around Kaydence where he sat, and held him close. Kaydence wept. There was no way in which to make Koscuisko understand. The thing about Andrej Koscuisko was that it had never been necessary for him to understand in order to be able to understand, nonsensical as that was.

After a while Koscuisko offered Kaydence his whitesquare.

Kaydence grinned, though his eyes ached. It was a joke

of sorts. Chief Samons had put him on extra duty for being out of uniform more often than any of Koscuisko's other Bonds. Boot-stockings not mended. A bit of seam come undone and not sewn back. A frayed under-collar not made right. Failure to carry a clean whitesquare at all times.

He had a perfectly good whitesquare in his blouse-plaquet.

He'd use Koscuisko's.

Tradition.

"Pyana, sir?" Kaydence asked, just to show that he'd been listening.

Koscuisko seemed to shrug, fractionally, uncomfortably. "Nurail are to Pyana as Sarvaw have been to Dolgorukij, which is to say cattle. Also, like Dolgorukij and Sarvaw, Pyana and Nurail are more alike than not so, deny it though they will."

Ethnicity and prejudice, then. Of course. Koscuisko spoke on. "In the history of the Dolgorukij Combine the most savage atrocities have been most constantly committed against precisely those people who are most like Aznir Dolgorukij. I do not mention Chuvishka Kospodar, Kaydence. But he was my great-great-grandfather."

Well, if the officer said so. "His Excellency would be interested in a staff profile, then." In order to be able to judge with more precision the extent to which Pyana held the majority of the influential positions in the prison. Affecting their potential willingness to commit murder in the full expectation of getting away with it, accordingly.

"Forgive me, Kaydence."

Kaydence froze, electrified. He had never thought to hear—he had never wanted to hear—but Koscuisko continued speaking in a quiet but utterly determined tone of voice, not waiting for an answer. Not expecting one.

"I never thought to sink to such a thing, not even with everything else that I have done. And I am so ashamed, but my shame cannot answer to your suffering."

He couldn't let Koscuisko talk like this.

He couldn't handle it.

"The officer is who the officer is." *You are what you are, your Excellency. There is no getting around it for anybody.* "It's just something we all have to deal with. Together. Sir."

This was too true to allow for argument or exploration.

The officer knew better.

Had the officer forgiven him for being alive, while Joslire was dead?

He hadn't realized he'd even been worried about it.

Now he could put the whole thing out of his mind and concentrate on pulling a report on prison staff for Koscuisko's use and analysis.

Robis Darmon's world coalesced gradually around him from a dark stifling mist of aching agony into a small cold stinking torture cell in the Domitt Prison, and he groaned aloud to realize that he was not dead yet. Not though he longed to be. Not though he waited for it. Not though his death was the salvation of those whose names he might have been able to remember once upon a time, lost now to pain and dread.

He was terrified of the sight and sound and smell of the torturer, who brought new pain with every breath.

His torturer, who tipped the cold sharp rim of a glass of water against his lower lip, lightly enough that Darmon did not recoil from the pressure against the broken skin but drank instead. His torturer was good to him, careful to see that he lacked for nothing that would preserve his life for more pain.

Still something seemed a little unusual.

He didn't seem to hurt.

His body ached, yes, and his flesh was sore, but where was the huge sharp transcendent all-consuming agony that had been his constant companion now forever?

He remembered this.

He could remember a life without pain, without physical pain, a world in which agony of spirit had been his only burden, grief for his dead, fear for the living, rage against the wrong that sought to grind them all into the mud and make good citizens of them. Yes. He could remember.

There was that glass again, and Darmon drank. The fluid caught a bit going down; his throat was rough. Screaming would do that.

"Talk to me," the torturer said, softly. "Your Shopes Ban, the one whose fate so troubles you. Describe to me this man, if you would, please."

Drugged.

That was what it was.

Drugged to put away his pain, but if the torturer was using drugs against him he was for it.

The desperation was swathed in cotton-wool, muffled in a resistance field; only dimly reverberating through his mind.

They had to have been powerful drugs.

"Thinking."

Because the torturer would know that he could hear, and speak. Shopes, poor Ceelie, what had been done to him? Of all the atrocities he'd seen since he had come to the Domitt Prison, it was this unknown horror that preyed most upon his mind. There was a point to be made. Somewhere.

"Middling tall for a Nurail, about your height, about. Dark in his features. Scar on his arm, from the fire, don't know how old he was. Couldn't have been above the age of twenty-five years, Standard."

"No, that won't do." Darmon felt a moment's panic; but the tone of the torturer's voice was light and humorous. And he was drugged. "That won't do at all. I have Shopes Ban outside this room right now, and he looks nothing like the man you have described. You simply must do better than that, for me."

This was a joke. It had to be. Yet if it wasn't . . . "Ask him about me, then. You will find. The man he knows is different. Let's bet."

"What do you say?" The torturer sounded genuinely startled. Darmon wanted to laugh.

"There are more than one of us. Shopes Bans. Marne Cittropses. None of us either Ban or Cittrops. Couldn't be. Not for months now."

There was a warmth at the wall beside him, and it made him uneasy. A sound of shifting fabric; the torturer sitting down on the floor beside him. Why?

"Explain," the torturer suggested. And tipped the tumbler to let Darmon drink, once more. Darmon hated himself for being so grateful for a swallow of cool water: but hating himself did not change the fact of his gratitude, or its shocking depth. "What is your experience of this place, that you should say such a thing?"

It had been so long.

He had suffered, since.

And still the anguished outrage that he'd felt when he had realized that Nurail were to be burned before they were so much as dead rose up into his throat and nearly choked him.

If Koscuisko wanted to hear, he could tell things that would make Koscuisko heartily sorry that he had asked.

"There were people in the cart. Fallen on the way. Young Haps, dragged. By heels. Not dead. They took him—to the furnace—"

He started at the beginning, and went through the middle to the end, when he had been taken out of work-crew to the torture. It took a long time. Every so often the pain began to build within his shattered body, from his savaged joints, his lacerated skin, his broken hands and feet. Every so often the torturer pressed him in his recitation and fed him a drink of water. And more drugs, he suspected, because the pain would fade away till he could almost forget he even had a body.

Years.

Centuries.

Centuries upon centuries, but Darmon kept at it, trying to remember, trying to make sure each man who had been drowned screaming in the water at the bottom of the ditch would be numbered, every man who had been beaten with shockrods until he bled from the eyes and ears and nose would be remembered, every man who had been worked and worked and worked—and tossed into the grillwork of the gravel-crusher, or taken living or dead to the furnaces, when he could no longer work—was named and tallied up.

The names of the dead. The names of the overseers. The names of the guards. The names of the dogs that had been set on exhausted prisoners to provide some amusement for their captors once they could no longer shovel earth.

And ever and always, the soft clear voice of his torturer, asking questions, probing for details, calling out the threads that formed the braid that was the Domitt Prison. Ever and always, the furnaces, smoking in the background of his mind.

Why did Koscuisko want to know?

Why should he care?

Finally he was finished, Koscuisko was done with questions at last, giving him to drink of cool sweet water in grave silence. And there was no pain. Nothing like the pain that here had been. Nothing like the pain that there would be, once the torturer tired of this game, whatever it was, whyever he was playing it.

Darmon drank the water and thought hard.

"You understand, such evidence must be tested before it can be freely relied upon," the torturer said. "I have in mind a speakserum, because you are very close to dead here and now, did you but know it. I will a dose of wakekeeper administer, excuse me for one moment to fetch it."

To confirm evidence was all very well, though Koscuisko had not confirmed any previously offered evidence that way. If Koscuisko had obtained evidence. Perhaps he hadn't. Darmon really didn't know, any more, what he might have said; and what managed to conceal.

One thing he had decided, though, during the long day's telling of his story. It was not the painease that decided him. It was because Koscuisko had heard the long list of the dead, and taken it into Evidence. Darmon had lived to the end of the Domitt Prison in at least that sense, howsoever small. He had survived for long enough to bear witness.

Longer than this he had no wish to live. So long as he could only get one final thing out of the way, before he died—

He remembered the first day, it had been two hundred years ago. Koscuisko had a book. Koscuisko was collecting weaves.

Darmon heard the torturer put the glass down, shifting to get up. And had sat beside him on the floor all of this time, leaning up against the wall, comforting him with the warmth of the proximity of another human body. Or a torturer's body. It had still been a comfort, in the cold of the cell.

"One thing the more, torturer," Darmon said.

Koscuisko stilled beside him. "You have something else to say about my parents, and how closely it was that they were related?" Koscuisko replied, gently, so that Darmon knew that he was listening. Darmon thought about smiling. But it would take too much energy to smile.

"If thy mother had but known. How much she could have saved us all, by hanging herself." But Koscuisko already knew that. "It's something I only imagined. I think I may have heard a weaver, once. Take out your book and write it down. If I can remember the weaver said it was the Shallow Draft.''

The torturer had dealt honestly with him, through all the obscenity of his craft. Had not forced the weave from him in all this time, that Darmon could remember. Had not asked him any questions about—

''Are you sure of what you do?'' Koscuisko asked, quietly.

''There's no telling. The weaver may have gotten the threads mismatched. But it was a persuasive weave. I can remember it almost as well as if it were my own.''

Blame it on a weaver. That would do nicely. Scum of the earth; with power that transcended it. It was a weaver who had first coded the song in the pattern of a piece of cloth, a way of writing before there was writing among the Nurail.

All a man could properly sing was his mother's weave, unless he was a weaver. A weaver could sing any weave; and make new weaves when the occasion warranted. Stricken with the calling from on high, destroyed and exalted at once; with the power to communicate any passion they felt to any Nurail within hearing distance, but powerless to control that communication—

Oh, had there been weavers here, to die in the Domitt Prison?

Koscuisko's book was like a weaver, then, if it held a store of weaves. That made the torturer a weave-keeper, and the thought was as good a joke as Darmon could imagine. Weavers were depraved, though it was not their fault; it resulted from the divine disaster that marked them as separate and apart, outside the secure ward of decency.

And weave-keepers, having weavers in their charge, participated only in the degradation; and had no share of the respect a man could not but grant the force within a weaver. Oh, sympathy, yes, that. Koscuisko a weave-keeper . . .

''Listen as the weaver sang it. It was about the clinker-built hull and the high curved prow of the ship that carried the daughter of the house over the chain and across the harbor, up the stream in summer muddy, past the shallows bottom-scraping to bring the wrath of the hill-people to take vengeance on Pyana for the burning of the houses down around her family as they slept.''

The Shallow Draft.

There was something of the weaver to Koscuisko, in a sense. He too was struck down, destroyed, and even in an obscene way exalted in the conduct of his craft. There was no accounting for all of the ways in which men walked in the world. Nor any understanding of what reason there might be for such a thing.

Waking and sleeping, dreaming and dozing, Robis Darmon sang his mother's weave, hearing from time to time the scratch of a stylus in Koscuisko's hand, the turning of a leaf of paper.

Now he had discharged his duty to the living, as well as to the dead.

Now he could die at peace with himself.

"Let the Record show twelve units of resinglas in solution for the purposes of confirming evidence received."

The torturer's voice was far, far away, and receding further moment by moment. "Three units of vondilong per body weight used for the purposes of wakekeeping for the duration. Adjusted downward in order to take the conservative approach, in allowing for dehydration."

It was only a whisper, now, drowned beneath the rising sound of the water cascading over Branner's Falls. And his wife dimly glimpsed just on the threshold of the family meeting-hall, with the child on her hip, his son, his Chonniskot. His daughters chasing around the corner of the building, the voice of the youngest brisk as a meadow-bird.

The sound of the falls was soothing in his ears.

He rested; and the trial of his life ended at last.

✧ Eleven

"How can you tell me that War-leader Robis Darmon is dead?"

Belan had seen Administrator Geltoi angry, but seldom so angry as this. He cringed in his heart for Koscuisko's sake: but the officer did not seem to feel the force of Geltoi's wrath.

Koscuisko stood politely in a relaxed position of attention-wait in front of the Administrator's desk. Somewhat closer than he had stood the first time he'd come into this office, Belan noted. As though there was more intimacy between them now . . . or less strict a gradient of rank to separate them.

"I am heartily sorry to have to report so distressing a reflection on my ability," Koscuisko replied smoothly. Too smoothly. "At the same time, Administrator. And I must point this out, at risk of seeming to excuse myself. It would not have come so soon had the drug not failed me."

Geltoi had hoped for great things from the testimony of War-leader Robis Darmon. Koscuisko had done such wonders with other, less promising prisoners. And for Koscuisko to come to report that the war-leader had revealed so little actionable information before he died was a blow. Belan didn't see what the failure of a drug could possibly have to do with it.

Geltoi sat back down, having half-risen from his chair in shock at Koscuisko's news. "Doctor. You are responsible for knowing your business. If the drug failed—isn't that the

228

same as to say you failed? To exercise professional judgment in the selection of application of specialized tools.''

All in all, Geltoi was more visibly upset than Belan could remember seeing him. It was a bad sign. Evidence from the war-leader was to have been of special value to Geltoi, since it would emphasize how deeply Chilleau Judiciary was obliged to the Domitt Prison for the resource. But it wasn't as though Geltoi had needed the additional leverage. Surely.

"Precisely so, Administrator Geltoi," Koscuisko agreed easily, with no hint of resentment. "The exercise of my professional judgment. The drug should have served as a wakekeeper, critical to that stage of the interrogation. It did not have the requisite effect, not even at a doubled dose. This is a troubling indication of potential adulteration of pharmacy stores, Administrator.''

Geltoi had been so angry when Belan told him of Koscuisko's words over the Lerriback confusion that Belan had half-expected him to call for an immediate reassignment. Belan was a little sorry for Koscuisko. He was probably accustomed to having his own way in everything—like a Pyana. When in the presence of a Pyana, however, Koscuisko was obviously outclassed.

"How so?"

Those two words were loaded with all the imperfectly suppressed outrage that Geltoi could bring to bear on a man. And yet Koscuisko did not stagger back from the force of Geltoi's contempt.

"These were stores I brought from the Domitt Prison's Infirmary, Administrator. When I brought my man Kaydence in. Based on the effect it had on my prisoner—lack of effect, perhaps, I should say rather—I can only conclude that the drug had been adulterated, but who would expect to have to do an assay on restricted stores here in the very heart of your Administration?''

They'd gotten off easy at the time, Belan remembered. Koscuisko hadn't said anything about stores. Belan had just assumed that the shift supervisor had been on top of things. Now it seemed that Koscuisko had not been as carefully watched in Infirmary as would have been prudent.

"Really, Doctor. Grasping at straws. As though a man of your caliber relies on drugs to effect his persuasion.''

Geltoi was trying to deflect the force of Koscuisko's point back onto the original problem, that of the war-leader's death.

It wasn't working.

"A man should be able to rely upon his tools. And it is my responsibility, after all. Given the circumstances I must either report myself as incompetent or conduct an Infirmary audit immediately. And I am not incompetent. I know my job."

Well, Belan told himself, Geltoi had walked into that one. He'd as much as told Koscuisko that he was incompetent. That had more or less forced Koscuisko to make the claim of adulterated drugs in order to defend himself against a bad report. Geltoi should rather have left the point alone.

"I hardly think that now is the appropriate time for such an audit, Koscuisko—"

Geltoi had seen the trap he'd laid for himself, but it was too late. Koscuisko merely insisted, with polite deference, on what it was Koscuisko's lawful right to demand on whim.

"Forgive me for saying so, Administrator Geltoi, but I cannot agree. I must know whether the stores in Infirmary are reliable. Only in this way can I protect myself from a recurrence of this shocking incident. To have lost so important a prisoner to death by systemic shock, because the wake-keeper was adulterated—it cannot be tolerated."

Koscuisko had a right to defend himself against accusations of incompetence, too.

Why hadn't Geltoi seen this coming?

"Very well." The Administrator had no real choice but to concede. And they all knew it. "You may conduct your audit two days after tomorrow. I'll send an escort for you."

Kitchen audit. And now an Infirmary audit. As far as Belan knew, Geltoi hadn't heard anything back from Koscuisko on the kitchen audit yet. On the other hand, Koscuisko had been busy.

"Thank you, sir. And good-greeting, Administrator Geltoi, Assistant Administrator Belan."

Day after tomorrow . . . so that Geltoi would have time to ensure that stores were rotated and replaced. A day in which to cover for themselves. If Koscuisko had meant to make trouble, he would surely have insisted on going now, and there would have been a scandal. Why had Koscuisko agreed to the delay?

In order to give Geltoi time to make the shortfalls good? What sense did that make?

Koscuisko would find no serious irregularity in his Infirmary audit. Geltoi would see to that. Or, rather, Belan would see to that, on Geltoi's instruction. That meant Koscuisko's story about losing the prisoner to an adulterated drug would seem the flimsiest of excuses: Geltoi would probably enjoy making that point with him, too.

"As you say, Doctor Koscuisko. Good-greeting."

Of course Koscuisko could always claim convincingly that the medication he had taken was one bad lot in an otherwise unremarkable stores inventory, and cover up his error that way.

It hadn't been an error.

They all knew that very well—he, Administrator Geltoi, Koscuisko, all of them.

Koscuisko would come out of this looking incompetent, surely.

Except nobody could take Koscuisko as incompetent on the strength of his previous performance.

Was this some sort of a signal that Koscuisko meant to transmit thus indirectly to Chilleau Judiciary?

And if it was—could he really trust Administrator Geltoi to see what was going on, in light of how easily Koscuisko had maneuvered him into the trap just now?

Administrator Geltoi watched grimly as Koscuisko left the room, glaring at the Inquisitor's back as though to plunge daggers into it. Large ones. Long blades. Sharp points.

The glare made no perceptible impact on Andrej Koscuisko.

The door closed behind the Inquisitor, and Geltoi turned his cold furious gaze to Belan's face, as though he were to blame for the scene, having witnessed it.

"You know what must be done," Administrator Geltoi snarled. "Get cracking. There isn't much time. Spare no expense. And be sure the documentation is in order, this time."

Still smarting over what Koscuisko had had to say about the Lerriback confusion, clearly.

Not to speak of the amount of money it was going to cost

to make Infirmary stores whole, after all of these months of harvesting prison stores for the black market. The drugs were there for prisoners, of course. But prisoners couldn't complain about their treatment.

Belan bowed in respectful silence and left.

He wasn't happy.

Administrator Geltoi had not come off the better in this interview. Koscuisko had handled the Administrator as easily as—as easily as if Geltoi had been Nurail, and Koscuisko Pyana.

What if he'd been wrong?

What if Koscuisko found out the things the Administrator had assured him would stay buried forever—

No.

Belan shuddered, and had to stop in the corridor, leaning up against the wall to steady himself.

They had been buried alive, he could still hear the screaming, and on late nights as the mist rose from the damp ground it was hard to avoid seeing faces in the night-fog. Nurail faces. Dead and half-rotted. Screaming in disbelief and terror forever, as they had died.

He had put his trust in Administrator Geltoi, and Administrator Geltoi knew what he was doing.

No other possibility could even be entertained.

Infirmary audit.

Yes.

If he went to see the senior staff physician now, right now, he could be well clear of the containment wall before the sun went down, and he would have nothing to fear from the tortured dead.

Mergau Noycannir could have shrieked in rage and frustration: but she had more control than that. It was just that the provocation was extreme.

Two of the prisoners were dead.

One of them useless for days to come, having bitten her own tongue clear through to avoid speaking. The First Secretary's censor might well claim it had been in response to an excess of pain: but if people bit their tongues through every time they were put to the stretcher there would be no evidence obtained from seven out of eight of the wretches.

Three prisoners, and no information.

Mergau slammed her fist down atop the open tray of doses from the Controlled List that were arrayed in the work-room, ready for her use. It wasn't fair. She was being watched too closely; this wasn't an offsite. She didn't dare spike the Levels with the First Secretary so interested in what results she might be getting, day by day. And she had lost three out of seven, two for good, and had got no useful information. Oh, information, yes, that. But nothing the Bench could use against the Langsariks.

She mastered her emotion with an effort. Her fourth prisoner was in the room with her, behind her on the work-table; and she had to maintain her superiority before him. Granted that he was probably not paying attention: There was never any telling when a prisoner might notice what, to the detriment of the exercise.

The whole difficulty lay in the fact that these people were accused on circumstantial evidence alone. The Protocols were clear. People could not be forced to incriminate themselves on the basis of circumstantial evidence; they could only be pressed to do so. If they were determined enough to withstand the maximum lawful degree of pressure, the Bench would grant them not guilty by default; and release them.

She was not allowed the efficient out, the obvious out, the one best technique for obtaining confession. The coercive classes of speaksera were only authorized at the Advanced Levels, and she wasn't authorized to invoke the Advanced Levels against these people. Yet.

The Bench required more evidence than circumstantial before it would allow the Advanced Levels prior to receipt of a confession. She was to be expected to obtain the high-quality evidence that only a speakserum could reliably deliver without the use of the only tools she had to obtain it reliably.

If she'd been offsite she could have cheated, gone off Record and invoked the Eighth Level. Then she could have her confession, and after that whatever speaksera she wanted. There were ways to invoke the Eighth Level that left no obvious visible physical evidence on Record; it had worked for her before.

She didn't dare.

There would be too many questions about the chronological gap, if she went off-Record in the middle of one of these interrogations.

Taking a deep breath, forcing herself to be calm and in control, Mergau started to sort the doses back into array on the dose-tray. They had been jarred ajumble when she'd struck it with her fist. The Controlled List, but what good did it do her? Wakekeepers were authorized, yes, but only at a very low level. Pain-maintenance drugs not at all. Nerve agents so moderate as to be functionally useless to her need, and speaksera restricted to the guarantee of candid speech, with no coercive aspect to them.

The doses had got mixed up.

It took some thought to get them sorted out again.

And when she had finished sorting the doses, she noticed that she'd inadvertently included an Advanced Level instrument in amongst the Intermediate Level drugs that the psychopharmacologist from Gatzie had selected for her use.

Nor was it just any Advanced Level instrument, it was her favorite, Andrej Koscuisko's finest contribution to the Controlled List, the one she used more than anything else. It worked on almost all classes of hominid, and in much the same way.

And if it frequently hastened the prisoner's death, what difference did that make, as long as she got the information? It was an Advanced Level instrument. Referral at the Advanced Level meant a death sentence one way or another, either execution for crimes confessed or death under torture to obtain confession in order to put the prisoner to death for crimes confessed.

And here it was, neatly replaced, in with her row of authorized and appropriate medications.

Did she dare pretend?

Advanced Level for most classes of hominid, yes; that was doubtless why it had been held out from her work-set this time. But Intermediate Level for some classes of hominid, and very effective in the Intermediate Levels at obtaining satisfactory results if a person chanced to make a small error and use it on the wrong people. Its inclusion in her work-set would not surprise her. She could easily have overlooked its sudden appearance in her work-set, in her concentration on her task.

She could make it work.

Even if the First Secretary reviewed the Record—and there was no reason to expect he would—no one need ever even notice. She had expected to use one drug. She would announce the drug she intended to use, on Record. It would take a psychopharmacologist or an autopsy to surface any small mistake on her part. Mergau anticipated neither; and once she had the information . . .

She picked out the stylus with the dose and turned back to her waiting prisoner.

She would prevail.

She was not Koscuisko; but she was as good as, and all that she was doing was exactly what he must have done, to have built up such an inflated name for himself.

"Let the Record show administration of six units of tincture of quillock per body weight."

Six units would do it, all right.

Yes, that would take care of the problem once and for all.

"So we'll get an Infirmary audit out of the way, all to the good," Administrator Geltoi sneered bitterly. "And we haven't had any complaints on the kitchen audit. Still our young Koscuisko makes demands, then calls for prisoners off of work-crew, and not so much as three words in courtesy to explain why he needs thus-and-such a soul."

Well, because the prisoners currently under interrogation had named the names, Belan thought to himself. Standing quietly beside Geltoi's desk, waiting for his instructions. Geltoi was annoyed about the prisoners as much because they had to be pulled from work-crew as anything else; and the work-crews were starting to thin out a bit. The Domitt hadn't gotten a good shipment of replacements in since Koscuisko's arrival.

"What are you going to do, Administrator?"

That wasn't exactly Koscuisko's fault. Or was it? They couldn't afford any irregularities, not right under Koscuisko's nose. Captain Sinjosi Vopalar seemed as little inclined to leave administrative details to locals as Koscuisko had proved himself to be. Their Port Authority contacts were worried about questions one of Vopalar's junior officers was asking, and it was rumored that Koscuisko had put him up to it.

Maybe that was actually Koscuisko's fault, come to that.

Rising from his chair, Administrator Geltoi turned his back to gaze out of the window toward Port Rudistal. "Losing money on work-detail, we can't supply the labor, not between Koscuisko and that Captain Vopalar. Losing money on victuals, the kitchen's gotten nervous and timid, insists on serving what we're issued for the duration. Losing a great bloody chunk of money just so Koscuisko can't find anything wrong in Infirmary. And he killed Robis Darmon, Merig, make no mistake about it. We could have had more evidence from him."

Which would have strengthened their hand at Chilleau Judiciary in case of any awkwardness: that was the unspoken subtext to Administrator Geltoi's argument. Belan didn't like it. Why did Geltoi feel the need for insurance?

The Port Authority and the kitchen might be excused for suffering a failure of nerve. But Geltoi was the mastermind. Belan believed in him. If other Pyana started to feel concern, did that mean that they weren't smart for Pyana?

Or that Geltoi wasn't smart for a Pyana?

If Geltoi wasn't really in control of this—

The idea was unthinkable.

"Perhaps if you were to make complaint to Chilleau Judiciary," Belan suggested, a little diffidently.

"And why the people he wants for the work-rooms?" Geltoi ignored the question, clearly more concerned about his own issues than what Belan had to suggest. "There isn't any logic to it. What's he up to?"

They could just ask.

Belan was tempted to propose they do just that. Koscuisko had been blunt enough about whether or not Darmon's death had been attributable to a blunder on his part. Maybe all they had to do was ask—and Koscuisko would tell them.

Maybe it was important that they know.

There were voices in the fog between the wall of the Domitt Prison and its containment wall, when the fog rose. It could be clear in front of the building. It could be clear at the north of the building. The fog would still creep out of

the ground on the south side of the building, at a little remove.

Right where the massive crane had been anchored in the
ground to lift materials onto the fast-rising floors of the Domitt Prison.

Right where the bodies of those dead were buried, but they
hadn't all been dead when they'd been buried, and the chem-
ical accelerant the Pyana had dumped into the pit to speed
decomposition ate into living flesh and burned like fire.

Belan had been there.

He had heard the screaming.

The voices didn't scream, they only hinted, teased,
warned, proposing riddles that drove him half-mad. He
hadn't gotten out of the building in time, last night. He'd
been forced to spend the night in his office, pretending to be
working diligently.

Now Geltoi turned back to the desktable and sat down
once again. Sighing deeply. "He's really left me with no
other choice, Belan." Geltoi's tone of voice was aggrieved,
as though forced into some action against his better judgment. "I'd rather we had been able to work things out, but
he's chosen not to bring his concerns to me before taking
official action. This isn't the sort of conduct one expects from
a ranking officer."

The words and phrases flowed in majestic measure. Rehearsed, almost. Maybe Geltoi *had* rehearsed. Artificial, one
way or the other—all except Geltoi's undoubted frustration
with how things had worked out for them.

"I can't accept a working relationship that's all take and
no give, the Administration does deserve some consideration,
after all. I'm asking Chilleau Judiciary to recall Andrej Koscuisko to *Scylla*. No Writ at all would be better than this
one."

One hand flat to the table's surface, Geltoi waited for a
response, staring at Belan. Oh. It was time for the chorus,
then.

"Such an undeserved disappointment." Yes, that had been
his cue; the look of irritation that had started to build in
Geltoi's eyes faded into bland self-satisfied self-pity. "After
you took every measure to see him comfortable and provided
for. Treated him with every evidence of respect."

Shut him up on the roof, and that so effectively that as far as Belan knew Koscuisko hadn't noticed yet. Koscuisko had taken guards from the torture-block to show him the way to Infirmary. Not their fault if Koscuisko had refused to wait even as short a time as it would have taken to call down to Infirmary and let them know Koscuisko was coming.

"Thank you. Good friend. You're a great help to me, Belan." And an accomplice, in this up to his neck. That was the way to translate Pyana. Praise was only given to point out the threat. "We should be through with Koscuisko's stunts soon enough. I can be gracious. He won't get the satisfaction of provoking me into undignified reprisals."

No, Belan thought, in sudden silent rebellion. *You'll get me to make them.*

"You're a true leader, Administrator." Aloud he only recited the lines he knew were expected of him. "It's too bad Koscuisko couldn't have learned from your example."

Else Koscuisko would be butchering his prisoners and demanding adulation for his hackwork. Rather than taking a slow and methodical approach, which yielded results for almost every death on Koscuisko's hands since he'd arrived at the Domitt Prison.

Administrator Geltoi waved Belan away in dismissal, a look of pained and patient noble suffering on his face. Belan bowed and went away.

Just in time.

He had had all of Administrator Geltoi he could take for now.

What if Geltoi wasn't smart?

What if the truth about the Domitt Prison should come out, somehow, some way, despite all the Pyana cleverness that had surrounded it from the very start?

It wasn't going to happen.

Pyana were smart, and Geltoi was Pyana. Also Koscuisko was leaving. Things would be back to normal in no time.

But he'd brought a nice length of good rope to the office, just in case he was mistaken after all.

" 'Multiple and egregious instances of behavior betraying a regrettable lack of delicacy and sensitivity to his position of responsibility within the structure of Judicial Inquiry.' "

First Secretary Verlaine read aloud, his voice remarkably light for such a deep bass and his tone emphatically less than serious. " '—Which would be in themselves unimportant if support for the Inquisitorial function was being exercised at an acceptable level of skill and professionalism.' Oh, my. He *has* annoyed somebody."

Morning-meeting, and Verlaine was sharing the new items on his desk. Mergau was resigned. Her disgrace was temporary; and could be best managed if she showed herself to be quite unconcerned about it. Not dismissing the gravity of the situation, no. Simply serene and confident that anyone could make a mistake.

Inquisition was an imperfect science at best, and it would all be behind her soon enough. The language the Domitt Prison's Administrator had used to complain about Andrej Koscuisko was unquestionably strong; if even Koscuisko could fail, that would strengthen her point. On the other hand, Verlaine was unquestionably not very upset: that would have rather the opposite influence on the question.

"Koscuisko's Captain wants him back," Bench Specialist Vogel observed. "There's a request in. To support his medical function, not his Judicial one, since *Scylla*'s duty status is still suspended. Maybe it would be just as well, but there's something that should be bothering us about all this."

The timing couldn't have been better had she planned it, Mergau congratulated herself. She could see the record cubes in Bench Intelligence Specialist Vogel's loose-fingered grasp; autopsy or Record or both, it hardly mattered. If Andrej Koscuisko, for whose reputed skills and talent the First Secretary had such evident if undeserved admiration, could lose a prisoner before time to a bad dose—why, any failing on her part was more than adequately covered.

"Bothering us?" The First Secretary leaned back in his chair, relaxed and receptive. "Please, Bench Specialist."

"Young officer, historical behavior pattern of doing first and asking later. Only look at what he's doing. The kitchen audit was mentioned in the First Secretary's morning report."

As part of the usual summary of daily activities at the Domitt Prison. Yes. Mergau remembered it, because otherwise very little had changed in the Domitt Prison's morning report for weeks.

Vogel spoke on. "Kitchen audit is standard operating procedure. I was reading the Fleet staffing reports for Rudistal, though, they've got an officer working on admissions reconciliation. Vopalar's got a lot on her hands and no reason to detail anyone to makework projects. I haven't asked, but I'm willing to speculate that Koscuisko's asked for a population movement analysis."

Bench intelligence specialists got into everything. Gluttons for information, no matter how inconsequential. Clearly Vogel felt called upon to come up with a story to justify the fact that he spent all of his time with his feet up on the furniture, reading laundry lists.

"Now this." Ivers picked up the thread as though she and Vogel were in the same braid. Maybe they'd rehearsed, to see if they could impress Verlaine's staff with their superior knowledge. "Koscuisko invokes an Infirmary audit, but he's given the Domitt Prison time. So he's not out to find something wrong. Gave them—what? Three days? To make any shortfall right."

Which was proof of Koscuisko's clumsiness if any was needed. He could have had the Administration of the Domitt Prison in the palm of his hand, if rather than tipping them off so far in advance he'd made a surprise raid.

Unless he knew very well that there was nothing wrong with the drug upon whose adulteration Koscuisko blamed the premature death of War-leader Darmon. That way when he found no discrepancies, he could claim that the Domitt Prison had cleaned itself up during its three-day grace period: His failure was covered.

Maybe she'd have to reconsider, reluctant though she was to do so.

Maybe Koscuisko was a little less useless at political survival than she'd thought.

"All in all, First Secretary, it looks like a signal. It's possible that Koscuisko is trying to get our attention. Learning from past mistakes, perhaps."

That went a bit far, Mergau thought. But the First Secretary sat up, leaning over the desk surface with his forearms propped against the edge of the desk.

"Something's wrong at the Domitt Prison?" Verlaine asked. "Or at least Koscuisko thinks there is. And is trying to get us to think about what he's doing, so we can get an audit team in there without embarrassing the Second Judge?"

No, Koscuisko was nowhere near so deep as that. And for once it seemed that even the Bench intelligence specialists realized it. Ivers knit her dark straight eyebrows and qualified, carefully.

"Possible, First Secretary. There's no way to tell for sure without either talking to Koscuisko or sending an audit team. The Domitt Prison hasn't stood an operational audit yet. It's due."

Verlaine frowned. "If we asked him . . . but there's no way to do it. Not informally. If he's trying to get us to send in an audit team on the whisper-run it's because there's something he knows we don't want on Record." The First Secretary should learn from the Bench intelligence specialists, Mergau thought. He'd been too impressed with Koscuisko from the start. "And it is due, you're absolutely right about that."

Shifting in his seat, restlessly, Verlaine took thought for the problem before him while Ivers and Vogel kept shut. As she did as well, naturally. She was in disgrace. She'd failed him.

"Mergau."

First Secretary Verlaine caught her eye, and stilled himself where he sat. She braced herself: but she wasn't too concerned, not right now. The conversation had yet to begin to touch on any delicate questions about how a drug that was lethal for a certain class of hominids had ended up in her rack. It was just bad luck, really. How was she to know?

"Yes, First Secretary?" She kept her voice bland and neutral; not blaming, but not accepting blame, either. If the doctor had excluded the speakserum because it was poison, rather than merely not authorized, the doctor should have told her. Accidents happened. And it wasn't as if more than one of the prisoners had died of it; that left four to be forwarded to the Fleet Inquisitor Verlaine had called for. One of whom should be able to speak again soon enough.

"We send in an audit team here and now, just as we're pulling a Writ on reassign, it'll raise a question or two,"

Verlaine mused aloud, looking at her. "I have an idea that could serve instead."

Vogel and Ivers were looking at her as well, now. It was difficult not to blush, just out of frustration. Vogel and Ivers blamed her: She knew they did. Too bad for the Bench specialists. Their Fleet resources would get them no further than she had done already. She had gotten very little information, but at least it had been timely.

Their decision to hold the remaining prisoners for the *Ragnarok*'s Inquisitor rather than suffer her to do her job only meant that what information they got in the end would be so old it would be functionally useless. If in fact they even got any more information, at all.

"Could control it that way," Ivers conceded, with evident reluctance. Mergau wasn't quite sure she believed what she thought they were going to propose to her: but if the First Secretary meant to entrust her with this—well, the Bench specialists could divert Fleet Inquisitors all they liked.

She was safe from challenges to her position, if the First Secretary was willing to put this into her hands: but Ivers hadn't finished with her thought. "One of us might accompany Dame Noycannir, in that case. Speak to Koscuisko in confidence, let him know that you heard what he had to say, First Secretary."

Verlaine nodded. There was relief in his voice, underlying the undoubted seriousness of the situation. "Very well. Mergau. We'll send orders to relieve Koscuisko, you take his place. Give us an on-site evaluation once Koscuisko's got out of there. We'll take a few weeks to get it cleaned up—whatever it is—and then we'll have an audit. We probably need one. But we don't need it public."

Keeping her face grave—she'd made a mistake with the speakserum, she felt badly, because even though it had not been her fault she was too professional not to take it personally—Mergau made explicit the job Verlaine seemed to intend her for. "I'm to go to the Domitt Prison, First Secretary?"

To be mistress of that place, after all. To hold the dominion. Even better now than it would have been before, because Verlaine needed her to manage a problem that he couldn't afford to let become public. Up to her to protect the Second

Judge from Bench criticisms over the irregularities that Andrej Koscuisko apparently thought existed.

She would have more influence than ever before.

"And right away, Mergau. Miss Ivers, if you'd do the errand for me I'd take it very kindly of you. Carry Koscuisko's orders by hand. No inadvertent miscommunication."

And wouldn't Koscuisko like that, to be turned out of the Domitt to make room for her?

"Four days, by courier," Ivers reminded him. "Do you want to send word ahead?"

Verlaine thought about it: but shook his head. "Can't risk it, Miss Ivers, or rather I don't want to risk it. He has a right to know it'll get fixed, whatever it is. It's just not reasonable to expect a man with his history to go home to *Scylla* without saying something, if we don't reassure him."

Reassure Koscuisko all you like, Mergau thought. *You and your Bench specialist. Coddle the darling dandy all you want.*

I will be mistress of the Domitt Prison.

Security escorted Shopes Ban from cells into the workroom, following Andrej. Once the door to the torture cell closed, they seated the prisoner on the block; and then came forward, standing to either side of Andrej where he sat in turn.

"Shopes Ban. My name is Andrej Koscuisko, and I hold the Writ to Inquire here at the Domitt Prison. There are some questions which I wish to ask."

No answer. Well, why should there be? He knew the crucial difference between simply stating that he held the Writ, and affirming that he held the Writ to which the prisoner was to be required to answer; but there was no reason to expect Shopes Ban to know.

Turning to his drugs-rack against the wall, Andrej checked his secures, out of habit; good. No one had tampered with these medications. If the Domitt Prison was as corrupt as he had begun to fear it was, it could well be that someone would take it into mind to thwart him of his purpose by silencing his sources before time.

Taking up an anti-anxiety agent to couple with the speakserum, Andrej turned back to the prisoner, who was looking confused. Still very worried. Sensible man, Shopes Ban. An older man, older by perhaps eight years or more than War-leader Darmon had been. Andrej put the dose through, and explained.

"This is a Fifth Level speakserum; it will not compel your speech, but will assure me that what you say is true. This is required for the Record to stand in Evidence, let the Record show administration of twenty-five units of eralics in sterile solution, five of dition to accompany."

The Record was secured. Only a Judicial officer could read it, since the Record was the basic legal document upon which all legal actions under Jurisdiction were founded. Administrator Geltoi was not a Judicial officer for the purposes of access to the Record. And the only Bench officer in Port Rudistal with a Judicial function was Captain Sinjosi Vo-palar, serving in the dual role in token of her command.

Andrej was counting on that.

"Dition is a soother, Ban. It should help you relax, be-cause although you are in prison and have been called here to me you are not here to answer to Charges, but to satisfy my curiosity."

Not as if that would mean anything either. Questions were questions. That was the real reason Andrej needed Erish and Code here with him: Their unspoken—but unwavering—support was his best help against temptation to put his ques-tions more forcefully than necessary, just because he could.

It would take a few eighths for the drug to take effect. Andrej sat down. He would use the time to establish the ground rules for this interview.

"I have of late with a prisoner named Marne Cittrops spo-ken. He has claims against the Domitt Prison, and they are damning. And also he was afraid that a man named Shopes Ban had been murdered, and yet the Shopes Ban he described to me is nothing like you."

Was it his imagination, or did the prisoner flash him a look of scornful mockery at that?

"His accusations were specific, and of a very serious na-ture indeed. For this reason I mean to question you about these allegations. The speakserum will guarantee the veracity of your responses. Also for the same reason"—the seriousness of the allegations, he meant, was he even communicating, at all?—"you are not to be returned to the work-crew, but sequestered here in holding till I have concluded my investigation."

He couldn't possibly keep them in here, in torture-rooms. And the Administration had filled the sixteen holding cells full of prisoners for the torture as quickly as he could empty them. There were eight cells up on the next level, however, where his office was, being used for storage.

There was obviously no way in which he could risk returning these people, once called out, to the general prison population. If he had been in Administrator Geltoi's shoes, he would have found ways to justify putting pressure on them outside of Protocol or in violation of Protocol in order to discover exactly what Andrej was doing with them.

"Can't help you," the prisoner said, suddenly. His voice sounded a little strained. Code drew a tumbler full of water and gave it to Shopes Ban to drink. Ban emptied it greedily and held the tumbler up, soliciting another go—testing the boundaries of this environment. Astute. Andrej nodded, and Code refilled the tumbler from the drinking-tap. This time the prisoner only drank half of it off: but he kept a good grip on it, declining to return it to Code. Still thirsty.

"I can't help you. I'm not Shopes Ban. Whoever Shopes Ban is, he's dead. It just happened to be my turn when the name was called."

"Even so." It was a disappointment; but one that he had half-expected, based on Darmon's testimony. "What is there to tell me of Marne Cittrops?"

"Now, there's an interesting question." The prisoner sounded bitterly amused. "When I came on to work-crew Marne Cittrops was this one man, big and square-like, eyes greengold. Changed midshift into some half-starved child, beardless, eyes as black as the lake-deeps."

As he spoke the bitterness seemed to lift a bit, replaced by simple enjoyment of his joke. Maybe the drugs were taking effect. "And more than that. Ten days ago, or thirteen. They called him out as Marne Cittrops to the work, and by sundown they'd changed his name, he was a different man. Imagine that."

Very much as Darmon had said. They'd arrested Darmon

as Marne Cittrops on evidence that Darmon had believed could only have come from Shopes Ban—who was almost certainly not Shopes Ban to begin with. They'd filled behind Cittrops with another man, but they hadn't bothered to change the name until they'd realized that Andrej was becoming concerned about accountability.

Thirteen days ago?

Had it been so long since he'd called Belan to account over that supposed Lerriback?

"Then if you would tell me what you know of Shopes Ban, if you are not he." If someone had gotten evidence out of Shopes Ban, it had been obtained outside of Protocol. Any special authorizations at the Domitt Prison had to come across Andrej's desk: and there'd been none.

The prisoner shook his head. "I've no threads in that weave, your Excellency. Is that what to call you?—Only that he went out on work-crew on one morning and was killed. Or died. Most likely murdered. And I called out to the work-crew in the afternoon, to take his place so that the count would be correct when we returned to prison in the evening."

Exactly as War-leader Darmon had said.

There was no help for it, then. He had to take testimony. The Domitt Prison had to be brought to account. And to do that he needed evidence.

He had the prisoners named in Wab's narrative to ask. He could ask the sixteen miserable souls who sat in cells waiting to be tortured. They wouldn't understand why he was asking. But he would still find out.

"Tell to me how you came to the Domitt Prison. How it has gone with you since. What you have seen. What you have heard. Tell me what you know about this place."

It would need as persuasive a set of interrogatories as he had ever prepared to bring him and his Security safely through the storm that would break over them if he declared failure of Writ at the Domitt Prison.

Three days, and Infirmary was ready to stand audit.

Merig Belan had checked the stores himself prior to calling on Koscuisko in the penthouse to escort him. Koscuisko brought his Security with him, his Security and his Chief of

Security all together. There were procedures for Infirmary audit: Among them, the requirement to team in threes, one to count, one to record, one to watch and attest by counter-signing. Koscuisko had to bring all of his people with him. It was the only way he could make two teams.

Down the main lift, where Koscuisko hadn't been since the day he'd arrived here. Out on the first level. When Koscuisko had come down to Infirmary before with his stricken bond-involuntary, it had been a different way. But that had been because he'd come through the work area. Unexpected. Unlooked for. And very unfortunately, in the end.

But why hadn't Geltoi expected this?

A medical officer, a pharmacy, what was more natural than that Koscuisko would feel himself called upon to certify stores?

Here was Infirmary, neater and brighter than Belan thought it had ever been. All the duty staff present and waiting. All of the uniforms clean. But Koscuisko wasn't interested in meeting staff; he let Belan introduce him, he was polite, but once that was over Koscuisko excused them all.

Threw them out.

Secured Infirmary stores against them, locking the pharmacy up. Belan didn't like it. It made him uneasy. And he was part of it; Geltoi would not for one moment tolerate such an audit of his stores without an observer.

Part of it, yet, but with nothing to do but sit or stand around and watch the procedure as Koscuisko and his people took dose by dose, store by store, exhaustive inventory of everything there. Belan wished they'd thought about the linen; there wasn't enough on the shelves, not really. But the staff didn't worry too much about linen for Nurail patients.

And why should they? Any patient referred to Infirmary came in dirty from work and left dirty for work, so what sense did it make to invest in clean linen?

Then one of Koscuisko's teams went on to keep counting while Koscuisko himself turned to assay-work. The lab setup at least could not be faulted; the lab facilities had scarcely been used since the Domitt had opened its gates to its first inmates. Geltoi needn't worry about the sufficiency of lab facilities.

Was that a problem?

Was there some point that Koscuisko could make about the fact that the lab was so little used, with a prison population of more than four thousand souls?

Not four thousand. No. He had to remember. Two thousand and four hundred, and no more. And maybe it was so few as that; it had been a while since there had been any new bodies.

Time wore on.

Shift changed, at thirdmeal.

Belan knew the work-crews were returning to the prison, being fed in the mess hall and hurried into cells. He was beginning to feel a little hungry himself. A good eight into thirdshift, the prison would be quiet, the guards would have eaten, the Administrative offices closed up for the night—

If Koscuisko didn't hurry, Belan told himself, he'd be stuck here till morning. Of course he could go out of the main prison gate, and avoid the Administration building and the fog beside it. Maybe that would work.

"Very well, Administrator Belan."

Koscuisko's people were finishing up, putting things away. Belan stood up stiffly from where he'd been sitting, bored and irritated.

"It's all in order. If you've got the report, please."

He could have told Koscuisko that hours ago. He knew it was all right. And how much it had cost to make it so. "Very good, your Excellency," he echoed, stupidly, then wished he hadn't used those exact words. Koscuisko might think he was making fun of him: and nothing could be further from his intent than that. "If you'd care to sign, sir. His Excellency doubtless knows where the validations are required?"

Setting the documents out on the countertop in the lab, Koscuisko bent over them. "There's for you as well, Administrator. Here. And here. Also on this back page, see the place, here."

Yes, attesting to the fact that he'd watched the audit. Affirming, alongside Koscuisko's statement, that a physical inventory had been made, and in proper form. The assay slips were all stacked to one side. Once Belan had signed, Koscuisko took the assay slips and sealed them in the documents-case with the rest of it.

Good, Belan thought to himself, wearily. *We can go home*

now. Of course for Koscuisko "home" just meant upstairs, back to the penthouse, and no problem for him if it was after the thirdmeal, there was a cook to feed him whenever—

"All quite correct." Koscuisko passed the entire package over to him; Belan took it in two hands. Koscuisko's Security had gathered around him, waiting for their officer. But it was a little odd; and suddenly Belan felt insecure. "Now, one thing else, and we won't trouble you further. I need to make an unannounced inspection."

"Of course." Belan's response was immediate and automatic. Unannounced inspection? Of what? Where? "His Excellency has only to direct. The Domitt Prison is open to you, sir."

There was some sort of an unspoken message passed between Koscuisko and his people, from him to his Chief of Security and to his Bonds. "You are very obliging," Koscuisko assured him, courteously indeed. "Take us then to the furnace-room. And I must insist that no one anticipate our arrival, Administrator."

The where?

The furnace-room?

The sound of the screaming grew louder and louder in Belan's memory till he believed that he actually heard it. Koscuisko must hear it, too. Why else would Koscuisko want to go to the furnace-room, if it was not that the dead Nurail cried out to him for vengeance?

"Quite impossible. Sir." He had to protest: He couldn't allow it. To take Koscuisko unannounced to the furnace-room would amount to betrayal of Geltoi's trust. He couldn't do it.

"But I insist." Cordially, politely, Koscuisko took his arm, and turned Belan toward the door. "Just the seven of us. Show us the way. There's nothing to hide, surely, Belan?"

Of course there was nothing to hide. There couldn't be. Administrator Geltoi ran an efficient prison. There was no answer for Koscuisko's question, none that would not compromise them one way or the other.

Koscuisko took Belan's silence for an answer in itself, or pretended to.

"Well, then. You see. Take us to the furnaces, Administrator Belan. Take us now."

There was nothing that he could think to do but comply.

◆ Twelve

Andrej Koscuisko had been dreading this since the moment he had begun to understand that it had to be done. There was no way around it. He had to see the furnaces, himself; and he had to see them as they were, at the end of the day's work, when the garbage was to be dumped into the incinerators. Before anybody had a chance to hide something that might be compromising. He hated doing it to his Security: but it had to be done.

He didn't want to see the furnaces.

Joslire was dead, and every time he thought about the furnaces he thought about Joslire. Things were getting confused in Andrej's mind: between Joslire who had been sent on high in fire at the hospital, and prisoners whose bodies were destroyed by fire here; so that he found himself confounding Joslire with Nurail prisoners, imagining the horrors he had heard in evidence these past few days as happening to Joslire.

And it was bad enough that anyone should suffer through such fearful horrors, without the accusing ghost of a dead man coming into the picture.

Strolling with casual purposefulness with Belan through the halls of the Domitt Prison, Andrej concentrated his mind on where he was and what he was about. Why would Joslire's spirit be accusing? Never in his life had Joslire found fault with him: and yet it was the feeling that Andrej had.

There was no one in the corridors to see them, to report to Administrator Geltoi; Andrej had had Kaydence select the time very carefully, taking shift-change and assignment into account. No one to talk to. Andrej wanted to talk, because he was afraid. But if he let Belan know how reluctant he actually was to seek the furnaces, Belan might feel emboldened to resist, or try to run away.

He had to keep his fear within himself. He was in control here, after all. He was the Writ on site at the Domitt Prison.

And if atrocities were taking place under his Writ, and he did not end them, his ignorance of their existence might protect him from legal difficulties, but he would be damned just as deeply as if he had himself planned all of the crimes that he feared he suspected—

Down stairs into the basement levels, avoiding the lifts to minimize the chances of being noticed. Two levels down from the ground floor. It was murky and hot in these maintenance corridors, poorly lit, poorly ventilated, and a rumbling groan within the very walls of the maintenance fans venting the smoke and the stench of the fire into the damper-vent system and out through the roof. There at the corner of the basement, where the walls above turned, there was a wide chute from stories up; a wide chute, and a conveyer, silent and still for now.

Miss Samons was keeping an eye on Belan for him. Andrej stepped forward, past Kaydence and Toska, to peer up through the darkness above to try to see where the chute opened from and how far up it went. No luck; it was black, above, but there was a draft that made Andrej think the chute vented into the Domitt's courtyard. Outside, where it would be getting dark, where the temperature was falling even as the sun set. A rubbish-chute.

He leaned too far over the lip of the chute, looking up. Andrej lost his balance. Falling forward over the base of the chute, he put his hands out to steady himself; but slid down against the slippery surface of the chute to fall heavily against the conveyer, before Toska had pulled him safely to his feet again.

The conveyer started moving.

Weight-activated.

Once it had started, it didn't seem to notice that Andrej wasn't on it any longer. Standing there, watching it, Andrej stared stupidly at the conveyer for a long moment before he realized what it was saying to him.

Follow me.

Nodding his thanks to Toska for the welcome reassurance of Toska's protective strength, Andrej Koscuisko walked alongside the conveyer-track to see where it might lead.

It wasn't far.

The sound of cursing could be clearly heard as he went down the length of the conveyer to where it passed through the fabric-fringed maw of a thermal barrier, into the furnace-room beyond.

"... filthy piece of Nurail trash. Move it. Get that stack shifted, you, there's more trash coming, who's out there culling the cattle at this time of night?"

Cattle. Nurail prisoners, he meant, whoever it was who was swearing. There was a hand-secure on the entrance gate beside the conveyer belt; Andrej gestured with his head for Erish and Code to bring Belan forward.

"If you would be so kind." Andrej pointed. "Open, here."

At this point he could set himself to ride the conveyer belt through the thermal barrier, but there was no telling what was on the other side. It would be better not to risk it.

Belan palmed the secure.

Nothing happened.

With a look of sickened desperation, Belan pulled a white-square from a pocket in his sleeve and wiped his hand. Belan would rather almost anything than be here: so much was evident from his face. So Belan knew what was in the furnace-room. And Belan was dirty.

Dirty, but cooperating, because he put his hand to the secure once more, and this time the lock recognized his now-dry palm and bowed to his authority. Disengaged. Opened the door.

Quickly, without waiting for Security, Andrej stepped across the threshold and went in.

The furnace-room was brightly lit, two stories high, and three times as long as it was deep. Andrej could see a work-crew toiling at a pile of debris under the whip of a Pyana overseer, another overseer belaboring a man who knelt—trying to cover his head, to shield it from blows—near to one furnace-gate; another sitting at a table near the door, at the back wall, with the remains of a meal spread out before him and a jug of what was probably a beer of some sort that he was using even now to refresh his glass.

None of these things could distract him or diminish the visual impact of the furnaces themselves. Five furnace-gates, stretched along the back of the wall. Five great grim doors, and darkness behind two of them, but the other three gate-windows aglow either red or yellow or white.

They'd been noticed.

The overseer who'd been eating put down his jug, hastily, rising to his feet. "Assistant Administrator Belan!" He called the name out loudly enough to be heard from one end of the room to the other, even over the noise from the furnaces.

The overseer who'd been tormenting the lone Nurail coiled his whip into his hand hastily, hurrying forward. The other formed his work-party up between the furnaces and the door, where he could keep an eye on them while speaking to their superior.

"This is an unexpected pleasure, sir." The Pyana overseer had left his table to greet them more formally. All the same, the emphasis seemed to Andrej to be on the word *unexpected*, and the Pyana looked keenly into Belan's face with an unfriendly eye for all of Belan's superior rank. Belan was Nurail. Andrej hastened to claim the blame for himself.

"The visit is specifically to be unannounced," Andrej answered, in Belan's defense. The overseer should know who he was, even if the overseer had never met him. "For this reason I made quite sure that Administrator Belan could not be accused of having tipped you off in advance. In this manner there can be no question raised about whether the Administration has passed the audit honestly."

It was duplicitous of him to imply that the furnaces would pass audit. But Andrej wanted the truth of what went on down here; that meant getting the Pyana overseer's cooperation. "Now perhaps you would to me the operation show, furnace-master?"

It seemed to work.

"Well. If you say so, sir. Excellency, your Excellency?" the overseer corrected himself, hastily, glancing to Belan for verification. Pyana were precise where titles were concerned: Every bit as concerned about correct categorization as Nurail, from whom they were—in the larger sense—culturally and linguistically indistinguishable. "No offense, your Excellency. Where to start. Well. Let's start here, then."

The conveyer. Where the debris to be burned was carried into the furnace-room. It had to be discrete chunks of debris, actually, rather than heaps of scraps and bits of things; because the conveyer's terminus was well short of the furnace-gates themselves.

"Waste comes in through here, bundled. The work-crew stacks it next to the furnace, depending on which furnace fires next."

Walking Andrej from the conveyer to the pile of debris that was being built next to the black mouth of one of the furnace-gates. The furnace-gates themselves were huge and heavy, by the looks of them, and got hot even past all of their thermal shielding; that was the reason for the clublike tool that leaned up against the hinges, Andrej supposed. To knock the bolt free when the furnace-gate was to be opened during use to accept a new pallet of fuel.

"Two kinds of debris to be disposed of, your Excellency. The office waste and such-like, that's no problem. It's these that take a bit more managing, if the officer please."

And "these" were the bodies of the dead.

Andrej had feared as much; it was not unexpected. And still the sight of the dead piled like kindling frightened him in some way that he could not quite explain to himself. It was not that it was indecent to burn the dead. He had burned Joslire, and it had been a comfort to protect the abandoned body by alchemical reduction to the ash; so it was not horror that bodies should be burned that frightened him.

There were too many bodies on that pile.

He'd done his research carefully, planning this inspection. He knew how many were on mortality report, day by day, over the past weeks. There should be no more than so many dead, waiting to be freed from the memory of their bodies in the fire. And there were more than there should be.

"In order to write the inspection report." His throat was dry. He wanted a swallow or two from the overseer's flask: but that was probably out of the question. "It will be necessary for me to examine these dead, and take a rough count. If you would provide for me the assistance of your work-crew, it would spare my gentlemen the unpleasantness.''

Surely this was not unreasonable. The work-crews had to do this work day by day, surely they were in some part inured to it—unlike his gentlemen. Unlike himself: but he could not hope to be spared unpleasantness, it was for him to take responsibility for it.

The overseer shrugged and bowed and gestured, and his fellow hurried the work-crew over to where Andrej stood waiting for him. That one lone Nurail prisoner who had been beaten as Andrej came in was lying on the floor, apart, ignored. Andrej wanted to go see how bad it was. But he had to keep himself in character, aloof and professional, else he would not be able to observe everything that he needed to take in evidence.

The work-crew unpiled their careful heap of bodies, laying the dead out on the floor in rows. "It will be necessary for my report to identify this work-crew by their names," Andrej lied to the overseer, taking his little notebook out of the chestplaquet of his overblouse. "It's customary to provide this information for the prison's protection, so that anything I may say in my report may be challenged by witnesses. Your name?''

Not so much a lie, perhaps. But more important than the audit was his need to try to protect the work-crew from execution once he'd left. The prison might destroy the witnesses on instinct. If he knew them by name, perhaps the prison would have to think twice.

"Shan Morlaps. Good, yes, and your mother's people hold? The Ringing Rock.'' Oh, in that case, one of Shan Morlaps's family was dead, Andrej had murdered him not three weeks gone by. He had the weave. At least he had the words, and as much of the music as he'd been able to transcribe to his satisfaction.

As difficult as it could be to speak under torture, to sing melodiously was all but impossible; but the tune could be corrected from the threads in the woven-weave, if necessary, so that was not so much at issue as the words. "And your father's weave. Yes, I insist. You may whisper it to me in confidence, I know how prudish you Nurail are.''

Better than that, if the overseers didn't know what name was given and written down it would decrease their confidence in being able to substitute. Andrej wanted these people alive.

The Nurail leaned closer, grabbing for Kaydence at Andrej's side to steady himself and keep his balance without giving offense by touching the officer's clean uniform with soiled hands. Whispering, he spoke, half-choked with grief or shame; or perhaps both?

"My father carried the Rose of Thirdmonth, in his life. Write it all down and witness to it, officer. These men are murdered outside of the Law."

The Nurail had no reason to expect Andrej to keep his confidence, no reason to look to Andrej for hope or help at all. But had apparently made up his mind to take the chance that Andrej would listen and hear. Andrej kept his face clear of distress. "Thank you, very good. And next?"

Yes.

He knew that murder was being done.

Once he had evidence, he would see the murderers punished under Law, as they had punished and killed outside of it.

Justice would be done, or his name was not Koscuisko, and Joslire—and Robert, and Kaydence, and Toska, and the rest—had never trusted him.

And yet the strictest justice under Jurisdiction could never make this right, what had happened at the Domitt Prison. . . .

Kneeling down next to the bodies, Andrej worked quickly. He didn't want to give the guards any cause to think twice: so it was important that he appear to be casual, even cursory, in his investigation. He was being watched, of course. But at least so far, the Pyana overseer didn't seem to have begun to worry.

And why should they?

Because they were the final damning link in the chain that was to bind Belan and the rest of the Administration over to the Bench for abuse of authority, and failure of Writ. That was why they should be worried.

Most of these dead seemed to have died of natural causes, not of trauma. Overwork and underfeeding, that was natural enough, wasn't it? Overwork, because hands were hardened and blistered beneath the callouses, torn even through skin toughened by hard physical labor. Underfed, because the muscle had wasted; and cardiac muscle would fail, under too great a strain, and leave the dead with just those expressions of surprise or startlement.

But there were also victims here of torture.

They were not people that Andrej knew, no names of weaves in his hand-book. How could they be? He'd been taking evidence on speaksera alone, these three days past. The Darmon was long since burned. And it hadn't been Protocols that had killed the men he found, but brutal treatment of the less formal, less effective kind. Ingenious and abhorrent, but that wasn't what separated it from Andrej's Writ; only the fact that this torture had not been sanctioned under Jurisdiction.

It made no difference.

Or at least these men, these two tortured dead, were as dead as if they had been killed under the exercise of the Writ to Inquire; so what difference did it make?

It made a difference.

As indefensible as the tortures Andrej had to hand, they were still ruled by Jurisdiction, subject to the Bench. Lawful, if intolerably unjust.

And the torture that had killed these men was not even that.

All right, he had been wrong to think that the detention block had ceased to operate outside of the Law on his arrival. Darmon had told him that, if not in so many words. Andrej himself had all but realized that it had to be the explanation for the story of Shopes Ban; but he hadn't wanted to believe it. All of these months. Should he have kept a closer watch on things?

How many had been brutally tortured by Pyana for no reason and with less authority while he had kept to the comfort of his penthouse, and indulged himself in the long drawn-out agonies of the punishments available under Protocol, and ignored any questions that might have come to mind about where the referral information was coming from in the first place, or how it had been obtained?

He'd sat still in one place for too long, staring at the wounded face of one of the dead. The overseer had taken notice: would be wondering. "It is always satisfying, to see a thing thoroughly done." Rising to his feet, Andrej kept his voice as light and cheerful as possible. It was easier than he had expected: There was part of him that meant every word. "And now I have made more work for your crew, but I have seen all that is needful. What happens next, furnace-master?"

As if he didn't know. He didn't need to number every one; he had the information he'd wanted to gain, from the bodies that he had examined. Both in their number and the manner of their deaths, the Domitt was condemned.

"His Excellency will have noticed that three of the furnaces are on line. Two of them off." The overseer was a little more reserved; Andrej walked with him, smiling and attentive, to soothe what suspicion might have started to arise. "Two, here, was fired yesterday. It takes each of them six shifts to run a cycle, and then we do preventive maintenance once the oven has had time to cool, that takes another shift."

Raking the ashes. Recycling stubborn matter to the next firing. The bodymill at the hospital had been much more efficient, but had only been intended to take one body at a time. To burn as many so quickly would represent too great a cost in extra fuel and in heat-shielding: and there was no way in which the Domitt could have been designed from the start to burn so many dead so regularly.

Could there be?

"The fire feeds itself, furnace-master?" Andrej asked, to keep up his part of the conversation. To the far right of the furnace-room, the work-crew were piling the bodies back up on a low sort of a trolley. There were tracks, from the furnace-gate out into the middle of the room. Andrej hadn't noticed them before: but now that the overseer opened one of the cold furnaces he could see that the whole floor of the furnace was on rollers.

Gridded.

A complicated apparatus, the furnace, with a false floor and a pit beneath as deep as his arm was long, nozzles and floor-vents and thermal gridding above. To capture the heat and inject oxygen, perhaps.

"Nothing wasted," the overseer agreed with a cheerful grin. "Any melt-off collected and added back. A beautiful piece of work if I say so myself, your Excellency, not that I had a hand in its design."

He couldn't grasp the implications of those words. He couldn't. He knew what the man was saying. His mind fled from the understanding: Andrej turned away, to walk back to the second cold furnace, before whose now-open door the work-crew were waiting with the loaded trolley.

"Such a conservation of resources can only be commended. Really, it takes one's breath away, furnace-master." If not in the sense it might be taken to mean. "They will fire this furnace for me now?"

The one prisoner who had been beaten had stumbled to his feet at last, and joined the others on work-crew. Pale and shaking, and bloodied on his face. The others tried to support him as best they could without being too obvious about it.

"Yes, your Excellency, we're going to put today's trash in the fire." The overseer had raised his voice so that it carried clearly; and his tone had become overtly threatening. Directed at the work-crew. "And if it wasn't for respect of his Excellency's presence, Mivish would go too. Right on top. Lazy. Filthy. Nurail."

That one prisoner, the beaten man. His whole body jerked, as if in a spasm of pure terror. The others restrained him from falling to his knees, holding his arms to prevent him from covering up his face in an agony of fear. The overseer smiled with savage pleasure.

"That's better. Professional bearing, Mivish. None of your malingering. Load the furnace, Mivish can stay out. For now."

It could be only a threat, cruel but never to be implemented.

And still it seemed too evident to Andrej that none of the work-crew took it for anything less than real, and near, and even commonplace.

It was getting harder by the moment for him to breathe, why was he stifling in this place?

The Nurail work-crew pushed the trolley from behind, guiding it forward with their hands against the bodies of their fellows. Fellow prisoners. Fellow Nurail. Family. Sons and brothers, fathers, nephews, cousins, brothers of mothers, husbands of daughters.

The trolley groaned beneath its burden of dead flesh, coming to rest within the furnace's oven with its rollers locking into place with a clearly audible report of metal against metal. The bodies had moved a little as the trolley tracked. The arms and legs were no longer as neatly stacked as they had been, although the work-crew had laid them down as decently as probably they dared.

Just this one final demonstration and he could be out of here, Andrej promised himself. He'd said he'd come down to inspect the furnaces. He couldn't really leave without standing to watch as the cycle was started with the day's debris. Only a few more moments and he could get out, get out and get away, and write the orders that would shut these furnaces down for good and all before a single Nurail the more could be so horribly threatened as Mivish had been—

But if the furnaces were on such a cycle, and if they had all the time they needed to cool down before they were opened up again for maintenance, why was a tool required to shoot the bolt?

And what was that clublike wooden instrument beside the furnace door if it was not needed to knock the furnace bolt back while the furnace was still hot?

Wondering, half-reluctantly, Andrej picked the wooden thing up from its resting place to examine it in the light.

Blood on the club-end of it.

Dried blood, and matted hair.

So now he knew, and was he any the better off, for knowing?

"There's sometimes sport to be had, your Excellency," the overseer called out. "Where's my friend Mivish? Come here, Mivish, I want you to see this, it will do you good."

Andrej put the club back down and went to join the overseer in front of the now-closed furnace door.

Secured and sealed, the furnace stood ready.

The overseer coded its initiate sequence.

There was nothing for a moment, except for a hissing sound—injection of oxygen, Andrej supposed, to fuel the fire.

Then the furnace seemed to blossom, inside, into a great strange flower made of red-gold petals quivering in profusion over the flower-bed of fuel that gave it life.

The furnace-window was wide, large and generous; there

was room for more than one to stand and watch. The overseer had the hapless Mivish by his side, now, one arm around
Mivish's neck; and talked to him.

"Take a good look, Mivish, how do you fancy being inside there? We have no use for boys who won't do as they're
told, Mivish, but you're a good lad, I like you. So I'm going
to give you one last chance to learn better."

And Mivish was no more a boy or lad than Andrej was.
Andrej stared into the furnace, dazed with shock in the realization of how badly wrong it had all gone; how oblivious
he had been to clues he should have pursued more aggressively, a long, long time ago. Blind and stupid with grief and
lust. Blind with grief for Joslire, ever and always turning his
face away from the furnaces, not willing to think about them.
Taking pains not to think about them. Stupid with lust to
make his prisoners suffer, and willfully unmindful of anything that might stand between him and the consummation
of that destructive desire.

Something shifted, within the furnace.

Andrej sensed Mivish recoil in fear, but the overseer kept
a good grip on the man. There was nothing to fear. Bodies
moved in a fire. Muscle warmed and relaxed or contracted,
joints worked as heat grew intense enough to stiffen tendons;
that was why poultry was trussed for the roasting, after all.
Bodies moved, but slowly, and there was no sentient spirit
that motivated them, it was only the heat.

Bodies moved, in the fire.

But not like this.

There was a man in the furnace, a living man, clawing his
way out desperately from the middle of the pile of bodies.
This was conscious movement, desperate beyond Andrej's
will to understand it, a living man inside the furnace scram-
bling across the top of the pyre right toward him. Screaming.
Reaching for the window as the skin of his palms blackened
before Andrej's very eyes.

Scratching frantically at the window with blackening fingers, his mouth stretched impossibly wide in horror and in
agony while the hair began to shrivel on his head for heat;
and then his clothes caught fire—

The fire bloomed around him, all around him, flowing
down his body like water as he screamed. Andrej knew that

he could not be hearing the screams through the noise of the furnace. But he heard them regardless. The Nurail prisoner Mivish was retching now, in horror, and the Pyana overseer—chuckling indulgently—took Mivish's head by the hair, forcing Mivish to face forward and look.

"There, now. That's nice and cozy, isn't it? All of that could be yours, Mivish. And will be. The next time you give the least, I mean the very least, trouble."

He had not checked them all. Nor had he checked that they were all really dead. He had not thought. Darmon had told him; but he had not thought. It was his fault, that there was a living man inside the furnace.

"Can you not do something?" Andrej asked; and knew it was the strangled sound of his own voice that startled the overseer into releasing Mivish at last. "Shut it down. Make it stop. There is a man alive, in there."

But even as he asked it, he knew the answer.

"With respect, sir, can't be done." Once the man was burned like that there was nothing to do but to let him go. "It's too much heat inside to vent out all at once, your Excellency. The secures can't be forced."

Yes, and in such heat as that a man would not know how he was suffering. A man's brain was soft tissue, vulnerable to heat, and with the fire roaring within there would be nothing for the man to breathe. There was nothing to do. He had put a man living into the fire—

He was trembling, he couldn't help it. He couldn't speak; his words would not have made sense had he been able to. He could no longer see the furnace in front of him, and raised his hands toward his face to steady his head so that he could focus. He couldn't focus. It was too much. He coughed, to drain the fluid in his throat before it crept in the wrong direction to his lungs; and his cough came out a cry, instead. Horror and dread.

He had put a man still living into the furnace.

He couldn't stop the cries in his throat.

Security tried to restrain him, hold him, but they could not begin to understand. It was even worse that people were put into the fire. He had put a man into the fire. If he had only checked them all, but he had thought that they were dead. How could he have imagined they would dare show a living man inside the oven, in the presence of an inspecting officer? He'd fooled them all too well—but it didn't matter.

It was his fault.

He could have saved that man, had he but checked.

Crumpling slowly to the floor, supported and protected in the arms of his Security, Andrej Koscuisko collapsed against the furnace-gate and howled with guilt and all-consuming shame.

It was his fault.

It was all his fault.

He should have known that something was wrong, and much, much sooner.

How many had been burned since he'd been here?

How many of those burned had been alive?

And why should he not go into the fire, here and now, and pay the price for all that he had done?

"And so I came straightaway, Administrator," Belan concluded, in utter misery. Administrator Geltoi hadn't cared to be called back to the prison after dark. It interfered with the party his wife was hosting for their second daughter's birthday: but there was no help for it. "Koscuisko has been down to the furnaces, I think he may have been counting the bodies. What are we to do."

He swallowed back his desperation. Geltoi would think of something. Geltoi was Pyana. Geltoi had everything under control.

Geltoi was angry with him, drumming his fingers against the desktop irately. "I don't know, Merig," Geltoi said flatly. "You've really done this one. I'm sorry to say it. Couldn't you have thought of any way to hold them off? Anything at all? Or were you only too happy just to do as you were told?"

That wasn't fair. He was supposed to do just as he was told. He was only Nurail. He didn't have Geltoi's brains. Geltoi would have come up with a way to avoid taking Koscuisko to the furnaces: but Geltoi hadn't been there.

Belan had no answer but to stand in silent agony, biting his lips.

After a moment Geltoi sighed.

"All right. I'll help you out of this one, Merig. It's our

honor that's at stake.'' Geltoi toggled into the braid on his desk. ''Administrator Geltoi. For the penthouse, please. And shut down all of the access routes first, the lifts, the emergency stairs, everything.''

The penthouse?

Why the penthouse?

When the circuit cleared, it was the voice of Andrej Koscuisko. A little strained. Emphatically wary. Belan thought about the look he'd seen on Koscuisko's face when he'd been watching through the window into the furnace-gate: and shuddered.

''This is Andrej Koscuisko. And you are Administrator of a prison in which much fault is to be found. What is it, your word to me?''

It was a voice-link; Belan was just as glad. He could hardly bear the sound of furious contempt in Koscuisko's voice. To see it in Koscuisko's eyes would be difficult: and yet Geltoi seemed unmoved.

''And good-greeting to you as well, Koscuisko. It has come to my attention that you have declined to support your Judicial function over the past few days, preferring rather to construct specious arguments against this Administration. You are to be replaced as soon as orders come from Chilleau Judiciary.''

Yes, well, but they hadn't heard from Chilleau Judiciary. They didn't know if Chilleau Judiciary was going to replace Koscuisko yet. Maybe it didn't matter. Maybe all that mattered was getting Koscuisko out of there, with enough time to clean out the furnaces and clean up the work-crews before the next inspection. If there was a next inspection.

''For the exercise of my Judicial function it is not my intent to even consider apologizing, Geltoi. What good do you imagine it will do, to send me to *Scylla* back? There is evidence to convict the Domitt of failure of Writ.''

Geltoi smiled. Koscuisko had stepped foot into a Pyana trap, it seemed. ''Which can only be cried by the Writ on site, Koscuisko. As of now I no longer consider you to be the Writ on site. You should be quite comfortable in the penthouse while you wait for orders. For your sake I hope it won't be long. Geltoi, away here.''

Grinning broadly with evident self-satisfaction, Geltoi

pulled the braid. Belan stared, confused and worried; Geltoi rose and stretched, signaling for his car.

"And that's—that. Security's shut down the penthouse, Belan, there was a reason why we wanted to be able to control access."

Shut Koscuisko up on the roof.

He could not cry for vengeance to the Bench if he could not gain access to the Bench.

And once Koscuisko's orders arrived from Chilleau Judiciary, he would have no standing to complain of the Domitt Prison; it would be only the new Writ assigned who could do that. By then they could be ready. This experience had been valuable, if too nerve-wracking for Belan's peace of mind. They knew better how to comport themselves in front of Inquisitors, now.

"Of course, Administrator." Belan didn't need to pretend, to be impressed and humbled. Geltoi had it all in hand. Why had he ever worried? "My instructions, sir?"

Because he had been down to the furnace-room with Andrej Koscuisko. That was why he worried. He was the one who'd seen. Who'd heard. He was the one who'd been there.

"Take the furnaces off line as they complete cycle, Merig, clean them out and let them stand. We'll dump the leavings underneath the dike-wall when we're ready to pour the next course, and in the meantime we can just get ourselves so sweet and fresh and pretty that there'll be no proving we ever burned so much as a scrap of steakbone in those furnaces."

"And in the penthouse, sir?" There were prisoners being held in the store-rooms by Koscuisko's office, prisoners secured under seals only Koscuisko could lift. There was water in the store-rooms, which had been built for cells. But who was to feed these people, if Koscuisko was to be prisoned in the penthouse?

"Oh, it won't be but a few days." Geltoi hadn't forgotten about the extra prisoners, surely. Geltoi had been too angry about them at the time Koscuisko had called for them: because they diminished his work-crews, and he needed every available man on work-crew to make his ambitious construction schedule work. And because he couldn't figure out why Koscuisko had called for these people by name.

Belan knew.

Belan knew that the fog had told Koscuisko.

Belan also knew better than to even hint as much, to a Pyana like Geltoi.

And Geltoi was still talking, as he moved past Belan where he stood to go back to his gracious home in Rudistal once more and enjoy his middle daughter's birthday. "Won't do them any harm. Have a schedule ready for me in the morning, Merig, we can discuss the furnaces, all right? I'm sure you didn't have anything else planned."

No. He didn't have anything planned. And Geltoi knew quite well that Belan couldn't leave the Administration building if he was caught here after dark. The fog rose. And there were voices. "Of course not, Administrator. I'll get right on it. The least I could do, sir, after failing you so miserably in the first place."

He had to say it. He did feel utterly miserable: though he wasn't quite sure it was because he'd failed Administrator Geltoi. How had he failed? What could Geltoi have done differently?

Why was it wrong to reveal the corruption at the heart of the Domitt Prison, rather than conceal it?

"Never mind that, Merig, we'll recover." Geltoi didn't think it was a problem. Geltoi only thought that other peoples' mistaken perception that it was a problem could create awkwardness. "We'll speak no more of it, but see you have that schedule in the morning."

There was work to do in his office, waiting for him.

And a bottle to drink himself stupefied as soon as he was finished with it.

Caleigh Samons rejoined the others in the officer's front room, shaking her head. "No luck, your Excellency. Locked down. Tighter than drunk-detention on an abstention ship."

Koscuisko sat on the couch, leaning well forward with his hands clasped across his splayed knees. He'd finally stopped shaking.

They were prisoners here.

Kaydence knelt down next to his officer with a cup of hot sweet rhyti, holding Koscuisko's hands around the cup as Koscuisko drank. All right, Koscuisko hadn't quite managed to stop shaking. As shocking as the impact of the furnace-room tour had been, she didn't think that was the entire explanation for Koscuisko's fit. This had to be something that had been creeping up on him, perhaps for weeks, possibly without his conscious notice.

"It is clear to me what must be done." Koscuisko's voice shook, even as his hands did. "Administrator Geltoi. I have given him too much time in which to understand. He means to keep us out of the way until he can get orders to relieve me."

The housekeepers had locked themselves into their rooms; Cook was in the kitchen, with nowhere else to go. The emergency exits were sealed shut: blast walls, solid across the floor of the stairwells. Solid as the lift-accesses were sealed, both of them.

This had been coordinated.

"What is happening? Sir." Ailynn was much more confused by this than anyone. She hadn't been down to the furnace-room.

"Thank you, Kaydence. Again, please." Koscuisko seemed to have recovered sufficiently to be able to drink his cup of rhyti on his own power. Kaydence hovered over him like an anxious parent, and it was always funny to see Security being protective of Koscuisko, when they could so easily have needed protection from Koscuisko instead. And not gotten it, being bond-involuntaries.

Beckoning for Ailynn to come and sit beside him, Koscuisko waited until Kaydence had come back with more rhyti, bringing the brewing-flask with him.

"Ailynn, I do not know what they say in service house about the Domitt Prison. I do not want to know," Koscuisko said quickly, to forestall a reply. "There will be time in which to provide testimony, later."

Chief Samons didn't think the penthouse was on monitor. They'd swept during the first few days, and periodically since. Koscuisko was being careful not to compromise Ailynn, just in case there were monitors that they didn't know about.

"We made an unannounced inspection of the furnace-room just now, Ailynn. We have seen things that will be difficult for the prison administration to explain, and you

heard Geltoi, they do not wish to be called to account for
any of it. I hope they feed those men in second-holding.''
The thought seemed to distract Koscuisko for a moment. But
he was surrounded by people waiting for his word; after a
moment he returned to his main stream.

"The prison administration is fatally corrupt, and the people who have been responsible must be brought before the
Bench to face extreme sanctions. It is called failure of Writ.''

Koscuisko was speaking so calmly and carefully for the
benefit of a woman who might not know the jargon that the
critical phrase almost passed before Caleigh snagged on it.

Failure of Writ?

With the sanctions the Administration potentially faced, it
was not out of the realm of imagination that the prison administration might try to arrange an accident—

"Administrator Geltoi must have me replaced before I can
go on Record, if he hopes to evade his responsiblity. Or face
the possibility of a Tenth Level command termination.''

Ailynn should have some idea. Surely. She had been the
one to translate the narrative, after all. On the other hand,
Koscuisko did not discuss the results of interrogation with
anybody: and Ailynn might easily have assumed that Koscuisko would take the torment of Nurail prisoners as
inconsequential, the way the rest of the Judicial establishment seemed inclined to do.

"Sir, have you found—all true—" Ailynn's horror
reached out and touched Caleigh's own feelings about the
furnace-room; and Caleigh shuddered. She'd read the narrative, too.

Koscuisko nodded. "And the evidence I have taken in
these last three days is damning. I have been blind to the
enormity of this thing, Ailynn. And now that I understand
what has been going on I must not fail in my duty. There
are so many dead to cry for justice.''

"If the officer, and his party. Should meet. With an unfortunate—accident—''

Erish had trouble getting the words out; Caleigh was surprised he spoke at all. It was a good sign, though. All of the
things that had happened to them here. And her troops still
knew that they could trust Koscuisko.

"It is an option.''

Koscuisko's frank endorsement of what she'd been thinking was a little unnerving, in its calm acceptance of the possibilities. Calm? They had pulled Koscuisko away from the furnace-room in a fit. Maybe he was just in shock. He sounded perfectly lucid. But shock could do that.

"It would create more problems than it might solve, however, and upon this I must rely for now. There has been one threat against my life in Port Rudistal already, if one may be excused for interpreting Joslire's death in so selfish a fashion."

Well, that was all Fleet and the Bench made of it. Security's job was to die in the place of senior officers of assignment. Koscuisko simply wasn't very rational about the issue. But he did have a good grasp on the official interpretation of the incident.

"The Port Authority would be called upon to validate that any accident was not sabotage or terrorism, and if it could be covered up there would still be my family to deal with. The Combine would be sure to take an interest in how an accident could be permitted to damage the management resources of the Koscuisko familial corporation."

This seemed to comfort Koscuisko as he spoke; he even smiled. "In fact it would be almost certain to invoke the Malcontent, and no secret is safe from the slaves of Saint Andrej Malcontent, gentles. They are the Bench intelligence specialists of the holy Mother's church. No. I do not think a prudent murderer would try it, and we have no reason to suspect that Geltoi is a desperate or imprudent murderer. For now I think we are just prisoners."

There were pieces in Koscuisko's logic that Caleigh didn't quite follow. That was all right. She had no need to follow his meaning. She trusted his judgment. And it was true that Koscuisko was a political figure in his own right, even only in the Dolgorukij Combine, even only as an inheriting son.

Geltoi might not know that . . .

"For now we are safe. I must cry my claim to the Bench before orders of reassignment are received by the Domitt Prison. And I must do so before Geltoi has a chance to destroy the evidence of his crimes. Miss Samons. We will need to get to the Administration building tonight; please explain how we are to do so."

Desperate men did desperate things. Anybody with a potential Tenth Level facing him could be excused for becoming desperate. Koscuisko was right, if for different reasons than Koscuisko might think.

Koscuisko was determined to declare failure of Writ while he still could.

Once Koscuisko was on Record, killing him would no longer be of any earthly use to anyone.

Night, and the sky was black and clear and cold. The breeze that had blown from the river to the land in the hours around sunset had fallen still and calm, but the damned furnaces still sent their plumes of milky smoke into the sky. Andrej shuddered at the sight of the white feathers in the night. To think. No. He could not afford to think.

"Miss Samons, please forgive me, and I hope to ask you this question only this one time." He stood a little apart with his Chief of Security, watching Toska and Erish secure the cable around the anchors they had built in the garden. "It is a reflection of my ignorance, I do not mean to challenge your judgment. You are sure that this will work. It is a long way."

He was the one who had said they had to get to the Administration building.

That she should go over the wall on a cable braided of torn sheeting had not been something he could have anticipated.

"It'll hold, sir. And the distance parses out."

Two eights until daybreak, two hours until sunrise. The lights had been on in the Administration building all night. There would logically be someone in there on night-watch, if only for appearance's sake.

For the rest of it, during all the time they had been here there had been no surveillance or patrol of the space between the prison and the containment wall that anyone had noticed. Chief Samons was convinced that that was reasonable, given Kaydence's analysis of the other securities built into the installation. Andrej could only hope that she was right.

The Administration expected anyone who managed to escape from the prison to make straight for the containment wall, not break into Administrative offices. Andrej leaned cautiously over the low safety barrier that spanned the vista gap in the wall, looking down. Chief Samons pointed. "And the fog is on our side, look there."

She was right.

There was a filled-in construction pit to the south side of the Administration building. And from the pit, a mist he'd seen in the early morning hours, rising in frothy columns from the ground, tendrils of moisture curling in the absence of any breeze. Fog rose strangely when it rose. Andrej had never quite understood what it was that caused the mist to creep or rise; something to do with warm moist soil and cold air.

The fog from the construction pit had risen much more thickly than he had ever seen it; or perhaps it was just the difference in time? It was a solid blanket in the night; not even the lights from the Administration building could penetrate far into that fog. The fog would cover them for most of the descent down to the ground.

Would they be able to find each other in the dark?

There would be the lights from the Administration building.

And his gentlemen had their gear with them, and that meant one of them was carrying the nightscope.

Toska went back into the darkened penthouse to fetch something or another, and Erish came up to salute.

"We're ready, sir. Chief. Cousin Ailynn to go with Kaydence, sir?"

That had seemed best. Chief Samons had assured him that his Security were fit to make the descent safely, and that he himself was not to lose his grip and fall upon pain of her displeasure. Kaydence was the man they all agreed had the most strength in his upper body; he was to carry Ailynn on his back. Leaving her behind was out of the question, because of the evidence she had in her mind. Andrej had rather hoped they would suggest building a harness of some sort in which to lower her down; but he had not been so lucky.

Here was Toska back. Security formed up at the wall, the coils of braided cable glistening on the ground. It was a very great waste of sheeting, in a sense, and they'd been lucky that the linen stores had held clean linen for the ten souls that had been expected to sleep there. Good quality sheeting it had been, too, especially that intended for his bed and that of Chief Samons. Excellent for load-bearing.

So Security was kitted up and ready to go. The house-keepers had been barricaded into quarters, to ensure that there would be no interference. Cook locked into the pantry for prudence's sake, and very understanding Cook was about it all, too.

"You have the narrative?" Andrej asked Ailynn, who stood close to Kaydence in the line. She opened her front-wrap and showed him: tied on a cord, and hung around her neck. Yes.

All right.

"Chief Samons, your action."

She had briefed them.

They all knew what they were to do.

"Switch on your nightscope, Code." Code and Toska would go down first. There were two cables, and Kaydence and Erish were letting them down over the wall in preparation for the descent. "Two tugs, then three, when you're ready. Kaydence goes next with Ailynn, Code, on your side. The officer next on Toska's side. Erish and I come down last. Then we move."

Didn't he know they could do it?

Didn't he know they would be all right?

Code and Toska saluted briskly and stepped forward. The braided cables were stretched taut between the anchors and the wall, now, and Code and Toska each sat down on the low lip of the vista gap. Feet to either side of the knots they'd set in the cable at intervals. Leaning well back to slide slowly down the other side of the vista gap and start down.

Andrej made a prayer to the fog in his mind. *Hide these people. Protect these people. It is no disrespect we mean to the walls or the grounds of the Domitt Prison. It is only what has been done here on these grounds, within these walls. We come to remove the shame of those crimes from these grounds and walls. Protect these people, hide them from un-friendly eyes.* .

They seemed to wait forever.

But the signal came up the cable strong and reassuring at last. Two long slow pulls at the now-slackened cable. Followed by three shorter pulls. Code and Toska were on the ground, and at least so far there was nothing they could see or hear that indicated the potential existence of a problem.

"Tuck up your skirts, cousin, and wrap your legs around my waist, now."

Kaydence's cheerful advice was carefully quiet, but the fun he had in his mildly suggestive comment was clear even so. It was too dark to see if Ailynn blushed. Kaydence took a moment, sitting on the lip of the vista gap with Ailynn pick-a-back, making sure of his grip, settling himself for the descent.

Andrej hated this.

Carefully, slowly, Kaydence edged himself over the wall, creeping down the rope in small controlled movements with Ailynn holding fast to his shoulders with her arms around his neck.

Kaydence could do it if anybody could.

Kaydence could do it.

The tension on the braided cable was terrible, and Andrej remembered the tests Chief Samons had insisted upon, unable to quiet his fear that it might fail regardless. He couldn't see them, when he looked; the fog was too thick. It had run well past the top of the Administration building; was it his imagination, or was it even thicker than it had been when Toska and Code had gone down?

Oh, clever fog, Andrej praised it, in his mind. *Gentle fog. Nobly born fog of a wealthy house begotten.*

The cable went slack.

Andrej stared at it in dread, willing his anxious gaze to travel down to the ground through the cable, desperate to be able to see what was happening.

Two tugs.

Three following.

Thanks be to all Saints.

Kaydence and Ailynn were down, and safe.

But now it was his turn.

Andrej sat down on the lip of the vista gap as he had seen the others do, and took the braided cable in his hands. Wondering what had possessed him to agree to this.

He had to get down from the roof, and his people with him.

"Find the rope between your feet, sir." Chief Samons had

crouched down next to him, encouraging. "Let yourself slide the first few eighths. You don't want to knock your hands or your head against the wall. You'll be on the ground before you know it, all you have to do is hang on and control the speed of your descent. Let's go."

The braided cable was soft-edged and cool between his palms. Which were sweating. It was cold, and he was afraid of the drop.

He could feel the thickness of the cable caught securely between the edges of the soles of his boots.

He couldn't sit here and stare at the fog below him forever. He had people on the ground. The longer it took to get them all down, the more vulnerable they were.

Be soft for me if I should fall, you princess of fogs, you prince inheritor of fogs, you well-bred fog of regal parentage.

He let himself slip down the length of the cable.

It felt too much like falling, and Andrej clutched at the cable between his hands in a sudden fright. No. He was not falling. He was climbing down. He had only his own weight to manage, and Kaydence had just done this with Ailynn on his back, and he was Dolgorukij. He had more than enough strength in his hands and shoulders to hang on.

Hand over hand, the cable held close between his feet, sliding past his ankles. Hand over hand, Andrej descended into the fog.

Once the mist took him, his anxiety seemed to vanish, his apprehensions evaporated, his fear gone.

He felt secure.

He could do this.

His people could do this.

They would see justice done at the Domitt Prison.

He felt the ground brush against his feet, familiar hands reaching out to him to steady him as he stumbled away from the cable, stunned to find that he was already here.

It was colder on the ground. The fog was wet; the chill of it went through to the bone. But Andrej embraced the dank discomfort of it; sound did not carry, they were safely hidden in the fog. It was a shield in the night. It would conceal them until he could reach his goal.

Within moments Chief Samons and Erish came shimmying down out of the fog; and they were all together.

Fine.

Time to make a surprise attack on the Administration of the Domitt Prison.

◆ Thirteen

Assistant Administrator Merig Belan had finished the furnace cleaning schedule at last. But it was still some time before the morning; and this was the worst time. The tide out in the Tannerbay was turning, down beyond the Iron Gate; and when conditions were right, the trouble of the waters echoed all the way up to Rudistal, eights and eights upriver. The chop on the water had always frightened Belan, for no particular reason.

Shuddering, Belan took another drink. He was safe here, far from the river, further yet from the Tannerbay. By himself, in his office, all alone. He didn't want to be alone: he could go and find the night-watchman, solicit a game of guesses or something. He outranked the night-watchman. He could insist.

And the night-watchman was Sentish, not Pyana, which would be all to the good; except that Sentish had been here when the Domitt Prison had come to Rudistal, and how was he to explain why he should be alive and here while the Nurail who had been part of Rudistal's life for all of this time were gone?

And no trace of them.

No trace except ash from the furnaces, laid down as drainage at the reclamation site and the roads leading from the prison to the work areas. No trace but for what might lie beneath the walls of the great dike that Geltoi was constructing to reclaim the land at the bend of the river from the water. Winter was coming; and after that, spring. How would it be if there was to be flooding when the snowmelt came?

The pontoon bridges across the river would be torn out, if they weren't moved in time. Rudistal might lose its land-bridge yet again. And if the reclamation site was flooded, if the river scoured beneath the foundations of the dike, if bone and hair and rotting flesh should surface in the black chop of the river as it fought its way through Rudistal toward the Iron Gate?

More liquor. Belan shook the bottle in his hand: empty, oh, this could not be allowed to happen. He was getting hysterical. Nothing was amiss. Nothing was wrong. Geltoi's request for relief of the Inquisitor had gone out on a standard receipt, normal priority. Business as usual.

No urgency, nothing wrong, simply a parting of the ways between a prison administration—whose documentation was perfectly in order, that had nothing to hide—and one over-young, arrogant Inquisitor with no respect for normal channels of authority or the common expectations of military courtesy. Nothing more.

So the recall orders would come soon. Administrator Geltoi would call a Fleet escort to see the Inquisitor out of the Domitt Prison. Whatever Koscuisko might say when he returned to *Scylla* would have to be referred through channels eight layers deep as a procedural complaint.

That process took weeks—sometimes even months—to reach the Bench level. There would be plenty of time to position themselves to answer any challenges from Koscuisko to the Bench's satisfaction. Geltoi was confident of his ability to smooth things over and explain any apparent anomalies for the simple misunderstandings that they were.

Perhaps they'd been a little careless, operating without any oversight for as long as they had done. Things would be different from now on.

Was Geltoi truly confident that he could survive anything Koscuisko said?

Or did he simply mean to put whatever blame on Merig Belan, and cry ignorance?

Geltoi had made him sign the kitchen audit—

No, Belan told himself firmly. He was not going to get paranoid. And if Geltoi meant to do that, there wasn't anything Belan could do about it to protect himself anyway;

Geltoi was Pyana, and Belan was no match for him. It was better to believe just what the Administrator said.

The orders would come, Koscuisko would leave. The woman would be returned to the service house, though they would have to question her about potentially compromising information she might have learned from the Inquisitor in bed. The cook would be questioned as well, if somewhat more carefully; they were not in too much danger from the cook, and the cook was to be paid, after all. It would all work out.

And once the sun but rose across the river he could leave, he could go to his little house and wash and eat and be away from here for a few hours at least. Administrator Geltoi would not be coming in before midmorning, surely, not after having been called back to the prison after supper. He could have five hours between sunup and return. But in order to survive till then he had to drink, because the trouble on the river raised the trouble in the fog, thick and white and murmurous on the south side of the building.

It had been Geltoi's idea of a joke to put Belan's office on the south side of the building. Belan was sure of it. That was just the sort of sense of humor Geltoi had. Belan turned on the lights, all of them, he shut the sun-shields to close out the night, but he knew that the fog was out there.

Waiting for him.

Wouldn't it be easier to take his life and go into the fog for once and all?

Wouldn't that be better than living in constant fear, fear of the fog, fear of Administrator Geltoi's ridicule, fear of the resentment the prison staff had for him, one lone Nurail in a nest of venomous Pyana?

Maybe if he got drunk enough he could find the nerve to do it, without having to think too hard about the irreversibility of the consequences.

To get drunk he needed liquor.

He'd finished what he'd had in his office hours ago.

He knew where he could get some more, though.

Administrator Geltoi kept several bottles of decent drinkable in his office. He wouldn't miss one of them. Belan could be sure it was replaced before that could happen. He could go quietly enough; the fog would not know that he was there, and it was nearly morning. The spirits would be losing their nightstrength and retreating to their graves anyway. Unquiet; but impotent, or nearly so.

Right.

Rising from behind his desktable, Assistant Administrator Belan went to open the closed door of his office, the door he had closed to shut out the voices in the fog. Someone had left a vent-shutter open, he was sure of it, he would have a search made in the morning; but once the sun had set he didn't dare get near any such vent that might let the fog in, and the spirits with it. With his door closed they wouldn't know where he was; there would be no reason for them to come in to look for him.

Quietly.

He almost thought he heard the whisper of the fog in the corridor outside, no sound of voices, but a sound of bodies. What bodies they had were rotted away by now, burned up by the poison of the accelerant even as the rest were burned in the furnace-fire. It was the night-watchman, surely. Only the night-watchman. He was drunk, Belan knew that. He was hearing things.

Taking care to make as little noise as possible, Belan eased the mechanical secures off the door-latch and turned the handle, opening up the door.

Only to fall back from the opening gap in horror and transcendent fear: because the dead were there.

Andrej Koscuisko, the demon Inquisitor, and who knew better than Merig Belan what Koscuisko could do with Nurail, when he chose?

Andrej Koscuisko, standing square in the doorway with the fog on his body and mist in his hair. People behind him, and oh, they might look like Koscuisko's Security, but Belan knew better. The fog gave them away. The fog surrounded them. They were ghastly and terrible with it, and the woman as well, the bondswoman from the service house, hadn't Belan guessed it would be a mistake to set her to serve a man who murdered Nurail?

"Assistant Administrator," Koscuisko said. Belan heard his voice echoing from a very great distance off, and far deeper than Koscuisko's voice had ever been. Because it wasn't Koscuisko's voice. It was the dead speaking, from beneath that weight of earth, their voices heavy and dark with death and rotting. "I'm glad to find you here, I need your help. Gentlemen, if you will."

The fog-policemen came into the room, came forward for him, took him by the arms to raise him up from the floor. The weight of the shackles they latched across his wrists was cold: but it would burn. He had seen the burning in the furnaces. He knew that Koscuisko had guessed, that it was not the first time.

And now he was just another Nurail prisoner, out of all the Nurail prisoners of the Domitt Prison. Merig Belan wept with hopeless despair as the Security brought him to stand before the Inquisitor.

"Very good," Koscuisko said, and he sounded mild-tempered and gentle, but Belan was not fooled. "We were told that you were in the building. I've a small chore for you, let's go upstairs, shall we?"

The fog-policemen moved him forward, out of his office, toward the lift. He didn't mind going upstairs, not so long as it was upstairs in the Administration building, not so long as it was only to Geltoi's office. Geltoi had created this, Geltoi had engineered the crimes that cried for vengeance, but it was Belan who would be punished for them. Poor Belan.

He had reviewed Koscuisko's interrogatories.

He knew what Koscuisko could do, with Nurail prisoners.

The dead men in the fog would have their vengeance . . .

Andrej put the dose through at Belan's throat, and the man relaxed at last. Not much. But enough. There was a look of madness to Belan's eyes, and a peculiar stink to his body that Andrej recognized. They were in the presence of a true psychosis. They would have to be very careful: There was information Belan had that Andrej needed, and he didn't care to lose it by inattention or accident.

That was one reason.

The other reason was that sentient creatures all responded to the near presence of great psychological disturbance by being disturbed themselves. And they were all stressed enough already. For everybody's sake Belan needed to be calmed and comforted, relaxed and reassured.

He needed much more than the emergency-set of medications that a senior physician always carried with him, divided up amongst his Security. But Andrej would make do until he got access to Infirmary. Belan needed help badly. Andrej meant for him to have it: but Andrej needed Belan's help first.

"Merig?" Andrej asked as gently as he could. Ailynn sat and held Belan's hand, stroking it soothingly. That was very good of her. Belan blinked; then looked up at Andrej, as though he was trying to focus.

"Koscuisko. Ah, your Excellency. Sorry, sir, how did you get?—Must have dozed off. What time?"

"Time to call the local Judiciary, I need a transmit. How do I find the direct, from here."

Administrator Geltoi's office was logically where access to the local Judiciary would be found, because only Administrator Geltoi—or his deputy—had business making direct contact with such exalted levels of authority.

Once Andrej but got to an appropriate transmit, he could cry his plaint, and be secure that it would be heard. He had to let Captain Vopalar know what was happening. But first he had to be sure he could get through to the Bench before anybody realized what was going on, to stop him.

"Oh, well, that." Belan struggled to his feet a little clumsily, staring at his shackled wrists in mild confusion. "Now, how did that happen? Oh, well. The Administrator's direct line here, your Excellency. Only be sure to engage the refer, or else Security won't get a listen-in. And, oh, the Administrator likes the recorder off, sensitive nature of the discussion. That kind of thing. Why, I remember, one day, I had to call to town for him about arranging for payment for the flour, and I forgot to set the recorder to null, and he was so angry."

Andrej nodded to Ailynn, and she drew Belan away with her to sit down on the low couch to one side of the room. Turn the Security refer off, so that nobody here would be on monitor, whether or not they happened to notice the communication going out. Turn the recorder on, to be sure he had evidence if necessary.

It took some moments for his transmit request to go through, since he was sending it as far as he was. He wanted to be sure to register his claim at the Bench level; there was too much at stake if he should complain only to Chilleau Judiciary. Too much of a temptation would exist to cover up, quiet things, hush it all over.

He couldn't risk that.

This had to be published: not to discountenance Chilleau Judiciary—though it was perhaps unfortunately certain to, whether justly or not—but in order to surface the wider question. Chilleau Judiciary was not corrupt. How could this have been allowed to happen?

The counter-validation code showed in the communications screen.

Bench access.

Personal attention, na Roqua den Tensa, First Judge Presiding at Fontailloe Judiciary. Or her Court; it was all the same in Law for the purposes of crying his plaint. Receipt validation requested from Chilleau Judiciary.

Still Andrej hesitated.

He'd never so much as spoken to a Judge at such an exalted level before, and the prospect of standing before the First Judge at Fontailloe to speak his piece was a daunting one.

". . . with sterile ash," Belan was saying. "Where was the harm in that?" Talking to Ailynn about whatever. Probably not about anything that anyone could even make sense of in his current state of mind, with the drugs Andrej had fed him taken into account.

The word "ash" caught in Andrej's mind, and gave him strength.

He was not standing alone in front of the Bench, to cry a claim like a private citizen.

He was a Bench officer, whose Fleet rank only betokened his Judicial function. And he was not alone. It was not his complaint. It was the cry of the murdered prisoners of the Domitt Prison that he made before the First Judge. It was the burned victims of the furnaces who put out their hands for justice, and not him.

"I am Andrej Ulexeievitch Koscuisko." It was to be spoken, because the Bench validated his identity on his voice as well as on the codes that had been assigned to him for his use when he had taken up his Writ. "I hold the Writ to

Inquire at the Domitt Prison. Due to the existence of multiple and systematic improprieties having to do with prisoner processing and documentation it has become necessary to cry failure of Writ at the Domitt Prison.''

He had no legal formula to declare failure of Writ. They hadn't really studied it at Fleet Orientation Station Medical, where he had received his training in jurisprudence and torture.

''The immediate assignment of a Bench audit team is respectfully solicited. I have made this Brief, and I will stand on the justice of the decision, and hazard what consequences may accrue should the Bench invalidate my finding.''

He waited.

If the Bench reversed his finding, they would be clear to interpret his withdrawal of his Writ as an act of mutiny; and for mutiny even an Inquisitor was vulnerable to the most extreme penalty in the inventory.

There was no help for it.

He could not go quietly back to *Scylla* and let those furnaces continue to burn, not to save his life.

Was his cry to be intercepted, refused, declined by some Clerk of Court at Fontailloe Judiciary, too radical a plea to be admitted?

Failure of Writ.

It had not been cried against a Judicial institution that Andrej could remember in his life.

There was a clattering of sound in the comaccess, and Andrej knew by the way in which the comaccess fought to recalibrate itself that it was processing a clear-signal at the extreme limits of its tolerance.

Koscuisko. This is the duty. Officer, Fontailloe Judiciary. Stand by for the. First Judge.

But it was weeks and weeks between Rudistal and Fontailloe Judiciary . . .

Every booster station between here and the Gollipse vector had to be on maximum override.

Andrej sat down, frightened of his own temerity, awed by the immensity of what he had done; and the voice that sounded next—and it was a voice, garbled and indistinct though it was—chilled him through to bones he hadn't realized he even had.

"What do you claim to have. Been done, young man. Be sure of what you say to me."

The First Judge.

Na Roqua den Tensa, Fontailloe Judiciary.

The First Judge Presiding on the Jurisdiction's Bench.

She had maintained the Judicial order all of Andrej's life: and her law was legend.

"Murder has been done, your Honor, to the great shame and disgrace of the Judicial order." He was so ashamed, to have come before her in such cause. This was the First Judge. And yet he knew that he was right. "Nurail are under Jurisdiction, they are not to be tortured and killed absent due and adequate process. The Writ has failed horribly at the Domitt Prison, your Honor, and we cannot in Law tolerate it."

How could he say such a thing to the First Judge?

He could hardly believe he was really speaking to her.

"What does Chilleau Judiciary say. Why take so drastic a step."

How could he challenge the First Judge, over a handful of Nurail lives?

Even if that handful should run to thousands, how could it compare to the greater good of all under Jurisdiction?

"I have cried direct, your Honor. I fear for loss of evidence."

Please.

He to whom so many useless pleas for mercy, pity, understanding had been addressed, he could not plead for mercy or understanding. He would stand or fail on the Judicial merit of his plaint.

"Do you know who I am, young Koscuisko?"

Was it his imagination, or was there amusement in that multiply transmitted and retransmitted voice?

"You are the First Judge." Before whom he could only bend his neck in humility. "Den Tensa, of good Precedent and grave ruling. Fontailloe Judiciary."

She was offended at him.

His cause was trivial, in the greater scheme of things.

He could not believe that the murder of guiltless parties was trivial, no matter how few. It was not an issue of relative importance. The rule of Law was absolute: or else it was not the rule of Law.

"Then be by me deputized, pending the arrival. Of an audit party. To you I grant authority in Port Rudistal, and any Fleet resources on call. Do your duty and uphold the rule of Law. Fontailloe Judiciary, away here."

The comaccess cleared, the words resounding in his mind and heart.

Do your duty, and uphold the rule of Law.

Andrej wanted to weep: and guessed that he was still in a state of profound shock from what he had seen in the furnace-room, compounded by this unforeseen development.

He didn't have time to weep. There was no telling whether the destruction of evidence had already begun; whether the furnaces were already being sanitized. No asking Merig Belan either. Andrej mastered his emotion with a furious effort of will. He had work to do.

The receipt of the boosted signal would have alerted the Port Authority and the Dramissoi Relocation Fleet alike, though they would not have been able to read it. There was no time to lose. The prison might be on alert. Andrej studied the standard-inquires on the comaccess for a moment: and made his selection.

"Andrej Ulexeievitch Koscuisko, at the Domitt Prison. For Bench Captain Sinjosi Vopalar, on emergency immediate."

He wanted a drink. Several.

But he needed troops, and Vopalar had them.

Oh, if it should give him second thoughts to assert his claim before the Bench, what was he to say to his father?

How could he ever excuse himself for challenging his lawful superiors?

He was already in disgrace for having so long resisted his father's will that he serve as Ship's Inquisitor.

He would never receive his father's blessing, now. Still less would his child gain acceptance.

"Skein in braid, your Excellency. Vopalar on thread, convert."

There was no help for it. He couldn't buy his father's blessing with the unavenged death of Nurail prisoners. He had no choice.

And utter despair was liberating, in a sense, because as long as there was no way in which he could be reconciled to his father—no matter how dutiful he strove to be—then there was no further use in duty; except to do justice. As he saw it. Not as his father would wish.

"Captain Vopalar?" he asked. "I beg your pardon, your Excellency. I have at the Domitt Prison a failure of Writ declared. And am in immediate need of your troops, in order to ensure that evidence be preserved."

The First Judge had spoken his name, and said that he was to do his duty.

For the first time in a long time, Andrej both understood his task and believed in it, completely.

Caleigh Samons stood in formation behind her officer of assignment, waiting for the gates to open.

It was sunrise in Port Rudistal; the fog was beginning to grow lighter, though as thick as it had come up from the river it would be hours before it actually burned off. And the fog had proved a valuable ally, during this past night.

It had concealed their descent from the penthouse from any stray observer's eye; it concealed the bulk of Vopalar's troops now. Three hundred troops, on either side of the containment wall. Belan had opened up the gate in the containment wall an hour ago. Now they were waiting for Belan to order the opening of the gates into the prison itself.

It was early yet.

The prison was still asleep.

Oh, the kitchen was awake, and the laundry, and the furnaces never stopped. The new shift had not come on since they had brought the officer up from the furnace-room. There was no way to be certain of what Administrator Geltoi might have told his staff; as far as they had been able to tell from what Belan had to say, Geltoi had left it all for the morning. They would be lucky, if it were so.

Almost unreasonably lucky.

Caleigh didn't like it.

It was more than the risk of destruction of evidence.

If Koscuisko could not find evidence, if Koscuisko's charges could not be proven out before the Bench—

The privilege of the Writ would not protect Koscuisko, if the Bench decided he had no cause to cry failure of Writ.

The knowledge that no other Inquisitor Caleigh had sup-

ported was capable of what Koscuisko could do with a Tenth
Level command termination made the prospect of Koscuisko
meeting his death that way no less horrible to her.

The fog dampened sound, as well as concealing troops.
She heard nothing from behind them, though she knew that
there were people waiting in formation, with Bench Lieutenant Goslin Plugrath to command them. Captain Vopalar they
had left in the Administration building with Ailynn to coax
Belan into what they needed from him; Caleigh wished
they'd hurry up. She was cold. She didn't care to be frightened for Koscuisko's sake.

Had it been less than four shifts since this had started?

Was it really just yesterday they'd gone down to Infirmary,
to audit?

Now she heard more activity up ahead; now she could
sense movement, from the gates. Guards speaking to each
other loud and careless, innocent of apprehension. So the
Assistant Administrator wanted them to open the gates early.
So what? Who knew what spooks that Nurail was seeing
these days?

The gate began to track, heavy and ponderous.

A sudden lance of light shot out into the dark and lay
across the graveled ground, widening moment by moment as
the gate opened. Light from inside the prison. The great
courtyard, empty now, and all the buildings dark except for
the lights in the mess building reflected against the east interior wall of the prison.

"Gentles," Koscuisko said.

They started forward.

Caleigh hated this, she hated it, it made her flesh creep.
There was no reason to expect a problem. She knew that.
And still she was letting Andrej Koscuisko walk into the
prison courtyard, functionally alone, unarmed, the man who
had cried failure of Writ down on the head of Administrator
Geltoi and everyone on his staff—

They didn't know.

Yet.

That was the only thing that made it even possible.

Calm and collected, Koscuisko crossed the gate-track,
stepped across the threshold with his Security, strolled toward the dispatch building to fetch the duty officer.

It was so quiet.

The fog seemed to follow them, pouring in through the gates. It could not penetrate: It was too warm inside the courtyard, with the lights. But still the fog came. Koscuisko waded through the fog up the steps of the dispatch building, and Caleigh followed in his wake. It was superstitious to imagine that the fog was following them. Fog had no volition.

The duty officer was sitting in the wide foyer of the dispatch building bent over a document on his desk. A narrative? Maybe he was working a puzzle; he seemed completely absorbed, one way or the other.

Koscuisko spoke.

"Good-greeting, duty officer."

It took a moment for the sound of an unfamiliar voice to register, apparently. Caleigh could sympathize. It was the end of the night shift; and what could happen within a prison, really?

"We have to effect a change in duty rosters, duty officer. Your assistance will be required. Please come with me."

Comprehension came slowly; but the duty officer knew Koscuisko's rank by sight, if not the officer himself. "Your pardon, your Excellency, didn't—ah—didn't hear you come in, sir. What's needed? If the officer please."

No idea. No hint of discomfort or dissimulation. Caleigh knew a sigh of relief was bottled up inside of her, somewhere: If the duty officer was unconcerned, no one had warned him about anything, put him on notice, tipped him off. It could be all right.

"Thank you, duty officer, I wish for you to come with me to meet the Bench Lieutenant. His name is Goslin Plugrath, and he needs to examine the day's order of duty. It will be this way."

Back out of the building, onto the steps. The courtyard was full of Plugrath's troops, the gate-crew held in a small cluster now near the gatehouse. Plugrath was waiting for them, and not very patiently. The sun was coming up. The day shift would be arriving soon. They had to be in control of the prison before that started happening. There weren't enough troops to relieve the current shift and turn the new shift back from the prison gates at the same time. Something would slip.

"Duty officer?"

Plugrath was too anxious about his task to think twice about protocol, but Koscuisko simply stood to one side to let him talk. The duty officer was pale now in the lights at the foot of the dispatch building. But he kept his voice low as he replied: No panic, no frantic attempts to give warning. Maybe the entire prison wasn't corrupt.

Or maybe there were people who were just as glad to be stopped, now that they were to be forced to stop.

"Bench Lieutenant Plugrath. The officer said you needed my assistance, sir."

Koscuisko was satisfied that Plugrath had things under control, one way or the other. Plugrath took the duty officer back into the building: He would get the location of all the night staff, who they were, where they were, and call them in one by one until Plugrath's people had replaced each and every one of them. Then they would be ready to receive the day shift: but Koscuisko wasn't about to wait.

"Miss Samons, one of those squads belongs to me," Koscuisko said. True enough. Plugrath had agreed. Caleigh called out the appointed squad leader with a gesture of her hand.

"Section Leader Poris, your Excellency."

And would have a rough shift of it. But had been warned.

"Let us to the detention area go." Koscuisko was halfway down the stairs as he spoke, and his Bonds with him. "I fear trying work for you all, gentles, but soonest started is soonest sung, and this cannot be left for moment longer."

Punishment block.

People had been tortured, there.

With luck they would find evidence: but Caleigh couldn't help but hope there were no prisoners.

It stank.

Pausing on the threshold to the punishment block, Andrej Koscuisko gathered his courage into his two hands and found it pitifully inadequate to the challenge that faced him. More than anything he did not want to go into punishment block. And more than anything he knew that it had to be done.

He turned on the lights, and someone screamed in terror; and once one screamed, others joined in, frightened by the existence of such fear. Fear born of agony was communicable, especially to other souls who knew what it felt like.

How many cells were here, in punishment block?

And, oh, how long would it be before he had well cleared it?

Evidence, Andrej reminded himself, firmly. He had to preserve what evidence was here, and seal the cellblock for the forensic team that the Bench would send. If there were prisoners here who could be healed, he needed their evidence. If there were men here who could not be saved, he needed to enter that fact into evidence. And if there was suffering, it was outside the rule of Law, unlawfully inflicted, unlawfully invoked. It had to be stopped by any and all means at his disposal.

He took a step, two steps, and the night-guard opened up the cell for him. He could hear the sound of the cell's inmate breathing, as though blowing bubbles in the water; and knew without needing to look what had been done. But had to go in. Had to loose restraints, and press the doses through. Had to look, and see, and note, and take evidence.

There was nothing else that he could do, not for this man.

"Let the Record show." He could hear the frantic horror in his voice, and choked it back into his belly. He was the officer in charge. He was responsible here. His report had to be complete and concise, too perfect to be challenged in evidence before the Bench.

"Nurail hominid, adult male. Unlawfully restrained, reference is made to the Eighth Level of Inquiry, partial suspension with restricted airway. Multiple lacerations, compound fracture at the left lower leg and upper right thigh, several days untreated to judge by necrosis of tissue. Administration of eleven units of midimic at jugular pulse, stabilization pending arrival of additional medical resources from Port Rudistal."

There, that was one.

And only one.

He could not stop and think. He had to go on. "Let the Record show."

And another. "Adult male hominid, Nurail or Sarcosmet."

Five.

"Burns of the third degree of severity, to the extent of approximately." Eight.

"No visible evidence, suspected use of psychoactive drugs. No intervention possible pending blood-panels. Patient to be restrained to await psychiatric evaluation."

Eleven.

"Consistent with employment of an instrument similar to a peony, dead for perhaps four eights at time of discovery."

Fourteen.

"With evident intent to mutilate. Partial recovery may be possible, cyborg augmentation to be implemented."

Seventeen.

The punishment block went on forever.

There were only twenty-three souls there.

And yet it seemed that there were three and twenty thousand of them, to Andrej.

And it was all his fault: because he was the Writ on site at the Domitt Prison.

And he should have known.

And he had done nothing.

It was a beautiful day in Port Rudistal.

Administrator Geltoi had overslept, his fond indulgent wife letting him lie until midmeal was on the table. He'd scolded her, very gently; his heart hadn't been in it, and besides a man didn't raise his voice to a woman. Let alone to his wife, who should be sacred to him.

Therefore he'd risen and washed, and dressed, and kissed his wife and the children who were at home; and now he was ready to face the scene that he was anticipating with Merig Belan. If he didn't hear from Chilleau Judiciary today, he would send a confirm message, and that would be enough. Chilleau Judiciary would send Andrej Koscuisko back to *Scylla* in disgrace. He would be rid of that concern.

There was a good deal to thank Koscuisko for: His impertinent curiosity had pointed out one or two areas in which potential for improvement existed in the documentation of prisoner processing. They would have time to recover from that. Koscuisko was going away.

Work on the land reclamation project would probably have

to slow down, with the new atmosphere of accountability. Scrutiny. He had been free from any oversight till now, and Administrator Geltoi could find it in him to resent Chilleau Judiciary for the change in his status. He was accustomed to being an independent agent. He had earned autonomy. Hadn't he built the Domitt Prison from the ground up, on time, under budget?

What good were Nurail lives to Jurisdiction if not to toil in its service?

But the world changed, and a prudent man changed with it. He had his earnings either way. There was no fear of losing the fortune he'd made, and no sense complaining about his fate because the next would come more slowly.

He was looking forward to the arrival of Koscuisko's orders.

Should he have an interview with Koscuisko, their formal debriefing? Koscuisko would be confused and resentful. Geltoi would explain that he had no choice but to comply with direction. He would remind Koscuisko that it was he who was in command of the Domitt Prison, and not Andrej Koscuisko. He would dismiss Koscuisko to escort with the contempt Koscuisko's behavior had earned.

A beautiful day.

The sun was brilliant in an ice-blue sky. It was cold, but Geltoi insisted on leaving the roof of his new touring car open anyway, enjoying the brisk invigorating stream of cold air in his face. A good coat was proof against any chill, and he had one, with warm gloves besides; and he never tired of the view, approaching the containment wall of the Domitt Prison, the peaked roof of the Administration building rising above it, the great black wall of the prison proper above that. The penthouse, crowning the wall.

Geltoi looked up at the penthouse and smiled broadly. Koscuisko would not have had an easy night of it, wondering what was to become of him. And then the summons to Administrator Geltoi's office would come . . .

There was the penthouse on the roof.

But—oddly enough—

Geltoi frowned, searching the roofline.

The flue-vents of the furnaces.

No smoke.

No cheerful hygienic column of white cloud to reassure him that garbage was being disposed of properly. Burned beyond any hope of recognition or identification. Reduced to undifferentiated ash.

No smoke?

Belan had been a little premature, surely. It was true that they had to do a little emergency cleaning, just to be sure that nothing in the furnace-room could create an unfortunate impression. But Belan was to have presented a schedule first.

Maybe he needed to have a talk with Belan.

Standing on the earth that covered the crane-pit, perhaps, to provide a little background.

The Administration building seemed strangely quiet, at first glance; it was a little eerie. The courtyard in front of the Administration building was deserted. No sign of movement or activity within the building—except that, if he craned his neck, Administrator Geltoi could see that his office seemed to be occupied by someone.

His office.

He couldn't tell much more than that there was someone there, standing near the windows.

Belan took such liberties?

He'd soon see about that.

Geltoi strode into the building with confidence and fury alike animating his step. Where was the staff? Of course. It was time for the midmeal break. There was a day-watchman on duty by the lift-nexus, and he should have been quick to come down the stairs and greet his Administrator with a polite bow. He hadn't come down at all. Geltoi ignored him with as much icy disdain as he could muster out of a cold fury.

The day-watchman could be dealt with later.

Right now he intended to find out what species of madness had overtaken Merig Belan and possessed him to make free with Geltoi's office in Geltoi's absence.

The lift opened onto the corridor, and his office was at the far end. The office doors wide open, both of them. There were Fleet Security posted at the lift, and again outside his office; they came to attention as he stepped out of the lift, snapping to with satisfying precision. Respect. What were they doing here? And outside his office, as well?

Administrator Geltoi hurried toward the office with all deliberate speed, pausing on the threshold to take stock of the situation.

His office was full of people.

There was someone in his chair, but Geltoi couldn't see who; the chair was turned to the window, with its back to the room.

Sitting on the couch to the left, a short blond man in a dark dusty uniform, slumped over on the edge of the seat with his shaggy head buried between the palms of his soiled hands.

Andrej Koscuisko?

There was that Security Chief of Koscuisko's, right enough, and Koscuisko's green-sleeved bond-involuntary troops as well.

Very good indeed.

Clearly orders had come in overnight, and Belan had wanted Koscuisko to be here waiting for his dismissal. Belan could be faulted on execution, but not on instinct. And it was enough of a relief to realize that Koscuisko's orders were in hand that Geltoi forgave Belan this misappropriation of his office in advance of Belan's explanation.

His role was to be that of the surprised senior administrator coming upon an unexpected occupation force: very close to exactly what he was, except that he knew what was going on, and was looking forward to playing it out.

"So. Doctor Koscuisko."

Koscuisko dropped his hands, raising his face to look at Geltoi as he strode confidently in. Koscuisko looked an absolute wreck. Perhaps the experience would teach him something; sober him, make him a better officer. As long as Koscuisko was a better officer far, far away from the Domitt Prison, Geltoi did not grudge him any good his brief imprisonment might have done him.

Geltoi stopped in front of the couch to put a point to the lesson. There were other Security in here as well as Koscuisko's; some Fleet security—but Geltoi ignored them.

"How unfortunate that it should have to end like this, Koscuisko. We acted in good faith, I remind you, and took great pains to see you lacked for nothing."

Koscuisko rose stiffly to his feet. His uniform was filthy:

and there was an unsubtle odor about it as well that Geltoi declined to identify. He had clearly been up all night; drinking, most likely. That would explain the blank hostile uncomprehending stare Koscuisko was giving him. It was a little uncanny. Stupid as Koscuisko looked, unkempt as he was, he almost did look Nurail to Geltoi.

The realization distracted Geltoi for a moment: What if Koscuisko had been found in the furnace-room, looking like that? Would it be so great a loss if his honest hardworking furnace crew made a mistake, quite reasonable under the circumstances, and clubbed Koscuisko unconscious to feed the furnaces?

Calling his fantasies firmly to heel, Geltoi spoke on. "While you have done nothing but engage in obstructionary and insubordinate behavior since you got here. The rumors we'd heard were right about you all along. No respect for honest decent working folk. No respect for authority—"

Failure to know his place and keep to it, stubborn refusal to honor the natural order and respect his superiors. Nurail in more than one way. And Geltoi would have told Koscuisko, too, but for some unaccountable reason he found himself flat on his back on the floor. Koscuisko kneeling on his stomach. Koscuisko's hands, locked around his throat, and the thumbs pressed deep into the pulse on either side of his windpipe.

What—

Koscuisko's face was a blue-and-white mask of furious hatred and indescribable loathing, and all for being told a few home truths about himself?

He couldn't breathe.

"Murderer," Koscuisko hissed at him through teeth clenched tight and bared in savage contempt. "Impious. Unfilial. Outlaw. Vandal. Murderer—"

Then Koscuisko was pulled off, finally, though it took all four of his slave Security to do it. Fleet Security helped Geltoi to his feet, and Belan decided to turn around, finally.

It was about time.

Belan hadn't jumped out of the great desk chair at the sound of Geltoi's voice, which was annoying. Belan was turning slowly from the window with no evident intention of surrendering his place to its rightful occupant.

"Your Excellency. You must wait upon the judgment of the Bench for that, with respect, sir."

It wasn't Belan's voice.

The man in the chair was Bench Lieutenant Plugrath, swiveling to square himself to the desktable's surface and toggle into braid. "Chanson, close the gates. Quarantine in effect for local staff. Good-greeting, Administrator Geltoi."

Koscuisko spoke, his struggle to master himself evident. "Yes, of course, Lieutenant. You are right." Security was not letting go of Koscuisko, holding him by his arms, standing close behind him. Oddly enough Security hadn't let go of Geltoi himself, either. "Geltoi, I never thought to believe it could be true. But I have learned. There is a crime under Jurisdiction that deserves Tenth Level command termination. And you have done it. I will have you, Geltoi."

Security appeared to relax as Koscuisko spoke. One of his greensleeves bowed, presenting a whitesquare that Koscuisko declined; with a quick gesture of his head, by way of thanks.

Geltoi stared in shock at the officer in Geltoi's chair, seated behind Geltoi's desktable, making himself perfectly at home in Geltoi's office. "Lieutenant. What is the meaning of this. Where is Assistant Administrator Belan."

Belan had been here late last night working. Why hadn't Belan warned him that Plugrath had come to visit? What were these Fleet Security doing here, if not to escort Koscuisko out of the Domitt Prison? Plugrath's escort, perhaps. Maybe the Dramissoi Relocation Fleet Commander had sent Plugrath with this escort in token of Koscuisko's rank. Yes. That could be. Geltoi felt a little better.

"Administrator Belan has been removed to a secure psychiatric facility in Port Rudistal, Administrator. On orders from the commander pro tem of the Domitt Prison, his Excellency, Andrej Koscuisko."

Koscuisko?

Commanding?

Impossible.

The carpeted flooring eroded like wet sand in a rising tide underneath Geltoi's feet. Shaking himself free from Security's grasp with an impatient twist, Geltoi staggered forward, catching at the fore-edge of the desktable for balance. "Let

me see if I take your meaning. Lieutenant. You have taken
my poor Merig to the hospital. What wild claims has he been
making?''

And what had Koscuisko said?

Security came up behind him, taking his arms once more.
But not holding them this time. Security pulled his arms behind his back, and Geltoi felt the cold kiss of the manacles
latching around his wrists without quite understanding what
it was.

What was going on?

Were these actually chains? Was this how it felt to be
made a prisoner? Interesting. But he was not a prisoner. He
was the Administrator of the Domitt Prison. Something was
not adding up.

''Quite an astonishing number,'' Plugrath admitted, almost
cheerfully. ''Not very coherent, any of it. His Excellency has
sent for a Sarwaw forensics team to excavate. There will be
physical evidence soon enough. And in the meantime—''

Sarwaw forensics? Whatever could that mean?

The construction pit.

The Nurail they had buried there.

Sarwaw forensics teams were top of the line for gathering
physical evidence from mass burials. Koscuisko was Dolgorukij. He would know. It was Dolgorukij that had mas-
sacred all those Sarwaw for the forensics teams to practice
on.

''I want him very carefully maintained,'' Koscuisko said
to Lieutenant Plugrath. Koscuisko hardly deigned to notice
he was there, any more. Koscuisko didn't have to. ''There
are reparations to be made, punishment owing too many
times over to count. I do not mean to risk escape of any sort.
I trust you take my meaning, Bench Lieutenant.''

''Yes, sir. I understand.'' Plugrath's submission to Koscuisko's authority was too absolute. Geltoi could hardly bear
to hear it. ''I'll pledge his safety to you personally, your
Excellency. You'll be wanting to move your people into
town, I expect.''

''Out of this place,'' Koscuisko agreed. ''Thank you,
Lieutenant.''

The furnaces should have warned him. The furnaces had
stopped. Koscuisko had people here to rake the furnaces out,

and number up the unregistered dead to claim vengeance against him. Belan had whimpered to them about the dead in construction pit, and Belan could tell a very great deal more to Geltoi's disadvantage. Belan was Nurail. He had no backbone, no courage, no strength of will to speak of.

Caught between a treacherous Nurail to one side and the prospect of being made to serve as Chilleau Judiciary's scapegoat on the other, Administrator Geltoi weighed his options as he weighed the stalloy cuffs that chained his wrists.

And decided.

"You're making a significant error, Lieutenant." He tried to sound sorrowful, while investing his words with as much aggrieved dignity as possible. "I don't know what allegations our poor Merig may have made, nor how much faith a prudent man should have in the ravings of a madman. I fear for your career; and you could profit by this instead, if you so chose."

He could brazen out the evidence somehow. He could see to it that Belan was silenced before evidence could be placed on Record. But if he once allowed himself to be removed as a prisoner, he was as good as dead. He was not in a very good position here and now: He had been taken by surprise. He could still make it work, if only he could walk out of his office a free man.

"Not my mistake to make, Administrator Geltoi," Lieutenant Plugrath said, respectfully enough, but with no hint of regret or uncertainty in his voice. "His Excellency has cried failure of Writ against the Domitt Prison. The Bench will decide if there have been errors made. Not I."

Plugrath gave Koscuisko the nod as he said it. There was no love lost between the two officers, perhaps, but there seemed to be little hope of making a wedge between them, either. Administrator Geltoi sought for the right words, the right thing to say, something that would work to break this intolerable spell. This could not be happening. He'd walked into a nightmare.

Lieutenant Plugrath nodded at someone behind Geltoi. "Ready to transport, squad leader. Secure your prisoner and escort to custody as previously detailed, secured psychiatric."

No.

"You can't do this to me!" Geltoi shrieked. "You don't—dare—do you know—who I am—"

They picked him up and carried him away, kicking and screaming, his dignity lost to him now as finally as his position. As his future. As his life.

It didn't matter how much prisoners screamed.

The Bench would have its evidence.

Koscuisko was petty and vengeful, and Koscuisko was Nurail after all; but Koscuisko was an Inquisitor, with the ultimate penalty within his power to inflict if the Bench ruled—

Administrator Geltoi sank like a dead weight in the grasp of the Security who carried him and wept like a man bereft.

His prison, his prisoners, his work-crews. His land reclamation project. His money.

All gone.

And nothing left—

Except that he could see to it that Chilleau Judiciary did not turn its back on him, he would give evidence.

Why couldn't they have listened to him, and called Andrej Koscuisko back to *Scylla* before any of this could have happened?

◆ Fourteen

Andrej Koscuisko stood on the planking that protected the lip of the pit being excavated, watching the forensics team at their painstaking work below.

From where he stood he could see the careful grid marked off with chalked lines, and the bracing that supported a partially decayed body with too precise a correspondence to how it had been uncovered for anyone's peace of mind. Clawing its way frantically toward the surface, the head thrown back, the jaw carefully wired into the openmouthed—dirt-filled—scream that had formed one last protest against atrocity.

There could be no possible hope of misinterpretation. Whoever it had been, it had been a living soul, buried alive, and fully awake to the horror of its cruel fate as it happened.

"Caustic losteppan, ground fine," the shift supervisor—Sarvaw, as was most of the team—noted, passing a closed vial of clear glass to Andrej for examination. "Broadcast into the pit before they started filling. Don't get it on your skin, sir, this stuff will start to dissolve flesh within moments."

Raising his eyes to the black wall that rose up in front of them on the other side of the pit, Andrej found he could not suppress a shudder. "What a fearful way to die." No one would challenge that, it was too obvious, but the horror he felt was too much to be held in. The excavation was too good. It was too clear. He could almost hear the screaming. "How many bodies in the pit? At a guess?"

But the shift supervisor shook her head. "No guessing yet, your Excellency. Imaging scans show too much confusion at

300

the next level to be able to sort it out. Going by bone density it could be upwards of three hundred souls.''

Andrej shuddered again, and it wasn't because of the cold or the smell of earth, heavy with decaying flesh. ''Thank you, shift supervisor. You should receive every assistance, speak to the Administration if help should flag.''

The woman bowed respectfully, but Andrej didn't think she cared what he said one way or the other. Why should she? She was Sarvaw, he was Dolgorukij. Worse than Dolgorukij, Aznir Dolgorukij, the twice-great-grandson of Chuvishka Kospodar. He could protest his outrage all he liked, in public or in private. No Sarvaw would believe him.

Or if they did, it would make no difference. This was still atrocity that the Sarvaw had learned to judge against the Kospodar rule.

Turning away from the grave pit, Andrej began to cross the planking toward the Administration building, and Security—Code and Erish—fell in to place behind him. There were people coming on foot from in front of the Administrative building toward them, a small group—six, and four of them Andrej thought he recognized.

He was not particularly farsighted. But Andrej knew his Bonds: and he had left Security 5.3 on *Scylla*, so what were they doing here?

Not only that.

It seemed to Andrej that Code knew more than just his fellow Bonds; and came as close as Andrej had ever known him to missing a step, near-stumbling.

Afraid.

As the party drew near, Andrej could get more of its members sorted one from the other. Cel Tonivish. Iyo Lorig. Hart Aicans. Specs Fiskka. Yes, Security 5.3. No Robert St. Clare, Andrej was grateful to see. It was hard enough for him to see all of these beaten punished prisoners who looked like Robert to him without Robert actually being here.

Two officers in Administrative grays, but Andrej wasn't familiar with the branch of service that the steel-gray piping on the uniform might indicate.

Erish was fearfully tense, all of a sudden.

Then Andrej knew.

These officers were dancing-masters.

And that could only mean—

"Your Excellency." The senior of the two dancing-masters brought up his detail and saluted, very solemnly. "News from the Bench, sir, perhaps you've been expecting us."

Dancing-masters were the people that the Bench put in charge of the difficult period of conditioning and training that a bond-involuntary underwent between the implantation of the governor and the first duty post. That was why bond-involuntaries were afraid of them. It was nothing personal. And very soon it would be over, at least for three of his Security; and it should have been four, but Joslire had claimed the Day.

Joslire.

"Indeed I hoped for you, in a sense." What was he to call them? He wasn't sure he was supposed to know that they were dancing-masters. He wasn't sure they knew what bond-involuntaries called them, come to that. "Where are the others? Because I think that they should be together."

He knew why they were here. Security 5.3 had clearly been briefed in advance as well, from the fiercely cloaked joy in their faces; and that had been kindly done. Code and Erish could not know: and still gave him so much honor as to have relaxed once more within their bond-involuntary's discipline, secure that they were in no danger of bullying in his presence.

"His Excellency's Chief of Security has taken the other Security assigned up to the Administrator's office, sir. We were to tell his Excellency."

They would be waiting for him, then. And not know what it was that they were waiting for. Andrej wanted to hurry. "With dispatch, then, if you please. Code, lead the way."

Code would be staying. Andrej was conscious of the dancing-masters taking their subordinate positions behind him, as Security gathered into formation around them to move into the building. It annoyed him to realize that the dancing-masters were evaluating the performance of his gentlemen with every step they took. It annoyed him even more that he was anxious for their approval: as though it meant anything at all to him.

They could not know.

There could be no bond-involuntary Security under Jurisdiction as perfect as his people; and yet Andrej knew too
well that to a dancing-master they might seem half-ruined.
A bond-involuntary might be said to lose the fine edge of
his discipline when he lost his fear of punishment.

But not where Andrej could hear it.

Upstairs in the great gracious office that had belonged to
Administrator Geltoi Andrej sat down behind the desk to see
what the dancing-masters had brought him. Chief Samons
formed 5.3 up in ranks outside of the office, in the hall; and
held Code back with them. Security 5.4 stood in the office,
with a blank space at the end of the line where Joslire should
have been.

The senior officer set the flat tray that he'd been carrying
down on the desk, and opened its secures. "His Excellency
will wish to see to these himself," the dancing-master said.
Safes. Three Safes, one for each of the surviving members
of Security 5.4 that had been on board *Scylla* for that fateful
event.

And each Safe on a necklace of fine chain to hang around
a man's neck, and sit close to the governor, and transmit its
carefully restricted signal to the governor to keep it lulled to
sleep until such time as the governor could be surgically
removed by someone with experience.

"Thank you." He still didn't know what to call them. "It
is a very great privilege. And orders?"

He would have liked to do the surgery himself. But he
wasn't sure he trusted the level of the technical sophistication
at the local hospital to support so delicate a thing. The dancing-master smiled; a very warm and confiding smile, really.
Andrej had not cared for the dancing-masters from the moment he realized that they frightened his people. The goodwill in the dancing-master's smile reconciled Andrej
considerably.

"To be read aloud, your Excellency, before, during, or
after. At his Excellency's discretion."

And it should be soon. At once. Immediately.

"Miss Samons, if you would close the door."

He would speak to Code and 5.3; but this was first. Rising
to his feet, Andrej gathered the Safes up into his hand and
approached the senior man on 5.4. Toska was as white in the

face as Andrej had ever seen in his own mirror, mornings that followed an excess of drink. He could have smiled. But this was solemn business: more so than anything in these peoples' lives.

"Attention to orders," the senior dancing-master began. Andrej raised an eyebrow at Toska, who realized finally that he was to bow so that Andrej could slip the Safe over his head. "In the matter of the petition of Fleet Captain Irshah Parmin on behalf of Jurisdiction Fleet Ship *Scylla*. For meritorious service above and beyond the requirements of duty, Revocation of Bond is granted to the following Bench resources."

Toska, then Kaydence. The dancing-master read their names; they were different than the ones Andrej knew. Real names. Who had Joslire been?

Toska Simmanye. Kaydence Varrish. Finally Erish Tallis. They were all on Safe; free men, and soon to be free forever, once the governor in their brains that enforced their Bonds was removed. Free: but still and stiffly at attention. Andrej stepped back to stand with the dancing-master, who was finishing his speech.

"The beforenamed therefore to travel at Bench expense to the nearest Fleet rated facility for restoration of organic integrity." Surgery, he meant. "Cadre officers Attis and Fisemost to accompany and arrange for adequate debriefing prior to return to civilian life. Accrued pay and benefits to be awarded in addition to Fleet meritorious service pension for life. By the Bench instruction, na Roqua den Tensa, First Judge, Fontailloe Judiciary, Presiding."

Free.

Andrej stepped forward on impulse, not trusting himself to speak; and put his arms around Erish, who was nearest. Kissing him formally, with heartfelt emotion, first on one cheek and then on the other. Feeling his way, through the tears that blurred his vision, to the next man, to embrace him in like kind and be embraced. They were free. And to him it had been granted, through no merit of his own, to see at least these many of his gentlemen safe and away.

But there was one missing.

Andrej stared at the empty place for a long moment.

Joslire was free, too; and had known the time and the place of his emancipation. And had rejoiced in it.

"I must to the others go out and speak." They all knew but Code; maybe Chief Samons was telling poor Code even now. "If you would stand by, gentles, it will be one moment."

Why should they?

He wasn't their officer any longer.

There was no reason they should listen to him.

But they would always have been his Security; and that reminded him, something of which he had only fantasized in years gone by. He could take care of them, as they had taken care of him.

"I will for you provide letters of introduction, you shall go to the familial corporation if you like." It could be that they would find themselves at loose ends, no matter how good the debriefing support to be provided. "That you are no longer bound to Fleet, I cannot but rejoice for you. And there is no claim I have to lay upon you for your service, but strong claim in your hands to make against my family, as it may please you."

He probably wasn't making sense. And they probably wouldn't get anywhere near anything that reminded them of him, not by choice, ever. Why should they? That they had shared an unequal partnership with him had been his privilege. But it had been their punishment. "For what has in the past been between us it is your right to claim honor and comfort, sustenance and maintenance and all due respect. For as long as you live, if you elect it."

And Joslire, Joslire was to be remembered in his turn. . . .

"You're wrong, you know. Sir." Toska was clearly struggling with something, swallowing hard on his emotion. "To say you have no claim. After these three years, sir. You can't expect us to forget everything you've done for us. Just because we get—to go free."

Oh, he was going to miss them. But he'd know they were free: not under some other officer's direction, to be subject to potential reprimand. "You are right, Toska, and I am a sinner." Toska had taken better care of him than that. No governor under Jurisdiction could make a bond-involuntary extend his unspoken support by choice. "There is no use pretending that you have not been good to me over and above your Bond, all of this time. The bond that is between us cannot so easily be revoked, no matter the distance that should separate.''

They would no longer be bond-involuntary troops, Security slaves. But they would always be bonded to him, and he to them.

There was no loss in them going after all.

Ailynn had seen the three reborn men on their way in the company of the dancing-masters. Code had introduced her to his fellows, the new team that had been sent to wait upon the officer, and gave her credence amongst them. Now it had been eight weeks since she had gone with Kaydence, who was no longer to be called Psimas, down the wall; and pleasant as her life had been, it could not last. She knew it.

Eight weeks.

First they had moved from the prison to a house in Port Rudistal, but the officer had not been satisfied with those lodgings; and had moved himself within days to a house he liked better. How he had come by it Ailynn didn't know, nor did she ask—she knew her place.

It was not so big a house, perhaps, but there was room enough for the officer and his Security and the house-staff besides. The officer had brought the cook from the penthouse at the prison to prepare their meals, but he would not have Pyana housekeepers, and had hired Nurail from the camps instead.

Left her to manage them.

Eight weeks, and she had ruled the officer's household as the keeper of his keys, and stirred neither foot nor finger to her own work except to see that the toweling was warmed for his bath and to warm the bed beside him while he slept. He'd mostly only slept in bed, these eight weeks past; busy at the prison and in the camps with the taking in of evidence and dispositions with speaksera, and no torture.

It wore on him, regardless. He was deeper into drink than he had been before: and why should she take a second thought for it? Except that he had treated her decently.

Still, something that Ailynn didn't understand was happening.

The officer had received his orders; he was called back to his ship-duty and due to leave Port Rudistal within three weeks. The business of the Domitt was not concluded: It was hardly well begun, but Fleet would have its Inquisitor back, a good indication that the officer was half-vindicated already. The Bench had sent audit teams, and the officer had given his evidence, his personal evidence, even as she had. Now the Bench audit teams would take the matter in hand.

It was the Bench, and not Andrej Koscuisko, that would continue the work of excavating at the prison and the reclamation site for physical evidence. It was the Bench, and not the officer, that would sift through what records could be recovered and cross-reference them with those available at the relocation camp to try to quantify for good and all how many had died, and how.

The Bench, and not the officer, to pursue the horror of what had been the Domitt Prison, and how it had been allowed to come about, and what was to be done to ensure that it would not happen again. The officer would come back to Rudistal to execute what penalty the Bench adjudged against whichever parties were eventually found guilty of actual crimes: but had his duty to Fleet in the meantime, and could not be spared past three weeks the longer.

So why was he furnishing this house?

Why had he troubled to engage a gardener to tend the salad-plot, and had the compound wall repaired, the black slate roof inspected and reproofed against the weather?

There had been workmen in the house all week with furnishings the like of which Ailynn had never seen before. Room by room, removing what had been there, replacing it all with strange rich alien forms that fascinated Ailynn.

It made her half-drunk just to look at such carpeting, as thick and wild and fanciful as its pattern was; drunker still to touch the roses that bloomed in well-oiled wood along the footboard of the small self-contained room that the moving-crew had put into the officer's bedroom.

They were all Dolgorukij, the work-crew, the furnishings from the officer's homeworld, and they treated her with a deference that Ailynn couldn't quite understand.

In the evening after the officer had washed and had his evening meal—a cold buffet, since Cook was struggling with an arcane toy in the kitchen, an intricate piece of machinery for the preparation and serving of rhyti—he drew her off with him to the side-sitting-room, where an immense divan had been carefully placed to afford the best view of the garden. Or of the draperies, which were closed.

"Ailynn, please. A conversation. Something which I should have mentioned weeks ago, I do not know quite how to approach this."

He was wondering about her tip, perhaps. Such things were usually figured on the number of nights a patron had hired her; but he had merely slept in the same bed for three times as many nights as he had exercised himself with her for pleasure. Extra spending money was always nice, and she was allowed to keep her tips for her own use; but it didn't matter so much.

She'd had months now of liberty with him. Months of sleeping with only one man—how was she to go back to servicing multiple patrons, and every night?

"One hears stories about the things that go on in a service house. It may be indelicate to ask, but I am curious. If pressed hard to it I might even admit to having played some fantasy story or another in a service house, for amusement's sake."

Leaning well back into the cushions of the divan. Staring at the drapes. She had always thought his rest-dress made him look much younger than he did in duty uniform. "It's actually something to look forward to, most of the time. Breaks the monotony." He didn't care to be called "sir," and she couldn't quite bring herself to say "Andrej." She compromised by not calling him anything. "And usually light duty, if you follow. I don't mind it, dressing up."

He knew exactly what she was talking about. And grinned. She relaxed a bit into the cushions herself: They were very tempting. "The standard range of taboo violations, I would guess, Ailynn. Gender identification. Prohibited degrees of relationship. Unusual accommodations. Religion."

And more, yes. "Yes, but what religion? That can make all the difference. You can't begin to imagine. With respect." Why, when she thought of some of the scenes that she had helped to stage—

"Very true." The lights were not very bright in the sitting-room. Frowning, the officer fumbled at the base of the nearest table-lamp for a moment; it grew brighter, and he relaxed once more, his hands deep in his pockets now and his feet stretched stiffly out in front of him. "I suppose that if one's patron wished one to merely pray it need not be too strenuous."

"Pray how, to whom, how long, and in what manner?" she argued, half-serious. She enjoyed the conversations that she had with him, infrequent though they were. If it hadn't been that he was just a patron, she just a Service bond-involuntary, she would have had to seriously contemplate missing him, when he was gone. Rather than simply missing the privileged life that she had led with him.

"Oh. Let us say, on one's knees four days in a week, and with full prostrations on fifth-days. For example. To someone's Mother who is probably not listening, but never mind." Head leaned back against the edge of the divan, now, staring at the ceiling. She could interpret neither his expression nor his voice. He sounded as though he was just thinking out loud; and yet she somehow felt he had rehearsed this. "In two periods of prayer, morning and evening, and in a foreign language. For an hour each time. Sometimes two hours at a stretch. Every day."

It certainly sounded commonplace enough to Ailynn. "A foreign language? And what if one couldn't speak such a tongue? What sort of patron do we deal with, here, who takes gratification in such things?"

Turning his head to look at her now; she still couldn't decide about his face. "This would be much easier if you came to sit in my lap, here, Ailynn. It would be very good of you indeed to do so."

It would be only what she was paid to do. But never mind that. She was almost happy to oblige him for his own sake. It was comfortable, settling into his arms; she knew his warmth and his smell and the scent of the soap he used. He had taught her body to trust itself into his hands. Ailynn put her forehead to his cheek and pressed the issue.

"Now tell me why a man would spend good money just to have somebody pray twice a day. Even with prostrations, and a foreign tongue."

It was very nice to sit in the officer's lap. The strength of his arms was a comfort, when she knew it was just to hold her. "Well. We will say, let's suppose. First. That a man is too vain to wish to realize that he is to be compared with others, when he's gone. And to be found wanting."

Whatever that meant. He wasn't serious, she was sure. Ailynn rested herself in silence, content to listen while the officer mused aloud.

"Next it would have to be that a man had been killed, and deserved prayers. Hypothetically this would be Joslire, whom you have not met."

Not met, but had come to know by the echo of his absence. Even now Code suffered. It was getting better: but why did Koscuisko use the present tense?

"After that it would have to be a man with businesspeople to negotiate, and make a contract. But then here is a problem. We would have to suppose that such a man is also bone-headed enough to have simply decided, and made arrangements, without even once asking the lady. Because he was distracted, and could not decide how the issue to raise. It would seem that he had no respect for her, to arrange things behind her back in that manner."

The hesitation and regret in the officer's voice were too genuine. Ailynn sat up, to look him in the eye.

"What. Are you saying. Exactly. If you please. Sir."

"Angry with me," Koscuisko murmured as if to himself, raising his left hand to stroke her cheek gently with his fingertips. "And has a right to be. I will come out with it, all at once."

It took him a moment to collect his thoughts regardless. Then when he spoke, it was dead serious.

"Ailynn, I have seen the four of my gentlemen free, and three of them living. I cannot buy your Bond from the Bench, you know that." Only a member of her own family could redeem her. And her family were all dead: not as if they could have found the price of her Bond in any case.

"And Joslire's memory is to be served in a dedicated establishment, by the prayers of a nun. A religious professional. A woman who has been procured for that purpose. You need not go back to the service house, Ailynn, but if you do not you must say the prayers. Twice a day. Every day. For the next twenty-six years."

She couldn't believe him.

The words were so strange they seemed hardly in Standard.

Twenty-six years?

The term of her Bond ran for twenty-six more years.

Koscuisko knew that.

Had he done this for her?

"Oh, it must have cost you—no, too much money." She was horrified at the magnitude of it. "Do you mean it? I don't have to go back?"

Maybe he had done it; but not for her, for his man Joslire. It didn't matter. If she didn't have to go back to that place, she would learn whatever it was that they wanted, she'd learn how to pray, and she'd do it wholeheartedly, in thanks for deliverance.

"No one can make you." Cupping her face in the palm of his hand, now. "I have seen the contract, it says that I hire you for all day, every day, until the Day dawns for you. If you consent you will be Joslire's nun. This house will be for you, and people to run it; you will be mistress here. It need not be too hard for you, Ailynn, I promise. The life of a nun in the church of my blood is not at base difficult."

It didn't sound hard. It could be hard; she didn't care. He was willing to hire her out of the service house, and whatever it was to be a nun—or whatever else—to be clear of the service house was more than she'd dreamt of.

"You. Cannot know. You cannot imagine." Or maybe he could. Maybe that was why. "I would do anything. Learn Dolgorukij."

"Are not angry?" He was kissing her, now, kissing the tears from her cheeks one by one, supping her salt tears with tender care. "Very high-handed, and to have bought you. When you cannot be bought. Even though the Bench sold you."

It was too much.

She had to shut him up.

There was a way she had learned how to do it.

She had to be sure that he stayed shut up: so she did it again, and more thoroughly this time.

After a while it was quieter, between them, and the officer held her, stroking her hair. "There will be a tutor for you."

As if he was thinking out loud, almost. Or as if he had kept
the details to himself for so long that he needed to get them
all out at once, since he'd finally told. "A Reconciler, of St.
Andrej Malcontent I think. Uncle Radu would insist on a
Filial Piety, but Joslire wasn't Dolgorukij, so I can get away
with it. He will explain what it is all about, to be Joslire's
nun. The word does not satisfy in the Standard phrase, does
it not imply that one is celibate? Dolgorukij nuns are not
celibate unless they like to be. I have told Kaydence. You
will slap me, now, and I will deserve it."

She'd do no such thing. So she kissed him instead. "I'll
be Joslire's nun for you," Ailynn promised. "I may even
remember you to your, how do you say it, to your holy
Mother. But only when I consider what this means to me.
Every hour of every day, for the rest of my life."

"No, only for twenty-six—"

He started to protest. She kissed him again, to silence him.
She knew what he was going to say. He wasn't paying attention. For an officer he could be very thick-headed.

Finally he yielded, and smiled and kissed back.

O holy Mother, she thought to herself. Just to start prac-
ticing.

Holy Mother, I'm free.

She could spend her life praying and never work off the
debt that she owed to Andrej Koscuisko.

ALEXANDER JABLOKOV

"An extraordinarily talented, interesting writer . . .
Jablokov's writing is both clear and scintillating."
Orson Scott Card

THE BREATH OF SUSPENSION
Stories
72680-7/$5.99 US/$7.99 Can
"A sparkling, diverse collection
of short fiction"
Denver Post

Novels by Alexander Jablokov

NIMBUS
71710-7/$4.99 US/$5.99 Can

A DEEPER SEA
71709-3/$4.99 US/$5.99 Can

CARVE THE SKY
71521-X/$4.99 US/$5.99 Can

And Now Available in Hardcover

RIVER OF DUST